THE MAN WAS DEAD

Asher's lantern caught the man's foot. He lay on his back at the place where the corridor shot upward, resting at a twenty-degree angle.

The man had been neatly skewered by a needler. He was, Asher saw, a Downer; the clothes had the off-style shabiness of the people he had seen downbelow. Other bodies were sprawled on the long ramp that faced him, six of them, men and women. He saw needlers, some still in holsters, some in hands. But he could see no signs that they had been fired before death had claimed the hands that held them.

Asher drew a long, shuddering breath. Some kind of automatics had done this. Something had aimed so well and moved so fast that the Downers had had no time to react, to defend themselves. Asher sent his mind ahead, questing for the mechanical thing that had killed these Downer agents.

PLANET OF THE DEAD

DON WISMER

BAEN BOOKS

PLANET OF THE DEAD

Copyright © 1988 by Don Wismer

A Baen Books Original

Baen Publishing Enterprises
260 Fifth Avenue
New York, N.Y. 10001

First printing, April 1988

ISBN: 0-671-65400-4

Cover art by Craig Farley

Printed in the United States of America

Distributed by
SIMON & SCHUSTER
1230 Avenue of the Americas
New York, N.Y. 10020

*To my sisters, Cathy Wilder and family,
and Mary Wismer, with love.*

The Galactic Index stood at 434,670.

Part I:

MISSION

Prelude

From the moment he landed on Surcease, Randolph Tarney had been afraid. A sense of dread had been building within him since the time, days before, he had walked into the passenger starship *Beyond Sorrow*, bound for this central world of the Castor/Pollux Sector.

At first it had been exciting to hear his native language again, for he had been born on one of the outlying planets of this Sector. But conversation had not gone well. The passengers travelling with him had been listless and demoralized. Most were oddly gaunt, and many limped from a disfigurement of the lower leg, a prominent bulge that was only partly hidden by the pantaloons they affected. Tarney had been puzzled and disturbed; he had wondered what disease or environmental mutation he might find on Surcease. Naturally garrulous, he had sought out first one, then another of the passengers, but there was something haunting in their eyes, and they responded in monosyllables, or not at all.

Tarney was looking in particular for drugs. The Bodyguard Guild had studied the decay in the Castor/Pollux Sector. Com Central, the galaxy's major information source, had scanned its trillions of informational levels and found no evidence of a cosmic disaster in that Sector—sudden white hole formation or a nova blast of hard radiation, for example—nor any sign of plague or unusual political repression. The likeliest cause, based on weighted attention to past rumor: the massive, endemic use of some new and ambition-stripping drug, possibly the Andalian lichen-derivative called Candy. But why had the problem not reached a high index in the Galactic Concourse newscasts?

3

Why, nowhere in Surceasean news, was Candy or any other drug identified, or even alluded to? Why did the news almost never mention the Surceasean Sector at all?

But statistics had told a tale, to eyes trained to read them and minds capable of seeing within them. Sector industrial output: fading. Trade: fading. Contributions to the arts: disappearing. Gross Sector Output (GSO): plunging.

The Bodyguard Guild had been interested. It had recently merged with the Guild of Thieves, and the Thieves had made it their frequent business to infiltrate drug operations, siphon off the profits, and close the druggies down.

Now, as the ship-to-shore shuttle touched the tarmac, Tarney felt an immediate prickling in the nape of his neck. The ship's shuttle had landed him in the most active spaceport on the planet, which itself was a sector capital; yet there had been few ships in orbit, and fewer shuttles on the ground. The terminal was almost deserted, cleaning robots moving listlessly about. Tarney cleared through automatic customs, his short, black body and his luggage scanned, inventoried and analyzed, and walked toward the plate walkway leading to the main terminal. Pastel colors surrounded him, but they were overlaid by a patina of yellowish film. Once Tarney walked past a cleaning robot bumping against a wall, again and again, and no service units in sight.

The prickling intensified, and he felt his warrior-trained body relax into preparation, summoning all its powers of self-protection. In his mind, he felt go up a wavering Shield, a Shield that had taken him eighteen months to learn, but which he was far from completely mastering.

The same eerie stillness dogged him out of the terminal. He had booked into an in-town hotel, and now from the automatic ground car he stared at the sprawling city around him, and wondered. It was mid-afternoon on a weekday, but he saw few people abroad on this level, though it was a fine day, green-hued clouds of water vapor puffing gracefully in a cobalt sky. The buildings he could see were low-slung—by planetary ordinance, he understood—but had an air of neglect, as if a ghetto had spread like a cancer to engulf the entire city. It was a highly carbonaceous world and the buildings were graced with a wood facade, but what stain or paint each had once sported was now spotted or chipped and rotting away. The buildings seemed too low and too few for a human city this size, until, coming to the top of an incline, Tarney looked over and realized that much of the city was below apparent ground level.

Tarney spent only a few moments in the autohotel—just long enough to stow his luggage. Then he began to prowl.

"Ding syrup," Tarney said, "is the sweetest thing in all the galaxy. Next to it, Earth's maple syrup tastes like urine. F'rup syrup tastes like industrial waste. There's nothing like ding in the known universe. I sell it, and I can't lose. When I let people taste it, people buy."

The barhands watched him lugubriously. Tarney ordered another round.

"And that's why I'm here," he said, slapping his dark palm on the charge plate. "Surcease needs ding; my company is willing to sell the first shipment below cost, because we know that once anyone tastes it, they will want more. As I said, we can't lose."

One of the barhands stirred. "You think so," he said, holding his glass under the automatic spout. "Dem." The drink Tarney had paid for spilled out into the glass, filling it half full.

The barhand drained the glass. His voice was cultured, but his face was white and emaciated and he was nearly in rags. Once he had been a big man, and the bony frame was still broad, but he was stooped now and his hair had receded until you could draw a line over the top of his scalp from ear to ear without encountering a hair. His right leg held the odd deformity that Tarney had seen on almost all the people of Surcease. The dem—nearly pure alcohol flavored with a whiff of musk, the thought of which made Tarney gag inside—was having no perceptible effect.

"I know so," the little black man said heartily. Another barhand, this one a woman, was standing at the automatic spout. "Aye, have another one," Tarney said. "There's plenty more where it came from." He slapped the charge plate again.

The balding man said: "You won't find any takers on Surcease, mister. We got something a lot sweeter than any syrup ever made."

"Now, my friend, that's hard for me to believe," Tarney said, putting a friendly arm around the other's shoulder and looking up at him. He winked broadly at the barhand. "Ding is sweeter than sex, my friend. Once you try it, my company knows that you will be hooked. That's why they let me pass out free samples. It's expensive stuff, but they don't care. It's not the first taste that makes the profit."

"Will my Ressie be hooked too?" the barhand said. The people crowding around the automatic spout hooted loudly, catcalling in cacophony.

"Your Ressie?" Tarney said.

"Blackie here, he don't have a Ressie," the woman called. She was weaving slightly, stringy grey-streaked hair peeking out under a scarf. Tarney looked at the crowd; its character had undergone a sudden, subtle change. In the eyes now looking at him, he saw . . . What? Sadness? Or, for heaven's sake, pity?

The balding man said: "Blackie, we got to get you a Ressie. Then you'll see what your ding syrup is worth around here." It seemed to Tarney that the crowd gave a collective sneer.

"What's a Ressie?" he asked again.

"Take him downtown," someone said.

The big, balding man reached for Tarney's arm. "Wait," Tarney said, almost desperately. "I want you to taste ding. Then you'll know." He drew a vial from his bodice pocket.

They passed it around. One after another, without bothering to wipe the bottle's lip, they tasted the ding. Tarney watched carefully, for ding syrup really was all that he had said. It was the rage of all the human galaxy. A single ounce was going for five hundred credits, even on poorer planets.

The first barhand licked his lips after the taste; his haggard expression did not change. The second, the woman, sipped, snorted and passed the bottle on. The third, a man, took an indifferent swallow, and without reaction, handed the vial to the next man.

"C'mon, Blackie," the big man said. He pulled Tarney out of the autobar and led him down the skylip.

"Where are we going?" Tarney asked, resisting a little. But the big man turned on him.

"Look, Blackie, I'm doing you a favor. Trust me. You got anything better to do? Don't you want to wrap up your business here one way or another?" The careful diction that Tarney had detected seemed to fade in and out, as if the man didn't care anymore.

"Don't call me 'Blackie,' " Tarney said.

"Hey, no offense," the balding man said, holding his hands up, palms outward. "We call yellow-hairs 'Blondie.' It's just the way of it here."

Tarney scowled. He didn't believe it for a minute; but now, as he watched the other limp ahead of him, he felt that he was getting somewhere. Ressie. Was that the name of the drug? But their syntax in referring to it had been strange, as if they were referring to a permanent possession that never ran dry.

On one side of them, the street's lip rose up and fell away into the depths below, dozens of building levels beneath them. Walking, Tarney could now see clearly what he had glimpsed from the car: that the great bulk of the buildings were below ground, massive caverns opening up between them like canyons in a desert of rectangular, upthrusting patterns. Tarney scarcely noticed the one exception until they were upon it.

"But that's Government Center," he said suddenly, recognizing it from his background studies of the planet. The big man was pulling him straight toward that monolithic tower that dominated the skyline.

"So what?" the man said curtly. "Look, bud, I'm doing you a favor. You'll thank me for it for the rest of your life."

Tarney subsided, but the prickling in his neck intensified again. He kept every sense he had on the alert, and maintained too the Shield that he had never expected to use.

They limped and strode through a side entrance in the granite tower, and all at once were rising in an antigrav

elevator. But they didn't go far. Even as they stepped off,
Tarney glanced upward and saw the shaft through a crack,
disappearing into dizzying distance.

"The Tower don't mean nothing," the big man said.
Tarney had the eerie feeling that this was a man of culture
gone entirely to seed, taking on the coloration of the
people around him, language and all. "The nearest Ressie
station is here, is all. Come on." They walked down silent
corridors. Again Tarney was struck by the unnatural stillness around him.

"Where is everybody?" he asked in a hushed voice.
The man ignored him, and hustled him through a door
marked in raised golden letters: TOURIST BUREAU.

"Got an interested customer," the balding man said.
"Just landed."

A man lounging behind a desk against the far wall
looked up at them. He was the first person with any flesh
on his bones Tarney had seen on the entire planet. He was
very young.

"Wait," Tarney said. "I want to know what a Ressie is."

The fat man's dark brown eyes caught his and held
them. And, to his horror, Tarney felt a mental probe
reaching out toward him.

"No," Tarney said. "No . . . !" He backed away from the
man. Despite his Shield, he had never really expected a
probe of mental Skill. The mental wizards of October had
fled the galaxy; he had seen them go.

The fleshy man's eyes widened. "You have a Shield," he
said in surprise. "You're no ding syrup salesman . . . no,"
he said, eyes narrowing, "you come from the Guild of
. . ." His eyes widened again. He rose abruptly and came
around the desk, moving with remarkable quickness for
one so large.

Tarney turned to run. The fat man lashed at him with
a whip of mental force. It shattered on Tarney's Shield.

Even the fat man, Tarney realized as that last glimpse
sank in, had that strange bulge alongside one leg.

"Stop him," the fat man yelled. The gaunt and balding
man who had been with Tarney whirled and flung his arms
around Tarney's waist in a movement belying his dissipation.

Tarney didn't even break stride. He simply let the natural movement of one elbow angle into the man's face with a sharp twist. The man's nose was smashed into his skull; he let go with a choking howl and fell.

Tarney's footsteps thundered down the silent hallway. He found himself straining with his mind. The feeble Skill that he could muster was almost entirely a question of concentration, of centering. He had no mental weapons of his own, just the one inadequate defense.

He was in the elevator; he reached the ground floor. Still the relentless mental probe thrust at him. Staggering for a moment, he burst through the door into an empty street.

"What now?" he thought desperately. He began to run, back the way he had come with the balding man. The probe seemed to follow him like a raven in the air, pecking down at him with a beak ten feet long, razor-sharp.

He saw a callbox, and called up an autocar, slapping his palm against the contact again and again.

Steps were sounding from the direction of the Center. Tarney turned and saw two men and two women coming at him. And the mental probe kept pounding, pounding.

The first woman reached him and . . . with the fluid grace of a warrior, Tarney avoided her grasping hands and buried one fist in her stomach. Her breath left her in an explosive gasp, and she fell. Her mouth opened and closed spasmodically, like that of a beached fish.

One of the men was upon him then; it was no time for niceties. Tarney smashed a palm against the other's ear. But before the man could cry out, Tarney's other fist had imploded his breastbone and the first had crashed in sequence against his temple, and the man was out.

The other two held back. The woman reached into her blouse . . .

Far down the skylip, Tarney saw the fat man coming. The mental probes still thrust and thrust at him, but the physical challenge could not break Tarney's mental centering; he was warrior-trained to the point of unthinking, automatic self-defense.

He fingered an ornamental button on his bodice, and a

weighted plastic blade shot out into the air as the woman's blaster cleared her clothing. The blade went into her neck, and her hands flew up, dropping the weapon. She fell back, and Tarney saw a gush of blood burst through her fingers.

He gave the last man a lunging, powerful push, and felt a rib break . . .

The man staggered, out of control, and fell against the lip. The weapon he had been bringing up in one hand dropped into the depths of the city as he clawed for balance. His hips the fulcrum, he seesawed for a moment on the lip. There was the briefest silence. And then the hum of the arriving autocar was occluded by a dopplering scream, receding into the sunken city.

Tarney was in the car and away before the fat young man reached the three bodies remaining on the skylip pavement. Only one was still alive.

An October wizard . . . who could have guessed, Tarney thought. They were supposed to be all gone, driven out of the galaxy. And yet . . . and yet . . . Once Tarney had dealt with a wizard, and had felt enormous Power—Power such that before it he had felt as nothing. He had not felt the same intensity from the fat man. Yet had those little warning bells in his mind not caused every possible alertness in him, the fat man would have struck him down.

Tarney had not wanted or meant to kill. He was trained to do so, quickly and quietly, but only when it could not be avoided. This time the mental struggle had befuddled him, and his body had gone maximum.

He didn't have all the answers, but there was only one option open to him now. He had to get away, had to communicate with the Bodyguard/Thieves. They had to know that a wizard was involved here, that an ordinary thief had almost no chance. It would take someone with mental Skill to figure out the riddle of Surcease.

No, he himself had to get off-planet as soon as he could. At the spaceport there would be a tachyonic holography booth. He would use it before grabbing the first shuttle out.

And then he was there, at the spaceport. He had palmed

the necessary credits long since, drawing on one of the Bodyguard's accounts to pay for the autocar. Now he was out, blinking in the late afternoon sun, and then striding under the canopied walkway toward . . .

WAUWMMMMMM . . . the mental bolt hit him like a sledgehammer on rock. His Shield still was up, and the blow rang it like a cast-iron bell. He reeled, clutching at a support post, almost falling. This was not the fat man; this was someone else, more powerful, more Skilled. Not like the October Adept he once had known, but . . .

WAUWMMMMMM! Prepared this time, he shook it off and broke into a stumbling run. The main terminal was thirty feet away. There were very few people about.

WAUWMMMMMM! WAUWMMMMMM! He was in the terminal. WAUWMMMMMM! WAUWMMMMMM! WAUWMMMMMM! He reached the auto check-in.

As he laid his palm on it, he looked wildly around, frantically working on his ringing mind, keeping it centered, keeping it concentrated.

WAUWMMMMMM! "Next shuttle out," he gasped. "Any destination. Any starship. Anywhere . . ." WAUWMM-MMMM!

"Clear for Gate 867," the impersonal autovoice said. "Proceed to Walkway 8."

Blow after blow hit Tarney's mind as he moved blindly onto Walkway 8. As the plate on which he stood picked up speed, he felt the blows pause for a moment, as if a watcher had lost sight of him. Looking in both directions down the interminable walkway, his tearing eyes saw no one. And then he realized that he had forgotten the holography booth.

He cursed himself for a fool. At that moment another bolt hit him, and Tarney almost lost it, for his self-flagellation had weakened his concentration. He suddenly found himself on his knees; the protective force fields had kept him from falling into the bed of the walkway beneath the speeding plates. He let his self-doubt fall away then in a convulsive letting-go, just as another bolt came down. And in that bolt, he sensed a triumph that turned abruptly to disappointment. "Hah!" Tarney growled out loud. "Not this time, baby. You didn't get me this time."

He repeated it, over and over. "Not this time. Not this time. Not . . ." The blows came faster now, but he was more centered than he had been before. He clawed his way to his feet and stood there, swaying, as the plate eventually found Gate 867.

There, right at the gate's entrance, he saw the universal symbol of a holographic transceiver. And . . .

A dog moved out of the transceiver booth. Tarney stared. The dog was as big as a pony, but with a massive mane almost like a lion's, lips drawn back over razor teeth like a Doberman. And its body was as red as if it had been dipped in blood.

The animal's growl came to Tarney like the snarl of a soul in rage. The beast seemed to flow across the floor, and leaped at Tarney's throat.

He flung his arms up, reaching for the mane—the only defensive move a man could make against an attack dog—to grab the collar or hair and fall backward, hurling the animal over and past . . .

But Tarney's hands grasped empty air. He fell on his back onto the floor.

Astonishment. The beast was ten feet in front of him again, snarling, ready to leap.

A holograph? No. A mental chimera? Tarney rose slowly . . .

And the dog said: "You are the last Bodyguard left in the galaxy. We have killed them all."

Alarm rang in Tarney's head, and fear welled up like vomit. Killed them all? How could that be?

The dog smiled.

WAUWMMMMMM! Tarney fell to his knees. He had let his control slip. He reached for it again . . .

WAUWMMMMMM! He reached . . .

WAUWMMMMMM! WAUWMMMMMM!

Chapter 1

"Is it true, Sensei," the boy said, "that you can stop an attacker with your mind?"

Asher Tye frowned. Sixteen boys stood before him. All hands were loose fists, dangling at their sides. All legs were sixteen inches apart, feet pointed directly ahead. All knees were slightly bent.

Cally, the boy who had asked, was in the front of the two rows. Like most of the others, he was in his mid-teens, and had been training with Asher for almost a year. His loose white, buttonless shirt was gathered at the waist by a cloth belt colored a faded yellow, almost matching his hair and nascent beard.

"No," Asher said curtly. This was one belief he could not allow to gain currency. It would destroy his effectiveness as a Bodyguard instructor, if his students believed his skills were due to mental trickery. "The more you train," Asher told them, "the more you feel the world around you, by its tiniest sounds and air currents and smells and vibrations, as well as by the eyes. The great Bodyguards seem to have eyes in the back of their heads, but they don't; they have normal senses exactly like each of you, trained to maximum."

Some of them looked dubious. Asher sighed inwardly. The vocational school was a for-profit cover for the real work that was going on: the training of members for the newly combined Guild of Personal Protectors (Bodyguards) and the fugitive Transfer Guild (Thieves). But the vocational school itself accepted nearly anyone who applied for its martial training. "Become a Bodyguard!" the ads screamed. "See the galaxy!" As a result, the school pulled in the young and rebellious of all kinds, macho-types and wallflowers and bullies and idealists, of whom perhaps three percent would eventually become full members of the Bodyguard Guild.

He wondered how the notion had become planted in Cally's head. Perhaps Asher had been careless at some point as he worked on the group of gangling novices. Once, for example, he had used a Shield to stop a knife from impaling one of Cally's opponents during weapons training. He had let the Shield push the opponent backward, and it should have seemed to Cally that his enemy had simply moved out of reach, as indeed he was supposed to. But maybe Cally had felt the Shield somehow, with his knife hand or even, if he had some natural talent in that direction, with his mind. Was he a Receptor, perhaps?

Asher pushed his brown hair away from his eyes in a habitual gesture, even though he never let it grow that long anymore. The sixteen brown and blond and red and black heads watched him fixedly, as they were obliged to do at all times during training; otherwise they were subject to surprise attack.

But this was not the time to leap at one of them, Asher thought. They would see him as avoiding the issue, and the seed that Cally's question had planted would grow.

"There are no mind readers," Asher said harshly. "I see the news too, and I heard about the October Guild and its destruction by the Galactic Police." Asher knew for a fact that the Police had entered the scene long after the real action had concluded. But the story had captured the imagination of certain holographic movie producers, and the resulting extravaganzas had been very popular. The basic plot was always the same: ravenous alien telepathic monsters from the Sculptor subgalaxy infiltrate the main galaxy, take control of everybody's mind, and rule with sadistic evil until thwarted by a hero and thrown back into the Sculptor. And in fact, the real events had had the same plot line; but the ravenous leader had been the subtle and manipulative October One, and the Sculptor itself had, in a way, taken back its own. As for the hero . . .

"You joined the school about that time," Cally said, and Asher scowled. He told himself that he had been an idiot to allow questions at the end of each class . . .

But no. The questions usually helped him understand what was going on in the heads of the class, subtle things beyond the words they said.

With the panther-like step of a Bodyguard, Asher strode to Cally and stood directly in front of him.

"Let's get this question answered, mister," Asher said harshly. Before the intense stare of Asher's brown eyes, Cally visibly flinched. But cowed he was not. He was nearly Asher's height and at least his weight, and besides, he had an audience.

"You see the shows," Asher's voice grated. "A wizard's mind shields him from all physical danger, right? By reflex, instantly, whether he wants it to or not. Right?" It wasn't completely true, but the movies had said that it was, and they were reality for the likes of Cally. "Right?" Asher shouted.

"Right!" Cally yelled, and, viciously, he slammed his knee upward into Asher's groin.

Asher saw it coming, of course, not with his mind, but by virtue of the intense martial training of the past five years from the greatest human warrior in the galaxy, the Nin Tova, founder of the Guild of Thieves. The tiny flicker in Cally's face, the instantaneous shifting of balance before the strike . . .

But deliberately, he suppressed his now almost instinctive reactions.

The slamming knee lifted Asher an inch off the floor, and as his feet hit again, he staggered backwards a few steps. Then he swayed, hunched slightly over, and let air in with an explosive gasp.

There was some pain, but not much. The class watched him, and he watched them. This was not over yet.

There was a question of respect . . .

"You see the value of the plastic protectors I make you all wear?" Asher gasped out finally. Then he let his eyes focus on Cally. "Come out here," he said.

Cally came. He could see that trouble was ahead, but he came.

They faced one another, beltless instructor and yellow-belted student. "Bow," Asher said. They bowed, never taking their eyes off one another. "Attack," Asher said.

Cally attacked in a flurry of fists, knees, and feet. Asher let the blows beat the air. With effortless grace he moved away from them, just far enough so that they almost hit, but not quite. He didn't bother to raise a blocking arm or knee.

At length Cally paused, panting. Then Asher extended a fist. Frantically, Cally drove an arm block against it, and . . .

The block bounced off. Asher let the fist move in, slowly. The second block bounced off. It was as if the arm were made of wood imbedded in the ground.

Cally regarded the arm confusedly, stepping back, and at that instant Asher kicked, one foot smashing forward into Cally's crotch. The cup protector was there, of course, or Cally would have died. But the ball of Asher's foot drove the cup itself deep into Cally's flesh, bruising the bone and leaving a circular outline that lasted three weeks.

Then Asher's leg snapped partly back and the same heel found Cally's solar plexus. Cally was flung backward onto the floor.

There was silence. Cally's face stared. He sat up. His eyes began to bulge, his mouth opening in frantic, useless sucking movements. He looked up in panic at Asher Tye, who looked down at him, the expression on his face saying that the discipline was now complete. And the seconds ticked by: twenty, thirty, forty . . . The class watched Cally and Asher in turn, horror coming into their eyes, restlessness into their feet.

"You won't die," Asher said softly. And Cally didn't. For all at once, his diaphragm lost its paralysis and came back into action. There was a gigantic gasp as air exploded inward, and Cally fell backwards on the mat, heaving off its surface as he drew in tremendous racking gulps of air.

"So now you all see," Asher said coldly to the class, "that I am not a wizard." Then he looked deliberately down at Cally. "And," he said wryly, "neither is he."

*　　*　　*

"Sometimes I wonder," Asher said to Clemmy that night, "whether anything I do is worth anything in the long run. Those sixteen kids won't last another year. Some will get lazy and drop out, some will run out of money and drop out, some will move away, some will get surface religion and misunderstand the point of the training, and drop out."

Clemmy regarded him from an inch away, one leg thrown over his body. Her narrow face was relaxed, cheek on one hand as her elbow supported her head.

"Some will become Bodyguards," she said.

"Oh sure, maybe," Asher said. "But most of them will drop out, and other ones will replace them to drop out themselves, and on and on and on."

She laid her cheek against Asher's shoulder, and Asher put his arm around her.

"Even the ones that drop out," Clemmy said in her throaty voice, "will remember. They'll always feel better because of it. They'll know some of their limits and know what they can do and what they can't."

"I guess," Asher said. He bent his head slightly and touched his lips to her hair.

"Anyway," Clemmy said, "that's not the only thing you do. Behind the scenes, you've trained the warriors to raise Shields in their minds. That's pretty impressive, and it might save their lives someday."

"But it's taken a year," Asher said with sudden heat, "and a lot of them can't do it at all. That's what I mean, Clemmy. When I was on the October World, it took the Apprentices less than a week to master, and I mean *master*, the Shield. Here it takes a year to learn to put up wobbly feeble Shields that take tremendous effort and then fall apart. I'm restless, Clemmy. I feel I'm wasting my time. There aren't any wizards in the galaxy to raise a Shield against, for heaven's sake, not anymore. If there were, the galaxy would rise up and exterminate them; the fear of them can still be sensed everywhere. No one likes the idea of someone else poking around in one's mind."

Clemmy turned her face up to him; his lips moved from her hair, across her forehead, down the bridge of her nose.

"You've taught me a lot of the Skill," she said, the last

word muffled suddenly. "Even the Green Flame—I can blast a tree to cinders with it already. It's incredible."

His cheek was back against her hair, then. "You have a natural aptitude," he said. "And you taught me a lot, too, about many other things." Against his chest, she smiled.

"What things?" she said. But his mind was elsewhere.

"Warrior-skills," said Asher. "You're a better warrior than I am, Clemmy. And also you taught me kindness. And integrity. And willpower."

"What else," she said.

"Running and swimming and jumping and tumbling," he said. "Juggling and acrobatics and fencing and knife throwing. You were one of my teachers in all those things."

"What else?" she asked, sighing.

But Asher wasn't entirely distracted. He smiled, but she couldn't see his face.

"Catching and hitting and waving and hiding," he said. "Pounding and skiing and handwalking and hopping on one foot. Eating and drinking and sleeping and mmphf." Her lips were on his and she shut him off, eyes twinkling.

"What else?" she said, and then covered his lips again before he could speak.

He broke away for a moment. "And being a husband," he said. "And I thought the teaching was mutual."

Late that night, Asher reached for Clemmy again. "No," she murmured blearily. "Want to sleep." He moved his hands on her, and she said: "No!" sharper now. She turned her back on him.

Asher sank back, hurt. It had happened before. Sometimes they seemed in perfect synch; other times they were off in different directions. How could sleep compare to love? Asher thought angrily.

Asher made up his mind as he was dressing the next morning. Clemmy was already gone, and as he left the tiny room that they shared on the fourteenth floor, he determined to see the Nin. He knew she was on-planet from the wrist computer announcement board. Whether she, the master of a Guild whose members worked on a little less than half a million worlds, would take time to see him, he wondered about briefly and then dismissed it. Maybe he would just be lucky.

He descended to her office on the sub-sixth floor. Outside the walls, in the bedrock, were tunnels and several escape ships. Even on this populated world, the Nin was prepared. Her former Guild was still sought by the Concourse Police, and if the Police became aware that she had absorbed the Bodyguards, there would be trouble.

He told the Watcher Com what he wanted, and it was only a moment later that the Nin herself came into the room from a rear door. She seemed to fill the space around her, a magnificent woman of perhaps thirty-seven, shaped as much by flowing muscular development as by a natural womanness. Asher tended to become tongue-tied in her presence. He resisted it now with determination.

"So, Asher," she said, her voice its usual casual presence, alien to pretense and deceit. "What do you wish?"

"You," Asher almost said, and found his teeth clamped on his tongue. He separated them with an effort, and was amazed. It was a thought that he had never articulated on any conscious level.

He told her some of what he had told Clemmy, and finished by saying: "I am restless and yet have no goals or plans. I don't know what I want to do next month or next year or for the rest of my life. The only thing I can think of is to seek out the great Teacher in the Sculptor sub-galaxy, but I don't believe I am ready yet for that. I might never be."

"Is there trouble between you and Clemmy?" the Nin asked. She had come around to the front of the desk, and now settled on a chair facing him. He could have reached out one hand and touched her. He wondered what would happen if he did. Maybe his hand would have touched empty air. Thinking about it now, he realized that on those rare times that he saw her in the flesh, usually in a meeting or assembly, he was never sure whether it was the Nin herself that he faced, or one of the hundreds of holographic amalgams with which she kept personal touch with Bodyguards on the thousands of worlds. Yet if today she were a sterile amalgam, the contact would not be entirely impersonal, for even with an amalgam some of her time was involved. At some point she had to scan the results of all the pseudo-meetings, no matter how condensed a summary the Bodyguard Com might present.

Clemmy . . . "Nothing really," Asher said slowly. "It's the one thing that seems right, most of the time. Two people are two people."

"But of course, you're both new at it," the Nin said. Asher looked at her sharply. "You will do very well if you can keep your feeling with Clemmy balanced toward the positive as you both age and change."

"This is getting away from the point," Asher said. He and Clemmy had been married for well over a year, partially because it had seemed right, and partially because the Nin had advised them to. Several times he had seen the Nin advise, even order, marriage between two of her Bodyguards when relationships reached a certain point, and he hadn't been too surprised when his and Clemmy's turn had come. But it was an odd thing too, marriage. He wasn't entirely used to it.

The Nin said: "No, it is the point. Restlessness has to do with your age, and sex is one of the driving forces for someone scarcely twenty-two. The problem will be, someday, to place it in perspective. Young men more than women have a tough time with it, Asher. Even in your happiest moments with Clemmy, have you ever thought of another woman? Your old flame Tawna, perhaps?" Asher opened his mouth to deny it. "Or me?"

He closed his mouth abruptly. She laughed softly, her short hair, alternating strands of brown and blonde, waving around her shoulders. She reached a hand out and took his shoulder, and looked into his eyes. Well, this is no computer amalgam, he thought.

"This is why human beings have brains," she said intently. "Your brain has to separate out the long-term value of everything you do, and decide what should get the most time and what the least. You yourself felt it first hand when you had to confront the October One that day that seems so long ago. We in the old Guild of Thieves had to teach you to separate your brain from your emotions, and that took a lot of doing, believe me, Asher Tye. Remember when you stood before October, and in the face of a power you thought was invincible you reached inside yourself and found something that gave you a chance against her?

"It's very, very hard to do at first. First you control the emotion; then you begin to plan, to separate immediacy from long-term gain. Children think sweet things have overriding importance; young men think sex does. They're both wrong. The two things have their place, but those places are down the list. And both can ruin the things higher up. Free access to sweet things can ruin health. Obsession with sex leaves you penniless and confused in the long run."

"This is not what I came to talk about," Asher said desperately.

"But it is," the Nin said. "It's practically the definition of restlessness in young men."

She released him, and leaned back in her chair again. "The only solution," she said, "is goal-oriented activity. You have to have action toward some goal, accomplish that goal, and see what you have learned. I think I'm beginning to agree with you this far, Asher: that it may be time for your first mission for the Guild. You're as good a warrior as you need to be right now. You need experience in the real universe."

Asher still felt her touch on his shoulder, and she saw it in his eyes. Softly, she laughed again. "No, Asher Tye, I am not for you in that way, and will never be. Look for the rightness in your reasoning mind. Clemmy is right for you, and it would be better if you both realized that there will be challenges to that rightness. Only if you both work hard can you conquer them all."

In a way, it was the same pep talk she gave warriors on the martial skills. But Asher felt let down.

"You can't have every woman that attracts your eye, Asher Tye," the Nin said then, still softly. "And if I and two hundred other women say 'no' to you, you can't let it bring you down. You're a married man, Asher Tye. Your peace of mind comes from what you do with it."

He left. In all his confusion of thought and emotion, it
was an effort to turn his mind toward the idea of going out
on a mission. He wondered what it would be.

That night, Clemmy came into their room in flowing tears.

"Oh Asher, Asher," she cried, and threw her arms around
him, as if by letting go she would fall a thousand feet.

"What's wrong, Clemmy? What's wrong?" Asher said in
surprise, smoothing her hair, kissing her eyes, her forehead.

"Hold me, Asher, I need you to hold me, so that I can
find the strength to hold you."

"Hold *me*?" But she was crying spasmodically now, and
it was long minutes before her breath was under her
control again.

"I knew him longer than you," Clemmy said. "He lit up
every room he came in."

A chill hit Asher's heart like a fist of stone.

"What is it, love?" he murmured, but his reason was
working it out already.

"Ran," she said. "It's Ran. Oh, Asher, he's dead."

Chapter 2

The Galactic Index stood at 434,671. Another intelligent race had been discovered.

Randolph Tarney. Asher had never called him that; it had always been "Ran." He had been Asher's first friend among the Thieves—sometimes roommate, sometimes partner. Asher could see with the vividness of a vision the round, smiling face, the immense, isometrically trained muscles, the friendliness and candor of the man. And above all, Ran had been a superb warrior. It was difficult to believe that someone could have blindsided him.

The Bodyguards held a memorial assembly, after their fashion. Ran had been a full-fledged member of the Bodyguard Guild, as all the "vocational school" teachers were, and the Guild gave two things to his memory. One was this testimonial, in which the Nin herself spoke about him, the image broadcast to hundreds of thousands worlds via tachyonic holography. The other was imbedded in the Code of the Guild itself: no Bodyguard was ever killed without the Guild discovering why. Sometimes it happened in the normal course of protecting some dignitary that had contracted with them. Rarely, it was capricious, because of some other factor. In the latter cases, the Guild delivered its second tribute:

Revenge.

The Guild of Personal Protectors had been in disarray following the disappearance of its top leadership during the October incident nearly two years before. Now the members saw the new Leader, and in watching her, knew why she had risen and prevailed.

"He was a Bodyguard like any other," the Nin Tova said, speaking quietly in the great stadium, the on-planet members of the Guild in the seats around her, a holographic transmitter before her. Quiet though it was, her voice penetrated the innermost consciousnesses of the Bodyguards as they watched on the myriad of human worlds. "And he pursued his duty like any other, with skill and determination and intelligence and strength."

She paused. All of the watchers could see the emotion in her, but they could also see that it was controlled, an integral part of the woman who faced them.

"All men die eventually," the Nin said. "They die of old age, of disease, of accident, of violence. Our job is to minimize the number of violent deaths by protecting those who contract with us. Our Guild of Personal Protectors was hired by powerful families in the Castor/Pollux Sector to protect the Sector itself. He failed, and we don't know why he failed. But we do know one thing: he was the best. The best! Many of you would have failed in his place. But I hope that many of you would have succeeded." The "powerful families" was a myth, but only the Nin knew that.

Asher watched her from a hundred yards away in the massive stadium at the outskirts of the city that housed the vocational school. Emotions flooded within him. Clemmy was at his side, tear-streaks creasing her cheeks, watching the Nin with shining eyes. Around them were hundreds of Bodyguards, and the students of the school as well.

"Violent death is a matter of chance," the Nin said, her blonde/brown hair moving with her head, her gestures at a minimum, but somehow the more controlled and powerful for all that. "The chance of the enemy encounter. The battle. The attack from the rear. The defense. Slippage. Third parties. Equipment failure. Exhaustion. Overwhelming odds. Many things determine a battle, and many of them are beyond the control of the warrior. We Bodyguards train ourselves to minimize the chance elements of a battle, but no matter how hard we train, random events surround us, inhibit us, and sometimes overcome us, as they overcame Randolph Tarney. He died in our service, and we miss him, and praise him, and mourn him. And, if necessary, we will avenge him."

There was no cheering. The Bodyguards knew when to speak and when to keep silent. But the tension in the stadium was almost tangible, caressing the bodies of everyone there, and of the watchers around the galaxy, too.

"I want to see Ran's body," Asher told the Nin. Hours had passed. Once again Asher was in the Nin's private office; this time he was certain that it was an amalgam that he faced.

"Why?" she asked. Then she said: "You will not like what you see, Asher. He was shot through the heart from behind with a needler."

But finally, Asher found himself looking down at the still husk of what had been Ran, his friend. The body was naked, stretched out on a slab of metal in a Bodyguard morgue.

The mark of the needler was clear enough. The tiny stream of coherent light had entered his back and cut through, wavering with the hand of the attacker, emerging in a ragged pattern from his dark chest. Bleeding had been slight.

The real Nin stood with Asher, looking down. And reluctantly, Asher reached out with his mind.

It was ghastly, this probing of the cold and dead flesh of the one who had been his friend. But there was in Asher a hidden fear, and to erase it or crystallize it he had to undertake this examination, looking for signs that automeds would always miss, for no automed had ever been among wizards as Asher Tye once had been.

It was entirely in Ran Tarney's brain that Asher moved, ignoring the rest of the body, for it was in the brain that the evidence would be found, or not found.

There were no traces of thought remaining in that dead brain, of course. There was nothing at all left of the entity that had been Randolph Tarney. All intercellular electrical activity had long since ended, potentials discharged, negatives having satisfied the positives now that life was no longer there to stop it.

At last Asher shuddered and pulled away. He felt permeated with cold, drained of heat to the innermost recesses of his soul.

"It was not a needler that killed him," Asher said hoarsely. The Nin started.

"Automeds have inspected him a dozen times," she said, looking sharply at Asher. "Cause of death was heart failure caused by the destruction of the heart muscle."

"Cause of death was 'heart failure,' all right," Asher said grimly. "But the heart failed because his brain failed; the muscle damage was later. Believe me, Nin; I see the destruction in his brain, the Skill-induced destruction of the protein barriers between the cells."

"The medicos said that that was a result of the heart stoppage," the Nin murmured.

"No. The other way around," Asher said. "I have seen this before. This is the result of a mental attack."

The Nin looked at him fixedly. "Do you know what you're saying? You and I both saw October driven from the galaxy."

"Aye," Asher said. "And now we see death brought by the likes of October, or some new Power with the same abilities. But what is to be believed? The October One herself canvassed the known human universe without finding any trace of such systematic use of Power. Does such use emerge now? Or is October somehow still among us?"

The Nin was silent. She was thinking of a long ago time when an emissary of the destroyed October Guild had come into her native solar system and had killed her mother and father.

"If this is so," she said at last, "and I believe you, Asher Tye, then only another wizard can locate and fight on an equal basis with the attackers of Randolph Tarney."

"Aye," Asher said grimly. "And the Bodyguard Guild has only one wizard."

"Yes," the Nin said. Then: "I think it time for your first mission, Asher Tye."

"You," the Nin said to the little group in private conference, "have been selected because, among your many skills, you hold the best mental Shields of all the warriors. You will need that Skill as you find out why Randolph Tarney died. Trace down the drug problem if you can, but above all find out who killed the Bodyguard and why. And unless the 'why' compels you otherwise, avenge the Guild—and avenge it with such decisiveness that no observer would ever again feel the slightest temptation to challenge it.

"You three humans will take on the appearance of spoiled aristocrats, rich kids with nothing to do but party and travel and play. The others will carry diplomatic pouches, and pose as bureaucrats exploring interplanetary trading compacts. You will travel always on the same ships—the three humans 'accidentally' together, the rest of you separately. You will not go to Surcease directly, but will pass from starship to starship as you penetrate the Sector, and ferret out anything about the region that seems unusual or threatening. Then, when you land on Surcease, you will know where to look and what to look for. And when you find out the truth, you will take whatever action is appropriate: from nothing, to the killing of the murderer of Randolph Tarney, to whatever your judgment dictates."

Asher stood before her. Beside him were Clemmy and four other warriors. One of them had known Ran in the old days: Dov—red haired and gangling, but lightning quick and loyal to a fault. The other three were aliens. All were warriors.

One was a Ghiuliduc called Spimmon. He was a foot high, spindly, and looked something like the base of an old-fashioned radio tower—a stick man without perceptible head on top, a jumble of rods as black as cast iron. To Asher's hypersensitive Skill, Spimmon's brain seemed a pool of turgid water, sometimes still, sometimes in motion.

The second was a Therd, a ghastly ochre-and-yellow being shaped something like a thickened and knobby cone, with writhing blue veins in the ochre areas, and three feet that retracted on demand. Its name was Adio-Gabutti, and Asher could not read its mind at all. That was its strength—that, and a certain obscure wisdom that escaped Asher most of the time. Sometimes Asher suspected that the Therd had come among the Bodyguards in order to write a Ph.D. dissertation or its equivalent; later, when he finally had a chance to study the Therd entry in the Galactic Encyclopedia, he found out that he had probably been right.

And the last was a humanoid. Nisha Scalli had a long, prehensile tail, but he stood on two feet, and his face had two eyes and a nose and a mouth in the right places, even if his ears were invisible and his head was a distinct downward-pointed triangle—wide mouth over abruptly squared chin. He was an Ekans, and was a shade taller than Asher himself. His hairless skin had an olive drab quality, but it was shiny and sleek with body oil. To Asher's mental probing, Nisha's mind seemed to be as clear as Clemmy's; if anything, it was even more transparent to Asher's scrutiny than human minds. For generally he could not read thoughts as logical verbal paragraphs unless the other was Skilled, too; rather, he had to piece together flows of emotion and scattered visual impressions when he moved inside an untrained mind. The comparison made Nisha's mind seem a model of clarity, although there were underlying currents that the Ekans seemed able to keep completely hidden.

The Ekans were a newly discovered race that had only just discovered interspatial drive, somewhere in an upper dusting of stars farther along the spiral arm near which the human worlds were centered. The Ekans were said to be pathologically aggressive among themselves, and the presence of Nisha Scalli here was something of an oddity: he had apparently journeyed alone for hundreds of light years solely to join the Bodyguards. But why? He seemed to need little training if he intended to offer his services in the protection of humans, for only the most advanced of the human Bodyguards might be able to take him one-on-one.

But his presence had led to an unexpected result, for there was something about the Ekans that excited a mental resonance with the little Ghiuliduc. Asher had never seen anything like it on the October World, where there had been no aliens other than the October One herself. For the result of the Ekans and Ghiuliduc interaction was a dual Shield far greater than either could raise alone—so intense that even Asher could not break through. He had only recently discovered the anomaly, and had reported it to the Nin immediately. The fit with the present mission appeared almost miraculous.

But there was also something in the Ekans that caused Asher to frown. For Nisha knew, *knew*, with the absolute certainty of experience coupled with racial awareness, that he was faster and stronger than any human warrior anywhere. Even than the Nin herself.

Why this human as a leader, Nisha was thinking even now, *when I could kill him with a flick of my tail. And that I will do . . . But how to deal with the Skill? Perhaps the Ghiuliduc and I . . .*

Asher shot a glance at Nisha. Was there hatred here for some unknown reason? The Ekans had a trick of hiding his underlying intentions beneath surface prattle that confused rather than revealed. *I will have to watch this one,* Asher thought.

"You will learn the Sector language," the Nin was saying, "for Ran Tarney was a native speaker and you do not have that advantage. And on your way there you can study the social system and general layout of Surcease itself."

"It will look suspicious," Dov said to the Nin, "for rich kids to be able to speak a language like Surceasean. Rich kids only know Basic; they carry a translator unit for everything else."

The Nin looked annoyed. One of the things she tried to pound into her trainees was to reason things out for themselves.

"Clemmy," she said. "You answer that."

Clemmy's narrow face flushed. Her crown of mahogany hair bowed as she focused inward, and then, almost immediately, she looked up again.

"We won't actually use it," she said, not looking at Dov. "It will be something we can take advantage of if translators are stripped away from us. The enemy will not suspect we have such knowledge behind us. We may learn something that might save our lives."

Dov's face was suddenly as bright as his hair, but he was not angry. Dov was often sarcastic, often willful and im-

pulsive, but almost never angry, and that was one of his
greatest assets as a Bodyguard/warrior/thief.

"You will leave in one week's time," the Nin said.

Two days into that week, Asher knew that he had a
problem with Nisha Scalli. The alien took his direction
readily enough, for that was expected of a warrior. But in
subtle ways he made his contempt for the rest of them
felt. And indeed, Asher was forced to admit that Nisha
moved with a fluidity and speed that no human being
could match. He himself avoided a one-on-one with the
alien, for he sensed that undercurrent of hatred in Nisha's
mind. He could not probe deeper for the cause, for the
alien would have sensed it and resisted. Nevertheless,
Asher decided, he could not allow the underlying attitude
to continue.

They spent mornings working on the intellectual side of
the mission. Language training is not difficult once fear is
set aside and time devoted to it. The online encyclopedia
offered a few million languages, and one of them was
Surceasean. They captured it in molecular storage and
subjected it to a training overlay; and from the moment
they began training, they spoke nothing else.

At nights they went to bed with subliminal sleep training all around them. The humans gathered in morning
classes and relaxed on couches while measured music played
in their ears, attuned to the rhythm of the human body
and mind, while instruction intertwined with and followed
the beat, one beat per second.

The aliens did something similar with their own biologi-
cal rhythms. By the end of the week, the words were
coming easily to all of them, human and alien alike.

Afternoons, they continued their Guild training; they
had all turned their "vocational" teaching duties over to
others. Now weaponry, hand-to-hand, aerobic endurance,
stick fighting, and concentration were pursued.

Adio-Gabutti, the Therd, could not move rapidly on his
feet, and nothing he did could be called running, but he
seemed to have an inexhaustible supply of tentacular arms
that would shoot out of his body when least expected, as

well as a stinging spray he could loose at will. The spindly little Ghiuliduc named Spimmon, only a foot high, could beat all three humans in short-distance runs, and when under attack, never seemed to be where the attacker expected.

Nisha Scalli could beat all of them in short- and long-distance runs, and, it seemed, any other physical contest.

Asher decided to bring it to a head one afternoon near the end of the week. All but the Therd had taken off on a fifteen miler, Spimmon after a short time riding on Clemmy's shoulder. Within the first mile Nisha had disappeared in the distance. When they reached their goal, a grassy knoll in a park-like area on the edge of the city, they found the humanoid sitting on his tail as if it were a stool, arms crossed, waiting for them.

None of the humans were breathing particularly heavily, for this sort of run was routine. They stretched out the kinks caused by thousands of foot impacts, and as they did so, Asher caught the thread of the humanoid's thoughts: "Slow, sluglike beings," he was thinking, "with minds just as slow. Any three-year-old Ekans could dangle them from his tail without working up a sweat."

" 'Shun!" Asher shouted. The humans and aliens looked surprised, but Asher was the mission leader, and at once, an arrow-straight line formed in front of him, Nisha on the right, followed by Clemmy, Dov, and the Ghiuliduc Spimmon.

"Combat," Asher roared. "Spimmon. Nisha."

The two came out of line. It looked ridiculous, the whipsaw, olive-colored Ekans towering over the foot-high, spindly Ghiuliduc. They faced one another, the Ekans' three-fingered fists tightly closed and hanging at his sides, tail thumping softly, and the little Ghiuliduc immobile, looking like nothing more than a structure of black tinker toys.

Asher sensed the Ekans' opinions, rattling around contemptuously in his brain. Yes, he and this Ghiuliduc together could raise a diamond-hard mental Shield, and that was a matter for respect. But as a warrior, the Ghiuliduc was excrescence, not fit to share the same mat with Nisha Scalli. But there was, of course, the other thing . . .

"Attack on count of three," Asher said savagely. "And
. . . *full contact!*"

Dov and Clemmy shot a horrified glance at Asher, but
such was the discipline of training that they brought their
eyes back under control and said nothing. Full contact?
The Ekans would crush the little Ghiuliduc like a pile of
straw.

Nisha's eyes flickered at Asher, and in that brief contact
Asher sensed a dilution in the other's confidence. What
was this? Did the human want the Ghiuliduc dead for
some reason? And might I kill him, even by accident, in a
warrior-heightened state of no-mind?

Asher felt something erupt suddenly in Nisha Scalli, and
it just didn't make sense. For it was fear, and he had never
associated tenderheartedness with Nisha Scalli before.

"Raise Shields!" Asher roared. Shields went up in Nisha's
and Spimmon's minds, and the resonance took hold between them. Both they and Asher now knew that Asher
could not interfere in the fight about to take place, even if
he wanted to or decided to. Touching the Shields with his
mind, Asher felt the ghosts of thoughts and emotions he
could not now affect. In the Ghiuliduc he felt an intense
awareness, but no fear, and that was what Asher was
counting on, for he had seen the Nin working with this
Ghiuliduc a dozen times, and hoped that what he had seen
could prevail here.

In the Ekans, Asher felt desperation. If full contact the
human wanted, and the Ghiuliduc dies, how then can I
come against . . .

Asher probed at the ghosts, unable to pierce through
into clarity, feeling that amazing hardness that could resist
any of the various forms of mental attack. The two comba-
tants would know with certainty that Asher could not in
any way interfere with the upcoming combat.

"One . . ." Asher said. No movement from anybody.
"Two . . . Three!"

The Ekans shot forward as if from a gun, step, step,
then a foot lashing out in blinding swiftness . . .

The Ghiuliduc had moved backward, and the foot struck
empty air.

Then the tail came, and again the Ghiuliduc seemed to quiver backward. But as the lashing whip of the tail reached its apex, Spimmon suddenly reached out and had hold of it, and as the Ekans followed through on his motion and shot the appendage behind him again, the Ghiuliduc was hanging on like a light bulb from a wire.

Nisha's other foot was already shooting toward where the Ghiuliduc had been, before what had happened sank in. With an animal snarl, he whirled, whipping the tail upward to smash the Ghiuliduc against the ground.

But at the apex of the whip, the Ghiuliduc let go and, driven by the force of the tail itself, hurled against the Ekans' face, pointy arms outstretched.

The Ekans howled and threw his hands upward to his eyes, and like a giant black spider, the Ghiuliduc flowed over his head to the back of his neck. Nisha's eyes were streaming tears and tightly shut, for Spimmon had poked them savagely. For the moment, the Ekans was blind.

Again, the tail. It shot up to grab Spimmon off his perch as the little black arms hammered into Nisha's ears, but again the Ghiuliduc was too fast for it. He slipped down Nisha's suddenly sweat-covered olive skin like a skier down a mountain, the whipping tail missing him by inches, and all at once he was on the ground away from the Ekans, and the lashing tail could not find him.

Asher felt the Shield dissolving from Nisha Scalli's mind. He did not enter the mind of the tortured alien, but kept it in view just as he kept its body in view with his eyes.

For Nisha was in pain: wracking, mind-numbing pain. Those dart-line hammers into the ears had destroyed his balance, shot agony through his head, rattled his thoughts and destroyed his battle no-mind. He found himself suddenly on the grass, one arm and tail holding him upright, streaming eyes trying to locate the Ghiuliduc.

And the Ghiuliduc was moving in . . .

"Stop!" Asher growled. "End of match. Bow."

Weaving, the Ekans reached his feet with an intense effort, and would have fallen but for the support of his tail. Finally, his eyes cleared enough to find the Ghiuliduc, standing before him like a glassy black statue.

They bowed. It was what they did at the end of a match. But Nisha Scalli was never quite the same again.

"You fought well," Spimmon piped hesitantly. The Ekans grinned and hissed, and the grin clearly had more in common with a tiger than a man. The Ekans was enraged, Asher thought.

"I had to stop it," Asher said gratuitously, "to protect Nisha." The hiss became a steam-whistle roar.

Then Asher did something which surprised even him. He suddenly reached forward and thrust a red-hot mental poker into the still water of the Ghiuliduc's mind. The little alien collapsed as if life had been taken from him.

Nisha saw him fall through streaming eyes. His rage evaporated and his mind said: "I need him!" Enigmatic, Asher thought. He slammed down on Nisha Scalli's mind too, then, and the Ekans fell like a tree, toppling off its stump.

Clemmy looked at Asher as if she were seeing him for the first time.

"So they won't get cocky," Asher said roughly. Then he thought that he shouldn't have said anything at all.

It didn't compute, Asher thought. The Ekans seemed to fear that harm might come to Spimmon, whom he had known for scarcely two weeks, but when in a formal match, it had looked as if he would have killed him if he had been able.

Respect? Toward Spimmon, perhaps. But not toward Asher, who cheated with his mind.

Chapter 3

The council on Surcease was deathly silent. Seventeen
men and women, humans all, sat around a circular table,
hands clasped above planted elbows, eyes fixed over fists
in unwinking stares at a point in the air above the center
of the circle. Despite the variety of physical types among
them, they all had several things in common. All were
very young. All were fleshy, from overweight to obese.
All, too, were naked.

Below the chairs from which rolls of flesh hung like
bread dough, the legs of the seventeen were wide apart. It
looked as if a foot-wide ochre ribbon were tied from leg to
leg in a continuous band around the circle, a ribbon shot
through with pulsing blue veins, writhing horribly in ceaseless, compulsive motion. Waves passed down the ribbon,
and on one leg or another the band would widen upward,
then down again, irregularly, spasmodically. Here and
there, thin red tendrils ran from the ribbon up a leg, to
disappear somewhere in the folds of flesh above.

The room itself was shabby. The moss-like carpet was
ragged from wear and stain and neglect. The windows
overlooked the city from one of the Center's higher floors,
but the scene was indistinct and crusty from the months of
film adhering to the lux. The odor was indescribable, but
none of the humans noticed, or if they noticed, cared.

Communication flowed. It moved on two distinct levels,
both independent of the other, both as alien to the other
as fire to vacuum. But both streams of thought had one

thing in common, and one thing alone: they were dedi-
cated to the same purpose.

"You should not have let the body leave Surcease," one
thought said.

"Rather that, than bring whoever sent him here," another said.

"Aye, but the Shield," said the first.

"Feeble and amateurish."

"He killed a woman and two men."

"And gave himself away. He was a Bodyguard. No one
else develops physical skill to that extent."

"But the Shield."

"Yes, the Shield. Why the Shield? The October One
suspected other Skill in the galaxy, but such was never
found."

"It was, but not within. It came from Outside; it came
for the October Ones, and dragged them forth from the
galaxy."

"Perhaps as it did so, it trained this Bodyguard for a
brief time."

"Perhaps it came back."

"If it came back, we would have been overwhelmed.
But no. It will never come back; I and we felt its intention
as it left. The Sculptor is its home, and there it intends to
remain."

"Perhaps the October Ones themselves have come back."

"Then we would already be among them again. Nay,
that cannot be. We would feel their Power moving in our
realm, and we feel it not."

"What if the Sculptor Being trained many Bodyguards
before it finished with October?"

"If this one was typical, we have no need to worry. His
Skill was primitive and easily defeated."

One of the men urinated; he scarcely noticed or cared.
Below him the salty stream reached the ribbon. It vi-
brated in ecstasy, which rippled around the ribbon in
dying harmonics. Above, the stream of thought flowed
uninterrupted.

"There is yet another possibility," a thought came. The
man who sent it, one Ash Medai, was powerfully built

beneath the overlay of flab, and unlike most of them, he paid daily attention to the maintenance of physical strength. It had set him apart from those around him since early childhood, and he continued it even now, in the face of the indulgence that had captured him as it had captured the others in the room. "And that possibility is that the teacher of the Shield is one like us."

A chorus of thoughts hit him.

"No."

"No."

"That is not a possibility."

"It cannot be."

"All October Adepts and Initiates left the galaxy with the Sculptor Being. All others besides us had long since been Erased. There was only us—three thousand two hundred fifty-two of us—and all are accounted for."

"Which brings us to another point," a mohawk-haired woman thought. "The Central operation says it needs another four hundred of us. It wants to reach beyond the compiled statistics of human space and alter the raw figures so that they add up. They also say that certain logical anomalies growing in the Encyclopedia threaten to reach the five-digit priority levels, and they fear that some being somewhere will begin to detect them."

A stony mental silence greeted this. Then Ash Medai angrily thought: "It would mean that over two-thirds of the 3,252 would be at Central."

"Yes," the woman said.

"How can we run our operations here then?" As said, shouting with his voice this time.

Again, silence. They all knew the answer; they all knew the priorities. The powerful man would have to see it, too.

"All right!" he snarled at last. "But only until we've reached ten percent penetration into human space. Then we and the Ressies will be so deeply entrenched that no force in the universe can dislodge us."

"You're concerned with economics," the mohawk-haired woman snapped, using her voice, too. "But the major issue has to be the safety of the Ressies."

Ash Medai glared at her. But all he communicated, by

thought this time, was: "They are two sides of the same coin."

"Please, please," thought the youngest and fattest among them. "Let us return to the point at issue. I was there, remember; this Network was not. And there was a Shield. We, to coin a phrase, are not alone."

The powerful man, strands of wet-looking black hair lying ropily over his high forehead, took it up, retaining dominance as he did so. "All right," he thought. He seemed to shake himself free of the chain of thought immediately past. "All right. Consider. What Skill does this incident reveal? Suppose you or I set out to train in Skill a human being without Skill potential. What could we teach him? Only one thing, and that is what Skill can be raised from the centering of the mind. And that was the type of Shield this black Bodyguard had."

The thought stream flowed emptily for a moment as they all digested this, looking for arguments against it.

"But," a thought came finally, "again, who is it? We have identified every such individual; who can such a one be?"

The room was very warm, and sweat beaded down the faces of the seventeen, forming rivulets as it merged with other streams further down the body, finally reaching the tendrils of the ecstatic ribbon around their legs.

"There are only these choices," the powerful man thought. "A trainee of the Sculptor about which we know nothing. Or one like us who somehow evaded our knowledge. Of the two, the first is most likely, in my opinion. But whichever it is, such a one is a threat to us all, for the greatest edge we have is the use of Power; and as long as we are unchallenged in that use, we will prevail."

"Then," thought the oldest man present, scarcely more than twenty-two, "we must know."

"Aye," came another thought.

"Aye."

"Aye."

"We must know, one way or the other," the powerful man thought. "Some of us must follow the body of the

Bodyguard, and ferret out this other, and destroy her, or him. And in the meantime, I myself will begin what we have long known must be begun. For the only organized human force that has the potential of interfering physically with us is the Guild of Personal Protectors, the Bodyguards, and they are the apparent source of this Shield problem, too. It is now time to move against the Guild as a whole, before they recognize what we are doing and try to interfere."

"But if you go to the Concourse, who will follow the dead Bodyguard and expose the Shield-teacher?"

"Who? Does it matter?" came the thought of Ash Medai. "Any of the several hundred of the most advanced among us still on Surcease. Any but yourselves, once you realize what it means. There are no Shields other than our own at the Concourse, and I can go in Shadow with my Ressie without fear of detection. Those who follow the dead Bodyguard must pass well beyond the sphere of Ressie space to reach the Bodyguard planet, and they can't use Shadow for fear of attracting the mental attention of the Shield-teacher. But without Shadow, even one Ressie that far out would attract attention that we do not want."

There was a horrified gap in the flow of thought.

"You mean," came a mental gasp, "that the followers will have to go *without their Ressies*?"

"We can route them through Dade Station on their way back," the big man thought, smiling thinly. "We are not entirely heartless. They can pick up Ressies there, two weeks before they could get to Surcease. Dade will soon be a hub of Ressie trade for us anyway."

"Who represents us on Dade?" a question came.

"Dal Gaskin maintains the Station Com," Ash thought. There was a collective shudder of distaste around the table which agitated the ribbon quivering below.

"He is, however, good at it," the big man thought.

"But . . ." quavered another thought, almost echoed by a third, wrenching away from Dal Gaskin: "Is it absolutely necessary to send a team out without Ressies?"

The big man did not have to answer. This time it was his colleagues' turn to reason it out for themselves.

And so, the decision was made. The thirty-four legs stirred then, and the broad ochre ribbon reluctantly oscillated, then broke into seventeen discrete pieces. As the pieces formed like flattened softballs against every other leg, the humans rose from their vinyl chairs with sounds like toilet plungers.

The Galactic Index still rested at 434,671.

Chapter 4

Four followers were selected, and once they realized what it meant, Ressie-wise, they fought with demonic desperation. But each was brought in separately by the seventeen, and against the combined mental power of the Network they could not prevail. All four were nearly as advanced in Skill as the Circle members themselves.

Ash Medai brought the four together for a last meeting as they were about to leave Surcease. They stood before him, four dejected people, three women and one man.

"You know what you're looking for," the powerful man said. He was fully dressed this time, in the careless tattered fashion that had recently overtaken Surcease. The four followers, however, were meticulously clothed in high-fashion travel apparel.

"The quickest way you can regain Ressies," the man said to them, "is to search out all the people to whom this dead Bodyguard was sent. Don't worry about any occurrences of the type of Shield that he raised against us; simply maintain your Network, and nothing can threaten you. But if you find someone with Skill beyond Shielding, Skill that might have trained those Shields, then you will kill that individual in the quickest way you can. Remain only long enough to discover if there are any others that can use Power. If so, kill them too. If there are too many for you, which I very much doubt, then contact us and we will send assistance. But our guess is that you will find one man or woman, and your four linked minds will be double the power to overcome such a one."

41

The emaciated followers stared hungrily at the bulge of the pantaloons on the powerful man's lower leg.

"And for heaven's sake, eat and drink as much as you can," Ash said. "Then, when you return, your Ressies . . ."

But he did not have to finish. They all remembered what it had been like when they had first encountered a Ressie.

"And if you cannot conquer the one with Skill, and feel yourselves in danger," he said with final grimness, "you can use this." And he reached into a large pouch at his side and drew forth a machine that looked like a half-sized juggling club. The four stared at it.

"Yes," Ash Medai said harshly, "a Skill jammer. You well remember the rebellion in our ranks that brought this hellish device into being. 'Use Skill for proper purposes alone,' the rebels said, as if we do otherwise. It was well that they were so few, and that we had the Surceasean Police under our control by that time so that we could destroy with unSkilled soldiery. Now *we* own the device."

"I'm not sure we can undertake that kind of work," the Nin Tova told Guteater. "We are personal Bodyguards; we do not function as a paramilitary force. We don't have battleships or heavy weaponry at all."

Guteater's image was as clear as if he were sitting in front of her, instead of in his own office three hundred light-years away. He was a humanoid alien of a common type, more like a fat, upright weasel than a man. Guteater was, of course, only an approximation of his name, or title, or whatever it was.

"I am not talking about interstellar war, Guildmaster. The attackers are not highly organized, but they make the word 'macho' seem like 'wimp,' " Guteater said in automatic translation. "They have their cruisers and light destroyers, but they use them only when attacked. That type of fighting is not the real thing, for them. They prefer to land and fan out and challenge every being they meet to one-on-one or small-group combat. Needless to say, they are very seldom defeated, although humanoids are resourceful enough to make it interesting for them."

"Emperor Guteater," the Nin said, "I would expect any humanoid to point grav cannon at these 'attackers,' whoever they are, and tell them to go away. Otherwise, they should call upon the Galactic Police to intervene."

"They will not do so—but please, you need not call me by title. I am Emperor to my own forty planets with twenty-five races only, but not Emperor to yours, and I have no expansion in mind. What I want to say is that these aliens don't seem understood by the Galactic Concourse. We ourselves know only rumors of the planets they have plundered—planets not able to use interspace, races without tachyonic science, which have simply disappeared. That the end result is the extinction of the other race is, again, only rumor; the Encyclopedia is silent on the matter."

"What you allege is impossible," the Nin said flatly. "Rumors, as you call them, will inevitably rise in priority in the Encyclopedia news channels if they are important enough, and certainly the death of races is plenty important."

"One would think so," the Emperor said, "but nevertheless the Encyclopedia is silent."

The Nin regarded the purple robe that hid the Emperor's ample physique. Parts of his throne were visible around the edges of the holographic transmission, and it seemed to be made of something like platinum or iridium.

She sighed. "So what you want me to do is to investigate an unknown race which doesn't interest even the Galactic Police, and somehow keep that race away from you?"

"Yes," the Emperor said; there was a note of desperation in the translated voice. "We are few, a few races on a few worlds. But you humans occupy over four hundred thousand worlds, and we thought that you, as the most effective fighting force per individual in human space, could . . . Look. My colleagues and I are convinced that we can persuade the Concourse eventually that the attackers have to be controlled. It is just a question of time, Guildmaster. You know that we are talking about four hundred thirty-some thousand intelligent races in the Concourse. Our problem will seem pretty insignificant in the face of the problems of a hundred billion worlds. But eventually we think that we can persuade the Police that what is happening out here is a menace to the peace and quiet of the galaxy as a whole. It is just our bad luck that they have hit one of the few underexplored Shroud areas, and have not impacted any Concourse races yet."

The Nin sighed again. "Emperor Guteater," she said, "there aren't enough Bodyguards in the human universe to randomly explore the Shroud stars where you believe this unknown race to be."

"Oh, but the race is known!" the Emperor said eagerly. "At least, we think it is the one. It . . ."

The holographic image froze suddenly. The Nin frowned. She waited, and all at once the image went two-dimensional, like a television screen, and then just as suddenly popped out of existence altogether.

"What the devil?" said the Nin's own holo image, a computer amalgam. "It's never done that before."

Asher faced his mission team—two humans and three aliens—in one of the training rooms of the school.

"Shields," he said. Five Shields went up. One by one, Asher probed them.

The strongest by far was Clemmy's.

"Dov. Harden that Shield. Center. Center." With slowly increasing force, Asher bore down upon the Shield with his mind. He pressed, harder and harder.

"More concentration,." he said with voice and mind to Dov. "More no-mind."

Dov's glistening face relaxed slowly as he forgot about his body and put all his attention into concentrating on a single point within his skull. Physically it might have been located in the pineal gland at the center of his brain, but such is an analogy only.

"Good," Asher said. It seemed to his pressing mind that he was encountering a globe made of solid diamond. When he had been an Apprentice in the October Guild, Asher would have been hard pressed to break through such a

Shield. However, he had since been trained further by the Sculptor.

"Relax," Asher said. Life came back into Dov's freckled face. "Excellent, Dov. Remember how to do that. Later we will train under physical stress. Above all, remember how to forget that body that you love so much. Spimmon!"

The little Ghiuliduc tensed his mind, and Asher moved in on it.

Again, Asher was struck by the analogy of a pool of still water, which he thought of every time he encountered a Ghiuliduc mind.

But this time the water had turned to ice. This was a test of each of them as individuals, and Asher would not permit Spimmon and Nisha to link together this time.

Asher pressed. He had a technique for piercing the ice, but he would employ it only after he had explored the strength of the alien's conventional Shield.

"Good . . . good," Asher said. His normal Apprentice attack was not breaking through. "Now concentrate, Spimmon, concentrate . . ." Asher turned his mind into a lance of fire and plunged at the lake.

And the lance broke through. Spimmon stiffened and uttered a plaintive scream, then collapsed into a pile of quivering rods.

The others would have moved to help him, but Asher stopped them. "He is but stunned," Asher said. "He will be back with us in a moment, and I will teach him further. Nisha!"

The olive-skinned alien's tail moved restlessly, and he put force into his Shield. Again, Asher caught a thread of contempt in the Ekans' mind, but it had been softened by his fight with Spimmon, and further sobered by the reality of Asher's Skill-trained mind. Physically, Nisha Scalli still felt the absolute confidence that he could crush Asher Tye. But as a reasoning being, he knew that raw physical power was not the only ability in the universe.

Nisha had been distracted lately. There was growing in him the certainty that he already had all the answers that he had come for.

Asher pressed. There was strength there, but it was

wobbly and uncertain. The alien had neglected Shield practice while working on physical development, Asher saw.

And so he hammered in. Not like a lance this time; instead, he smashed against the Shield as if he were a sledge striking stone.

The Shield shattered in a thousand fragments. Nisha's eyes went blank, and like a tree, he toppled forward on his face.

"Adio-Gabutti," Asher said. The Therd seemed to be facing him, although it was hard to tell. "Raise your Shield."

"It is raised," the acidic voice of the alien came. And then Asher found it, a glassy invisibility as transparent as glass, revealing behind it . . .

Nothing.

Try as he might, Asher had still not been able to penetrate a Therd's mind. In one key way, however, it made the Therd invaluable in any encounter with October. For if October Skill could not detect a Therd, then it could not directly attack one. A Therd's mind could be hammered or lanced, but first the attacker would have to know that the Therd was there, and then cast blows all over the place until the Therd was hit.

WHAM! Asher smashed at Adio-Gabutti's Shield, and it held. He hit it again, and it held.

"Excellent," Asher said. He closed his eyes for further concentration, and . . .

The Therd's Shield was gone. Asher cast about with his mind, and . . .

"Ooof!" he exploded, and staggered backward. The Therd had moved up on him and smashed him in the stomach with one of its tentacular arms.

Asher laughed. "Adio-Gabutti—very, very good!" For against hostile Skill, the Therd had realized that its Shield was a liability, enabling as it did the attacker to pinpoint its mind. The Therd had taken the logical step, and Asher knew that he had an apt student in the person of the ghastly yellow and writhing red-patched cone.

Clem . . .

"Ahhhh!" Asher screamed. For something had seared

the edges of his mind. He threw up his own Shield, and felt another burst of mental fire pour over it.

Then he opened his eyes, and was just in time. He side-stepped Clemmy's hurtling heel, and struck back with his right fist. But she had recovered instantly and was already out of reach.

WAUWMMMMMM! came her mental hammer blow. But with his mind, Asher reached out and grabbed her feet and upended her with a convulsive jerk. Her head came within an inch of impacting with shattering force on the ground.

"You advance," Asher said to her, "but there is much yet to learn."

She reached one arm toward him, and the others, recovering from their lesson, were astounded to see a sort of green aura form around the wrist, focus around the palm, and . . .

A tremendous bolt of green fire leaped at Asher. He laughed, a mentally induced physical Shield between himself and the pouring flames, which cascaded off into nothingness.

"Bravo!" Asher said. "A perfectly focused Green Flame. But watch your head." And he dropped her from his mental grasp.

Clemmy was ready. Her head was bent and she took the fall on her shoulders, letting the floor roll down her back, and then she came springing upright.

Perhaps she would have attacked him then, as would have been expected, but Asher uttered the Word. Hypnotically implanted, any October-trained Apprentice knew the Word, and Asher had made certain that Clemmy had internalized it early in her training. It was a Word that stopped all activity, ended mental and physical attack, bringing the hearer to a frozen standstill. October Adepts had used it to control their students. Now Asher used it the same way.

Clemmy froze. Her thin, strong body stiffened into immobility, and the life went out of her eyes.

Asher clapped his hands, and she started, conscious again, and . . .

"No," Asher said, laughing. "No attacking now. End of lesson."

They all, Asher thought, are doing very, very well. But he was uneasy still. Someone with fair Skill had killed Randolph Tarney, and such use of Power would challenge to the limits any of his mission partners, and perhaps himself as well.

And still he felt that trace of contempt in Nisha Scalli's mind.

Chapter 5

Confusion grew in him, and he went to the Nin.

"Send me alone," Asher said plaintively. "Or send me with Clemmy and no one else. The rest of them can't help me; they will just get in the way."

The Nin frowned. "I send them for reasons that have only partly to do with backing you up, Asher Tye," she said. "I send them for their own learning, too."

"Send me alone with Clemmy," Asher insisted stubbornly. "Leave the rest here. It's less complicated that way."

"You've led squads in training," the Nin said. "But it's different on a mission, and you're finding that out, aren't you, Asher Tye?"

"Yes, and I don't know why," Asher said miserably.

"I wanted to speak with you before you left anyway, Asher," the Nin said gently. "Spimmon complains that you have some kind of grudge against him. Clemmy doesn't much want to talk about it, but says that you seem more ruthless than she's ever seen. Nisha Scalli says nothing, but in his short time here he has a history of landing on human instructors whenever he can. Only the Therd's attitude is wholly positive. Adio-Gabutti is ready to follow you anywhere, as long as he can sneak up on you with that invisible mind of his."

Asher had always been able to lay out his soul before this woman. Now, even though it hurt, he tried to do it still. The trouble was that much of what he felt inside was

49

emptiness, blankness without certainty or even content. How could he articulate that?

"I know something of what it is that's going on in me," Asher said. "It's anger at the death of Ran. That's part of it. But there's also a part that doesn't care. The purpose doesn't drive me like the war against October did. That was a menace anyone could see, and against the entire galaxy. Here it's just revenge, and I'm not at all sure that it . . . it . . . it *feels* right."

The Nin sighed. The endless self-analysis of the young, she thought.

"You're a Guild member, and you have a duty to uphold," she said severely. When Asher didn't react: "And the problem that Ran was looking into is not so insignificant as you seem to think. An entire human Sector is stagnating, and we don't know the full story yet. Whatever is moving in Castor/Pollux could be as galactic a threat as October, or as local as a new upper. Revenge is only the surface; the core is unknown."

Asher was still despondent. He thought about his parents, whom he had seen only a year ago. Strangers now, they had sent him to the October Guild years ago, and had developed lives in which he was not a factor. The meeting had been awkward, and Asher had fled as soon as he decently could. And he still felt guilty about it.

"Roots," Asher said suddenly, again articulating something that had popped into his mind only an instant before. "I need roots somehow. I don't know what I'm going to end up being. I don't have a long-range goal. I'm interested in a thousand things, and none of them is enough."

He fell into moody silence. The Nin regarded him sadly, memory moving in her. She had been driven by revenge against October in the beginning, then by the exigencies of leadership of a complex Guild. But Asher Tye had lost course since the destruction of October.

"Asher, I wanted to see you about something else, too," the Nin said, trying to force his mind in another direction. "You know that I keep watch on the newscasts with many

key words. One of them is the Sculptor sub-galaxy, Asher
Tye. Are you listening to me?"

"Yes," Asher said dully. *With my ears, anyway*.

"Something is happening out there, Asher Tye. All background tachyonics from it have . . . disappeared."

She tried to make it a dramatic flourish, and for a
moment her tactic worked.

"What?" Asher said, head jerking up. "Disappeared?
But that's impossible. All galactic bodies radiate tachyonic
background noise like beacons."

"We've never received anything like coherent tachyonic
transmission from the outlying members of the galactic
cluster," the Nin said, " 'we' being the Concourse races as
a whole. And the few ships that the various races have
sent out to the nearer of the few dozen sub-galaxies have
never come back. The distances are so immense and the
gravitational and string forces so unknown, that the Concourse hasn't worried much about it, since there didn't
seem to be any threat involved. But now there is an
uproar among the tachyonic scientists. It's as if light itself
had stopped coming from out there."

Such vast distances, Asher thought, even between the
Milky Way and its satellite galaxies, multiples of the gigantic distance across the Milky Way's own disk. So far away
that even the tachyonic transmissions of civilizations would
be drowned out by the static of the star groups themselves. The Sculptor, with its million loosely bunched
stars, was one of the closer of the satellite galaxies,
with Fornax and Leos I and II, for example, much farther
away.

"Can it be, Asher," the Nin asked quietly, "that this
phenomenon has something to do with your Teacher, the
one who brought October back to the Sculptor these several years ago?"

Yes, it had to be that, Asher thought. It had to be, in
some way, a sign of the being who had taught him beyond
October for a very short time, and then went away. But
what was happening out there? Was there some titanic
war between October and the Teacher that somehow interfered with tachyonics? Was something else at work?

Asher shook his head. He was tired. More than that, he was about to embark on a mission. He could not afford, he thought, to indulge in cosmic speculation.

And he was human, too. He felt the emotions piling up in him more directly than he did the abstract events in the universe. The lash of criticism from his own squad was hurting.

"Yes, it may be the Teacher," Asher said, "but Spimmon and the others should not have come to you. They should have confronted me face-to-face."

The Nin gave a despairing sigh. It had worked for a moment, anyway.

"That is not the way I run my Guild," she said. Her face took on now the seriousness of certainty. "Yes, they should have come to you, but also yes, they can come to me whenever they wish."

"And what about Dov?" Asher said, still looking down, hands on knees as he sat in the Nin's office. He could not bring himself to look her in the eyes.

She smiled. "He complains," she said, as Asher's spirit prepared for another blow of criticism, "that it is not fair for you to bring and enjoy Clemmy on the mission, while he has no one to share his cabin during the weeks to Surcease."

Asher was surprised, since he hadn't considered that factor at all. Then he was paranoid: "You know what that means?" Asher said, alarmed. "He will want to move on Clemmy; I can feel it." Meanwhile, his mind was analyzing itself: I have mostly conquered anger and hate, but jealousy is still lurking in the shadows, ready to spring at every turn.

"Perhaps, Asher Tye," the Nin said quietly; then: "Look at me."

Asher looked at her. Brown eyes met grey, and Asher felt the confusion of attraction and respect and awe and loss, knowing that he moved on a different level than the remarkable woman before him, and believing in all his heart that hers was the superior of the two. If he could distill her confidence and serenity into liquor, he would drink it down in a single swallow.

"Perhaps Dov will move on Clemmy," the Nin said, eyes penetrating as if she held some occult Skill. "Perhaps Clemmy will move on Dov. Perhaps Clemmy will not move on Dov, but will no longer have you. Perhaps she will remain with you without change. And perhaps you will all meet new people on this mission, and your relationships will fragment into new patterns that would horrify you if you knew them now. But understand this, Asher Tye. It is up to her. And it is up to you. In the long run, we all die."

The last, short sentence was said so fiercely that Asher felt coldness wrap around his gut. The Nin seemed to recover something, eyes losing their intensity for a moment as she looked inward, then coming back into focus on Asher Tye.

"No, that is not the immediate point here," she said, an undertone of savagery in her intonation, "although it lies at the root of everything. The point is that if you are finally able to seize control and point yourself in some particular direction, your destiny will flow and you will know what you have to do. And if you do not seize control, your destiny will flow regardless, and you will do what you have to do, one way or another. I, who all my life have inclined toward taking control and seizing the day, cannot say whether that is for the greater good, or whether passivity and acceptance is. All I do know is that if you do not decide, events will decide for you, what you will be and what you will become."

She had her finger on it, Asher thought. "But how," he said plaintively, "can I seize the day, when the options are so vast and the results so unknown?"

"You seize it regardless, or you don't," she said. "This is getting us nowhere, Asher Tye. You are leaving for Surcease tomorrow with a crew of uneasy partners, and your immediate job is to carry this mission through. You can worry about all the rest of it all you want, but you must do this particular job now."

"And then what?" Asher moaned.

The Nin threw her hands up into the air. "Who

knows? You'll find out soon enough; you've got to learn to wait."

It must be better to seize the day, Asher thought, than to drift like a stick in the ocean. It must be better to take control. It must. It must.

But why couldn't he seem to do it?

Chapter 6

Suppose you had control of 430,000 separate species on 100,000 million worlds. How would you govern them?

The founders of the Galactic Concourse had done what you eventually would have had to do. They had thrown up their . . . er . . . hands and let each species go its own way.

However, with an average of 42 planets, moons, and moonlets per star, it was inevitable that species would clash with one another. In a given solar system there might be three or four methane worlds, a couple of oxygen planets, and a chlorine and carbon dioxide planet or two, with appropriate temperatures and sizes. Some would be satellites of others. Still others wheeled in eccentric orbits around double or triple or quadruple stars, freezing and thawing and earthquaking and generally raising hell. And the vacuum planets: some had had atmosphere once and had lost it through freezing or lack of gravity; others had never had it. On some of those that had had it at one time, life had evolved and then adapted to the growing cold and the gradual freezing of the gases, and such beings now lived in near-vacuum as happily as an aphid lives on a leaf.

And so the species shouldered one another like bowling pins in a rack as populations expanded and interstellar travel became as common as walking to your car. The differences in physical need had a dampening effect, luckily, or the galaxy would have exploded into interplanetary and interstellar war.

A singular rule of the galaxy played its fortuitous part, too. For some reason there seemed to be a common technological ceiling. Throughout man's own history, it had been a truism that new technological ideas would often pop up in several countries simultaneously. When they reached the stars, man had found that the same thing held true among advanced races galaxy-wide. A newer race might advance rapidly until it caught up with the rest of the galaxy, but from then on no race could far outstrip another and, when a new idea did come, it hit millions of worlds at the same time.

But despite this trend toward uniformity in technology, there were conflicts. What if you had to distill the desires of 430,000-plus life forms into a central government. What would you have to do?

Lots of local autonomy; that went without question. No centralized social services, for example—the variations in aging alone would have driven a central social security administrator bananas, if that happened to be the fruit of choice for his, her, or its ape ancestors.

No, in the long run there were only two things that each species demanded of the central authority, and those were both in the interests of self-defense.

The first was a Police force to inhibit overly aggressive races.

The second was information.

And the Index stood at 434,675. Four new races . . .

Shadow. Not the darkness cast by an obstacle to light, but a conscious deflection of photon energy. Within Shadow a trained individual could move without detection, and if the individual were sensitive to magnetic and gravitational detection, the Shadow could deflect those forces, too.

Into the Galactic Concourse Ash Medai came, travelling on a gigantic passenger starship which spun into near-circular orbit about the bizarre world that housed the central government, such as it was. The early pioneers among the 430,000 races had sought a planet that could cater to most of them, and they had found it near the

Core, the central bulge of the Milky Way where densely packed stars raged and an immense singularity grew and grew.

Someday the black hole around the singularity would devour most of the central Core, the spiral arms breaking up and spinning into new configurations as the galaxies of the Local Group reacted with one another. But that was millions of years distant, and the swarming sentient progeny of the galaxy were unworried. The time would come, and in the meantime there was work to be done and lives to be lived.

The planet: you would call it "terraforming" but, thinking about it, you would back away and try to find another word, and fail. It was not large, nor was its sun distinguished, except perhaps for its stability and for its relatively close proximity to the Core, though the latter peculiarity was shared by millions of other greater and lesser stars. But this planet had:

An ocean, cold by terrestrial standards, saline and stormy;

A land mass sealed in an energy shield in which the greenhouse effect had been allowed to run rampant, in an atmosphere of contaminated carbon dioxide;

Another continental land mass open to the oxygenated sky, in an atmosphere with too much hydrogen cyanide for a human being;

A number of islets enclosed in energy shields and sporting an incredible array of environments and gravities and atmospheres;

A couple of vacuum moons of divergent sizes;

A sister planet that was really two, farther from the mediocre sun, a large ammonia world and a slightly smaller chlorine world in eccentric orbit about one another, spinning around the sun like the twins Pluto and Charon;

And about half a dozen cold methane moons around two outer gas giants.

And even so, not all species could be accommodated. But most of them . . .

To one of the oxygen planet's islets came the powerful man from Surcease, swathed in Shadow, his Ressie cling-

ing to his left leg. This particular islet catered to oxygen
breathers who could not tolerate hydrogen cyanide, such
as human beings and Trarrian Ventrapods.

The man was not alone. A Surceasean agent had met
him at the shuttle. The agent was a woman, and she would
soon have to be replaced. Her body weight was danger-
ously low.

The Human Information Office stood on a damp street
near one edge of the force field surrounding the islet. A
tongue of shimmering transparent force stood out over one
part of the sea, taking in an area almost equal to the islet
itself and housing a few water-breathing species with needs
similar to their air-breathing colleagues above. Around the
Office, the streets were densely packed. It was a shanty
town, in fact, and its inhabitants were shift workers from
Surcease, all with Skill, all with Ressies. The squalor was
indescribable.

The powerful man stood, and breathed the fetid air
deeply. He would get used to it, he thought. He could get
used to anything.

With the woman, he moved in Shadow to the Office,
and eased inside its canopied doorway. The lobby area was
vast and jammed with people. But it was not an ordinary
lobby situation. Most of the people were part of a vast
circle around the room; most were naked, emaciated, sitting cross-legged a few inches above the floor. From ankle
to ankle there ran an ochre ribbon of pulsing Ressies. The
room stank of excrescence and sweat, but was almost
silent, save for an occasional subdued plopping noise.

"Five hundred twelve of them," the old woman said
with a faint pride. No, Ash Medai caught himself, she was
not old, could not be old; she only looked that way. She
was as young as he was.

"Four shifts," the woman said. "And the complexities
still grow on us."

The air fairly shimmered with mental energy. Phan-
tasms moved liked shaped cigarette smoke among the
circle, dissipating and forming at random as the energy
flowed and channeled.

"Amazing," Ash breathed. "The largest Network in the history of the galaxy, and the aliens swarming around this islet and this planet don't even know that it is here."

The woman shot a glance at Ash Medai, but said nothing.

"I will follow the energy stream," Ash announced, and moved toward the back of the lobby. He knew he, as one of the Seventeen, would not be denied, and he was surprised when the woman ventured a question in which lay a faint reproof.

"You would be entering the protected circuitry of the Galactic Com," she said, not looking at him.

"I will see the human fragment of the Encyclopedia," he said roughly. "Now."

They circled around the Network and passed into another room, a half-dome affair. Ash Medai paused in the doorway, searching the room with his mind, pausing to influence this circuit here or that bundle there. The woman watched, her lips in a twisted smile.

There was no one in the room. An automatic receptionist sat like a tree stump in the middle of the floor.

And suddenly it spoke, sending a sword-cut of surprise through the powerful man.

"May I help you?" it said in sixty-three languages, human and non-human.

Ash Medai had thought that he had neutralized all of the warning mechanisms of the room. The early races who had built the Com and set it upon its self-perpetuating journey of knowledge had been thorough in its defenses, but there was nothing physical he couldn't handle, Ash Medai thought with arrogant confidence. He cast his mind like a spike, here and there at random around the room. It was nearly ten seconds before he found and desensitized the offending detector.

It had been a weight detector beneath the doorway. The big man allowed his bulk to rise via levitation, once he realized what had happened. The woman's feet, he now noticed, were fractionally above the floor, and probably had been so all along. The continuing inquiries of the receptionist stopped.

"Are you flying?" it now inquired, drawing the logical conclusion. But its infrared and motion detectors detected nothing; nor did its electric eyes and sound pick-ups and radio frequency and microwave scanners. The man's mind met and redirected all of the energies from those units, so that they seemed to pass unimpeded through the air space that he occupied.

"You are good," the woman finally said, grudgingly.

"I have to be," Ash said. The sound waves their voices made hit the Shields they were maintaining and echoed about inside. Outside, there was nothing.

Like a wraith, the man moved around the receptionist and through another opening in the rear, the woman behind him. The vaulted metallic walls rose around him as he floated into a much broader, copper-tinged room, in which intricate mechanisms captured the official reports of the human worlds, news and governmental alike, sorted them out and blew them into the on-line encyclopedia of the Concourse itself. The mental energy from the Network was palpable, pouring in like a two-way stream of jet-propelled lava.

And meanwhile, the Encyclopedia, available to every citizen, poured out of the galaxy in a super-light tachyonic stream. Nearly the entire bulk of the planet was taken up by the molecular storage and tachyonic transmitters of the Concourse, powered by the star-resonated energies implicit in the mantle of the planet itself.

The powerful man easily bypassed laser weaponry; electric, magnetic, gravitational fields, and various combinations thereof; and eight savage were-dragons from Thraxillin, which could sense a fly at a hundred kilometers. He had a moment's trouble with the violent, oscillating force field that protected the central sorting unit itself, but his mind finally found a way of spreading the field apart for an instant, like opening a curtain, and in he went, the woman with him.

He found himself in an enormous cavern where he could feel the pouring input of the human and para-human planets throughout the galaxy—the official words of several hundred thousand human worlds and another 75,000 worlds of species in the same classification, uncontaminated water/oxygen and oxygen breathers, all beaming blathering fact and fancy from planet to Concourse. The unceasing tachyonic stream of the Concourse caught the words, processed them, remembered them, ranked them, and broadcast them omnidirectionally. And citizens of the galaxy were free to seek out keywords or any defined types of information.

But with a byte outpourage of multi-quintillion pieces of data, currency was almost impossible. Men could read the encyclopedia and gain galactic expertise, but in fields so narrow that it was the rare individual indeed who had useful knowledge of even a few of the 430,000-plus oxygen and non-oxygen species that filled the galaxy.

The defenses deflected, the powerful man sent his mind into the central processor. At once he was appalled. He could not absorb such an outpouring even if restricted purely to human news, much less insert his own priorities into it. The woman watched, smiling grimly.

"Now perhaps you stay-at-homes will understand why we have asked for greater and greater numbers of Networkers," she murmured softly.

For a moment, he felt fear. His Ressie stirred against his leg, and made as if to move upward, but the big man caressed it with his hand and it subsided. The fear produced chemical seepage from his pores that the Ressie liked, and it wanted to spread itself more thinly across the man's body in order to absorb more of it. With complexity such as this, how could a Network, even one of 512 and more, even begin to handle it?

Still in Shadow, the man moved slowly across the floor of the immense cavern, touching with his mind one after another of the receptors from the human portion of the galaxy. As he did so, he traced the millions of terabytes coming in. Here they arrived, there they were sorted, there they were categorized, there they were ranked, there they were sent on to the central transmitter . . .

There they were ranked . . .

That was the focus of the Network—not the bytes themselves, though false information could be entered. But mostly, the work was one of realizing priorities of reranking. That was why Surceasean news was almost never ferreted out by the citizens outside. It was there, but buried so deeply by the Network that literally no one in all the galaxy scanned it.

"This you will arrange for Network insertion," Ash Medai told the woman, "that the Bodyguard Guild intends the long-range takeover of all human governments, and once established will rule with terror and fear. Two thousand eighty-eighth priority."

Intelligence units on many thousands of worlds would pick such a high-ranked item out of the information chaos, and pass it on to paranoid planetary governments . . .

The great luxury starship *Bonnie's Best* carried Asher and crew away from the Bodyguard planet. It wasn't long before Asher encountered Dov's message on the wrist-accessed ship's bulletin board. The transmission was routed directly into the receiver implanted in the mastoids behind his ear, a device commonly used by nearly every human in the galaxy.

"Foot race, racquetball, squash, tennis, karate, judo, archery, juggling, bridge, chess, whist, et cetera," Dov's smiling, three-dimensional face said. "Any passenger interested in enjoyable competition with a fun guy, please leave a message at suite A-214."

"I say, old man," Dov said to Asher Tye, meeting him on cue in one of the lounges, approaching with an outstretched hand and an air of hearty good fellowship. "Thank you for your response to my response to your online note. Let's 'do' handball, shall we?"

"Quite," Asher replied dryly. He had to remember: they did not know one another.

Asher scanned the court; it was empty of detectors or listeners of any kind.

WHAP! The ball struck the wall and hit the floor energetically, leaping into Asher's naked hand. He scooped the ball violently against the wall in a looping, upward arc.

"Nothing," he said, *sotto voce*.

WHAP! The ball slammed into the center of the wall and shot high behind them, hitting the rear wall before bouncing on the floor. Asher caught it as it came up and hurled it forward. Dov said:

"You have the freak mind." He rose on his tiptoes and swung at the ball, catching it on the tips of his fingers. "Ouch," he said.

The suddenly flaccid ball barely made it to the wall, hitting the floor an instant later. Asher dived forward, but missed in a wild swing. The ball bounced one, two, three behind him, finally hitting the back wall then and re-bounding forward, rolling like an eviscerated marshmallow.

"We make planetfall tonight," Asher said.

"Aye, the first planet of the trip," Dov said. "Though it's a hydrogen/helium world and would crush us flat and freeze us into sheets of red glass if we disembarked there."

"It's the Station that counts," Asher said.

WHAP! Dov served the ball against the wall. Asher caught it easily in a left-handed blow that sent it up into the top right corner of the court.

As it bounced high, Dov leaped into the air and snagged it.

WHAP! Asher's attention wandered. The ball careened off his head and he lost the point.

Rubbing a point above his earlobe, Asher said: "You did that on purpose."

"Stay out of my mind," Dov grated.

"I'm not in it," Asher said. "As I told each of you, I will not enter your minds unless there is a grave reason."

"And who decides what is a grave reason?" Dov said, his red hair almost matched by the flush creeping up from his neck. But Asher suspected a put-on. Dov might be edgy sometimes, but of real anger he had always had, apparently, complete control.

Asher was silent. The answer was obvious, of course, but he said at last: "A handball to the head is not a grave reason."

"How," Dov said, a bitter edge slicing the corners off his words, "is Clemmy?"

"There are travellers aplenty on this starship," Asher

said carefully. "Even a few . . . uuuuhhhh!" He sagged
suddenly to his knees. The ball Dov had just served shot
past him to impact loudly on the rear wall.

"What is it?" Dov asked, his simulated anger gone
abruptly, reaching Asher in two long strides. Asher shook
his head from side to side, bowed forward almost touching
the floor, still rocking on his knees.

"Interspace," he moaned, clutching his head. "We have
left interspace, and I had my mind all around the ship."

"Uh huh," Dov said, standing and looking down at
Asher. He understood, a little. Interspatial travel involved
the creation of a tiny universe that skimmed down the
center of a two-dimensional gravity string. What would
happen to a hypersensitive mind if its universe were suddenly expanded to infinity in the blink of an eye?

He grasped Asher by the shoulders and heaved him to
his feet. "Sometimes I feel better off having an ordinary
dim-witted and insensitive mind," he said in Asher's ear.

"You need a woman," Asher groaned, scarcely aware
that he was speaking. Dov scowled, still holding Asher
upright.

"Stay out of my mind!" he said.

"I am."

That night, as they reached the depths of the gravitational well that signalled the waystation, Asher told Clemmy
of the incident.

"He needs a woman," Clemmy mused. A shot of alarm
passed through Asher.

Clemmy glanced over at him, across their ornate and
richly appointed cabin.

"I think I know why the Nin arranges marriages," Asher
said then. There was a strain in his voice that he could not
hide.

"There are religious planets that set it up between people who've never even met one another," Clemmy said
quietly. "But I don't think the Nin is ready for that."

"For the religion, or for marriage?" Asher asked. His
mind was churning, a garbage disposal in high gear.

"Marriage," Clemmy said. Asher held her narrow, black

hair-haloed face in both his eyes and mind. He ached at its character and, to him, unwavering beauty.

"I love you, Clemmy," Asher said desperately. His ears heard the words and he was surprised, and in his heart the ache that had brought them forward almost overwhelmed him.

"I love you, too," she said softly. She came to him, and tried to relieve the chaos in his mind. And she did, for the moment.

Chapter 7

Ceal Carnak remembered the October World, but it seemed a thousand years behind her. When she had been brought there as a girl of eleven, she had been awed by the mental powers she had seen displayed all around her. And she had been a talented pupil.

But now her memory was tinged with distaste. It was as if she had not been alive then, she thought.

"I know the same thing," the man Score told her. She stared at him through fevered eyes, her anorexic body as tight as a drumhead.

"You look like hell," she said. And he did; they all did. Their appetites had been slow coming back on their outward journey, and self-pity had crippled their will to force it.

Score's stringy black hair lay unwashed, streaking across a largely bald head. In their common cabin, the man and three women regarded one another morosely, each wishing to be far away, back the way they had come.

"It proves one thing," the shrill voice of bald-headed Sanda grated at them.

"Yeah? What's that, you bat-throated . . ." It was the third woman, Larla, speaking, but Sanda's voice overrode hers like a siren over a piccolo.

"And that's that a Ressie's not some kind of drug you're glad to get off of," Sanda shrieked.

"No one ever said it was," Ceal Carnak said.

On Tenn, the Mother Regent gathered her flowing robes

around her in a way that made the air swish with decisive
finality.

"You have served me long and well, Holbart Card," she
said. The man kneeled before her, his costume simple
white, a black sash striping from left shoulder to waist. He
held his head bowed.

"It is my contracted duty," he murmured. In truth, he
would not necessarily have chosen this matriarch as first
among the seven equal rulers of the planet. But then, the
other six were at minimum incompetent, and at worst
repulsive.

"When the unity fanatics attacked the summer palace, I
believe I might have died were it not for you." Even as
she said the words, she sounded mildly surprised. It was
the idea of dying, Holbart knew. It scarcely ever crossed
her mind.

"Your advice on the false magicians was so valuable that
I would have given you a kingdom, had you been born on
Mother Tenn," she mused. They were in her private
chambers, and as always he was feeling a faint alarm at the
presence of her massive, down-filled bed. But she had not
yet challenged him with it these dozen years, and for that
he was thankful, for there were many rumors that count-
less others had not been spared. "As an outworlder, of
course, it would have been impossible," her voice moved
relentlessly on.

"And yet, I might have done it anyway," she said, "and
I almost did. Perhaps it is just as well that the xenophobia
of my world has spared me the task of killing another
king."

Holbart looked up sharply. She regarded him levelly,
her green eyes startling in the largeness of her face.

"Yes," she said softly, "painful it is, but I must now end
your services to myself and my house, Holbart Card."

He felt foolish on his knees, but he could not bring
himself to breach the protocol of the planet to which he
had been assigned. He bowed his head again.

"I will miss your service," he said, his trained body
coming to maximum readiness. "I trust, however, that my
Guild will send a replacement more worthy of your trust

than I evidently have been." Blast it, he thought. He had
let bitterness creep out, and he did not yet know the full
story behind this.

"Your Guild," said the Mother Regent, "is interdicted
from Tenn from this day forward. You can carry that
message back to your Guildmaster, Holbart Card. I have
paid out your contract, sir, and today you and the sixty-
seven other members of your Guild who soil this planet
are leaving Tenn forever." It seemed to give her a kind of
joy to say it. Holbart was amazed.

"Your Grace," he said in confusion, "may I know the
breach we have committed? Perhaps we can repair . . ."

"You are all fortunate," she broke in coldly, "that we do
not gather you together and exterminate you. But we
know your Guild's reaction in such cases, and while we do
not fear you, we do not invite your retaliation when our
purpose can be served quite well otherwise."

She turned away from him. "Go," she said. "A shuttle
awaits you."

He climbed slowly to his feet. Her broad back showed
him nothing, and to speak after dismissal was a breach of
planetary custom and would have landed him in jail, at
least.

He turned away. What is going on? he thought.

The Nin felt the first trace of mind-touch as she lay
asleep in her bed. She was like a sea captain sound asleep
in a storm, who even through unconsciousness could detect the shifting of cargo or the tiniest abnormal change in
the movement of the ship.

She had little talent for Skill, and all she knew was the
centering technique for raising a mental Shield. But she
had one of the most disciplined minds in the human
portion of the galaxy, and when she centered a Shield, it
was backed up by a will of tungsten steel.

"Watcher," she said, belting the weapons harness of the
final level of Guild training. "The entrance of the school,
please."

A holographic image appeared, two-dimensionally, against
the far wall of her sleeping chamber. It showed the appar-

ently empty entranceway of the massive Bodyguard Head-quarters, glass doors magnetically and mechanically locked as tightly, as she herself had left them on her pro forma rounds.

There was a rear entrance, and she called it up, too. She also called up the corridor outside her chamber where, unbeknownst to the Watcher computer, her main escape tunnel lay concealed; but again, there was nothing and no one.

"Motion detectors," she said.

"No movement," the Watcher said. The weapons were belted on now. She strode out of her chamber and entered the long basement corridor, the holography moving stead-ily before her.

The mind touch came again, very faintly, a probe of infinite delicacy feathering around her upraised Shield.

"General alert," the Nin snapped, breaking into a run toward the elevators. "Radiation bath on front and rear entrances. Roof weaponry on kill. Heat detectors on maxi-mum." As she ran, the holographic image before her split into groups of telltales, showing the locations her words brought forth, showing the energy drain as each responded to her commands. "Vacate first floor. Prepare gas and fire on my command . . ." And then her voice slowed. She took a few more inertia-filled steps, and paused.

The holography seemed correct. The telltales read as they should. But . . .

Where was everybody?

The Nin looked back over her shoulder at a door-studded corridor that stretched into dimness. In five stories above her, reaching to street level, similar corridors lay. Each contained over a hundred bedchambers, and in each bed-chamber was a warrior/thief from the old days, or a loyal member of the Bodyguard Guild that had absorbed them. And above that there were three hundred stories yet, filled with trainees and instructors.

Mouth suddenly dry, the Nin said: "Watcher. Show me each bedchamber corridor, one per second."

The images began to flash. The attackers, the Nin rea-soned, might know how to control mechanics and their telltales. But they probably did not know what she expected to see.

No one had emerged. The Watcher showed alarms going off all over the underground; she could hear them, feel the screaming vibrations in her ears. But the only one who stirred seemed to be a late-night lover who was making furtive way in one of the Level 2 corridors. He, apparently, was hearing no alarms and . . .

"Watcher, tell Candless there to meet me on Level 4." Candless's image suddenly frayed into distortion, and then cleared suddenly, showing the Level 2 corridor. But now it was empty.

I do not know how to Shield anyone else, the Nin thought, much less how to Shield all the minds and mechanics of the entire building.

Would that Asher Tye were on-planet. For this was an October attack; it had to be. No one else could mount an attack with such coordination, meeting every defense and deflecting it, probing for danger while still far away from it, with something so intangible as a mind touch. No one else in the galaxy save Asher Tye, and to a lesser degree Clemmy, even had the mind touch, as far as she knew. Though, of course, there was the matter of Ran Tarney.

Were the October Ones back among us? the Nin Tova thought. Then God help us . . .

The main elevator suddenly clicked on. The Nin turned away from it and ran back toward her bedchamber.

And suddenly, the corridor was empty no more.

It was filled with howling beasts. Great fanged creatures—lions with shark mouths and dinosaur claws—bounded out of the far reaches of the corridor and ran savagely toward her, filling the walls with an echoing din of snarl and scream.

The Nin laughed. She ran straight at them, weapons untouched in her harness.

And as she had known they would, the beasts melted away even as they seemed to spring on her.

She laughed again, and in her centered mind the Shield suddenly stiffened. The laugh died in her throat, and she felt a sudden pressure against the Shield, as if something were leaning on it with a weight of many tons.

Two somethings. Three somethings. Four somethings . . .

She was under multiple attack. There was more than one October presence within the school, and somehow they knew that she was outside of whatever net they had spread over the warriors around her.

If it were four October Adepts, the Nin knew that she would be lost. It surprised her that her Shield had not already been breached.

She reached her bedchamber and barked a command at the Watcher, calling up a hidden routine that he had not known, to this moment, was there.

No. He still did not know. For he did not respond at all anymore.

The solid parts of all modern buildings were intricate channels of duplicated optical fiber intertwining the memory-affected molecules, so that if one portion were damaged, the rest would take over and pursue without interruption whatever the task of the damaged portion had been.

But the Nin had one additional, non-electrical and non-photonic device. And she had long since directed the main power bundle outside of the diffusion network and . . .

She drew a blaster from one of the pouches of the harness and pointed it at a particular spot on the floor. Hoping that the unseen attackers' mental control of energy was not all-encompassing, she pressed the firing stud.

The disintegrating fire tore through the circuit bundle beneath the floor.

The lights went out.

And behind her, the elevator stopped. The doors had just begun to open.

The Nin pulled a magnetic key from the harness and turned it in a spot in the corridor wall. A hatch fell away at her feet. She heard it rather than saw it, for the darkness was absolute, except for the retinal image that the blaster fire had left.

She stepped forward and let herself drop, body instinctively assuming the position of maximum fall self-protection, head and knees both tucked into chest, hands clasped over head and elbows protecting temples.

The elevator door groaned open and light shot into the tunnel.

"I'm losing her," Larla said from the elevator. "Wait. She's stopped falling. Now she's . . .ahhhhh!"

She lost contact as the escape ship ripped down its hidden tunnel and tore into the air, far away in an instant.

"Never mind," Ceal Carnak said. In the light from their lanterns, the four could see the outlines of the corridor disappearing into darkness. "There are minds here aplenty to probe. Some of them will know from whence she and Tarney learned their Shields. I only wish that the Apprentice we sensed on our way in was in-system." The after-taste of Asher's Skill was all around, but it was only a lingering shadow in his absence.

Their minds attuned to the ebb and flow of energy, they were not prepared for the purely motion-driven mechanicals that the Nin had triggered on her way out. But they did have Shields up, both mental and mental-driven physical . . .

Ink seemed to fill the corridor. The light of the lanterns was fading, driven back toward them by a tangible darkness that flowed and moved.

"What's going on here?" Score said, panic in his voice. The three women probed with their minds, as did he. But the clockwork mechanism that had released the gas was already still. It, in turn, had triggered something else, a sort of wake-up call to selected chambers . . .

All at once, a needler beam came lancing out of the darkness. It cascaded against the physical Shield, bounced off, and spent itself in the wall in bubbling fury.

"Something's out there," Sanda shrieked. "But I don't feel a mind!"

"A robot?" Ceal asked. But no, she thought. A robot's brain is as easily detected and smashed as any human's.

Blaster fire came from another place in the darkness and sprayed off the Shield.

"Up the stairs," Ceal ordered. They wrenched open the doorway to the stairwell. Darkness poured out of it and over them like a flash flood.

Like blind men the four struggled upward, detecting

the outlines of the stairway with their minds, but able to see nothing at all with their eyes. The Shield held the black gas off, and kept oxygen around them.

"What is that stuff?" Sanda complained. Then something sharp and heavy shot down from the darkness and careened off the Shield. They could feel the Shield shake from the weight and force of it.

Yet they could detect no active minds above them, or anywhere around them.

The nightmare journey upward seemed to take hours. Intermittently, their invisible attackers would hurl blaster or needler fire at them, or more primitive projectiles, from axes to crossbow bolts. And never once could they track down the minds behind the weapons.

"If we could only Network, we could kill everyone in the building," Sanda said hopefully. Ceal just scowled at her. In motion as they were, the configuration and its reinforcing Ressie link was not feasible. They had Networked in the streets, and since had been able to hold and even extend the interference they had initiated with the building's Com, but they had wanted living, rational prisoners, not the dead, so they had not aimed a killing blow at the Headquarters.

Finally, Ceal Carnak stopped them. They had reached the last floor below ground level. "We've got to take one of them with us," she said.

They groped their way to the first chamber on the floor and blew the door away with blaster fire. The man within was on his feet, facing the door, a practice sword in hand, but already the black gas had poured in on him and cut off the glowing edges of the doorway.

Ceal moved instantly, fearing that any of the others might overreact and kill. She hammered at the warrior's mind with hers, one carefully controlled blow. His Shield was so weak as to be almost nonexistent. On this planet at least, they would not need the Skill jammer she now carried with care in a pouch at her side.

They dragged him up the last flight and then out of the main entrance, and as they forced open the outer doors, the black gas flowed with them until they clanged the doors shut behind them.

In the opacity within, five Therds clustered at the top of the stairway. One was always on duty on each floor, hired especially for that purpose by the Nin. One of the Nin's mechanical devices had alerted each of them, and they knew the drill.

The Nin and Asher Tye had planned carefully, preparing the little they could against October attack, and it had evidently worked. But the Nin, orbiting the planet now and waiting for the first report from the Therds, wondered. It had always seemed to her that an attack by October Adepts could not be resisted. She had seen one of them attack hundreds of warriors hidden underground in the original planet of the Guild of Thieves, and stun them all from a parsec away. No Shield she could raise would be effective against such Power, she well knew.

But this attack . . . there was something incomplete about it, as if October were just a feeble remnant of what it once had been. Even so, as she mobilized her forces, she guessed that the attackers could not be detected or met with any of the physical weapons at her command.

And the Galactic Index still stood at 434,675. It had not risen in thirty-eight days, which was extremely abnormal.

Part II:

BLOW-UP

Chapter 8

Dade Station wheeled around the silver-grey planet like a faceted ball-bearing around a tremendous marble sphere. The station was as large as a moonlet. It was an ancient waystation from the early days of the interstellar human explosion, built up endlessly, layer upon layer like a metallic onion, with cellular rooms and irregularities here and there that, from a distance, merged into one huge, mottled iridescent splendor over the towering gas of the disk below.

That disk was the hydrogen/helium planet Dade itself. Only traces of oxygen bedevilled its atmosphere, and for the few bizarre visitors who emerged from one of the nonhuman areas of the ship nearest the drive and entered a planetary shuttle, the minus 400 degrees F surface temperature would be a breath of fresh, comfortable air after having been transported wall-to-wall within the frightening heat of a human-oriented starship. Gravity on the planet stood at nearly two standard gees, and Asher, who was used to .8, would have found the extra weight troublesome if he had been able to notice it after having been strangled by the atmosphere assuming he had been so foolish as to go down there in the first place.

"Martha," Asher announced ponderously after they had studied these indicators, "I believe I will forego the pleasure of a visit to yonder galactic wonder."

"Me, too," Clemmy said.

"Instead, m'dear," Asher intoned, "let us repair to the comforts of yon Station, where pleasure is to be had for the taking, I hear, and money disappears in puffs of delirious delight." He drew the last word out until it made Clemmy laugh and lighted his own face with the reflection.

He took a step back and regarded Clemmy critically. She was wearing an outfit that would have crushed comfortably into a bottle cap, and he knew that his own regalia came to even less than that.

"The latest . . . er . . . fashion," Asher stammered, "becomes you, Martha." Indeed, the only false note he could see in their facade was the warrior-trained muscles that rippled unconsciously beneath both their skins. But the idle rich were not necessarily the flabby rich, with handball just one of many vigorous activities available.

Clemmy became serious for a moment. "Asher," she said, "what about the aftertaste of Skill you've been sensing. Is an Adept in near space?"

"I wish I knew," Asher sighed. "The taste is there, all right, but weak, like that of a beginner in Skill. Perhaps an Apprentice at the most, but a feeble one. A full Adept? I don't think so." And, thought Asher, I will make it my main business to track down the source of this taste. An Apprentice, perhaps? What, after all, had happened to all the October Apprentices after the destruction of their Guild? There certainly could still be some around, even in a place such as Dade.

"Warren, dear," Clemmy twinkled as they strolled out of their cabin. "Let's invite that dear man you met the other day. What was his name—Gadby was it? Or Canby?"

"Ah, yes, Gadbois. Nice fellow. Popping handball player, too," Asher said. Dov as Gadbois couldn't wait for a visit to the notorious Dade, he thought. The only question is whether we can catch up with him in time. "Gaddy will just love it, I'm sure. Call him up, m'dear."

Bonnie's Best hung in near proximity to the Station, following an adjacent orbit around the cold green planet, pushing against the Station's tiny gravitational attraction from time to time with brief bursts of gas. A long tube snaked from the great starship toward the greater Station, a tube that seemed as thin as a thread when viewed in perspective, but which carried inside it bus-sized passenger cars. But that particular tube never made it to the Station, for it soon entered a forest of similar tubes from the swarms of starcraft, large and small, that surrounded the Station proper. It took computer routing to get each car at last to the Station itself.

Elsewhere in the *Best,* the few non-oxygen aliens, out of place on the mostly human route followed by the great passenger ship, went about their peculiar pursuits. So did oxygen-breathing aliens such as Adio-Gabutti, Spimmon, and Nisha Scalli. Dade Station had some small facilities for them, though it was mostly human and purely corrupt. Nisha, Asher knew, was planning an excursion, though Spimmon and the Therd were not. Spimmon had reported that Nisha had wanted Spimmon to visit the Station with him, and seemed violently put out when Spimmon refused.

It was Dade's good fortune that it happened to fall on one of the illogical interstices of dozens of illogical interspatial routes, and had grown accordingly. It attracted people who drank and smoked and ate and rutted in every aberrant way human beings had so far devised. It was, therefore and of course, one of the most popular spots in the human galaxy.

When at length their bus disgorged them onto a huge lobby, Asher, Clemmy, and Dov (whom they had indeed almost missed) gaped at the swirl of humanity around them. The first thing they saw was a huge sign in Basic, with words they would have reason to remember later: YOU ARE BEING SCANNED, it said. ENERGY AND PROJECTILE WEAPONS PROHIBITED ON DADE STATION. DO NOT ATTEMPT ENTRY WITH SUCH DEVICES UPON PAIN OF DETENTION.

Behind them, bus after bus drew up, one after another, some empty, but many filled with partygoers and shysters and drunks, pouring out to join the gigantic throng in the lobby proper. Bodypaint was much in evidence. Most of the visitors were dressed as scantily as the three of them, but some would have made a peacock blush.

Asher was not used to crowds. "Garr," he said. He had felt a sudden, intense stab of fear. The swirl was too much for his mind to encompass, the babbling press of close-packed human minds too oppressive for coherent thought. He drew himself into tightness, and realized all at once that he had placed a physical Shield around himself, and that Clemmy had sensed it and was trying to signal him with her mind.

"Warren, dear," her mouth said. "Come along, away from all these people; I feel faint. I need to find a lounge and relax a minute." Her mind said: "Asher, drop the Shield. You can't float like a bubble in a crowd like this without drawing attention." Indeed, he saw, she herself could not touch him with her hands, and was trying to avoid seeming to try, even as she pressed her body against the Shield to be as close to him as she could.

Dov was looking at them, puzzled. "I say, old man," he said, "are you all right?"

I, Asher thought, don't like crowds, and it's the first time I've really realized it.

He forced the fear aside and dropped the Shield. "Yes," he said feebly as Clemmy fell suddenly against him, "perfectly fine, thank you, Gaddy, and thank you . . ." he bussed Clemmy on the lips, ". . . Martha, sweetheart. Love ya."

"Love ya," she repeated mechanically. Seizing his arm, she threaded them with remarkable skill into a less densely packed part of the crowd. She had said that she felt faint; she looked about as faint as a fullback, Asher thought. At length they reached an area of bars and lounges and entrances to less expensive eateries. They found the most deserted lounge they could.

I'm no good at the rich playboy bit, Asher thought. I don't know how to act. But Dov, he noticed, seemed as polished as a crystal ball. Some people, it seemed, had an intuitive grasp of elegance.

Asher was jealous.

"Good heavens," Dov said nasally as they sat heavily into too-soft upholstered captains' chairs around a table the size of a dinner plate. "Robot waiters, by all the stars. How quaint." And indeed, instead of the delivery mechanisms built into automated bar tables, there were black-liveried figures moving stiffly through the smoky haze, delivering drinks and snackfood, metallic voices speaking stiffly in the slightly variant basic dialect that was practically the native trademark of Dade Station.

"Dear, dear Martha, may I suggest Polarian brandy?" Dov said with oily ingratiation to Clemmy. Knock it off, Asher thought at him, but if 'Gaddy's' mind received the message, he did not visibly react. He was keeping to the script, all right, in character with "Gadbois."

"Ooh, how exciting," Clemmy squealed. Asher winced.

But he looked at Clemmy's excited eyes, and thought suddenly: maybe she's serious. She has never seen anything even remotely like this. Her life to this point had been nearly as sheltered as a nun's. And for that matter, he himself had never seen anything like this either. Dissipated partying was not one of the underpinnings of either the October or the Bodyguard Guilds.

Dov's natural coloring made his face seem even more inflamed than Clemmy's. He slapped a palm on the table's sensor and said: "Polarian brandy for the three of us!"

A waiter moved out of nowhere and slid three glasses down in front of them with smooth rapidity. It had a face of respectful politeness, badly painted, with a chip at the side of the nose, making it look as if it had a zit.

This is not the high-rent district, Asher realized.

Outside the lounge, the swirling chaos continued without pause, the noise filtering past imperfect dampers.

"Gaddy, you're an absolute genius," Clemmy trilled. Asher cast her a sour look, but his critique softened as he saw the obvious delight in her eyes. She had tasted the brandy, and following her lead, he now did, too.

Something thick and liquid that seemed to lack wetness altogether slid down his throat. It left a faint fruity taste and a tingling at the sides of the tongue. And then, like a surprise wave at the beach, a feeling of fatuous benevolence closed over him, and radiated upward from his belly in the blink of an eye.

"Not bad," he said gruffly, fighting it, and Clemmy shot a harsh look at him. "Er . . ." he amended quickly, "not the quality of Caldott's, but a fine aroma nonetheless." Aroma . . .should he have said "bouquet"? He looked nervously around, but the few other patrons were taking no notice.

Then, without forethought, he leaned forward and the other two automatically bent their heads toward him to catch whatever secret he was about to reveal. "Confidentially," he whispered, and the message was carried to their minds directly, rather than by the hissing words themselves, "I feel like a horse's ass and can't wait to get out of here and on with the mission." He stared into both their eyes for a fractional moment, and then raised the glass to lips that had suddenly become a hard line. But it was mostly a facade; for all his outside grimness, inside, the brandy had made him feel a trace of placidity for the first time in a long while.

"Martha" squealed, "Ooh, I just love that barracks talk," and Dov roared "Nonsense!" and delivered such a hearty slap to Asher's back that half the brandy went into his nose and he fell back, snorting and gasping. "We will not spend only one DAY here, my good man," "Gaddy" said for all to hear. "We will spend all the time we NEED, and fully sample the delights of this marvelous place! Martha, my sweet poppy, am I right or am I right?"

"Er . . . right! Absolutely!" "Martha" said firmly, smiling straight into Asher's eyes. "We must keep up appearances, after all."

Asher wiped his streaming eyes with a handkerchief (plucked out of nowhere by the robo-waiter). Somehow everything was getting away from him again. What would the Nin do in this situation? he wondered. But he knew. She would do the job at hand, and their job was to seem like aimlessly wandering jet-setters, and no jet-setter would pass up Dade Station unless he or she were sick or dead.

And then Asher's watering eyes, flickering restlessly about the room, fixed on something odd, taking his thoughts suddenly away from the contemplation of his own predicament. Clemmy and Dov, noticing his gaze, followed it.

"Holy sh—er, I say!" Dov breathed. "What in the universe?"

There was a couple alone at a table about twenty feet away. Both were nearly naked, which was not unusual in this place, although theirs was not an elegantly trimmed nakedness as was their own. And both were hollow-eyed, unlike the three, with eyes moving as restlessly over the crowd as two ferrets. But it was the thing on the woman's leg, sticking carelessly out from under the table, that drew their eyes.

"It's some kind of disease," Dov whispered.

"No. It's alive," Clemmy murmured shakily.

The thing adhered to the woman's leg, low down toward the ankle. It was thicker than the leg itself, of an irregular roundness a little bigger than a softball, and it writhed. Not rapidly, not convulsively, but with a ghastly terrible regularity, blue veins moving under a deep redness verging on purple, and there was something about it that made the three visitors swallow nervously and move uneasily on the contoured chairs.

Dimly, they could see around the pedestal of the chair that the man had something similar on his leg.

"What is it?" Dov whispered.

Asher reached out toward it tentatively with his mind. For a moment, he thought that he felt an answering something from the grotesque softball, an intelligence peeking out from behind the alienness. But then he realized that it was a reflection of the woman's mind that he was seeing, —the reflection of something quiescent and desperate at the same time, but with detail absorbed in the reflecting material somehow. He probed deeper, trying to separate out the squirming little entity from the overlay of the evidently sick woman, but he could get a handle on nothing.

Then the woman's eyes caught his, and Asher found himself staring into pools of deadness, seeped through with a sort of dirty shrewdness that made him turn his gaze abruptly away. Clemmy and Dov too had jerked their attentions suddenly elsewhere, he saw.

If ever Asher had felt a miasma of dread, it was at that moment, sitting in a lounge on a Station known for its shrieking delights.

"Let's get out of here," Dov muttered, and they shot through the door as if prodded by an electric whip.

*   *   *

By the time they sat down inside a fifth bar, they were at least twenty floors down into the Station, and Asher was dizzy from the substances churning away inside his stomach for the first time in his life.

"Let's not overdo this decadence thing," he mumbled at Dov and Clemmy.

"Impossible," Dov hollered, drawing all eyes toward their table, a self-server this time. "The night's not over until the lights are out," he yelled, and the crowd roared. "And the lights are never out on Dade!" he screamed, and the crowd roared again.

This bar was crowded, and Asher was again feeling a pang of claustrophobic fear. But, overlaid as it was by three Polarian brandies and a couple of smoky things whose basis was not alcoholic, which seemed to be gently pressing the lobes of his brain apart, Asher felt he could handle it. In fact, he felt he could handle almost anything.

Clemmy had tossed off everything Asher had had plus a few dizzybeers, and even now was chewing on a whackstick, but to Asher's dazed eyes, she seemed entirely unaffected.

"Detox soda," Asher whispered into the server.

"DETOX SODA?!" Dov yelled at the top of his lungs, and the entire crammed-together population of the bar turned and looked at Asher Tye, who suddenly felt himself shrinking in his chair. "Can't you handle good liquor, boy?" thundered Dov. "Cancel that! Give him a double witslap rye, by all the devils. Everyone! Everyone! Forty witslap ryes for all my friends!" He gestured expansively around him, and the crowd, hearing the freebie, pressed inward in clamoring friendship, reaching for the frantically working table server.

As glass after glass popped out and was grabbed and spilled and sloshed and handed back, Asher felt himself take hold of one, put it to his mouth and down it in a single swallow. Fire seemed to explode in his midsection, radiating bolts of heat lightning along every nerve in his upper body, while at the same time, everything below his waist became as remote as the next star. The claustrophobia was a memory now, flaring feebly as the crowd pressed in. Clemmy shrieked gleefully as a jostled hand dumped a glass full of rye down her cleavage, drawing Asher's momentary attention. Had it been as accidental as it looked? he wondered dimly, trying to focus on the one who had done it, but the hand had disappeared into a forest of other hands reaching and clawing at them. "Forty more!" Dov roared.

Thank the stars that the bar couldn't hold more than a hundred people or so, thought Asher. The numbered account they were drawing from was deliberately huge as a part of their cover, well supplied from the coffers of the defunct Guild of Thieves. But Asher had an idea that Dade Station could inhale such an account in a single night, were the owner so foolish as to permit it.

And then they were dancing. Asher had no memory of getting to his feet, but suddenly he found himself pressed up against an androgynous something whose eyes batted at him and doughy body left doubt in his mind as to whether this were a woman or a man. Asher shook his head to clear it, to no effect, and nearly dislocated his neck as he craned it around, looking for Dov or Clemmy, just as a dance step landed him hard on the floor with both jarring heels. Then he was in the arms of another. This one was a man without a doubt, towering over Asher and hairy as a blanket, with other indications as well, not the least a long beard that poked into Asher's eyes. Mercifully, Asher felt himself whirled away into another partner, and then another, and another. Three or four were distinctly women.

And then, reeling, he felt something like water gushing along the insides of his jaw, and with a sudden intuition as to what was about to happen, surged through the bouncing bodies toward the door.

He didn't make it. He hit the floor on hands and knees, and thought that the sound of his vomiting could be heard on the planet Dade itself.

"Shriek!" Someone female slipped on the viscous mess and careened into someone else, and then a body hit Asher and tripped backwards over him, but didn't fall. It couldn't; the crowd was too thick. Then Asher felt a jarring blow to his ribs, and realized that it hadn't been the first time. Dancers were kneeing him and bumping him and

stepping on parts of him, and if they noticed, they did not
particularly care.

I could get trampled to death, Asher thought through a
mind that had only slightly cleared from the retching.

Then a knee struck him on the temple, and his mind
rang like a giant bell. He felt his arms and legs collapsing,
and knew if he were to fall flat on the floor he would be
stomped upon without mercy, and when the dance was
finished, they'd have to scrape him off the floor with a
snow shovel.

Shield! He used his mind at last, and threw a physical
Shield around him, but he was not in full control and he
made it too big. To the rest of the crowd it seemed as if,
all at once, half a dozen dancers had made incredible
five-foot leaps straight into the air, to land on the heads of
other dancers in a hysterical flurry of arms and legs. For a
brief moment, there was a completely empty space around
Asher Tye.

He staggered up and cancelled the Shield. Those nearest him, who had been pressed against it like children
looking at puppies through a plate glass window, suddenly
fell inward in a great tangled heap of arms and legs, sliding
through the vomit to those brought in by the implosion
from the other side.

Asher threw himself at the crowd and bulled through it.
He knew that using the Shield had been a mistake, but he
hoped that the rest of the revellers were as stoned as he
was. A broad-chested figure loomed before him just short
of the door, wearing some kind of synthetic leather vest.
Asher tried to elbow his way past, but the man moved to
block his way.

Asher scarcely glanced at the man's meaty face as it
opened its mouth at him. He lashed out with one foot, his
body's training taking over for a moment, and hooked the
sole of his shoe against the other's ankle shooting the leg
sidewise. The man shouted in surprise and fell heavily
onto his backside, one hand clawing into his fake leather
belt. It came up with a stiletto six inches long, as thin as
an eyelid, as sharp as a razor.

The crowd was thinner here. Asher turned his back to

the doorway and drove backward as the man came to his knees and lunged at him, knife held underhanded in skilled street-fighting position. Slipping it into Asher's belly was the obvious intent, and Asher, trained as he was, was suddenly afraid that the alcohol and dope had thrown his concentration, and therefore his reflexes, out of whack. But the danger had cleared some of the fuzz away, too.

The man came in low. Asher feinted, grabbed the thrusting wrist with his left hand, turned the other arm so that the elbow impacted the man's eye, and brought a knee suddenly up into the knife elbow. He heard the crack, felt the tendons give way and the joint turn inside out, and knew that he had put too much force into it. But all at once, he didn't care.

Perhaps it was the frustration of the game he was having to play; perhaps it was the shame of losing control. He dropped his knee and, still holding the wrist, slammed his other hand into the inverted elbow and pushed. Dimly he felt the big man's frantic blows from his free hand as they rained off his back and neck. He looked into the man's eyes and saw agony there, but hatred too, the determination to kill. There was some sort of glassy bundle of threads in his hair . . .

Asher pushed violently an upthrusting palm. The force nearly lifted the man off his feet. The elbow surged upward in a sickening, grinding V. And the man's scream was like a cry from hell.

Asher let go and stepped back, and he was out of the bar and in the plazaway. Inside, most of the dancers seemed to be gyrating on, but there was a crowd of open-mouthed onlookers facing him in front and on either side, while just through the door the leather-clad man convulsed on the floor in a U made by other watching bodies.

"S't one de Cleos boys," one of the crowd said in awed horror, hissing his s's in the peculiar dialectic variation generic to the Station. Asher saw Dov and Clemmy working their way toward him through the mob. He turned and walked rapidly off, not wanting to draw attention to them, too. He weaved and bobbed and twisted through the throng, head gaining a modicum of lucidity, and at length found himself before one of the hundreds of lift tubes that penetrated the Station, open shafts of the naturally light station gravity passing through the artificial one g-gravity of the layered floors. This shaft had huge relief letters embossed into the wall next to it in maroon metal—the letters GCQ.

They had agreed that if separated, they would meet at this shaft, and now Asher waited for them as he brushed detritus off his sweating body, trying to restore his appearance to a ghost of its former elan.

And as he waited, he kept his befuddled mind as alert as he could, scanning for stray hostility and rancor among the passers-by, even those in the shaft; and though he found it in the milling multitude once or twice, he did not find any that was directed at him.

But his mind kept slipping away from its task, blearing as much as his eyes, and he felt again, much more faintly, an incipient nausea.

Then he saw that just across from the shaft there was a stand-up, hole-in-the-wall refreshment stand. It took a moment for the implication to register, but when it did, he nearly ran across to it, staggering into a passing fat woman who glanced at him with a come-hither look, and slapped his palm on the sensor. He missed, and tried again.

"Detox," he said hoarsely. His hand made it this time, and a liver-colored flask popped out of the counter while the machine deftly deducted the cost from the account that matched the palm print and imbedded password.

Asher popped the top and drank it down with a long, convulsive shudder, and for a moment he thought that he was going to bring it back up in projectile form. But suddenly he felt the tension that he had not known he had twist away. The nausea disappeared, and he could feel his vision clearing.

Dov and Clemmy stood near the shaft opening. He saw them before they spotted him, and stepped carefully over. He found that his unsteadiness had faded.

Clemmy spotted him first, and for a moment Asher

could see a rapid-fire series of emotions trace themselves over her face: gladness, concern, anger, concern, puzzlement, relief.

"Yes," Asher said. "I'm okay; I look like hell; I shouldn't have done it; no, there is no hidden reason; I can't figure out why I did it; and yes, I seem to have sobered up."

Clemmy was probing with her mind, but found that he was not probing hers.

"All of that," she thought at him. "But mostly, you showed off back there, and if there are any October Adepts on Dade Station, they will have felt your use of Power. You might have blown our cover."

Meanwhile, Dov was saying: "Warren, there you are. Where were you during all the excitement, old man?"

"Excitement, Gaddy, old fart?" Asher said wearily. "Whatever do you mean?"

Dov launched into a florid description of the fight. Since there would be no reason to do so to one of the fighters involved, any listener's thoughts would be led away from the hint that Asher had been involved.

"I have felt no use of Power," Asher thought-beamed at Clemmy while he directed a clench-toothed smile at Dov. "I can't even detect that Apprentice aftertaste."

"You are sure?" Clemmy thought. Asher nodded.

"You hurt a Station citizen," Clemmy thought. "What about Dade Police?"

"We all studied the in-house database." —Asher. "The Station's full-time inhabitants are mostly on their own. The Police move in when some group or other gets too far out of line. Otherwise, it's hands off."

Clemmy— "If you had killed him . . ."

"I didn't. And the Police would have gotten excited only if he were a rich tourist. He didn't look like one to me."

"Hist!" someone said at Asher's elbow as Dov took a breath, and Asher jumped as if stung. His mind shot to the intruder as fast as his eyes did. And then he realized that he had not detected this mind because there was no hostility in it, at least toward them.

The man was average in every way: height, weight, hair color, complexion, handsomeness. He was dressed a bit more conservatively than they were, and his light brown eyes were without guile or cleverness.

"I say, you spoke to us?" Dov said, frowning patronizingly.

"Nay, I zpeak wiss zis," the man said, thumbing at Asher. "Less you's'r wis him?"

"We are, my good man," Dov said stiffly.

"Zen I tell you all," the man said, and now there was a furtive something in his demeanor. "He's," he said, thumbing at Asher again, "done ze job on a Cleos boy. Soon zay come, and zay not kill him, no, for he's Outzide, but zay roazt him, shall we zay?"

"You are saying," Clemmy cut in, "that some group of thugs is after A . . .Warren here?"

"Zat I zay," the man said nervously, eyes darting. "Und I zay zat zay will take him and put him off-ztation and ranzom him for what he did."

Well, that was plain enough.

"Good heavens, Warren, old boy," Dov said, "I think you're right. Off to the ship with you." He gave a broad wink. "Martha and I will party for all three of us."

But Dov was not serious, and Asher did not have to read his mind to know it. Any gang assault was warrior business, was Bodyguard business, and Dov would protect their lives as a warrior would, and would move in on Asher's wife only later.

"Nay, nay," the brown-eyed man said. "Zay zwarm zrough ze gates, and have your pix by now. Nay, muzt hide, come to ze zhip anozer time, anozer way."

"The Station Police . . ." Asher said. But the man was shaking his head. "Zay cannot move fazt. Cleos take you before you come near zem or zem you. Nay. And," he said, looking at Clemmy and Dov, "if zese were wiss you in bar at any time, zen Cleos knows. Nay, you muzt come wiss me, and soon, for zay will come out de ze shaft or down ze lane any zecond."

Clemmy triggered her wrist computer. "Dade online," she said. "Who is Cleo?"

"Cleos," the unit corrected, the receptors under their ears answering promptly. "Gang leader. One of the seventy most powerful ruling factions on Dade. Member,

Privy Council of Dade Station. Controls the following concessions . . ."

"Stop," Clemmy said. She looked at Dov and Asher, and then frowned at the brown man. "But we don't even know this guy . . ."

At that moment the decision was snatched away from them. A hoarse shout came from the shaft, and four people came surging out of it. All wore imitation leather vests and calf-length imitation leather pants.

"Run!" the brown-haired man screamed, and was off down the corridor like a frightened rabbit. The three looked at each other, and shrugged. The Nin had always told them to avoid a fight whenever possible, for fights are full of uncertainties and, no matter how well trained, the most skilled warrior can sometimes lose to the most un-skilled novice because of a slip or a distraction or some other form of beginner's luck.

But Asher and Clemmy and Dov were young. And they felt immortal. And they were half stoned. And they had trained so hard . . .

Chapter 9

Which among them made the imperceptible movement that triggered the other two? Asher never figured it out, thinking it Clemmy some times, Dov other times, and yet again wondering if it could have been himself. What they should have done was follow the example of the brownish man and shoot off into the crowd, separating with some meeting place in mind, determining to reach *Bonnie's Best* by the quickest route possible. But their minds were clouded, and Asher at least was frustrated by the role he had had to play, and by the depths that it had led him to. Dov was surprising him at every turn, and Clemmy, he suspected, was simply reacting. He wondered whether the celebrating had affected her more than she was showing. Then again she was angry with him, and he never knew what to expect when that happened—what conclusions would eventually emerge from an emotional process as opaque to his understanding as a rock's.

This is stupid, Asher thought, diving at a six-foot-five bearded fellow holding some kind of club in an outstretched fist. That thought was the only one he had time for. The action was happening too fast, and Asher reacted with unconscious no-mind rather than reaching for October Skill. Or perhaps some part of him did, but it was by-passed by violence.

The unnatural position of the man's arm barely warned Asher in time. The club was not in the air coming down at him, or coming up in an underhand cut. Instead, he was prodding it outward. Asher twisted aside as a foot-long blade shot out from it and touched the muscles of his left arm, shaving off a few hairs.

And then Asher was under the outthrust arm and barreling into the man's body, catching him in the lower belly with his shoulder. This is martial skill? Asher's dazed mind demanded. It was more like hockey technique.

But the man staggered backward and went over the edge of the shaft, arms flailing for the handholds and missing them. Unless someone reached out and grabbed him, or he "swam" through the ventilated air until he reached a handhold, he would fall, but slowly, toward the bowels of the station.

Asher turned and his head reeled for a moment. He flung out his arms for balance, and one hand touched something. Like an inchworm, he recoiled into a fetal position as something heavy swung past where his head had been. Dimly, his positional sense functioned. He pivoted on his hip and shot a foot out. He took someone on the ankle, with a snapping blow that would have shattered the joint but for the fact that the other's weight was not fully on that particular foot at that particular time. But he heard a yell nonetheless, and as his vision cleared, he saw one of the men in a limping stagger backwards, away from the shaft, holding some kind of knobby thing in one of his hands. Asher looked away and did not see the man catch himself.

He looked for Clemmy and found her standing over a still body, and was just in time to see Dov up in the air, both legs wrapped around the head of one of the enemy. The man reached up with clawing hands, shrieking, as Dov slammed both palms against the man's ears with brutal force. The man's scream shook the walls as he fell, Dov rolling nimbly off.

And then Clemmy's eyes widened. She leaped forward at Asher, and . . .

WHAM! Asher was thrown forward. He felt his mind go and then leap back in again. His head seemed to lose its hearing and bury itself in a great roaring, and Asher found his cheek pressed against the plasteel of the decking. His body rolled over, and above him he saw Clemmy in a gigantic leap, an impossible leap. Skill? he thought, or only perspective? But the blade edge of one of her feet was shooting out in a perfectly timed snap, exploding into the man's throat, and he was thrown back into the shaft. They saw his hands shoot to his neck and horror come into his eyes as he disappeared downward.

That one would be lucky to survive, his shattered larynx, Asher thought, unless someone got to him in time. We should go after him and save him—but the thought was dim and far away.

Then, lazily, a knobbed metal pipe appeared from the top of the shaft, moving in a rapid spin as it fell feebly past the opening and downward. Evidently the man had used the club on Asher, and then, in the course of Clemmy's attack, had thrown it upward, where it bounced off the corridor wall and up into the shaft, as he had reached for his own crushed throat.

Alcohol. Drugs. A lapse of attention. Accident, the Nin had said. Slippage, beginner's luck, random events. Martial skill, but always at the mercy of chance.

Asher suddenly felt his head lifted up. Dov had hold of it against his thigh and was looking down at him.

"Asher, Asher," he said. Not "Warren, Warren?" Asher thought, but his lips did not move. He saw real fear crawling into Dov's eyes, but he was disinclined to say anything in return, content to look blankly upward as Dov's face swam in and out of focus, an unusual effect that caught his attention.

Clemmy's face swam into view. "We've got to get away from here," she whispered to Dov. Always practical, Asher thought, far away. But he couldn't hear her voice, actually, and he blinked his eyes only when they swam with tears and the memory crawled into him that that was what he should do.

"Can you walk, A . . . Warren, old pal?" Dov asked, bringing Asher to his feet with surprising gentleness. Asher answered nothing. There were, he saw, many people around them, staring at them.

"Move," Clemmy hissed, supporting Asher by a shoulder, and they walked, Asher mechanically, without coordination. It took all of Dov's and Clemmy's concentration to keep them all upright and moving through the crowd.

It gave way before them and swallowed up behind, and Dov and Clemmy blessed, for once, the population density of the artificial moonlet, for in moments they were anonymous again. People jostled past them like waves of solid perfume and sweat, many as disoriented as Asher appeared to be.

After a while they reached another shaft and, stepping to one of its edges, Dov grabbed a rising handhold passing along a vertical track in the shaft wall. A moment of vertigo seized first him and then Clemmy as they passed from earth-normal gravity to the feather-lightness of the Station's natural g, and Clemmy caught hold of a handhold lower in the same track that Dov was using. Toward the center of the shaft a few people were falling unconcernedly, almost all equipped with magnet-attractive rods for catching the side of the shaft at the floor they wished to enter.

Asher, one of Dov's hands tucked into his armpit and Clemmy leaning against his hip from below, watched the people rising and falling, downward swimmers in a watery pit, upward reachers in a sodden ballet as they themselves moved upwards. Sound penetrated for the first time—faint echoes that drifted with the wafting scene around him.

Clemmy's wrist computer sounded quietly below, and Asher heard the Station's latest news, but no details reached his understanding. "No Police Alert," Clemmy's voice came then, quietly, carrying upward easily past Asher's ears to Dov's, and Asher thought that he should recognize the person to whom the voice belonged, if he bothered to think about it. But the roaring in his head was there too, and nothing stayed long enough to come into focus and be recognized.

Then a hand reached out from a shaft opening and yanked Dov inside by the belt. Asher was dragged behind by Dov's suddenly tightened hand. The sensation of sudden weight hit Asher's mind unpleasantly; he felt a distant stab of pain and was dizzy again.

"Ze top level crawls wiss Cleos," the brownish man hissed out of the side of his mouth, as if that would

prevent anyone from noticing that he was talking with
them. Clemmy appeared at Asher's side in a fighting stance,
but there was no one there but the inoffensive-appearing,
nondescript, brown-tinged man. "Zay all know you; zayr
wrizts huv holo'ed your miniature images. One by one,
dizguized only, might you make it. But might."

He let the two of them finish the thought. Together,
Asher hurt and his mental Skill out of action . . .

The brown man touched Asher's head with one finger,
gently. "Ahh," he said quietly as Dov stood rigid with
indecision. "Zayr iss . . .yahh!" He yelled in sudden outraged surprise as Clemmy's hand reached his sleeve and
yanked him toward her and past, straight into the yawning
shaft.

And around herself, Dov, and Asher, she threw the
Cloak of Unnotice.

Of the two techniques that involved hiding in the midst
of people, Shadow was more often used by those with
Skill. In Shadow one could hover around the edge of
things, blending into the background like a chameleon. It
was most effective in backgrounds of extensive color and
light variation. But Shadow was an individual Skill, a reactive Skill, and involved the dampening of the observer's
attention at the moment it was being triggered. An October Adept could have extended it beyond himself, but
Clemmy, barely an unofficial apprentice, could not.

The Cloak, on the other hand, cast an aura of unimpor-
tance around an area as wide as the esper could control.
Pedestrians would see those in the Cloak and step out of
their way, but would attach no significance to them.

Clemmy hissed at Dov what she had done, and they
began moving off down the corridor, Asher mechanically
in tow, seeking another shaft for the last few levels upward.

Then they heard a voice behind them, and looked back.

"Why you do zat? Where you go?" shrieked the brownish man, propelling himself in from one of the upholds.
They became aware of angry, shouting voices from below.
The man must have pushed off one of the fallers, and used
the propulsion to reach the side of the shaft only a few feet

down. Probably any native of the Station would be good at tricks such as that.

The man ran frantically down the corridor yelling, drawing bemused and bored glances from the passers-by.

"You cannot make it!" he screamed, darting from one corridor opening to another, peering down them one by one. "Zat one wiss you, he die zoon!" he yelled. "Feel hiss head; it be *dented*, for Sizz zake. You get you zhip, he maybe dead before." He had almost disappeared, and then was back among them, running frantically here and there, knowing they could not be far, but with no idea where they could have gone.

With trembling fingers, Clemmy felt Asher's skull. The indentation was there, a roundness the size of a half walnut near Asher's left temple, near where the bone was weakest and the brain most vulnerable.

"My g-d," Clemmy breathed. "If it's swelling inside, he may go on us." Asher heard the words, but he was not listening. The roaring was getting louder again, and he was worried about something maybe, but could not bring it into focus. There was blueness around the dent, and to Clemmy's fingers the skin felt hot.

"Quick, in here," Dov whispered, and they stepped into a side corridor just ahead of the brown man as he came scurrying toward them. Then Dov reached out and snagged the man by the shirt, and dragged him, yelping, into the Cloak.

"I zought I looked down here," he wailed, trying to brush Dov's hand away. It was like swatting a tree.

"The nearest medico or I wring your neck," Dov hissed at him, looking like a well-bred, red-haired savage.

"Let me go, let me go!" the man said. "Yess, medico firzt, but you muzt follow me and you muzt do what I do and you muzt truzt me, or Cleos will zlice you good, I tell you. Top corridors, no. Even here, zay own half ze people."

"The Station Police . . ." Dov began.

"Zay will not come," the brown man said.

Clemmy and Dov looked at him, and then at each other. Asher suddenly reeled in their arms.

"All right!" Clemmy said. "Go!"

The man peered up and down the main corridor, and Clemmy knew that he had no idea about the Cloak. She wasn't about to enlighten him. "Come," he hissed. They moved out behind him and found themselves heading back toward the shaft. Asher was stumbling now, and Clemmy and Dov could feel his coordination going with every step they took. The shaft opening loomed in front of them.

"Habba," Asher said. His eyes had suddenly brightened. "Habba conda blabba." He faltered for a minute, and his eyes focussed on something in the far distance. "Spabba babba d-d-d-d . . ."

Clemmy shot an agonized glance at Dov as Asher staggered, and she saw in his green eyes the same fear she knew radiated from her own.

"Faztezt way, ztraight down!" the man told them. "Cleos keep to upper, moztly. Ziss not one of zayr uzual zhafts. Hope, now . . ." He pushed at them with hands that had little strength, but fear made Dov and Clemmy pliant. They stepped off into space, Asher squirming and babbling between them.

And they fell. It seemed as if they were falling through molasses to Clemmy, and even though they picked up some speed as they descended, the terror in her made each second seem like a prolonged pain, stabbing at her insides like a hot wire.

Around them, passing ascenders eyed them incuriously, looking their way only when they heard Asher's babble, and even then they apparently saw more peculiar behavior every day. Clemmy had turned off the Cloak now, and with that part of her mind freed, tried to probe Asher. It was like probing into a melange of randomness, thoughts coming at her like a meteor shower, no purpose behind them and no guidance giving them coherent direction. She drew away finally, aware that she was not equipped for deep probing, aware too that emotion would have interfered with it even if she had been trained for it.

She looked up, focusing on distance. It seemed to her that in that towering, hazy dimness there were black-

vested miniatures, all coming down. But the blueness and
haze wavered, and the images faded in and out.

Another part of her kept watch all around, her eyes
peering down corridors as they slipped silently or noisily,
darkly or glaringly past. The deeper they fell, the more
violent the partying down the corridors seemed to become, but the fewer such corridors, too. More people
lived down here than in the uppers, Clemmy thought, and
most made their living up above, but could not afford to
live there.

The brown man was just above Clemmy, falling with
them, and if he spoke, neither she nor Dov could hear it
over Asher's increasingly raucous babbling. Fragments of
sentences were coming from him now, more and more
urgently, but making as little sense as the nonsense sylla-
bles of a few moments before.

"Can't we go faster?" Clemmy suddenly screamed, a
controlled, tight-toothed scream timed when there was no
one close enough to hear but the brownish man. But he
did not say anything, and Clemmy, glancing upward, saw
something that barely registered through her terror over
Asher Tye. It was the first time she had looked at the man
from below, and she could see the cuffs of his flaring
trousers billowing in the air. The near-bellbottom style
had concealed it before, and she hadn't been looking for it.

A lumpy reddish something, affixed to the outer skin of
his left calf.

Another one, Clemmy thought. Then something jarred
her from below—Dov's hand against her hip—and her feet
hit the grated deck of the shaft. She let Asher fall gently
beside her. And now it was she who was babbling as Asher
faded: "Please, please, please . . ." The brown man drew
them into a dark space, a corridor that seemed not to have
been serviced for many years.

As they moved, Clemmy saw closed and open doors
all around them. Inside the open doors there were people
in various stages of dress, sometimes leering out at them,
sometimes in various poses of sleeping or eating or whor-
ing or drugging, and several times hands reached for them,
only to be stopped as if burned by a hiss from the brown-

ish man as he pushed them along. The people were mostly gap-toothed and dirty. Those who looked toward them did so with predatory, avaricious eyes, and more often than not Clemmy saw the leg things, sometimes flattened out like a pie plate wrapped halfway around the leg, sometimes huddled in a rough sphere attached somehow to the skin.

Then she felt Asher's full weight on her arms. She looked at his face and saw his eyes half open, pupils rolled back, Dov a dim shape on his other side dragging him forward.

"In here," the brown man said.

Chapter 10

It was a medico unit, all right, though it looked as if it were vintage 500 years before. But it seemed to be functional, and as they laid Asher on its table and pulled the cowling over him, Clemmy found her hand on Asher's throat at the last moment, feeling for a pulse. She thought she found it, but had to snatch her hand away as the cowling fell into place. Somehow she did not dare let her mind inside Asher's. She was afraid she wouldn't find anything at all.

"Payment," the brownish man said, and looked at them penetratingly as Clemmy placed her encoded hand over the medico reader. The machine hummed reluctantly into life, and they stepped back as it coughed loudly. They smelled anesthetic fumes leaking out.

The brownish man was speaking rapidly into his wrist computer. Clemmy sat down heavily on a bench running along one wall. Dov was there in a moment.

"What can we do?" she asked, watching the medico as if it would blow apart.

"Nothing," he said. "There's nothing we can do now." He was about to say more, but all at once the opening to the corridor filled with people, perhaps a dozen cramming forward from the outside. Looking at them, Clemmy thought: predators. A pack of vultures circling above the pickings.

The brownish man held up a rigid hand, palm outward, and for a crazy moment Clemmy thought that he was

going to blast at the little crowd with the Green Flame.
But it was meant solely as a gesture of authority, it seemed.

"Back home, friends," the man said. "Zeze'r under ze
Downermazter's protection, if you pleaze."

A tough-looking woman built like a walk-in refrigerator
snarled: "And you will ztop uss from zelling zeze to Cleos,
all by yourzelf, Ponger ze Great?" They laughed, a chorus
of howls, but they did not move forward.

"I remember, Chorda Sclene!" the brown man screamed.
"I lie wiss ze Downermazter, and zhe liztens to me!" The
woman laughed again.

But she and those around her faded back into the corridor then, and Clemmy and Dov, who were on their feet
and ready, saw that the brownish man carried some influence after all.

"We could have taken them," Dov growled, and Clemmy
dropped wearily back onto the bench.

"Who knows," she said. "That's the kind of thinking that
got us in trouble in the first place. We must have been out
of our gourds. I'll never eat a whackstick again."

"StaCom," Dov said quietly into his wrist. "Who is
'Downermaster'?" Clemmy triggered her receptors and
listened.

"One of the seventy," the computer said. "Her Group
controls the oldest power sources in the Station—crystalline
nuclear cores in the center of the original Station structure, controlling about 11 percent of the circuitry in the
lower levels as they presently are wired."

"*Crystalline* cores?" Dov said, aghast. "I thought they
went out with blunderbuses!"

"Listen," Clemmy said. The computer was still talking:
"Known participant in blackmail, kidnapping, and drug-
running schemes. New drugs often under her Group's
control until taken over, if in demand, by upper groups."

"Aye," Dov said acidly. "The poor always get the new
drugs first, and the drugs that kill are left with them
while the richer folks grab hold of the safer ones. It's like
a giant testing lab with the poor as self-employed guinea
pigs."

"Shh . . . Will you be quiet?" Clemmy hissed. But the computer was launching into an elaborate history of the Station from its earliest beginnings.

"Stop," Dov said.

Clemmy mouthed: "This doesn't make sense. Kidnapping? The tourist trade would die in a week. The news would be on the database, and Poof! No one with bucks would take the chance."

Dov consulted the computer. After a moment, he said: "So. You have to analyze it, Cl . . . Martha, dear."

" 'M'dear,' " she said.

"Yes. Rather," he said, then whispered: "I'm going to call up the Station Police; I don't care what this brown guy says. We're supposed to be rich kids, right? No Police would let people with our money get sucked up into some kidnapping scheme."

"Wait," Clemmy said. Then, into her own wrist computer: "StaCom, describe the function of the Station Police."

"One function," the computer said. "By ancient covenant, the Police keep ruling Groups at seventy, with membership in each Group within ten percent of all others. This social structure is directly descended from the original seventy founders of the Station, who perpetuated their families' control by . . ."

"Stop," Clemmy said. Then: "Who protects tourists?"

"Tourist abuse controlled by charter," the computer said. "The seventy regulate one another by . . ."

Clemmy said: "Stop," and Dov said: "Shee-it. It's every man for himself."

After a moment's silence, Clemmy agreed bitterly. "If we get out, we get out by ourselves, and we've got to wait for Asher."

They looked at one another. The fuzzying effects of the alcohol had entirely disappeared.

Bonnie's Best leaves in three days," Dov said.

"Aye, but these people don't know that. They don't know who we are or where we come from. All they know is that we fight pretty well for rich kids."

Dov let it slip out before he could catch it: "Perhaps it's

just as well that Asher took a good one," he said. "It's something an inexperienced rich kid would have done, but not a Body . . ." Then he saw the look on Clemmy's face.

The brown man sat on a bench across from theirs, head nodding and apparently asleep. Clemmy had expected him to be a motormouth, but after he had chased the spectators away he had closed up like a clam. She and Dov sat. After a while, Dov stretched out on the floor and was asleep in seconds, but started awake after forty minutes. Clemmy tried it, and was surprised at how heavy her eyes were, but after a moment of relief upon closing them, she found her mind talking to her and could not pass the gateway of sleep, no matter how she tried to still herself.

From time to time, sound came from the medico as it did its job. Once it sounded like a toilet being unplugged. Another time it was ice cubes down a garbage disposal, and a little later a slurping moan like a giant dog licking blood. The digital readout on the unit's side should have showed elapsed time and expected time remaining, but the figures hadn't changed since they had fired up the old machine.

Clemmy, lying on her back, found her mind on the planet where she had been born. It had been a small planet, slightly less massive than the human standard, and with significantly more oxygen in the air. Her mother— she had never known who her father was—had been caught in the explosion and buried under hot ash when one of the dormant volcanoes on the active planet had unexpectedly blown with the force of a minor bomb; of the family suller-fur operation, nothing had remained but a smoking plain of hot ash and cinders. She, however, had been on a field trip to the planet's major spaceport. The guilt of the survivor had been with her ever since.

That same awful day the field trip company had turned her over to a cult orphanage; she had been eleven years old. From the moment she entered she had fought with the rationality of her young mind the blind rote approach of her tutors, for her mother had fostered in her a need to know the reasons for things. The tutors had often had no reasons except force.

The tutorage fell upon hard times. When the orphanage closed, the directors had brought the four remaining children, those without relatives or friends, into space with them as they headed back to Salvation for reassignment. Used to the rich air of her home, she had had to wear a trickler, and she had still been wearing the oxygen device when she ran away from them at the first planetfall, knowing that she was taking the chance that she would die if the trickler ran out and she could not find another.

She remembered the scene well. She had been running through the streets of a gigantic city, trickler hanging from her back, its nearly invisible mouthpiece in place, ragged clothes streaming behind her, when she had hurtled full tilt into the stomach of a man leaving the fanciest eatery she had ever seen. The man had taken an interest in her and had brought her home to decide what to do with her. He had a wife, but she seemed to be on perpetual vacation at an island resort hundreds of miles away. Clemmy did not understand the relationship.

But she was not left alone in the big house, for there were servants who took a shine to her, in particular the man's Bodyguard, a kindly man she called "Big Fist," making him laugh. It was rather nice for the few short weeks she lived there, but then the rich man's wife began a legal attack on her husband; the woman had been on her way out of his life for a long time, Clemmy rather sketchily perceived. The man had lost interest in child caring, and much else, and had put Clemmy up for adoption. That he hadn't any kind of legal custody of her in the first place his lawyers swept aside with the force of his money and consequent power.

But Big Fist had seen something in the wiry, narrow-chested little girl, and he persuaded the rich man to let him send Clemmy to a Bodyguard training facility. One of the trainers too recognized her potential, and that trainer was a covert member of the Bodyguard offshoot known as the Guild of Thieves. So he had sent her to the Nin, and with the Nin she had finally achieved enough aerobic development to do away with the tricklers. The day she had done so had been a day of delicious lightness, of body and mind both.

On her home planet, schooled at home as all modern children were in houses that were practically sentient themselves, she had been protected and challenged and had excelled. In the orphanage, too, she had shone with quickness of mind, much to the annoyance of the directors. On the Nin's Warrior Planet she had become a weapons expert, master of unarmed combat, and technical genius; she could fix almost any device, whether thinking machine or strictly mechanical.

And on the Warrior Planet, of course, she had met Asher Tye.

But what was next for her? she wondered. She had reached most of the minor goals she had set for herself, and they were fine. But what place would she occupy ten years hence, or twenty? Would she be off on another mission for the Bodyguard Guild, and then another, ad infinitum, until one failed? She had no aspirations to Guild leadership, but the Guild did give her an identity that she liked. Perhaps she should leave, and have a few babies. What would she do for a living? Would Asher go with her?

Asher . . . he had been her first lover, and insofar as she was concerned, her permanent one. She knew that such was by no means the case in the universe around her, but she felt no crises of sexual identity and no desires beyond Asher Tye. Well, almost none. She almost felt guilty about it, as if she *should* develop a wider sexual experience beyond this one man. But when she reasoned it out, she failed to see the point. It didn't, as Asher sometimes said, compute.

She opened her eyes suddenly, and found Dov sitting on the bench next to her head, staring down at her. The expression on his freckled face was unreadable, but his very attention sent a minor shock of awareness through her. It was sexual awareness. She recognized it with interest, and at the same time realized that it was not the same thing as desire.

"How much longer?" she said. Dov did not answer, staring down at her with brooding intensity, his features harsh in the downer light. He was still young, still had the underskin fat of youth, but she could see the cragginess beneath that skin, and knew that he would be far more ruggedly handsome in the years ahead.

"We are idle rich kids," he said suddenly. Looking up at him, she felt no wish to sit up and regain the bench. The floor felt just fine.

"We are the idle rich," he said again. "We must behave that way." And he bent suddenly down and kissed her on the lips.

She could have avoided it, but his words had cast doubt into her head, and she wondered how idle rich kids would behave in such a situation, pursued in the upper reaches of the Station and at the mercy of the downers. She let confusion delay action and his lips reached hers and moved, feeling for response.

Then she did act, turning away, breaking contact. She smiled hollowly.

"What?" Dov said.

"You are bent over like a pretzel," she told him as she looked away. It was true, but they were not the words he wanted to hear. He flushed and drew back.

"I, idle rich kid, am too worried about my husband to kiss," Clemmy murmured. "Of course, I kiss everyone in sight most of the time." She smiled, and the smile was not at her own words, but at what she felt inside, had felt when his lips were on hers. And that was . . .

Nothing. No fire in her belly, no tingle down her spine, no stirring at the nape of her neck.

Nothing.

She looked back up at Dov then, saw his frowning face, and smiled languidly. She raised her arms.

"Help me up, Gaddy," she said. "Let's gambol around the room."

"Gamble around the room?" he repeated, puzzled and a little angry. He seized one wrist and drew her upward.

A man came in with a needler in his hand. The brown

man looked up, then leaped suddenly to his feet. The intruder glanced at him, then at Clemmy and Dov.

"Zese zem?" he said. The brown man said: "Yez, yez, and I found zem, remember pleaze, and I want . . ."

"Zhut up, Ponger," the man said wearily. He was a good six feet, dressed in formal vest and drawstringed, bell-bottomed slacks, and impeccably groomed. His face held something that Clemmy could not read, a mindless something, as if intelligence were subservient to something else in all he did. But his black eyes were as alert as a bird's perched above a snake pit.

"Hey," Dov said loudly, "you can't bring that thing in here. I'll call the Station Police! That's an energy weapon, my man, and the rules . . ." The man cut him off with a wave of his wrist, the wicked muzzle describing a short arc that took both Dov and Clemmy in.

"Ziss ain't ze upper," he said, harsh and flat. He pushed a stud on his wrist computer.

And three more people came into the room, crowding the area in front of the doorway. Two were men, both scarcely distinguishable from the bird-eyed man, but their eyes were flat and ruthless. The bird-eyed man was a watcher, Dov thought, a scout. These were soldiers; their faces were without mercy.

And the third one coming in, the woman . . . Neither Dov nor Clemmy had ever seen anything like her, even among the motley throngs in the upper corridors of Date. She held no weapon, and she didn't look as if she needed one. Clemmy's first impression: a servant of some kind, a nanny perhaps—someone who took orders and never, never questioned them. But then her warrior-trained eyes took in just how this woman was using her five foot eight, heavyset matronly body, grey hair flowing in two long braids down her back. She was moving as if she had never bumped into anything, never expected to, and would move right through whatever the obstacle was if she did.

Why did she strike them as so unusual, Clemmy wondered, and then realized that it was because she was so usual-looking—at least, would have been on most of the human worlds. Here on Dade Station she stood out precisely because of her apparent plainness. And then, when the observer saw the way she moved, and saw those black eyes piercing bulkheads with their steely fixation . . .

"Downermazter," Ponger's voice came wavering to them. Looking beyond the three guards and the woman, Clemmy couldn't see the man at first, and then realized that he was bowing so low that his torso was at right angles to his legs.

"You will be rewarded, love," the woman said, not looking his way. "Go."

One of the bodyguards looked toward Ponger, and that was enough for him. He went out the door like a brown mouse. Clemmy caught a glimpse of someone else outside in the hall, a striking red-haired woman facing away, needler loose in one hand.

But Clemmy's attention was elsewhere. Her partially trained Skill had become aware of a questing *something* in the Downermaster's mind, a sensitivity, a constant search for mental emanation. The older woman was not casting her mind, seemed unable to; but there was some sort of underlying suspicion there. Was she a Receptor perhaps, someone who could sense thoughts but could not cast her own into another mind? If so, Clemmy did not dare employ Skill in her presence; the woman would have felt it like a slap in the face.

The medico gave a sound like a safe rolling down metal stairs.

"It's almost done," one of the bodyguards said, but the woman ignored him.

"I am Downermaster," she said to Clemmy and Dov, her voice as smooth as oiled soap. "Welcome to Downer. I regret your trouble with Cleos, who is not well liked by any of the uppermasters, much less by us below. I regret that you slept on the floor; Ponger the Great will regret that, too. Welcome to Downer. When your friend awakens, we will escort you back to your yacht at your convenience."

Dov and Clemmy were staring at her, not grasping her

words entirely, and not believing what they did understand. They had walked a few of the downer corridors; they could not take the words at face value.

"Where's the 'zese' and 'zose'?" Dov said through his nose then, and Clemmy shuddered inside. His acting was certainly consistent.

The woman's eyes flashed, and both of them sensed fury inside. But they had only the slightest glimpse, buried instantly under a courteous veneer. The two guards, eight feet apart, stood like statues, with the birdlike man making the apex of their watchful triangle, his eyes darting.

"I speak standard Basic to visitors," the Downermaster said shortly, "and twenty other dialects as I need them. Ah . . ."

The medico unit gave a sudden gasp, as if it were relieved about something, and then the canopy popped up with a twang, bouncing on its hinges so hard that it nearly locked closed again on the downward bounce.

Clemmy rushed forward. Asher was lying there, apparently in peaceful sleep.

Her hand trembled again as she felt his head; the indentation was gone. She looked at the temple closely, and where the injury had been, there was now a disk of almost invisible plastic.

The hole was no longer there. The machine had applied just the right suction with a thousand feelers, pulling the bone fragments outward, fitting them in place like a jigsaw puzzle while sharper probes went inside and drained off the fluid pressure and circulated anti-swelling solutions where danger threatened.

It had been routine. The only thing that machine could not have done was to revive dead brain cells. Clemmy could only hope that the damage had been contained and any destroyed cells unimportant.

"He will sleep for a long while," the Downermaster said. "Now please come with me. I would offer you the hospitality of Downer while your friend recovers."

"See here!" Dov yelled. "You get us back to our ship, woman. I am tired of Dade Station and I'm going to tell all my rich friends, you can bet on it." He went on in this vein for a minute or two, and then the woman cut in.

"Your ship. And which might that be?"

"The *Marblehead*," Dov yelled. "The *Springer*," Clemmy said in chorus.

"You are not together, then?" she inquired.

Inwardly, Clemmy cursed her own inventiveness. Perhaps she should let Dov do all the talking, but she was afraid that he would be carried away in an excess of acting ecstasy. She spoke rapidly on as Dov paused for breath.

"No, Warren and I met Gaddy in the uppers," she said, "and he has been a dear. But he might be going on with us in the *Springer*; we had been having so much fun, until this." And she gestured at Asher. Then she threw in the key question. "And please, do you know when he will be up and around? I would so much like to get back to our ship and away from this Cleos, no offense to the Station."

The solid woman was looking suspiciously at Clemmy. The guards seemed to sense it, stiffening. Was I overdoing it the other way, she wondered, opposite that of Dov?

"Forty-eight hours is the average for injuries of this type," she said.

"Forty-eight hours!" Clemmy said. But the woman was telling the truth. For a single fleeting instant she whisked her mind across that of the Downermaster, looking for a lie, looking for suspicion, looking for danger. She caught the truth in the last statement and whisked on in fear that the woman would somehow sense her touch. And indeed, she saw the woman stiffen almost imperceptibly, but whatever had been felt, she evidently could not put a finger on it, and could not even be sure that she had felt anything at all.

But Clemmy had caught the edge of her mind, and found the suspicion and danger she had been looking for—cargo shipfuls of it, planetary masses of it—and she knew then that there was no way they could avoid being suspected of something or plotted against by this one. All they could do was to carry the act forward as consistently as possible, and see where it came out.

Seventy local guildmasters, Clemmy thought, all fighting for a piece of the riches that Dade Station brought in every day. No wonder at least one of them had a suspicious mind.

"You won't kidnap us?" Clemmy found herself saying in a quavering, little girl voice, and heard Dov's feigned outrage next to her: "Martha. Really." And she saw the woman stiffen, too, in transparent indignation.

"My dear, what you must think of us!" the Downermaster exclaimed. "Please believe me when I tell you that I and sixty-eight other masters are in the process of accusation against Cleos for the type of action to which you refer. How long do you think Dade Station could survive a reputation for kidnapping, dear? Even we, here in the downers, want each and every one of you to enjoy our Station and come back again." Her puffy face radiated offended sensibility, but Clemmy guessed that she was as sensitive as a clip of light needles from one of her soldier's needler guns.

Clemmy passed the back of her hand over her eyes. "I am so tired. Please, I must rest." And she made as if to lie down on the floor again.

"Dear, dear!" the woman gasped, and clasped her hands. "We have proper quarters awaiting you!" Sitting on the floor, Clemmy had a momentary glimpse of the lower legs of the loosely clad four.

Red blobs held their now-familiar position on two of the men's outer calves. The Guildmaster and the bird-eyed man had none.

Later, the Downermaster was alone with Ponger the Great.

"Zere's zomezing odd here," she said, scowling.

"Are zey October?" Ponger ventured.

"Maybe. Maybe," she said contemplatively. "I felt Power moving in ze Ztation beyond zat of zat Cleos pig Dal Gazkin. But ze zing zat doezn't fit wiss zeze is zat zey were fighting Cleos. If, as I believe, October controls Cleos . . . Perhaps the dizturbance did not come from zeze. Probably Cleos has October guezts out in a bubble as he always has before."

"We will not be killing zese zree rich kids, zen?" Ponger asked, disappointed.

She looked at him with momentary disfavor. "If zey *are* travelling rich kids," she grated at him, "we will make money off zem, as uzual. But if zey are October . . ."

Ponger nodded happily. "I hope zey are," he said.

Chapter 11

"This," Clemmy said in amazement, "is 'ze unders'?" She looked around. For as far as could be detected by normal vision, they were outside, on a planet's surface, standing in a field of grass as finely tended as a golfer's green.

Overhead was a confused blueness that could have been the sky on any of a billion thousand planets. They seemed to be standing on a flat-topped hill, dropping gently away on all sides to join the slopes of other grassy hills that rolled away into the rippled distance.

There was no sun. The illusion was imperfect.

Dov was standing there with her, his wild red hair haloed by the intense blue light that seemed to come all over the inverted bowl of sky above them. And next to them, as if its legs were imbedded in the turf, was the medbed on which lay Asher Tye, a half hour into the forty-eight that the healing would take.

"Ponger," Clemmy said loudly. She hadn't seen him since the medico, but she had an idea that he was somewhere about, protecting his investment.

"Yess, miss," she heard at her side and jumped. And there he was, as if he had popped out of the air.

Dov moved in like a mind reader. "I don't like this place," he said, grabbing his arm, grabbing Ponger's arm and wheeling him face-to-face. The brown man stiffened as if pressed into plaster. Dov could feel the skinny muscles vibrating under his grasp. "Ponger. Friend Ponger," Dov said, "I don't like open sky. It makes me nervous. Bring

114

me back to my ship, Ponger the Great; I get paranoid in places like this. Every time I feel this way, someone punches me in the fist with a chin. Know what I mean?"

Ponger was getting the message. "No," he said. "No no no no. Pleaze." He reached into a pocket and took out a handheld. "Look. Zee. You can do it yourzelf. Zee." He twirled a knob and the sky caved in.

Clemmy shrieked. But in an instant the collapsing blueness was gone, and they saw instead a standard plasteel ceiling, no higher than a normal Station cabin's. And the walls were there, too. They had popped out of the green hills like holograms, but they were reality; the hills had been illusion. Where Ponger had pulled his magic, there was now merely the corridor door.

Dov reached out and haughtily accepted the handheld. "So. Yet I still insist that I must call my ship . . ."

Ponger yanked his arm out of Dov's grasp and stood vibrating, nervously smoothing skin with his other hand. "You forget Cleos!" he said indignantly. "Ze Downermazter I zerve, and zhe zay you muzt be cared for properly. But zhe zay too that we move on Cleos only when zat one awaken. Not before." Dov followed his pointing finger to Asher's medbed. When he looked back, Ponger the Great was fading backwards through the door.

Clemmy stalked about the cabin, noting the overlarge bed along one wall, the autoservice for food, the stingsprayer for showering. She guessed that if she chose, she could call a whirlpool spa out of the floor with the unit that Dov held in his hand.

She turned toward him and found his gaze upon her. She looked at him levelly, black eyes meeting green. "There's something wrong here," she said. "We've told them we're from different ships, Gaddy. Why then did they put you in the same room with us?" Dov's eyes narrowed, and a look came into them that caused her to say hastily: "Wait. I know. They want to blackmail us, Gaddy. That's it," she said excitedly, moving suddenly up to him and taking his hand. "They're watching us, Gaddy. They think we'll . . ."

"Let's," Dov said.

She sighed inside. If she was doing all she could to keep up the act, Dov too was doing nothing that conflicted with the character of the playboy Gadbois. The trouble was that in her case, Dov could make Gaddy's goals a mirror of his own.

"Martha," Dov said softly. Was there a twinkle in the rear of the eyes, as if he was well aware of the convergence of goals and enjoying it? "Martha," he said, "you are an enormously beautiful woman. Now, I would like to enjoy these forty-eight hours with every bit of joy that I bring to everything else. Why don't we . . . ?"

"We must not," Clemmy said flatly. Then she yawned gigantically, which shattered the romantic nose-to-nose closeness that Dov had been trying to maintain. "Give me the handheld, Gaddy." She took it from him. "Sleep is what I need, Gaddy. I'm sorry."

And for an instant, she almost regretted it. His face did not change expression in any easily identifiable way, but without mental probing of any kind she could see an ego on which a bruise was growing.

"I'm sorry," she said again. They stood for a moment uncertainly, and then Clemmy moved.

"Good night, Gaddy," she said. "Ponger. Show Gaddy his room." And she turned and flopped on the bed, fully clothed, such as it was.

Dov stood looking down at her. Then he abruptly clenched his fists and reached the bed in a single powerful step. His hands moved, then paused.

She hadn't been kidding about one thing. For Dov could see it plainly.

Clemmy was sound asleep.

"Ahem," a throat cleared behind him. Dov whirled, and Ponger shrank back into the doorway. "Zir, pleaz, ziss way to your room." Dov scowled at him, but after a moment he followed the scuttling brown man.

I can't sleep forty-eight hours, Clemmy thought, staring upward at the fake wood-panelled ceiling she had called into existence moments before with the handheld. I've slept fourteen hours already, according to my wrist computer. But that's enough; I couldn't go to sleep now to save my life . . .

Beside her, on the care-giving gurney next to her bed, Asher slept in dark oblivion. She sat up, and wondered what would happen if she conjured up the Cloak and wheeled herself and Asher to the nearest airshaft?

Cautiously, she began moving her mind around the room. She checked for electronic surveillance devices, sensing the tiny magnetic ripples they caused, and found at least three, plus two more that she was not certain of.

She let her mind drift outside the room. She couldn't "see" the physical surroundings away from the vision of her eyes, but she could sense mental activity and certain electrical and magnetic forms. There was no one in the corridor . . . wait. A little way down there was a dozing mind. Ponger? Yes, for even his dreams carried the aura of the man. As to their contents, they she could not read; she had not the Skill. It all seemed to be a contained soup of flashing and cloudy images.

Straight through the wall by the bed she sensed Dov. He too was sleeping, his mind at near stoppage as he lay between REM cycles. She guessed that he had awakened for a while sometime during the fourteen hours, for his sleep to be so deep. Or perhaps he had delayed sleeping for some reason. (That was it, of course. The cold needle-shower had been useful, but had had the annoying effect of shocking his body to full wakefulness. So he had ordered a couple of witslap ryes, and they had had the unexpected effect of invigorating him, so that he had paced around the cabin like a caged lion. Ponger had dared to linger upon delivering a third rye, and had been pushed roughly out the door. Whatever Dov wanted, it had not been conversation with the servile man.)

Clemmy's mind moved slowly along in a widening circle. Soon she was sensing other minds, awake and asleep. She began searching for images of herself, for someone thinking about her or Asher or Dov. But none of the minds were concerned with them.

She widened her range, but her training was elementary and it began to show. The closer minds overlay the

farther ones, and she could not fully suppress the near
ones in order to see those farther with clarity.

Dov was up. She felt his awakening as if it were a
leaping overlay on a part of the mental chaos around her.
Something had alarmed him, evidently; he had come fully
awake with warrior speed. Ponger . . .

Yes, Ponger was in the room with Dov. Clemmy could
feel his awake mind now, though it lacked the sharp clarity
of Dov's.

Then there ensued a dialog that Clemmy only partly
understood.

Dov, belligerently: "What do you want?"

Ponger, courage tight in hand: "I offer you any zervice
of ze Ztation courtezy Downermazter, young zir. Women.
Men. Uppers and downers. Drinks. Foods. Smokes. Snorts.
Games. Gambling. Any holographic performanze from ze
lazt zouzand years, we pay ze royalties."

Dov: "Women, eh?" Clemmy sharpened her attention. "How many?" She raised an eyebrow.

Ponger, expansively: "As many as you like."

Dov seemed to be considering. Clemmy frowned. Yes,
appearances were important, but . . .

Dov, savagely: "Then I want you to drug Martha next
door and make her think I am her husband and she has
just married me."

"What!" Clemmy yelled, appalled. The walls, of course,
carried no sound to the other side. I thought I knew him,
she thought, raging. Then a tiny fear shot through her.
What if Ponger agreed?

She refocused her mind in the adjoining room, and the
first thing she sensed was Dov's sardonic mood. Sardonic
. . . But wait. What was its source?

And then she linked it with the cynical humor that was
lurking in an inner layer of his mind. He was not entirely
serious! But then . . .she felt a great relief. He was kidding the brown man!

But Ponger was speaking. She strained to understand
the words and their inner meanings in his understated
mind.

"Downermazter would veto zat, I am afraid. You muzt remember zat zhe is a woman herzelf. But we can obtain women much more zkilled than yonder puppling."

Puppling! Clemmy thought indignantly.

Wait. What was that she was seeing in Dov's mind? Disappointment?

"Damn!" she cried aloud. Human minds were so complex! Yes, he was treating the whole thing with sardonic humor. But also yes, somewhere in him, some part of him was disappointed that she wasn't going to be gassed and he wasn't going to be her husband-for-a-day.

But the key element, she thought to herself, wasn't there. For suppose Ponger had said "yes"? Then what would she have seen in Dov? Because if she then saw dismay, or hesitation even, she would know that he was as fully complex as she guessed him to be, torn by conflicting impulses and desires and character.

Say yes, Ponger, she almost beamed into the brown man's mind. But he would have jumped as if stuck with a stiletto, and would have known then that she had mental Skill.

Apparently Dov had demurred on the skilled women suggestion. Clemmy had missed some of it as her mind whirled around. Now she sensed him in an attitude of intense listening.

". . .zomezing zat is better zan women, you know, my young friend. Better zan any drugs, too."

Dov: "And what, pray tell, might that be?"

Ponger, hissing: "Rezzies."

Dov: "Rezzies."

Ponger: "Rezzies."

Dov (now Clemmy could see that he was, if anything, bored inside, that all this byplay was not greatly interesting him. She could see that he was immensely frustrated by something, but the underlying cause was not visible to her, for he was not thinking about it in particular, just feeling the frustration that it had engendered): "How much?"

"Gratis. On houze. If you like Rezzies, we can zell you one later."

Dov: "And if I don't like?"

Ponger: "You will like."

Clemmy felt Ponger's mental aura receding out of the room, and then she felt Dov's mind go blank. She recognized the blankness. He was reaching for no-mind, trying to let his turgid emotions flow away.

But then she felt the other's presence again.

Ponger, proudly: "Rezzie."

Horror. She distinctly felt it welling up in Dov.

"What . . . is . . . that . . . thing?" his thoughts came, matching his words. "It looks like . . . it looks like . . ."

"Like what you zee on my leg and others? Yess. And zere is a reazon. You will zee."

Dov: "No. Take it back. I'd rather have a woman."

Ponger, sighing: "Takes courage, ze firzt time. But no harm, only pleazure."

He couldn't have used a more potent argument, Clemmy thought. Not the pleasure part, but the courage. She could feel Dov's aura stiffening at the mere breath of the word.

Dov: "What does it do?"

Ponger: "Let me leave it here. I guarantee zat no harm will come to you, young friend. You could kill ze little zing with bare hands, anyway." Clemmy sensed a quaver in that last thought, as if the idea were nearly too appalling to contemplate.

Dov, after a long moment: "Leave it."

Without another thought, Ponger's aura faded and disappeared.

For minutes, Clemmy could sense nothing from the other room. Dov had entered a state of no-mind again, and Clemmy knew why. Altered consciousness proceeded much easier when begun in no-mind, and Dov had no idea what to expect from the Ressie. That it was one of those ochre round things she had seen on people's legs, was obvious. But what it would do was not.

She thought about beaming a thought to Dov, to let him know that she was there and watching. But no, he would only resent it. He hated anyone entering his mind. But she would keep watch, just in case there was danger in that room with him.

She felt a tickling on her left calf, and glanced at it. There was nothing there, and suddenly she knew that she had felt Dov's mind, not her own. She transferred perception slightly, and the sensation became more abstract. She was not in full resonance with it for the moment.

The tickling continued, expanding around the leg. It reached the knee, carressing over the fineness at the back, sending shivers upward. Then it too was whispering upward, passing along the outside of the thigh now, while below, the gentle, infinitesimal massaging continued without a break.

The flowing warmth reached the waist, having avoided the genitalia and surrounding area, but still as gentle as a baby's breath. And then it was moving upward still, and Clemmy felt herself drawn back into resonance. For a moment, she was another body, and she recoiled from the unexpectedness of it. Then she was back in herself again, with the memory of strange hardnesses and shapes out of round.

The warmth reached the neck. It had avoided the chest, and Clemmy felt a delicious shiver as the neck felt the soft, probing, million-fingered touch. Then, ever so slowly, the creeping warmth moved across the chest and touched the nipples.

Clemmy felt a double electric jolt through her body, and realized that again it was not her body anymore, but Dov's. He was sweating now from the warmth of the enclosing Ressie, and suddenly it was on his tongue. Clemmy thought about gagging, and then felt the certain knowledge that the Ressie would not permit it, that that was not its intent. And suddenly she was tasting something sweet and savory at the same time. The Ressie could manipulate taste buds with such fine accuracy?

Yes, and olfactory equipment, too, for there came into Clemmy's head such a pleasant smell that . . .

Jolt. Something tore through her—something so exquisite that she shot upright in her bed. Her lips were half open, and she licked them, finding them dry. She realized that she was sweating like a stevedore, too. This wasn't right, she thought. The Ressie entirely covered Dov's body now. She could feel its total embrace, and waves of ecstasy—oh, the jolting, twisting power of it.

And she thought of Asher. She thought of Asher, and twisted around to look at him, but he still lay unmoving on the gurney. She looked at him, and then a jolt of sympathetic wonder hit her and she fell back on the bed, gasping.

The door opened. Ponger stood there, his face without expression.

"You zomehow feel it, mizzy," his voice came.

She nodded. They knew now, from watching her. They knew that she could at least receive another's thoughts. They knew that she could feel in synch with someone else, could feel specific sensations. And she was feeling them now, an alien maleness, wave after wave of intensity, and she suddenly wanted him to get out so that she could sink back into it.

She began to say so, but then she saw what he held gently in the palm of one hand.

She licked her lips again, and felt fear. But the crests rolling in from the next room seemed to go higher and ever higher.

"Give it to me," she croaked then. He smiled and brought it over to the bed. He treated it as gently as a kitten as he placed it next to her leg. And then, without a word, he turned and moved quickly out of the room.

And the Galactic Index stood at 434,675.

Chapter 12

"Zhe be Receptor," Ponger wheedled at the Downer-master. "Zhe muzt be October!"

"Zo zhe be Receptor. Zo what?" the woman grated. "I be Receptor, too. Does zat mean I be October? No, love. We wait."

By this time, seventy-two thousand planets had fired, expelled, or taken some other hostile action against its resident Bodyguards. The Nin had lodged a formal protest with the Concourse charging Com manipulation. Since it was well known that such interference was physically impossible, no one had believed her.

She came up out of a deep sleep, and for a moment did not know where she was. She sat up abruptly. She saw the panelling above her, and the plasteel walls.

She became conscious of a raging thirst. She moved off the bed, feeling languid and fluid all at once, and called up nearwater, which had a few useful electrolytes. The carafe that popped out of the server seemed small. She drank it down and signalled for two more.

She looked around the cabin. It seemed as she remembered it. The medbed was there, and Asher asleep. She called up the time; she had slept for seven hours.

And then, in a rushing moment, she realized that she felt wonderful. She felt agile and light. She swept around the room, imagining that she was wearing a voluminous, gauzy dress that swept with her, scarf-like trails behind.

123

She whirled onto the bed and lay there, hands behind her head.

"Get hold of yourself, Martha," she said out loud, happily. Inside she said the same thing, only a tiny bit more seriously.

She sat up abruptly and looked around. There was no sign of the Ressie.

"I couldn't take another bout, anyway," she said, falling back again. "Not now . . ." She remembered what had happened to her, and saw that there could be disgust in it, if she could let herself define it that way. But she couldn't. What she remembered was too exquisite.

And it had seemed to go on for a long, long time. When she, writhing, had thought that she could not experience any more, could not feel or tolerate any more, the Ressie had forced her up another rung of ecstasy, until she had shrieked and begged for respite. But the Ressie evidently did not understand, and now, to tell the truth, she was glad that it hadn't. For each plateau had seemed to have another just above, each mountain peak not a peak at all, but just another step.

She remembered wondering whether her heart would give out. It had seemed so intense that even with her aerobic tolerance, she had wondered if a heart, any heart, could live through the wrenching and quivering force of it all.

But it had, of course.

She had sweated; oh, she had sweated! And the Ressie had just sopped it up. And when it had finally disengaged, she recalled with surprise that her skin had been bone dry, roughened as if rubbed with terrycloth.

The sexual part of it—that was what she might find disgusting, she thought. But she couldn't bring herself to feel it so. It had not been entirely sexual anyway. There had been tastes to satisfy hunger, tastes that made the finest food seem insipid. There had been some kind of eardrum manipulation that had caused a low background sound, a kind of bass music that had soothed and stimulated at the same time. And there had been vision too, a kind of massaging of her closed eyes to produce colors, very vivid at times, moving in and out. She wondered if the thing could slide between the eyeball and its socket to the optic nerve. And then she realized that she could not explain the kaleidescopic visions she had had in any other way.

But certainly there had been a sexual component, she thought, shivering. In her mind she had a sudden vision of Asher. No, it had been much different from that.

The gurney made a growling sound and Clemmy looked at it, surprised. Evidently there was a mechanism under Asher working on him in some invisible way.

She stepped over and looked down. Asher seemed utterly at peace, brown hair falling loosely, the curve of eyebrow to temple beautiful to her eyes. Somewhere inside there, Clemmy thought, is that set of habits and ideals that I love. How totally helpless he seems right now.

"May I come in, Martha m'dear?" a disembodied voice said.

Clemmy looked toward the door and felt a shadow pass across her face. With a pang she remembered the maleness she had felt before her own Ressie had come. She remembered the incredible feeling of being inside someone else's body, and that of a man besides.

She sat on the bed and drew her legs up, cross-legged, knees upright, hugging them with her arms as if she had a cramp in her stomach.

"Come in," she said. And Dov bounded into the room.

One look, and she knew that he felt as invigorated as she did. She smiled sardonically, arms hugging her knees.

"You had a good time last night," she said, watching him.

"Did I have a good time?" he exclaimed, hands gesturing but seeming unable to hit upon the right combination. "Did I have a good time? Let me tell you, Cl . . . Martha. Good time doesn't say it. I . . ."

Then he caught himself, and stood looking down at her. "And how would you know that?" he whispered hoarsely, his face altering.

She just looked at him. He turned away from her and

paced toward the wall. "Only two ways," he said aloud.
"Either Ponger, or . . ." He whirled. "I've told you to stay
out of my mind!"

Clemmy laughed.

He seemed not to know what to do. He stood there,
arms held slightly away from his body, swaying.

"Gaddy, Gaddy, Gaddy!" she said. "I cannot enter minds.
Yes, I told you when I met you two days ago that I could
feel them. Yes, feel them, Gaddy. And believe me when I
tell you that you were radiating like a star last night. Even
if I could have gone inside your mind, I wouldn't have
needed to. You were like a holographic beacon. Now
smile, Gaddy. It was terrific, wasn't it?"

"You mean . . .?" he said, his eyes rolling around to
indicate the Station itself.

"Yes, it's no secret, Gaddy," she said. "The Downers
must know that I am a Receptor; why not? There are
millions of us around."

"Ahh," Dov said. He obviously knew now what she was
getting at. Receptors did not raise Shields. Receptors had
no link with October.

"And I . . ." Dov said. "You mean that you . . . I mean,
you felt what I was feeling?" He stopped, confused.

"Yes, Gaddy," she said softly. "Come over here and sit
down next to me."

He did so. She sat up straight, and regarded him levelly.

"For a moment, I thought that you had a woman. But
then it was plain you didn't, and yet . . . and yet . . .
Well, they could see that I was in synch with you somehow, Gaddy."

He turned slightly and let his green eyes peer directly
into hers. "I was thinking of you, you know."

"Not all the time," she said. "Not even much of the
time." He blushed. She thought about telling him what it
was like, sharing his body for those brief moments. But
no, confound it. There was too much intimacy between
them already.

"Then, Gaddy, Ponger brought me my own Ressie, and
I lost interest in what you were doing."

"Your own Ressie!" he said. For a moment she was

taken aback. He was appalled, for heaven's sake! His face
began working, and he stood up suddenly.

"Are you telling me that one of those . . . those . . .
those *things* was crawling all over you?" She looked at
him, and let a bemused smile come onto her lips.

"Yes," she said softly, "just like it was crawling all over
you."

"But you're a woman!" he exploded. "That thing would
. . . would . . ."

"Tell me this," she said, still softly. "If I invited you to
make love with me, right now, right this minute . . . could
you do it?"

He spluttered, beet red, his face flaming. Then he said:
"That's beside the point. You . . ."

"It is the point," she said, still smiling. "But anyway,
I'm not inviting you; you can relax."

He sat down again. She had thrown him totally off
balance. And still he was moving his hands spasmodically,
gesturing into the air in ways that lagged or led his words,
but never seemed in synch.

"I don't know, Martha," he said, no longer looking at
her. "I didn't want to do it at first, but with you right here
next door, so close and unavailable . . . well, I wanted to
do *something*. And when it first began crawling up my leg,
I wanted to scream and tear it off. Do you know what I
mean?" She nodded, but he probably didn't see it. "But
why did I feel that way, Cl . . . Martha? It's a small thing,
after all, and if I wanted to I could have ripped it apart
with my bare hands. Well, maybe not; it is incredibly
elastic, as you know. But, boy, it knows what it's doing! I
can see why every third person we see on Dade has one
for a pet.

"Tell me, Cl . . . Blast it, I keep trying to say someone
else's name! You remind me of someone, Martha."

"Who?" she asked sweetly.

"Oh," he said vaguely, "someone I once knew. Anyway
. . . Martha, you say I was radiating last night. Were the
Ressies radiating, too?"

She considered the question. She knew what he was
getting at. Were the Ressies intelligent aliens? Was there

a reasoning mind under that almost infinitely stretchable body?

"If so," she said finally, "I did not feel it. Sometimes I wish I could go inside of things, but I can't, Gaddy. But listen: why don't we look it up on the Encyclopedia?" No observer would wonder at that, she thought.

They did so, using Dov's wrist computer. "Ressies," the machine intoned, probing the arranged molecular pattern of the Station, feeling the thrust of the tachyonic stream as it poured past them and out of the galaxy. "Lifeform" (the holographic image of a Ressie appeared) "from the Draco Sector at the edge of the homo sapiens portion of the galaxy." (There appeared before them first a 3-D visualization of the galaxy, which took them spinning down toward one of the spiral arms until it focussed in on a smallish planet in the covering shroud of stars; and then a man and woman, walking hand in hand, Ressies on their legs.) "Parasitic in nature, the Ressie feeds upon bodily fluids of host creatures, without apparent harm to the creature. Ressies are valued as pets by certain races, notably the homo sapiens (humans) of Draco Sector. No danger to hosts has been reported."

"That sounds a little glib," Dov commented. Clemmy shushed him, but the computer was silent.

"That's all?" she said incredulously.

"Auxiliary files show Ressie anatomy and physiology."

"I want to see the holo that the original expedition took when it discovered the Ressie world," Clemmy said.

"One moment," the computer said. Then there popped into view before them a reddish planet, whose relative size was impossible to gauge with nothing nearby for comparison. The scene, much speeded up from the original event, showed the ship sending its exploratory shuttle down. The point of view switched to that of the shuttle as it entered the atmosphere (average in cyanide-free gaseous structure) and spun downward toward the surface. They saw mountains and wide plains, and as they went downward there came into view what seemed at first to be black dust spread out in clumps around the wide plains, which then resolved themselves into herds of herbivores whose physical details could not yet be ascertained.

Then the shuttle was landing, and the scene shifted again to an image of an explorer, a short, belligerent-looking fellow, standing in front of the shuttle holding a Ressie in his hand.

"Wait," Clemmy said, and the image froze. "Show me a picture of the host carrying a Ressie."

Another pause, longer this time. Then: "That was not holoed."

"Not holoed?" Dov sat beside her, but two or three feet away. "Why not? It would seem to be an important part of the exploration record to me."

"The exploration company maintains a small station around the Ressie planet," the computer told them, "and exports to the galaxy from it. Homesteading has not yet begun, but will ensue in a few hundred years if past patterns on other planets hold true."

Again the computer fell silent. "That's all?" Clemmy exclaimed again.

"That concludes the exploration record," the computer said. Clemmy had an idea.

"Computer," she said. "Are you concealing any aspect of this Ressie thing from us?"

The pause, this time, was even longer. "No," the computer finally said.

"That'll show you," Dov said out of the side of his mouth. Clemmy frowned.

"Now computer," she went on. "Would you tell me just how the Ressie paristisizes . . . er . . . feeds off a host?"

"Hairlike tendrils," the computer said, "which can operate in clumps or singly, are implicit in the Ressie body by the billions. The Ressie can penetrate the skin to nerve endings, and may have a slight psychic receptivity in that it always seems to know what the host desires. In detail . . ." The computer launched into an illustrated, clinical presentation which they watched, open-mouthed.

Clemmy realized that she was sweating. "Computer," she said then, "what is the Ressie penetration? I mean, how many people own Ressies? On which planets are they concentrated? Are there any planets on which the majority of people own Ressies as pets?"

"The Ressies," the computer said, "have not penetrated beyond a few scattered individuals on the edge of the Sector."

"I beg your pardon," Dov began. Clemmy said: "Please rescan, computer. What you said cannot be complete. We ourselves have seen Ressies in increasing numbers as we approach Surcease. We've seen dozens of them here on Dade Station alone."

"There are none on Dade Station," the computer said.

Dov and Clemmy looked at one another.

"None on Dade?" Dov said. "But . . ."

Clemmy motioned for silence.

"Computer," she said. "Is this information up-to-date?"

Again, a long pause. Then: "Yes," the computer said.

Clemmy shook her head.

"It just seems to have so little on Ressies," "Martha" told Dov as they ate together on the pop-up table in her room. Ponger had not visited them all day; no one had. "Look at any other racial listing, and there'd be hours of coverage. Here, almost nothing."

"Dear Martha," Dov said. "They do not seem to be all that intelligent. I'll bet the encyclopedia covers dumb animal life with short listings only. There are so many species, multiples of the 430,000-plus intelligent races galaxy-wide—far too many to cover in real depth."

"I don't believe that," she said. "Com Central can handle all that and more. You know how it was built. It uses the molecular structure of entire planets for its memory."

They had spent the day talking, looking at Asher, and for an active three hours indulging in Tai Chi Chuan, which rich kids would be expected to know, and which exercised all the right muscles for the rest of the skills they did not show. The needle shower had felt very, very good afterwards to Clemmy.

They didn't say much at the meal. Clemmy feared that Dov would press his attentions, but he did not, and in fact she had the impression that he was hurrying through the food. It was a large meal, for both of them. Dov excused himself then and disappeared into his own cabin.

And shortly thereafter Clemmy, seated on the edge of her bed, felt what she had half expected, and half hoped for.

"Ponger," she said in a voice that was barely audible. He came in without a word, and gave her a Ressie.

The next morning she felt equally languid to the day before, but also a little drawn. The raging thirst seemed unquenchable, and she drank until her belly was as hard as a drumhead. She felt excitement, but it was an excitement of another kind, for Asher was due to awaken in about three hours.

Dov came in, and they ate a desultory breakfast. He, too, seemed as languid as wet spaghetti, and they said little to one another. Finally, when the server had just finished sucking up their plates, the door sprang open and the Downermaster's birdlike guard hopped in, looked around, and then was out again.

The Downermaster herself strode in and stood in the middle of the floor, and Clemmy wondered if an armored tank would be strong enough to push her aside.

"Martha and Gadbois," she said in her flat voice. "I trust you have enjoyed our hospitality? Good. Now to business, I'm afraid."

She looked and gestured like somebody's tough grandmother. But Clemmy would have wanted a grandmother like this one.

"Cleos," the woman said, "has offered 850,000 credits for anyone in the Station who can come up with you."

Asher's medbed coughed, and they looked toward it, startled. But nothing further happened for the moment.

"It's a matter of business," the Downermaster said. "That *is* a lot of money. I regret that I must accept the offer, unless you exceed it."

"Of course I can top it," "Gadbois" said contemptuously, "if you guarantee our departure from Dade to our ships."

The woman smiled thinly. "Guarantee," she quoted, "is

perhaps too strong a word. But we would accept a locked fund transfer. You sign the amount over to us before you leave, providing that after a three-day period you verify the transaction. If not verified, the money reverts to your account. We, of course, have no access in the interim."

"Accepted," Dov said at once. "One million credits."

Why not? Clemmy thought. The Nin's autoaccountants would go berserk, but if she and Dov demurred now, there would be some sort of unpleasantness. She eyed the Downermaster's bodyguards. They were obviously not members of the Bodyguard Guild, but the three of them were scattered around the room in just the right places.

"Apiece," the Downermaster said, eyeing them.

There was a momentary silence.

"Of course apiece!" Dov said disdainfully. "But we cannot speak for Warren."

"Warren?" the Downermaster said mildly, and the gurney burped. She glanced toward it. "Oh, yes. Warren. Just take him. Your fee covers him."

"All right," Clemmy said quietly.

"But there is one thing," she and Dov said together. She looked at him. "Go ahead," she said. "No, you go ahead," he said. "Well . . ." she said. "Throw in a couple or three Ressies," Dov said.

"And tell us where to get Candy," Clemmy rushed out, feeling warmth in her face and trying to suppress it.

She glanced at Dov. She thought: I just threw that Candy thing in to make him think I wasn't somehow fixated on Ressies. But even so, she thought defensively, isn't Candy one of the foci of our investigation?

The Downermaster barely glanced at her. "You won't be interested in Candy if you own a Ressie," is all she said. Then she rocked back on her heels, as if considering. "Two million credits," she said finally. "One million for each of you, above our agreement. If Warren wants one, we can talk about it later."

They gaped at her.

"A million credits for a red softball?" Dov exploded. "Are you crazy?"

The Downermaster smiled unpleasantly. "No," she said softly, "I am not crazy."

But she is, of course, Clemmy thought. She could sense it around the edges of the Downermaster's mind. She dared not go in, with the crudeness of her Skill. She had already seen how this woman could sense mental movement. The Downermaster seemed to be a Receptor of at least moderate sensitivity. And she would probably kill them out of hand and deliver their bodies to Cleos if she sensed even the slightest hint of October, for all leaders everywhere in the galaxy feared October.

"I . . . apologize," Dov said stiffly, obviously with great difficulty. "And I thank you. You have been generous to us up until now. I think that I, for one, will accept your departure guarantee. As to the Ressie, I will buy one elsewhere, if indeed I buy one at all."

The medbed gasped.

"Computer," the Downermaster said loudly, making them jump. "These two were quizzing you about Ressies earlier. Tell them now: what is the going price for a Ressie on Dade Station?"

They waited. Dov and Clemmy knew that this was something that could not be faked. Their own wrist computers, vastly and uncreatively intelligent, would sense such a maneuver. As far as they knew, there was no way to influence the information in the Encyclopedia.

"One million credits per," the computer said. Dov had the friendliness factor tuned to a minimum on his own wrist unit, and he saw that the Downermaster had done the same to hers.

Wait a minute, Clemmy thought. Just yesterday it had denied that there were any Ressies on Dade at all. What was going on?

"Ridiculous," Dov said huffily. "If that were so, we would have seen almost no Ressies among the common people of this Station. But we saw many such."

"Such instances represent indenture," the computer said.

Dav and Clemmy looked at each other. "Indenture?" Dov said. "Do you mean slavery?"

"Indenture," the computer said as the Downermaster

watched, cynically. "For a term of twenty years, commonly. All production save necessities goes to the master."

"Enough," Clemmy said wearily. They could sort all this out later. She was not about to . . .

"Oh, all right," she heard Dov say petulantly. She looked over at him, eyebrows arching. "I accept. Here." And he slapped his palm down on a sensor.

Clemmy almost said: "That's Guild money you're throwing away," but thought better of it. Dov, she thought, will need instruction in fiscal responsibility before he's turned loose again with someone else's money.

"You understand that a locked transaction," the Downermaster said, "means that when the three days are up, the very next time you make a credit transaction our arrangement will go into effect? Automatically?"

"Yes, yes," Dov said.

Clemmy was gaping like a fish. She snapped her jaw shut.

"Not me," she said. "I'm surprised at you, Gaddy. This is extortion, plain and simple." Again that thin smile on the Downermaster's face. Gaddy said:

"Ah, Martha m'dear. Since first I met you, you've been reading me like a book."

"I . . ." Clemmy said, then paused. "Reading me like a book." It was a signal of some sort.

She let herself drift into his mind and, as usual, she found it difficult to sort out what was going on, but he clearly knew that she was doing it, clearly had something to communicate to her . . .

Go along . . .

Was that it? Yes, it came through more distinctly for a moment. Go along. Why antagonize the Downermaster?

She struggled inside. What would a real rich kid do? He had not set the pattern, but . . .

Then again, a Ressie . . .

She moved a hesitant tongue over dry lips. She said: "Eight hundred thousand." The Downermaster's smile broadened; she said nothing.

Clemmy made a show of it. She licked her lips again, then licked them a third time. She brought her hands up toward her breasts, then let the hands drop and squirm nervously against the outside of her hips.

"My own Ressie?" she said finally, weakly.

"Bring them in, Ponger," the Downermaster said.

Ponger the Great appeared at the door, a satchel with a handle in his hand. Clemmy slapped the sensor, and Ponger transferred the satchel to Dov's eager hand.

It was long later that she realized, in a burst of intuitive understanding, that this had been the first sign of the destructive power of the Ressie: in all the Ressie transaction, she had not thought about Asher even once.

Asher's gurney belched a gigantic belch, and he sat up.

Chapter 13

"Where am I?" Asher said, and in his eyes there was incomprehension. He tried to focus, but the room swam around him and he felt himself falling backward again.

Dov caught him.

"Warren, old thing!" Dov yelled in his ear. "You're with us, Gaddy and Martha. Thank heaven you're all right!"

"Gaddy and Martha?" Asher mumbled. He shook free of Dov's arm and sat upright again.

Dumbly he looked around the room; dumbly, he scanned his own body. Then, automatically, he sent his mind outward, touching those in the room. Clemmy was shaking her head violently at him, but he had no idea why.

Dov and Clemmy he knew; that birdlike fellow and the other two were strangers. Something about them brought his martial awareness to the fore. That fellow in the doorway; he had seen him before, a brownish kind of guy. And that heavyset woman . . .

Asher shuddered. His hypermind was taking in too much at once, sucking in the essences of everyone around him, and the woman's essence had been like septic quicksand.

She was looking at him fixedly now, her blue eyes wide, graying hair rigid in its styling.

"So," she said in a whisper.

"My head," Asher said, bringing his hands to it. The martial alertness was not fading; it was increasing, step by step.

"Entirely fixed, old boy!" Dov enthused. Clemmy was looking toward the Downermaster, apprehension on her face.

"Kill them," the Downermaster said.

There was the barest instance of total silence. And . . .

The birdlike man reacted first. He snapped his wrist and a fingerneedler appeared. He fired point blank at Clemmy, the savage coherent stream making an arcing sound in the air.

It hit her Shield and neutralized in an incandescent splatter.

"Asher!" she screamed. "I can't hold it!"

Asher regarded her in dazed wonder. The Downermaster screamed: "They are October! Kill them!"

The second soldier was a hair too late. Dov had been more finely trained than he. Dov kicked the other deep in the stomach with all the snapping power of a dozen years' practice behind him.

The soldier was wearing some kind of plastic body armor beneath his clothes, of course, but the force of the kick threw him backward and ruined the aim of the handheld needler he had plucked from his waist. Laser light sprayed around the room, and the Downermaster fell to the floor, nails scrabbling.

"Be careful, you fool!" she screeched.

It's like a holo melodrama, Asher thought, detached.

Clemmy seemed rooted to the floor. Blood streamed from a shoulder wound, a hit from Dov's opponent, not hers. From his belt the birdman was bringing up a blaster, a far more potent weapon than any needler, in a jerky, snatching motion, the finger weapon discarded and skittering across the floor.

Ponger the Great had disappeared.

The third guard fired his own blaster at Asher Tye, who remained sitting on the gurney, apparently oblivious to everything around him.

Hiss! Everyone in the room felt the fire of it as it reached a point in the air about a foot from Asher's face, and disappeared into sudden, impossible darkness.

The same foot Dov had used before connected with a solid thud in his enemy's breastbone; they could hear a simultaneous pop as something inside gave way.

"Asher!" Clemmy screamed. The birdman levelled the blaster at her and . . .

She raised both arms at him, outstretched, hands at ninety degrees. Fire wrapped around her wrists and the Green Flame erupted into the air before her . . .

The blaster's fire met the Flame and both seemed to pause, violent cascading forces struggling for mastery, one entirely physical and the other an amalgam of substance and Power.

The Flame engulfed the fire and the blaster and then there was a man with nothing above his waist but a black thing in a gout of greasy smoke and fire. The legs stood for a long moment in remembered equilibrium, and then they toppled suddenly in red and black excrescence onto the plasteel deck. Clemmy choked convulsively.

Asher gestured with his left hand; his opponent dropped his blaster and reached with both hands for his own throat. But before he could reach it, the throat seemed to compress, and suddenly it was squeezed to half its normal size by something that none of them could see. The man's face exploded into redness. His eyes bulged horribly and his tongue stood out as if suddenly inflated. Tiny drops of blood stood out all over the engorged face as capillaries burst. Asher held him suspended there as if he could not figure out what to do next.

Clemmy had turned an ashen face away from what she had done, and now found herself facing something shot through with equal horror. The Downermaster was staring upward, a maniacal excitement on her face; Dov was looking at the doorway and reaching for a fallen blaster.

Clemmy sobbed. "Asher, let go!" she wailed, and tried to force her mind between him and the dead man, but it was like encountering a shiny steel rod.

But he did let go, then. Intelligence was flowing back into his eyes, and he let the man drop leadenly onto the cabin's deck as he brought a shuddering hand to his forehead.

A klaxon sound reverberated down the corridor outside, and running feet could be heard converging toward the doorway.

From the floor, the Downermaster cackled and said: "Ze Under, zhe iss awake!" She had lapsed into Station dialect. Asher looked at her then, and once again encountered the cesspool of her mind.

"I feel zat," she said, sitting up, grinning. "I feel zat, Octoberman. I felt it when you woke up and zcanned, and I feel it now. You will never ezcape."

Asher spat. Clemmy's eyes widened in surprise; she had never seen him do that before. And then Asher hammered down on the Downermaster's mind with a mental blow that would have felled a dinosaur.

"I should kill her," he said savagely. His detachment was abruptly gone. Rage was boiling up inside, and his body shook with the force of it. Clemmy grasped hold of his sleeve.

"Asher," she said desperately, "what's wrong with you? You conquered this kind of thing years ago."

He shook her free and towered over the prostrate, gray-haired woman. "No!" he yelled. "She caused me to kill a man!" And then he turned agonized eyes to Clemmy. "And I didn't have to." It was a grating whisper. "You know I didn't have to, Clemmy." He grabbed her shoulders. "I could have disabled him, but I still had the reflection of her mind in me, and it somehow had control as I reacted to attack. Clemmy!" It was almost a wail. "I never wanted to do *this*." And then he had let her go and was kneeling beside the corpse of the man he had strangled.

He hadn't noticed the wincing on her face or the blood that had seeped through his fingers from her wounded shoulder. Perhaps in another situation she would have gone to him and comforted him. But . . .

"Get up!" Clemmy said harshly, and heaved Asher upward with her good arm. "Get out of yourself. I killed a man, too; and you could have Shielded me so I didn't have to do it. And instead, you just sat there like a lump." He looked confusedly at her.

Dov said: "Oh, shut up, both of you. I also killed a man. So what? They were going to kill us, and so are the ones coming up from outside . . ." Suddenly he levelled the blaster and fired, and a stream of energy hit the door frame and splashed outward. A needler beam shot through the door and winked out; there was a cry of pain from the hallway outside.

Asher isolated the room they were in and cast a mental hammer for two dozen yards around it. The noise of movement outside ceased abruptly. What remained was the klaxon, still sounding its warning throughout the downer realm.

Shadow. The Cloak of Unnotice. Clemmy helped as best she could as Asher raised confusion between them and all observing eyes. He stepped over the snoring body of the Downermaster and took Clemmy and Dov by the hand. Dov, holding the smoking blaster, glanced at him irritatedly, and then saw tiny flickerings at the base of Asher's brown hairs. Static electricity? No . . . something else.

They moved into the corridor. Perhaps twenty people were fallen that they could see, one the striking red-haired woman, and the weapons fallen with them were all heavy versions of the blaster Dov held in his hand. All three wondered at the brazen willingness to destroy walls and floors and ceilings and whatever lay beyond them, for blaster fire would pass through perhaps half a dozen bulkheads before dissipating, which was why it was almost never employed in starships or space stations.

Clemmy pulled gently, and they moved toward the place where she guessed the nearest lift to be. And then they came upon Ponger the Great.

He had fallen heavily over a mobile weapon of some kind. It was a moment before they could discern what it was, and then a moment more before they could believe it.

"Grav cannon," Dov growled. "Short range, assymetrical pattern. We wouldn't have lasted half a second against it, and neither would any living thing for forty rooms in its way." He gestured at all the weaponry around them. "So much for the Station's rules on projectile and energy weapons."

Asher held his silence. He could have Shielded them from the grav cannon, but it would have been a close thing, and he still felt shaky from what he was already handling.

Footfalls. A dozen people tore around the nearest corner, and Dov, Clemmy and Asher flattened themselves against the wall so that they would not be blundered into while in Shadow.

"Faster," Clemmy said, and they began to run.

They met four more groups of Downers, all heavily armed, all racing toward the place where their master lay, before they finally passed beyond the immediate vicinity of the combat.

"This place depresses me," Dov grunted as they moved along. "All closed in. No wonder they have handhelds to make artificial skies and fake outsides."

"Shut up," Clemmy said.

And then the lift opened up in front of them. Looking up, they could see the almost familiar smoky blueness, human figures drifting like balloons. For a jolting moment, the Cloak fell away and Shadow rippled, and they suddenly felt as light as a feather.

"Sorry," Asher said. He had not anticipated the change of gravity to Station natural. He should have; he still wasn't fully in control.

Up. Asher found himself still holding onto Clemmy's hand. She was looking at him with a disturbed expression on her face.

"Whisper only," Asher said. She nodded.

"How long was I out?" She told him. "You're kidding me," he said, and she shook her head. "*Bonnie's Best* must be on its way outward already," he said, but she shook her head again. "Not for four more hours," she hissed. "We should make it."

All the way to the top they rode, hopping off at the gaudiest of gambling corridors in close proximity to the gigantic entry lobby.

Cleos agents were everywhere, their black vests distinctive. At the edge of the lobby, Clemmy held back.

"We can't get through that!" she gasped. "They won't be able to see us, but they surely will feel us." And indeed, so closely packed was the mob of partying humanity that a broomstick would have had a tough time getting through.

"Just hang on," Asher said grimly. He gripped their hands even more tightly and . . .

They rose into the air as if on a magic carpet.

Clemmy suppressed a shriek, and then let some of it out as she realized it would be lost in the din around them anyway. Dov's hand tightened until Asher was afraid his own bones would break. Far above them, the faintly curved shell of the station appeared dimly through the banners and pyrotechnics that constantly flowed over this, the welcoming entryway to Dade Station.

"Levitation," Asher told them. "Not difficult, but with it and the Cloak and Shadow all at once . . ." It was a strain, Clemmy realized; she could feel it in the flow from Asher's mind—a flow that she was trying to add to and aid.

Twenty feet below them, people accosted one another and laughed at one another and conversed and giggled and had a damn old time, and they could feel the heat of their bodies and smell them, and see the riotous colors that they displayed, with flesh tones predominating.

Dov, Clemmy saw, had put the blaster away, but he was still holding something . . .

With an anticipatory chill, Clemmy recognized the satchel containing the Ressies.

And the Galactic Index abruptly fell to 434,650. The Galactic Concourse exploded into uproar. It was the first drop in the Index's history. Twenty-five races had been wiped out or disappeared somehow. The news rose to priority one in the newscasts, and the myriad citizens of the galaxy scanned, and demanded action.

Chapter 14

Once in the transtubes, there was little chance that Cleos or anyone else from Dade could catch them. Nevertheless, Asher kept the Cloak around them as the bus filled up; people were subliminally aware that they were there, and did not try to sit on top of them, as might have happened had they been only in Shadow. Only when the bus had moved away and lost itself in the tangled web of tubes networking around the Station did Asher finally let the Cloak relax.

Then, at last, they signalled for *Bonnie's Best*, and watched silently as the bus moved from yacht to starship to yacht, while now below, now above, now from one side or another, the glorious green vastness of the planet came into view randomly through the interstices of the tubes.

Asher watched the Station as parts of it appeared and disappeared through the tangle of tubes. The mission was not going well. The stop on Dade had been a disaster, and he had not even traced out the source of the faint Skill presence he had detected on arrival. Why hadn't the Nin listened to him? He and Clemmy alone would have done better than this. He hoped.

"Was your stay on Dade a pleasant one?" a crewman inquired of them solicitously as they disembarked at *Bonnie's Best*. Dov grunted rudely and Clemmy said: "Yes, thank you."

There was little chance that either Cleos or the Downer-master could have traced them, but nevertheless they held to the public areas of the ship and avoided their cabins for the moment. Once the *Best* had entered interspace and Asher had scanned as many minds as he could, only then might they relax.

"What's in the box?" Asher asked Dov as they sat in one of the observation lounges.

Dov and Clemmy exchanged glances. Clemmy said: "Let me.

"Ressies, Asher," she said. "Two of those things we saw attached to legs here and there. They're called Ressies."

Asher's mind was flying here and there, scanning the tube, part of which they could see out of the viewport, looking for hostile minds.

"Ressies," he said. "What are they, after all, pets or something?"

Again Dov and Clemmy exchanged glances. "Something," Clemmy said.

"Asher," she said gently, laying a hand on his arm. Her wound had stopped bleeding, and she had covered it with a shawl she had bought from the ship's stores, but the wound was stiffening and the pain was growing. "Asher, this is something I have to describe to you in detail. Please . . . once we're in interspace, I have many things to tell you, and show you." Dov flushed and turned his face away.

Asher saw it, and looked at her. In his mind he saw, starkly, the staring, bloated face of the man he had killed.

"You two were together for two days and nights," he said savagely. She said nothing, but her dark eyes flickered.

"Aye," he said bitterly. "Maybe we had better wait. I . . ."

His eyes narrowed suddenly, and he said: "Wait . . . wait . . . there's something coming in. Ahhh."

Dov was paying attention now. "What is it?"

"A communication from the Station. Simple video," Asher said, and closed his eyes. Dov imagined the chaos of electromagnetic impulses around them, and wondered how Asher could distinguish any particular one of them.

"My brain scans up and down the spectrum," Asher muttered, and Dov realized that his own thoughts had been broadcasting. "Now . . . now . . . it is an alert that the Station is seeking three fugitives who robbed one of the boutiques. Images of each of the three follow . . ."

Dov and Clemmy leaned forward tensely.

"The first one," Asher said, eyes closed, concentrating. Then a smile flickered at the corner of his mouth. "The first one weighs three hundred pounds, name of Leroy. The second one, Lester, has a beard hanging down to his waist. The third one is a female dwarf named Esmeralda."

"What!" Clemmy and Dov said in one voice. Dov expostulated: "Asher, you can actually alter electromagnetic information?"

"Yes," Asher said slowly, his smile disappearing. "But . . ."

His eyes were vacant and he fell silent. Clemmy said in a low voice: "I think we'd better leave him alone. The transmissions are digital and full of redundancy. His brain must be in some kind of no-mind overdrive to handle the speed. And they'll probably be repeating the message for a while."

They regarded Asher silently for a time, but he never changed his close-eyed, watchful attitude. Clemmy found her eyes sliding over to the box at Dov's side. Dov caught her gaze and mouthed: "Your place or mine?" "Oh, shut up," she mouthed back.

Asher suddenly relaxed. "I think I've taken care of it," he said wearily. "I programmed an overlay on the ship's Com. If the fugitive message arrives again, the overlay will be triggered and make certain the descriptions remain the same, completely unlike us.

"You know," he said, leaning back, suddenly thoughtful, "this is the first time I've realized that I could distort a Com, even for a short time."

Both Dov and Clemmy regarded him with a kind of awe. Clemmy felt a trace of fear moving inside her.

"Asher," she breathed, "is there anything you can't do?"

His eyes snapped open and she could see pain lurking inside.

"I," he told her, "am the merest Apprentice of the Power. I had not enough Skill to reach Initiation. If a group of Apprentices were to attack me, I would probably fail. Were a full October Adept to come against me, I would wither like grass before a flame." His eyes were burning, tension lines around them, and both Clemmy and Dov could see that he was torn by some inadequacy inside.

"But you were taught by the Teacher," Clemmy said.

"Aye," Asher said, still bitterly, "and to this day I do not know what he taught me. Some of it is still buried. I do not feel integrated; I do not feel complete. I got drunk. And I killed a man."

They were silent. There was nothing to say, though Clemmy wanted to reach for him. Dov, however, looked impatient.

"This is your last chance to contact the Nin, Your Squad Leadership," he growled, "before next planetfall." Asher ignored the sarcasm; Dov was right. They had been out of her reach for nearly three days. Much could have happened. And once the ship was in interspace, they would have to wait until it exited again to communicate via interspatial holography.

"Wrist computer," Asher said. "Please list any messages for . . ." And he gave their full, pseudonymous names.

The machine almost leaped off his wrist.

"Whew!" he said. "We'd better see what those priority messages are all about."

He stood up. "I'll go first. Clemmy," he said. She looked up at him, hoping for something personal, but there was only the squad leader there. "Dov. Watch the tube. If Cleos or a Downer comes, neutralize them any way you can that doesn't draw attention. Clemmy." She was still looking at him, her narrow face pleading. "No Green Flame," he said harshly. It brought back the image and the blood drained from her face, from her soul.

Dov shot upward. "Asher, you bastard," he said, fists balled. Asher just glanced at him, and turned away.

In a holo booth he paused. The urgent message to call the Nin was in his mind, but so too was the need to rest, to gather himself together, to master all that had happened to him. He reached up a hand and touched the transparent plastic seal on his temple. There was no pain, only numbness. The numbness was physical; it had no reflection in his mental chaos.

I cannot solve it all now, he decided. I need a long talk with Clemmy first; I need to find out what happened when I was out. And I need to know if this injury has any future implications.

He called up the Nin.

Her image cascaded and firmed before him. He had evidently awakened her; there was no telling without asking the computer what the time was on the Bodyguard planet.

A full robe hid her magnificent body. It's just as well, he thought.

"Asher, we have been under October attack," she began, and that brought him to full attention. She described the event in detail, and he listened without interruption. "You must return, Asher," she said at last. "I cannot count on the Therds to repel another attack. As it was, they kidnapped Wayne Rangeley and did something to him. We found him on Outer Moon Station in the psycho ward. He was a babbling idiot, Asher. His mind is hopelessly destroyed, the medicos say."

"They were looking for Skill," Asher said. He remembered Rangeley, and was immensely saddened. "They were looking for me, and they emptied him to do it."

"He couldn't have told them much," the Nin said. Her hair, with its odd alternation of blonde and brown, seemed disheveled, though the only comb he had ever seen her use was her fingers. "All he knew was that you were on a mission. But Asher," she said, and leaned forward slightly, her face taking on a look of scraped bone. "They as good as killed a Bodyguard. I do not need you only to protect the Guild, Asher. I need you for revenge. *No one kills a Bodyguard.*" This was definitely no computer construct.

"Aye, but I *am* on a mission," Asher said. "Is it now aborted?"

"Absolutely not," the Nin said. "I am transferring Leadership to Clemmy. My Guild never abandons a contract. You should know that, Asher Tye. But you are unique, and the event here threatens the Guild as a whole. You must return."

Separated from Clemmy . . .

I could refuse, Asher thought. But then what?

"As you wish," Asher said.

"And another thing, Asher Tye," the Nin said. "Have you heard the news about the drop in the Index?"

"Drop in the Index?!" Asher exclaimed.

"It just happened in the last few hours. Asher . . . my people are scanning continuously, and I see signs of an effort to lay the genocide of twenty-five races at the door of the Bodyguard Guild."

"But that would be absurd," Asher yelled.

"Tell that to races who have trusted the Galactic Com for millennia," the Nin said.

Asher waited for Dov and Clemmy to finish their own conversations with the Nin. Clemmy came out looking sober. Dov looked elated.

"Nisha, Spimmon, and Adio-Gabutti have been informed," Clemmy said. "I don't think I'm ready for this, Asher."

Asher took her by the shoulders, and she cried out in pain. He snatched his hands away.

"You're ready," he said. He was finding it hard to look at her. "You have enough Skill to recognize Skill, and you have enough to raise a respectable Shield. And you have Spimmon and Nisha Scalli and their diamond Shield, and the Therd and his invisible mind. Just be careful. If you sense October, draw inward and pretend you're a normal woman."

Tears sprang to Clemmy's eyes. "I am a normal woman, Asher," she said.

His hands twitched. She had injured her shoulder somehow, he recalled now. He dropped his hands to her waist.

"Find out who killed Ran," he said. "And find out what's happening in the Surceasean Sector. That's all. Save revenge for later."

"Yes, Asher," she said meekly. He kissed her then, oblivious of Dov.

"And watch out for Dov," Asher said. "He's a horny bastard."

Clemmy opened her mouth, and closed it again. She didn't know whether to laugh or cry.

Neither did Dov.

"Take care of each other," Asher said to Dov. "You're a good man, my friend." He chucked Dov under the chin with one fist, and then he turned and strode away, headed back toward the tubes.

"Final call: visitors must disembark," the ship told them. They watched Asher's back, tired, upright, but with shoulders hunched, as he moved through the hatchway and disappeared.

"He's going back to Dade, back to Cleos and the Downermaster," Clemmy said dully.

Dov took her hand. "They don't have a chance against him," he said.

Chapter 15

Xenophobes always stayed huddled in the human areas of *Bonnie's Best,* but most of the young elite had enough of a sense of adventure to sample the interracial facilities in the bowels of the great starship. Thither went Clemmy after the *Best* had entered interspace, and thither too went Dov. Ostensibly they were casual samplers of exotica. Actually, they had arranged a meeting with Adio- Gabutti, Spimmon, and Nisha Scalli.

It was accidental, of course, or would have seemed that way to the casual observer, but at length the three of them were bending the elbow (or its equivalent joint) and toasting the universe and all in it with happy good fellowship. The place: The Spider's Web, a watering hole in the afterdecks. It was raucous and small.

"So what's a Therd doing in human space . . . slumming?" "Gadbois" hollered, regarding Adio-Gabutti with a banal expression of hail fellow, well met.

"Yes," Adio-Gabutti and Nisha Scalli said in unison.

There was an awkward pause.

"Clibbyclibbyclibby," said Spimmon.

"Eh?" Dov said.

"He's laughing, you ninny," said Clemmy.

"Oh," said Dov. He regarded Nisha and Adio-Gabutti for a moment, and then, sotto voce: "Hey, you guys, live it up, for the love of Mike!"

Nisha Scalli hissed and whipped his tail, which was hanging through the rungs of the human chair he was astride; it struck a passing Andalian Snail with a ringing clang.

The Snail didn't notice.

"What does this red one mean?" Nisha hissed. "'Live it up?'"

"He means," rumbled the Therd, "to disembowel your opponent, but only to imagine it, not actually do it." Nisha frowned.

"No, I don't," Dov said indignantly. "I mean get drunk, laugh, have a good time." Nisha was grinning now, he saw, and Dov gulped. He had never associated an Ekans grin with joy and camaraderie.

"I have drunk five standard liters of your witslap rye," Nisha hissed, "in the past half hour. Is that what you mean by 'drunk'?"

Dov and Clemmy studied him. His skin had darkened into an olive green. He looked as if he could pluck a fly out of midair by its nose hairs.

"Not exactly . . ." Dov ventured.

And then he and Clemmy noticed something else. Affixed to the base of Nisha's tail, as if it had always belonged there, was an ochre, pulsing Ressie. They looked at each other.

Spimmon, who was sitting on the table itself, now broke in in a way that made them all take notice:

"Asher is gone," he said in his fluty way. "He may never return to us." Clemmy paled, but of the aliens only the color sensitive Ekans noticed it. "Now we must act as if he were never here. Ms. Clemmy is now Squad Leader; to her we now turn our allegiance and respect."

"Allegiance," Nisha hissed. "Yesssss."

"And respect," Spimmon insisted.

"Honk!" A bellowing sound came from behind Nisha. They all looked, and saw a Canshaw's Cylinder bent slightly out of true where Nisha's tail had caught it. The foot-thick alien towered over them all, perhaps ten feet high and armored like a fish.

"Put your tail, composed of waste products, in your . . ." The Cylinder faltered. He was looking at Nisha through his ring of chest-high eyes, and the Ekans was grinning broadly. "Yes," the Cylinder honked, subdued. "Well, good-bye," it said, and wheeled away.

Nisha half stood, but the Therd placed a restraining tentacle on the back of his neck. "No, my friend," the Therd said, a voice like low and distant thunder. "A Bodyguard does not initiate an unnecessary battle."

"I wish we had remembered that on Dade," Clemmy muttered. But they all heard it, and they turned back to her and Dov and demanded the full story.

Clemmy began to tell it, but Dov interrupted: "C'mon, Clemmy! You're leaving out the good parts." Then he launched into a lurid account that brought snarls and hisses from his audience.

But when, in the middle of relating the confrontation in Clemmy's room, he reached the climactic battle: "And I kicked, I mean *kicked*, my guy, but when I turned around there was Clemmy, this frail-looking, narrow-chested, black-haired Clemmy, about to be blasted away by this chirping character with the mean face, when . . ."

Clemmy reached over and poured a pint of dizzybeer into his lap.

"Oops," she said, "how clumsy of me." Dov leaped to his feet in a splatter of droplets. "Hey!" he yelled.

"Wait, Gaddy, please!" she said, looking up at him, teeth clenched in a ferocious smile. "Go ahead with the story. We are captivated."

Dov saw the aliens watching narrowly, and suspected suddenly that he was being disciplined, with the aliens fully aware of it and watching to see what he would do.

"She, er," he said grudgingly then, lapsing into slightly more formal language, "defeated her opponent then and helped lead us all out of there." Abruptly he sat down and continued with the story, but the expansive gesturing had gone out of him.

Later he escorted her to her room and, outside of it, grasped her suddenly by the shoulders. She gasped and he let her sore arm go.

" 'Squad Leader,' " he grated. "Just like something from a holo melodrama."

"Yes," she said, looking him levelly in the eyes. "Just like that."

He let her other arm go, and turned away from her.

"It's always Asher Tye, isn't it?" he asked, shoulders hunched, "or is it now the Ressie?"

Eighteen days to Lisbon Station, the edge of the Draco and Castor/Pollux Sectors.

"No offense, Gaddy," she said then, her voice very faint. "Asher is my husband. And you . . . what do you want? Me? The Ressie?"

He kept his back to her, and she let the silence last just long enough.

"You see, Gaddy?" she said.

He took a step, then another. "I'll get it for you," he said dully.

It was better than the first time, now that she knew what to expect. She let herself fall into it, and again could not believe that her heart had withstood it and survived.

Then, panting and dry, she called up carafe after carafe of nearwater, the Ressie a fat round ball resting on the bed, and she felt the first faint stirrings of guilt.

Why? she asked herself. I could understand it if I had indeed taken Dov in; that for certain would have been a betrayal of Asher. But this little round pet . . . how could it ever be any kind of rival to Asher and me? Rather, it's like taking a bath, as impersonal as the water that warms me.

She liked the comparison. She went over it again in her mind.

Still . . .

Asher waited. He was deep in Shadow, tucked against a beam along the inner wall of the outer concourse of Dade Station. There were still three hours until the next ship out toward the Bodyguard planet was due to dock. In the meantime, he meant to stay away from the hordes of Cleos agents still milling through the far greater hordes that were Dade's human space communicants.

A light-hour away, a ship was about to burst out of

interspace. It was a liner as big as the *Bonnie's Best*—a sister ship, in fact—on its scheduled run, with a pause at Dade, to the Roil. The *Ann's Best* was on a sightseeing excursion, booked by a corporation as an annual bonus for its chief executives, who were making merry in oblivious ignorance of the four Surceasean agents who had climbed aboard at a maintenance stop at the Bodyguard Planet.

The ship switched into non-existence the little artificial universe that had sustained it within the interspatial string; in a flare of incandescence, *Ann's Best* was back in real space.

Aboard Dade Station, Asher Tye suddenly tensed. He felt the sudden stirring of Power where only that elusive trace had been before. Somewhere relatively nearby, someone was using the Cloak.

No. More than one.

He turned toward the support beam and simultaneously dropped out of Shadow, facing away from the seething mob behind him. He would have seemed to pop out of thin air to anyone looking toward him, but no one happened to be doing so.

On the incoming ship the inner lounge was empty, save for a weeping woman hunched over one of the far tables. Save, too, for the unnoticeable foursome gathered at another one.

"I felt something," Score insisted. "Didn't you feel it? There is some use of Power nearby."

The other three scanned, mental powers straining to rake the ether.

"The trace of Dal Gaskin," Ceal Carnak said slowly. "But I thought I felt something else, too." She fingered the pocket of her bodice where the little Skill jammer was tucked. It was still there.

"Maybe it was just the leap out of interspace," Sanda said shrilly. "That always blows my mind."

"Shh . . . keep it down!" Ceal whispered.

The weeping woman was looking with tear-filled eyes around the lounge, where she had fled from her cavorting husband. She saw the four of them, but it did not register.

She bent her head down again and tried to make the tears flow some more.

"Me," said Larla, "I'm having another pudding steak." The others groaned as she slapped her palm on the sensor. Larla had gained more weight than any of them during this enforced trip away from the Ressies.

The buttermilk-yellow, quivering mass rose out of the table steaming, on a platter garnished with greenweed. Her body concealing the steak from the weeper, Larla began to shovel it in with her hooked fingers. Naked fingers were the fashion of the day, for that particular food.

"Hey, you!" a bass voice said, and a hand grasped Asher's shoulder and spun him around. The man's eyes widened as he saw Asher's face. Asher could see the thought leaping into the Cleos brain: "It's him!"

The man was as tall as Asher, and much thicker of body. His arms were watermelon thick, his hands hamlike. He opened his mouth to yell.

Asher thrust four rigid fingers into the man's solar plexus. The man coughed, and would have bent over, but Asher had one arm around his head then, and a knuckle poised above the nerve along the bottom edge of his jaw. "Keep silent and still," Asher said, and dug the knuckle in for a brief moment. The man opened his mouth to scream, and Asher forced the man's arm against it, muffling him.

"Take me to a safe place," he hissed into the man's ear. He let go of his head suddenly and grasped him by the left wrist, bending it back in a peculiar way.

The man couldn't believe it. He was used to pushing other people around. Only Cleos and the bosses just below Cleos had ever pushed him around, and then not this way, not by sheer technique. But when he tensed himself to break free of this very young man who held him, he felt his wrist nearly break in two.

"All right," he growled. He looked frantically around for help. The throng around them surged and milled. Both he and Asher scanned it piercingly. There were no other black-vested people in sight.

They jostled through, no more or less aggressively than

many around them. Asher's mouth was like a line of rock.
He did not dare use Skill, for he knew that those nearing
Dade Station would detect such use with instantaneous
certainty. He wondered, momentarily, whether the Downermaster was awake below and able to feel the stirring of
Power that the incoming ship was bringing. For it had to
be an incoming ship; nothing else could account for the
suddenness of that fourfold rippling of the Cloak, belching
out of nowhere.

It looked like a maintenance corridor that the thick man
took Asher into, but there were still people around them,
and now they saw some of Cleos' other servants, scuttling
past. Asher twisted his face in a desperate attempt to turn
it into something unrecognizable, but it only caused a
passing woman to eye him curiously.

"Caffeine," he croaked, and the woman's eyes arched.
Then she was past.

And then they were around a corner, and another woman
heading toward them looked at him, and frowned. Then
recognition dawned and she whipped a needler out of
nowhere and danced backward, out of range of Asher's
hands or feet.

"I found him!" the hamlike man in Asher's grasp yelled
at her.

"I'll break his arm," Asher rasped, and gave a slight
twist. The man howled.

But already there were four or five other Cleos agents
upon them, ringing them with needlers. "So break it," the
woman said.

Five minutes later, he met Cleos.

The man was wired. A few million optical fibers glowed
hideously in multicolor array as they sprouted out of his
head like glowing hairs, and disappeared into a transmission field hovering above him. Were the field lower, it
would have fried his synapses. Higher, and he couldn't
have moved out of the room. But the room itself was big.
From the scarring in the floors and walls, it had evidently
once held some large machine, now rendered obsolete by
a change in technology. A haphazard effort at redecorating

had been made, with a few scatter rugs and softly upholstered chairs and couches.

The man had once been big, too. Now, however, his
body was emaciated, hidden by a long tunic. Around his
shoulders was the trademark leather vest, hanging loosely.
His eyelids jumped like spiders on a griddle, while below
them moved glassy and washed-out orbs in ceaseless, open-
eyed REM motion. His beard was as white as the belly of
a fish. He was sitting in an easy chair, but his body was
still with muscular tension.

Around him five or six other people stood, and they too
were wired, but less grandly than Cleos himself. One,
taller than the others, whose few crimson-glowing wires
pulsed in ceaseless cadence, approached as Asher was led
in.

"I brought him in," the thick man began. The woman
snorted. A movement of the tall man's hand cut them both
off.

Then Asher got it. He understood what the fibers meant.
He glanced to his right and focused at the hamlike man's
hair. Yes, it was there, a tiny bundle of fibers ending in a
tiny transmitting pod, not forcefield-generated and not
needing to be.

It was not like October's manipulation of the brain. That
was remote, invisible, and as far as anyone could determine, apart from the electromagnetic light and radio spectrum. This used that spectrum to impose neural control on
everyone with the proper feelers imbedded in the proper
parts of individual brains.

Cleos could direct his agents with more certainty than
the October One herself could have done. She had oper-
ated with interstellar distances and thousands of Adepts,
but it had been threat and loyalty that had led her forces.
Here, in a far more limited spatial environment, the
Uppermaster was touching the brains of his few hundreds,
seeing what they were seeing, commanding directly into
their minds.

But not feeling their pain, Asher thought. He had known
where I was from the moment the thick man had recognized me. But he had not felt the solar plexus blow, or the

wrist hold. And he had caused the thick man to waltz me right into his inner sanctum.

"I speak for the Master," the tall lieutenant said. "We would know one thing."

"Tell the light show that my father will turn this Station upside down if anything happens to me," Asher snapped. It sounded good, anyway, just like a rich kid. He hoped.

Cleos was evidently paying attention, for his weary eyes were focusing in and out in Asher's general direction.

"We had had the impression that the Downermaster, rot her, had you hidden somewhere," the tall man said levelly. "But the agents we have down there are giving us some wild reports. This we want to know: how did you escape her? How did you kill her three guards exactly? And . . . *who are you?*"

How easy it would have been to use Skill on such as these, Asher thought, to rip the fiber kaleidoscope off of Cleos' head, sending everyone in the room into mental-hammered darkness. But the rippling in Power was still there, and his own use of it would have been like a neon sign to whoever was exercising it.

He had no resources left but the physical. The doorway was just behind Asher Tye. It might as well have been a hundred parsecs away.

"Suck space," Asher said, and sneered.

The tall man's throbbing fibers changed their rhythm slightly. He nodded at his boss. "Cleos is investigating the Downer uproar," he said. "If we harm you now . . . We do not know enough. Perhaps a trade with Downer . . ." The words were becoming more and more disjointed.

Cleos closed his eyes.

"Sell you," the tall man said. "To Daddy. To Downer. But hide? Can't hide on Dade. We know everywhere. But. But . . ." And then the man signalled somehow, through the fibers probably, since Asher never caught it. "Until we know more," was what he thought he had heard, but it was probably his own conclusion, based on what was happening.

The woman had put the needler away. Asher turned and stiff-armed the hamlike man. Out of the corner of his eye, he saw the Uppermaster react. Could he after all feel his slaves' pain?

He heard a hiss. He didn't see the sprayer that the woman behind him had gotten from somewhere. He blacked out instantly.

One hour later: "Zhat one!" the grey-haired woman screamed. She pointed a rigid, iron-steady finger down the table at the haloed man. "He," she hammered, her voice controlling the scream and modulating it, every syllable a punctuation, "is ze one who has corrupted ze Founders' plan. He is ze one who has turned ze bulk of you into znivelling, crawling lackeys."

"Oh, come now," one of the seventy there assembled said feebly. The table was gigantic, so that so many could sit around it. It was a holograph, of course, as were the figures themselves. Each reclined comfortably in his or her area of Dade Station as the images were transmitted, compiled, and received. The table and the room itself were a fiction.

Once the table had been round, years ago. Now it was oval. The computer reflected the power change that had evolved. No, not really oval. More pear-shaped.

At her place at the smaller end of the pear, the Downermaster thrust her finger again, this time at the coiffed and bejewelled man who had just spoken.

"And you!" she roared. "You, of all people, object! You, who have taken ze Ztation Police itzelf into ze Cleos fold; you, who have allowed ze Zeventy by your zell-out. You are ze worzt of zeze, but you be all at fault, in ze long run. Each of you has a hiztory, a lineage to uphold, damn you all. And you have betrayed it mozt contemptibly."

"You," Cleos said from the other end of the table, his eyes clear, as they always were in such meetings, his fiber halo dull, his neural control over his forces for the moment relaxed, "have developed your own allies, my dear Downer." His voice was like the whisper of a cold wind. He indicated the small group, perhaps a dozen, clustered at the far sweep of the pear. "And we do allow you ze bulk of ze Rezzie traffic."

"Aye," she said bitterly, looking at them. "Culture, for g-d's zake. In charge of live entertainment for Ztation perzonnel. Hah! And zweepers. And pickpockets. And ezcorts. Ezcorts! And you have air and gravity and mozt of ze power and ze Police itzelf! Let me tell you, Cleos. I am appealing to ze Com directly. Directly, do you hear me? You know how ze Founders dezigned it. Zey knew zat ziss kind of power imbalanze could happen, and zey gave ze Com ultimate control. Zee how far your hairfire carries you when ze Com finally intervenes!" She was goading him. She already knew that the Com would not intervene.

"If ze Com finally intervenes," Cleos said, so softly that it seemed an echo in her mind.

"Yess!" the Downermaster hissed, her grey hair loose around her face, hanging like dirty rain, framing her eye-shocked pale face. "If. Zat is ze reazon I invoked ze charter and called ziss meeting. Becauze, all of you Cleos people, you are ztill of ze Zeventy. No matter what power Cleos has over you, you can ztill, in ziss forum, in ziss official meeting of ze Zeventy, break him. Break him, do you hear me? Becauze zere is only one pozzible way zat he can zay 'If.' "

She was silent for a moment, letting the assembly, the nominal executive power on the Station, ponder her words. Some even appeared to do so. The rest fidgeted or slept or stared vacantly into space.

"If," she said then, her own voice soft now, but with an underlying ferocity that kept a few on the Cleos side from dozing off. "If, zomehow, he has taken control of Com itzelf!"

The bombshell—there it was. She threw it out angrily, defiantly, hopefully. That she was thereby revealing the cause of a crisis that went far beyond Dade Station, that could threaten the galaxy as a whole, she had no idea.

"Zat be impozzible," another of Cleos' men, a well-oiled, nearly naked specimen said, his voice firmer than the Police Captain's had been. "Ze Station Com be like ze Galactic Encyclopedia: nozing and no one can affect it."

"Yet zere was one forze, one time, zat could have done

it," the Downermaster went on, hissing. "And zat be . . . October!"

The assembly stirred at this, but only for a moment. The oily man said: "Nonzenze! Everyone in ze galaxy knows zat ze October Guild be no more. Zhe be gone— zip! Out of ze galaxy. And whezer zey could affect ze digital flow . . . lady, permit me to doubt it."

"Doubt it and be damned!" the Downermaster shrieked. "I have felt it, I tell you! I have felt October minds puzhing and zhruzting on zis Ztation. And it was only a little after I firzt felt zem, before I knew what zey were, zat Cleos began to move, and zucked you up like zewage zrough a ztraw while ze Com ztood zilent."

"Hogwash," came a voice. "Nonzenze," came another.

The Downermaster was afraid, now. She had seen the day coming when Cleos could not be defied any further, and this assembly, this Seventy, and the Com, had seemed the only way out, short of violence. She did not, ultimately, want a bundle of fibers sticking into her brain.

"All of you, lizten," she begged. "Lizten to a Com zat is not right in ze head.

"Com!" she commanded. "Tell me, tell us all: how many Rezzies zere be on zis Ztation?"

They all waited. A few of them began to stir uneasily, for the wait itself was abnormal.

The Com said: "There are no Ressies on Dade Station."

The Seventy looked at one another. On their faces was not outrage, however; not enlightenment, not horror. Only a little surprise. Most of them were wearing Ressies of their own.

"Do you zee?" the Downermaster said desperately. "Zomething has mezzed it up. And if zere be any Receptors among you, bezides me, let your minds feel, for even now, zere is October in Dade Ztation zpace!"

The dramatic announcement stirred them, just a little. But none of them were Receptors; they had only heard of such abnormal people. Deep down, few really believed in the October legend, and Receptors seemed as bizarre as talking cats.

"I azzure you, Madame," Cleos said in a silky, distracted voice, "zat zhould any October wizards appear among us, each and every one of us would kill zem out of hand, as would any dezent zitizen of ze human galaxy." There was a murmur of assent.

"Perhaps," Cleos continued, his halo brightening as he moved his thoughts away from the meeting, "perhaps ze Downers are unhappy wiss ze tazks zey are allotted. Perhaps we zhould, zay, remove ze Rezzie trade from zeir jurizdiction?"

The Downermaster caught her breath. That would wipe out one of her largest income areas.

"No . . ." she said. And for the first time, her composure wavered. Only for an instant. But a few of her supporters saw it.

By the next meeting, she knew then, the pear would be sharper at her end, the balance of power all on Cleos'. Unless she could somehow reveal the October/Cleos link in all its clarity. Or . . . but an attempt at violent revolution within Dade had never been made.

Chapter 16

"Asher. Asher Tye," the Nin's lonely voice called through the tachyonic ether. Station Com could not locate him; it was willing, however, to take a message.

"Warships, Asher Tye," the Nin relayed, and she seemed, for the first time in her life, staggered by the magnitude of what was happening. "Warships are on their way to the Bodyguard Planet. The Galactic Police is moving against us, and such are its numbers that we cannot, dare not resist. Our only hope is through the Police investigation itself; they intend to interdict the Bodyguards until Com Central rules. Already, Asher, there are things on the Com that I cannot believe. Blasted planets in Emperor Guteater's space for sure, but signs of the Guild? How can that be, Asher Tye? We don't have heavy ships, but the Com says we do. What is going on, Asher Tye? I need you. I need you . . ."

The Downer attack would be swift, sudden, and would take advantage of the hidden ducts and airshafts with which the Station was riddled. They knew exactly where to strike, where the October miasma was localized; the Receptor Skill of the Downermaster herself told them that.

The four Surceaseans had been in a lather of anticipation as they approached Dade. Dade, and Ressies. But in the last hour of their approach, Ceal Carnak had been called into one of the *Ann's Best* holo booths.

It was Dal Gaskin, as she had expected. She had read his dossier, and it had made her wonder how mankind had survived these millennia. For Gaskin was one of those highly intelligent people who believed that intelligence alone should bring success. He believed that he was better than other people. It wasn't that his opinion was entirely wrong, because in fact he was intelligent. But somehow it had never sunk into his mind that such factors as character and generosity had to be developed before anyone deserved respect from anyone else. Gaskin believed that the scintillating light of his intellect should bowl others into obeisance. Instead, his arrogance had bowled them into hostility, the why of which baffled him even when it was directly pointed out. He could not admit to inadequacy in any field of life because he was smarter, he thought, than the bovine mass of living humanity.

"You earn your way in society by actions, not qualities," Ceal Carnak had muttered to herself while reading the dossier. When the Seventeen had been forming, Gaskin had behaved as if he was an inevitable part of it. But they, the emerging rulers of the Apprentices, had not agreed. Sensing a man who disrupted the peace of mind of those around him, they had sent him to Dade Station, they had told him, to sharpen his Com manipulation skills. In truth, his Skill was rather feeble, though he would have been the last to admit it. That he had been drowning his sorrows in the drugs and Ressies and other diversions of the Station had been clear from the dossier. That had been why Asher had had trouble detecting him; much of the time he was not in a state of lucid activity.

Gaskin began without preamble. Ceal watched his angular, rusty-haired face as he spoke, scarcely moving his lips, as if verbal communication were beneath him. There was a scraggle of mustache on his upper lip that looked like winter-blasted dead moss.

"An event is about to occur that demands Skill," Gaskin said. Even in imparting information, he made his tone supercilious. "The presence of the four of you is fortuitous. You will assist me."

"Not fortuitous," Ceal said. "The renegade has passed through this space in recent days. You yourself must have detected him; and we must alert Surcease."

"I felt some faint stirring," he admitted. Ceal thought: I'll bet. She doubted he had felt anything at all during the time the mysterious wizard had been in-system. Probably he had been engaged with a Ressie.

Gaskin rushed on: "Listen. A situation is coming down on Dade and you must join me to cope with it. The moment you arrive, we must Network and influence the Station Com. Our allies on Dade demand it, and I demand it."

"Cope?" Ceal inquired cruelly. "You cannot cope with this yourself?"

"Of course I can cope with it," Gaskin snapped. "But a Network is quicker. Report to me when you arrive."

"But I can't sell that to the rest of them," Ceal protested. She felt bitter disappointment twist her insides. Come off it, she thought. Whatever this was, it would delay their reunion with Ressies for only a few hours.

"They have no choice," Gaskin said flatly. "I am the only one stationed permanently on Dade. There are just not enough of us to go around, and the Seventeen have not given Dade sufficient priority. Now one part of Dade thinks that October is upon them, and they're going to attack our allies and try to reveal us to the Station as a whole. I've jimmied the Com, but there's too much to do here for one man, even me. I've had a request in for assistants for months, but the Seventeen won't listen." Gaskin said it bitterly. He was, he thought, the equal of any of them, but Networked, the Seventeen's will had been irresistible.

"I must have a Network now," Gaskin continued. "The machine is spouting irrationalities, and raising suspicions among our allies' enemies. You will help me in bringing it back into line. You know how badly the Seventeen want Dade for Ressie commerce."

Ceal sighed. "All right," she said. "But I'll have a tough time selling it." And it was tough indeed. They would have Ressies, but could not enjoy them as they wished until after the Network. The convincing of the three came hard and slow.

When they had finally detubed, the Surceaseans were escorted by Cleos agents to an old bubble observation cabin on the outer shell of Dade. There were many eruptions of such lux-glass relux bubbles all over Dade's surface. Most of them were hotel rooms, more expensive than the ones below. For despite the wonders of holographic imagery, the knowledge that a particular view was the real thing had financial value, even when the view itself could be simulated exactly in the rooms below.

The bubble was like a twenty-foot-diameter glass pimple thrusting out of the rectangular surface that was the outer wall of the room. Despite its appearance to incoming ships, which caught glimpses of the Station proper through the forest of transtubes around it, Dade was not a spherical shell. It was, rather, built of hundreds of thousands of rectangular surfaces, welded together at the slight angles needed to create the apparently round envelope.

Cleos and his tall lieutenant met with the four upon their arrival in the bubble.

"When ze attack comes," Cleos said dully when he had described the situation, "keep on top of ze Com. My people will take care of ze Downers." His eerie voice, like a banshee howling in a storm, cut into them like a knife.

Key Com decision circuits had been routed to only feet away. Long ago the same circuitry had been housed in the Downer area. But as layer after layer had risen over it, the Dade planners had integrated Com circuitry into every structural member of the Station, on the theory that multiple redundancy would ensure the Com's inviolability. No one had expected Skill to come along.

Ceal Carnak said sharply: "Let's get on with it. Where are Dal Gaskin and the Ressies?" The other three seemed to be holding their breaths.

"He is almozt here," Cleos' tall lieutenant said, his own fiber bundle pulsing like a fire alarm on his head. "Ze cuztomers muzt know nozing of ziss. We don't want any outward dizruption of Ztation buziness."

Cleos' eyes were almost closed. His vast halo was shimmering in colors too fast for the eye to separate. So frantic was the activity that the effect was a dazzling whiteness.

"Nor does Surcease," Ceal Carnak said.

"Nor," said the lieutenant, "does ze Downermazter, I believe. Any damage to ze Ztation be damage to us all.

Anyone who damages ze Ztation would be labelled a traitor and executed out of hand by any Ztation citizen. It has to be zat way in a population much greater zan any available ezcape tranzportation."

"We do not approve of the way you have handled this," Ceal said grimly. "There should never have been a confrontation with the Downers. You should have moved more subtly."

Cleos was lost to her words. His eyes were closed, and in his mind he saw a thousand separate images, the scenes viewed by a thousand pairs of eyes, and he had to relax, had to free his mind to sort and choose and focus and pass on. Anything involving will had to be pushed away. Instinct was in charge now. Asher and the other warriors would have recognized his condition at once: no-mind.

The lieutenant said: "If you wizards had done your wizardry properly, ze Downermazter would not have known what we were doing until it was too late. Inztead, the Com malfunctions wiss your man poking around in it, and as a rezult ze Downermazter knows zat zomezing is wrong. It was becauze of you Zurceazeans zat Cleos was able to control ze Com in ze firzt place; and now your incompetence is putting us in danger."

"How could Gaskin have known that the Downermaster was a Receptor?" Larla said hotly, her jowls quivering. "She must have known there was Skill around from the first time a Surceasean visited you. And anyway, the four of us weren't even involved in all this."

"How could _we_ have known . . ." the tall man began.

"We want our Ressies," Sanda shrilled suddenly. Her bald head glistened with a sheen of sweat. Unlike the other three, she had, if anything, lost weight during her time away from the Ressies.

"Yeah," Score began. "We want . . ."

"Shut up," Ceal said. "We wait."

"No!" Score shouted. His hair always looked like stringy black slime no matter how often he washed it. "First Ressies. Then Network. That's how Sanda and I are going to do it."

"Yeah," Sanda said.

Ceal sighed. "Lieutenant," she said then, "I am advising you to hide every Ressie on this Station until this Network begins." Score and Sanda paled. "As for you," Ceal said, facing them, "you know that a Network of four or five can defeat any average Skilled individual. Three may not. Two may not. We need you, and you must work with us to keep the Com coherent and stop any hint of the Downer action from being known to the visitors of the Station, above all others, and to the Seventy, as well. If we gave you Ressies first, you would be out of action for an entire day."

"A day," Sanda breathed. She moved a slow tongue over her lips.

"You have to wait!" Ceal said sternly. "If you do, then you can have your Ressies for the rest of your lives. If you don't, I myself will crush your minds if Cleos doesn't blow you away first, and then you will never have Ressies."

The thought of death was not compelling to these two, she knew. But the thought of an eternity without Ressies . . .

It shook even her.

"Zey're coming," Cleos panted suddenly. He made a gesture.

"We muzt go elzewhere," the lieutenant said hastily, taking Cleos by one arm. "You are perfectly zafe here."

"You bet we are," Ceal said grimly. "If you let any danger within forty feet of us, we will blast the brains of everyone in a hundred-foot downward and sideways slice of the Station, and if you and Cleos were caught, we wouldn't give a damn."

"Juzt control ze Com," the lieutenant said. He and Cleos disappeared through the door even as Dal Gaskin floated in on an anti-grav dolly. One by one he studied them, lips curled. Their eyes, even Ceal Carnak's, were fixed hungrily on the softball-shaped beings that Gaskin carried with him on the sled. A wet sob erupted suddenly from Sanda.

"Remember," the Downermaster whispered into her wrist communicator. "If you zee anyzing zat's doing zomezing weird, like moving zings wizout touching zem, or making green fire come out of zayr hands, or anyzing, blazt zem. Burn zem down where zey ztand."

She turned and looked at Ponger the Great, who stood nervously against the wall of her operating center. For the briefest moment, a softness came into her fierce and unbalanced eyes.

He looked back at her, eyes flickering away and forced back again with an effort of will.

"After ziss," she said, "you will take off zat damned Rezzie and come to me."

Ponger gulped. It was never easy. He would reach the point soon, he knew, at which he would no longer be able to force himself to disengage from the Ressie. How he would cope with that, in front of this grim, demanding woman, was more than he could imagine. If only she would try a Ressie, even once. But she seemed to know better; she was a teetotaler in everything but him.

"I look forward to it," he said quaveringly, and she thought it was from a combination of fear and desire. He was perfect for her, she thought.

Behind the public bulkheads, back in the little-used service shafts and corridors, storerooms and robot tunnels, an unnatural hush fell. The Servicemaster (one of the Seventy) had ordered his staff away from the likely areas of attack, at Cleos' instruction. Robots had been retired into their niches and deactivated. Outside, the shrill partygoers continued their uproarious fun.

"Lights," Cleos whispered. The command moved from his brain, out a fiber, and to the Powermaster. The maintenance areas of the upper Station went dark. Nothing could be done about the Downer areas yet. They were powered by their ancient crystalline reactors, and could not be influenced from above, except, perhaps, by the Com, and the Surceaseans had had no time to investigate that possibility.

"Ze fool," the Downermaster whispered, below. "We live downbelow, in ze darkness already. We know how to handle ze darkness."

Some of her agents had been circulating in the upper

areas as if they were tourists. They now moved toward the bubble hotel entrance.

Others were rising directly into the hotel in service gravity shafts.

Cleos waited. He had every detail of the Downer plan in hand, from an agent down there. He wished that he could simply evacuate the atmosphere out of the maintenance tunnels, but it could not be done. The tunnels had not been designed to be airtight from the rest of the Station.

The Network formed. Ceal, Sanda, Larla, Score, and Dal Gaskin sat cross-legged in a near-circle, knees touching, minds touching, a ribbon of ochre forming a pulsing band from leg to leg. They probed each other's Skill with mental tongues, wove a net of Power from what they each had learned as October Apprentices, linked together into one. Where one had strength, they gathered collective strength. Where one was weak, they plugged the weakness.

"We are," Score exulted, silently in his mind, "the equal of any Adept that ever walked the stars!" They all felt the words, and in the power of the moment, they all believed it.

And, like a five-headed, one-brained thing, they entered the Com.

Asher woke up suddenly. He was in utter darkness. His ears strained, but before his Skill could be awakened to roam the areas nearby, he stifled it. Carelessness upon awakening less than a day before had caused the deaths of three men.

He took a moment to inventory his body. Unrestrained, he found. And unmonitored.

Something was wrong. At least, it would have been wrong from his captors' point of view. The drug dosage had largely worn off. Why hadn't his awakening triggered some sort of alarm?

He sat up and let the expected wave of dizziness wash over him and subside. And as he sat there, feet dangling off the edge of what was apparently a bed or a couch, he became aware of the stirring of Power.

It was nearby, and it was strong. And it was of a nature that he had not encountered before.

He sat passively, letting the harmonics reach him. After a moment, he recognized the taste of one of the four he had felt Cloaked, coming in on a ship, just before Cleos had taken him. Then he recognized the taste of another, and another. All four of them! And the source of that faintness he had first felt on Dade, too. But all were intertwined in a peculiar way. Combined somehow, focusing on something as one mind. And an alien something was reinforcing it.

A Network, perhaps?

He had been dimly aware, all through his October training, that Networking was possible. But the October One had never allowed it. She, a solitary figure herself, had never permitted her people to organize in any way that might, someday, evolve into a threat to her. So the idea of joining minds in coherent purpose had remained implicit in the Skill they were learning, though never articulated. In fact, once in a while, it was warned against by their Adept teachers.

But here it was being done. Asher analyzed it, and quickly became aware of two things:

One, the strengths did not lead to new Skills among the four. They could not collectively go beyond what each had learned as an Apprentice. Learning a new Skill required a teacher who already had the Skill. All they could do as a group was strengthen what they already had.

And two, here were Apprentices only, as he himself once had been. If they were the group who had attacked the Bodyguard Planet, then something about Ran's death was clarified. For Asher had known that all October Initiates and Adepts had left the galaxy along with the October Ones during their encounter with the Teacher.

Who had been left behind? Only those students who had never reached Initiation—Apprentices, relative beginners in Power. What had happened to them after they no longer had an instructor who could bring them to further Skill?

Now, as he thought about it in depth for the first time, Asher realized that they would either disperse . . .

Or they would gather under the strongest and most advanced among them.

I've been blind, Asher thought. All wrapped up in my own development as a warrior, I always believed that the legitimate authorities could deal with any rogue Apprentice that arose from the dregs of October. The possibility of Networking never entered my mind.

But there must have been hundreds, even a few thousand, Apprentices on the October World when it had fallen. What if they had banded together in the aftermath?

Why had he not heard about it through the Galactic Encyclopedia? The one thing he *had* done was maintain a continuous scan of topics relating to October and to magical skills of any kind. Why had nothing ever arisen to account for the activities of leftover Apprentices?

The more he considered it, the more Asher realized how abnormal it was. Even if they had organized somehow, their activities would inevitably have appeared somewhere in the galactic record. He would have perceived the significance of any Skill-related event. But absolutely nothing had appeared, and the logical scan that he had ordered had been extensive and deep.

And what they were doing now . . .? In taste it felt similar to the digital image-changing he had done on *Bonnie's Best* with the all-points bulletin that had been circulating on himself, Clemmy and Dov.

Asher's jaw dropped open. Could they be working on the central logic unit of the Station's Com itself? But he had always thought a unit like that would be too complex for . . .

Wait a minute. Reason it out. A Com like this one would have miles of imbedded molecular circuitry throughout the Station. No mind or group of minds could control the electronic flow in so vast and complex a situation.

But what if the logical unit itself was the target? Was it as diffuse as the memory of the machine? He himself had placed an "overlay" on the Com. Suppose a Network could go deeper in? Wouldn't the complexity defeat any Network, no matter how strong? Would it?

Suppose the attackers could abstract the activity somehow? Suppose they could gain a collective awareness of the activity of the Com's logical routing circuits without actually influencing each part of it? After all, when he went into a mind, Asher was not conscious of each synapse and nerve bundle that was involved in the thoughts he was seeing.

But if they could do that, they could literally read the mind of the machine, route its thoughts, change its thought patterns, without the need of altering the impossibly complex circuitry itself.

Asher stood up. These must be the people who had attacked the Nin on the Bodyguard Planet. His mission as a Guild member was to confront them and find out why. And then find out, if he could, the details of the death of Ran Tarney.

And they had now shown him the danger that such minds could wreak, working together. The implications . . .

But now now, now they were locked in a concentrated manipulation of the Station's Com. Their minds were fully occupied, so he was free to employ Power with little fear that they would notice him.

Asher found the door. It was locked, but he reached easily with his mind to the molecular deadbolt and drained the power from it. The door swung open; light from a portable lantern flooded in. A startled guard leaped to her feet from a chair that faced the door.

Asher slammed her brain. It was not a killing blow. As the woman slumped past him to the floor, he picked the needler out of her hand, half drawn from its holster.

Asher picked up the lantern too. Darkness stretched away from him on either side. To the left, and above, was the sensation of the Network at work.

The time for concealment was over.

It was time to attack.

Chapter 17

A dozen men and women moved into the lobby of the hotel. They were dressed as typical tourists, which is to say in a wild confusion of styles and colors. They casually entered the lobby, movements at odds with darting eyes and nervous fingers, and paused.

It seemed business as usual at the front autodesk.

After a time, one of the newcomers—a man—reached the main grav shaft to the hotel rooms on Dade's outer skin. Then another man, and then a woman. No one impeded them. There were no discordant black vests among the mingling throngs of the wealthy.

The first man stepped into the shaft, the others pressing behind. From that moment they were a group, separate from the men and women already rising above them, and from those pressing toward the shaft behind.

Delicately grasping handholds, each took the abrupt change of gravity easily, and in short order a half dozen or so parallel risers were occupied by two rows of nervous intruders.

The first man, the leader, glanced downward. Below the receding lobby level, he could see no one else in the thickening blue haze rising or descending. He had been told that only maintenance and service personnel found any reason to venture below the lobby level into the fifteen food service and customer support floors. But some of the Downer attackers should be infiltrating from those same support floors right now. He frowned.

In the lobby, just as the last of the attackers disappeared

over the lip of the shaft, a suave young woman moved from an office behind the hotel check-in desk and intruded upon the next group of revellers about to enter.

"I must apologize to you," she said with an elegant gesture, "but there is a maintenance emergency further upabove." A translucent, grey plasteel door was already sliding into place over the shaft entrance. "This way, please," the woman said. "We have an auxiliary shaft across the lobby."

As she led them toward it, she glanced casually at the closed doorway behind her. The emotion that stirred behind her almond eyes never reached her face.

The first man was high above the lobby level now and had moved up a few handholds, while his companions remained in their two rows not far below. The lack of people below them was definitely abnormal. There should be hotel patrons, at least. Above, patrons were getting off at the cheaper floors, though most were hanging on, waiting for the bubble level.

He saw it then, high above but moving steadily closer. It was the most active entrance by far.

No one, however, was coming into the shaft for a downward journey.

He glanced downward. Any guests who had been on their way down had already disappeared. He was too high now to see the lobby opening. The down-travelling guests had, in fact, disembarked a floor below that, directed there by an attendant standing on the lip between the lobby and the grey steel door that covered it.

"We apologize for the inconvenience; the problem should be resolved shortly," the man had been saying. He had followed the last of them down and through the opening.

The Downermaster, deep in the center of the Station, listened to the whispered report of the lead man in the shaft.

"Zayr is zomezing happening," she hissed into her wrist. "No one below, no one coming down from above . . . zis is unnatural. Be very careful; ze lazt guezt dizappears above, ze next head you zee will be a Cleos man. Shoot zen, I tell you."

On the bubble level, a liveried man inside the corridor was shooing downward-heading guests to a smaller side shaft.

The last of the guests above stepped onto the bubble floor.

There was silence, emptiness, a sense of oppression . . .

Then a man's head poked out and peered downward. The Downer agents were only twenty feet away, and to their fevered eyes the man looked too competent by far. The leader already had his needler out; instinctively, he snapped a shot at the head above. Even in his worry, the leader was good. The shot tore the side of the watcher's head, and blood erupted into the low gravity of the shaft, drifting lazily outward with a few optical fibers.

Suddenly, the blood droplets became rain. The gravity in the shaft switched abruptly to one g Station normal.

Most of the Downers were taken by surprise. The weight their hands had supported with loose circlings of the riser handholds went in an instant from a single pound to a hundred or two. The leader heard screams; his own body slammed with stunning force against the side of the shaft. The risers ground to a stop, and the gun spun out of the leader's other hand as he clutched wildly at the wall.

His reflexes had been good enough—the first hand had a solid hold on the riser handhold, and the second now reached the same handhold. But he felt as if a mule had kicked him in the belly; he recognized acrophobic terror.

He looked downward and saw the bodies falling, arms flailing, screams dopplering downward, faces contorted, figures spinning upside down and over.

There was only one other who had kept her hold. She was about ten feet down, bringing one foot upward, already in a climb, needler still in one of her hands. The shock of relief was as enervating as the fear. *She was alive!* He could see the intensity on her face, red hair framing its whiteness as she climbed. She looked up, and her green eyes tried to reassure him, to reach into the maelstrom in him and comfort him.

A splash, darker red, hit her forehead, and almost simultaneously the leader felt warmth splat against the back of his own neck. He cringed, closing his eyes before he realized what it was.

The man above was still bleeding on them.

The Downermaster was screaming at the leader now, the sound radiating through the implants behind his ear. But the terror twisting his stomach was still there, unrelenting. He could not move to save his life. The woman climbing up from below was made of ice, he thought. No, not ice; there was nothing cold about her. Spring steel, he thought, spun in fire.

Opening his eyes, he saw that she had almost reached him, but that she was thrusting herself to full arm's length, hand with the needler jerking outward. In his terror, he thought wildly that she was going to shoot him. Then she did shoot, and coherent light twisted the air as she fired away from him, across the shaft.

Far below, the last scream ended suddenly. In his mind the leader thought he could hear the sickening crunch, and he felt vomit in his mouth, but he could see nothing except the blue haze, and the woman firing.

Firing at . . .

He twisted, and saw the enemy then, saw the black vests and the grim, mostly bearded faces. At least a half dozen, peering out from a wide opening directly across from the bubble door.

And then, all at once, he was in free fall. He looked, shocked, at the hands that had been grasping the handhold, but they weren't there. Both arms ended peculiarly just past the elbow.

He caught a last glimpse of the red-haired woman, and she seemed to be falling too, feet first, in a weird, controlled way. No! he thought.

There wasn't any pain.

The gravity switched in five other shafts that had direct or indirect access to the bubble level. The Downermaster heard the screams, abruptly cut off, and from the few words that reached her before cut-off, guessed what had happened.

She cursed softly, relentlessly, words pouring past her

in a cadence that shocked even Ponger the Great, who alone was attending her in her command center near the center of the Station.

"I've got to call ze ozers back," she said at last. "If zey knew zo exactly ze shaft plans, zen ze climbers won't have a chanze eizer . . ."

The climbers were the other wave of attackers, making their way upward through layer after layer of station corridor, scrambling up maintenance ladders and rampways, avoiding the shafts.

The Com began to say that there were gravity malfunctions in six shafts, and that tourists had apparently been hurt. The Com tried to call the Servicemaster and the Medico crews.

But the Network rerouted the messages. It studied and let some go through, but stopped those that might affect the Station newscasts, and reach the public. They also interdicted those to the tachyonic transmitters that fed the galactic databases.

At Central, an alien told another alien (not in so many words): "There is an interruption on Dade Station."

"Where and what is Dade Station?" the other alien inquired, pollinating.

The techie said that transmission interruption was highly abnormal. But his vibrating boss did not consider it so, even when the techie tried to describe the safeguards built into all the Coms.

"Let the humans handle it," the boss said at last, and turned to greater pleasure.

It seemed like a long way. Asher moved through darkness impenetrable, though occasionally he would see light leaking around an out-of-flush door or a badly welded wall plate. Once he heard revelry, and later an incoherent gargling and a heavy, irregular thumping. He fought down a mad impulse to peek into a crack in the wall.

He felt the Network wax and wane, and Asher was certain now that they were working on the Com itself. A flood of associations began to build in Asher's mind. He kept his attention away from them, but still they kept coming, and he kept wrenching himself to warrior awareness and wondering if the mental distractions would cause him to lose his edge at a critical, near future moment.

Normally, with his Skills, he could have attacked the October minds above him, slamming against them like a hammer on a melon. There would have been individual attempts at Shielding, of course, but he was trained beyond any Apprentice in some ways, and this was one.

But a Network, he was sensing, had a side effect. It was rather like the diamond-hard mental Shields that Spimmon and Nisha Scalli were somehow able to conjure up together. Whoever had perfected the Networking technique had built this into it as protection against interference. He had to get closer, to see their bodies, see their auras directly, to have any hope of breaking through.

But there was no point in needlessly alerting them, so he did not employ Skill much. Intent as the Network was upon intricate work, its members were, must be, as constantly aware as Asher of the ebb and flow of Power in their near vicinity. It was something that any October-trained man or woman had—a kind of background awareness that served to inform and to warn.

Asher did send tiny, darting shafts of awareness into the spaces beyond his pool of lantern light, probing into side rooms and into the tunnel ahead and behind for any hint of danger. Not far, just a few dozen feet each way; anything more intense would have involved too much Power.

Clang! A door opened a few feet in front of him, and Asher threw a hand out to call up the Green Flame. He was surprised. He had probed that room, and found nothing except some background mechanics . . .

A robot on wheels shot out of the room and spun toward Asher. Long ago, before he had failed the Test of the October One, he would have blasted the machine to spare parts in hysterical reaction, using the Flame and alerting every Adept within six cubic parsecs. Now, though, his mind was on top of emotion. He measured the size of the machine and the corridor walls in an instant and plastered himself against the right-hand wall as the unit thundered up and past without a mechanical glance.

Asher peeled himself off the wall; the machine droned into the distance behind him. He wondered what had triggered it, since the one thing that had struck him as abnormal in the extreme, besides the absence of light, was the lack of mechanical action in the corridors.

As he thought it, the charged relux panels in the ceiling flickered on, then died. Then the lights flickered again. Asher froze, probing with his mind.

Up ahead he thought he saw a short, wide, human figure at a point where the irregular corridor curved abruptly upward.

The lights went out again.

Asher moved forward cautiously. Something was wrong, for the mental aura of the human ahead of him was escaping his low-level probes.

More carefully, he honed in, and then he stopped, still thirty feet from the unknown figure. For now he knew why he could not make contact.

The man was dead.

There was a ghost. It was nothing coherent, nothing tangible, certainly nothing intelligible. But the man had died within the hour, and there still hung around him an unnameable something that Asher had seen several times before in his life. Tiny electrical charges still flickered in the man's brain, but most of the cells around them were dead, or dying.

Asher moved until his lantern caught the man's foot. He was reclining on his back at the place where the corridor shot upward, resting at a twenty-degree angle. Asher had seen him from a point of view that had made him seem foreshortened.

The man had been neatly skewered by a needler. Asher bent, looking for a pattern of holes on his chest. He found just one short line, right below his left pocket, upward at an angle toward his shoulder.

The man, he saw, was a Downer; the clothes had the off-style shabbiness of the people he had seen downbelow.

He became aware of more ghosts then, more tiny, dissipating sparks in the mental darkness, and he shot his lantern up and ahead.

They were sprawled on the long ramp that faced him, six of them, men and women. He saw needlers, some still in holsters, some in hands. But he could see no sign that they had been fired before death had claimed the hands that held them.

Asher drew a long, shuddering breath. This was too neatly done to be human work. Some kind of automatics had done this. Something had aimed so well and moved so fast that the Downers had had no time to react, to defend themselves.

One of the bodies had a peculiarity to it that made Asher peer more closely, though he did not move beyond the first sprawled body. It was about halfway up the ramp. It looked as if it were encased in some kind of purple-red coating, under the clothes.

A small, squirming aura came to him. He probed it, and recognized it.

A Ressie? Those aliens were popping up everywhere. But what was this one doing?

Perhaps, like a dog, it was snuggling up to the body, mourning its dead master. But Asher detected no emotion of any kind—no mourning and no anger. If anything, the Ressie was exuding . . . sleepiness?

He could not afford to study this further. He sent his mind ahead now, questing for the mechanical thing that had killed these Downer agents.

And it was easy to find. It was plastered against the wall like a limpet, just over the top edge of the ramp so it could see all the way down—a sensing body with a tiny mechanical mind and a timer that had been set by hand. It was about two feet in diameter, and would have been entirely unnoticeable to anyone walking these corridors in the light, much less in darkness.

Asher studied it, not moving. Whoever had set it had instructed it to turn itself on at a certain time, wait for movement at the top of the ramp, and then let loose on it and anyone else to its limit of vision.

Anyone. And now it was watching him, waiting for him to move.

Asher did not move. He resisted the impulse to spring backward. No doubt it was programmed to react to that by an instant stream of pinpoint needler fire.

He erased the machine's mind.

It wasn't hard, but it disturbed the Power, just a little. In the Network, Ceal Carnak stirred.

As he passed the body with the Ressie, Asher reached down and touched the ochre film over the body. It was, he saw, that of a woman, and the Ressie layer was quite warm, warmer than body heat. A subdued pulse moved under his hand from the Ressie, but the mental leftovers in the woman's brain were almost all gone.

The lights flickered again. Asher reached the top of the ramp, questing with his brain. If there were some kind of Downer infiltration of the upper levels going on, someone apparently knew all about it and had prepared well. Asher found two more limpets, spaced along the corridor walls as backups for the one he had blanked. He blanked these, too. He twisted the action in time-sense, so that it would be undetectable to the nearby sensitives, or at the least seem physically far away.

The stray thought, surprisingly, came from Larla.

Yes, the others responded. We felt it.

We must break Com contact and concentrate on it, Larla said. But she made no move to initiate such disruption herself; she was not the deciding authority here.

Yes, thought Sanda.

Yes, thought Score.

Yes, thought Dal Gaskin.

No, thought Ceal Carnak.

It was then that Dal attempted to assert command. He failed immediately, the four of them against him. In an immediate sulk, he tried to withdraw; they would not let him.

Concentration was not threatened, but the potential was there, from both Dal and the unknown below. Ceal let herself work on two levels—one engaged with the others on the Com, the other leaking the directives that led the other minds.

No, she thought. We are Network. We will follow the Cleos' instruction. We know that Skill is at work somewhere nearby, and we will move against it soon. Unless it gets close to us, we will continue our work.

Cleos, in his chambers, heard the withdrawal order of the Downermaster, the signal registering directly in his brain via an optical fiber. He would wait a dozen minutes, peering out of a thousand eyes, to be certain that the Downer attack was over.

Asher was thinking about the placement of the limpets as he moved cautiously down the corridor. The Network was close now, not more than fifty yards ahead and one level up. Whoever had set the killing machines could have done it in one of the long, straight stretches of corridor, and if there had been a hundred people in line, a hundred would have died. But the ramp placement meant something. Whoever had done it, had had mercy in his or her heart. The idea was probably that a few would die in the limpet's line of sight and the rest, having seen them fall, would flee. Maybe that's exactly what had happened, and Asher had entered the corridor after the flight. The only ones who fit the circumstances were Cleos and his agents. Perhaps there was some humanity left on Dade Station.

As he had done from time to time, Cleos now probed with his remote electrical feelers, testing all the defenses he had installed; that was the cause of the flickering corridor lights that Asher had seen. Cleos was a believer in isolating defensive machinery from central power supplies, so that an attacker could knock out no more than one machine at a time. But Cleos did monitor those defenses. The energy bursts he sent out touched and evaluated the machines and carried the responses back to him.

Something was worrying Cleos. In the last few minutes, three limpets had gone dead. That was highly suspicious.

He had concentrated his human forces on the shafts that riddled the Station; now he ordered the nearest squad into the corridor in question. It was alarmingly close to the Octobers. He turned on the corridor's lights.

Asher had thought he heard something behind him, and was turning when the lights went on. They dazzled him for a moment. When his vision cleared he saw nothing, from where he was to the downward edge of the ramp. Perhaps if he sent his mind that way . . .

A clang sounded ahead of him. He spun and threw himself into Shadow. Thirty yards away, a door had opened and black-vested figures were pouring through it.

Asher broke into a run. He would pass right through them, and they would never see . . .

One of them had a needler rifle with a dozen orifices—one that could spray like a hose. He lifted it as if to spray the corridor . . .

Asher struck. He had no choice. He delivered the mental hammer on all of them at once. Ten dropped, and through the door Asher could feel more of them falling. He rounded the doorway, his footsteps echoing behind him in eerie discord.

A ramp. Bodies sprawled along it, six or seven sleeping minds, distinctly alive. Among the needlers that had been in the Cleos agents' hands, he saw a few blasters. He picked one up.

The Network had felt the blow; he was certain of it. But even in his haste, he had continued twisting time-sense, and the blow had seemed, even to him as he delivered it, something far in the depths of Dade Station.

Cleos was on his feet in his chambers. The tall lieutenant was ranting into his wrist computer, shuddering as a flood of orders passed through him and around him. Cleos agents from all over the Upper rushed toward the bubble level, while the tourists gaped at them and murmured among themselves.

When Asher had struck, Cleos had felt as if a wall of darkness had descended onto a part of him. It was a small part—seventeen wired minds were no longer with him—but whatever had felled them was very close now to the October agents.

There! Asher pinpointed the undulating mentality behind a bulkhead door. He pointed the blaster at it and fired.

PLOOM! The door blew inward into molten fragments. Asher went through it and into the bubbled room. And there, in front of him, was the Network.

Chapter 18

As he burst into the room, Asher leaped to the side so that his body would not be framed by the doorway. He had a blaster in one hand, a needler in the other.

He was in a relux bubble, he saw at once. The entire room was one gigantic bubble, beginning about three feet up each wall and rising in a smooth dome. Outside, the magnificent panorama of intertwined transtubes shone like transparent plastic worms in metallic shades of green and blue and red. The heart-stopping green of the planet could be glimpsed here and there, while directly across from Asher there was a gap in the tubing through which he could see a few brightly tinted stars.

The five people were in the center of the room, sitting cross-legged in a huddle that would have been a circle if there had been more of them. The mental chaos pounded like surf, and all at once, his perspective shifting, Asher saw them with three eyes: the tiny group hovering a foot above the cushions below, around them a pulsing ruby haziness while static electricity seemed to flicker in their hair, twinkles on Sanda's bare scalp. And with his October-opened eye, Asher saw the aura of rubiness as a solid gemstone wall, the flickerings as the pinpoint sources of waves, rays of force pouring from each of them to a point in the air above, with a suppurating flow blasting from that central point into a near wall, below the bubble.

And in the flow, as it beat in discordant flares of basso mental sound, he could hear the dialog with the Com. It was like a torrent of monosyllables, a river of bytes that

pierced his brain and, for an instant, overwhelmed him
with detail and complexity and chaos; but then the instinctive, trained Skill took hold, and he sorted and compart-
mentalized and, eventually, understood . . .

They were partially disengaging from the Com. It had
not yet been fully controlled, but they had no choice but
to face the danger to themselves. The Downer attack at
least was over, but they could feel their own immediate
peril, far closer than they had expected. They were
wrenching free of the Com . . .

Asher attacked. He delivered the hammer blow, putting
all the force of his mind into it, knowing that with it he
could kill any ten thousand normal human beings all at
once, could batter through any single Apprentice Shield
like an axe through a soap bubble . . .

The ricochet was so painful that he cried aloud, even as
he tried it again, and reeled as it rang off their mental
shell like a mallet off a bell.

The scene was going negative. Asher had seen that
effect once before, and now it scared him, for that other
time it had been the side effect of an attack by the October
One herself, and before her power no one could stand.

This Network . . . it was far more coherent than he had
expected. Far more disciplined. Far more integrated.

Asher pointed the blaster and felt the five minds react
to it, ready themselves to resist it. But behind the five
was the bubble, and while the transparent relux might
absorb a needler beam, it would disintegrate under the
full force of a blaster, puffing them all into the awful
vacuum of empty space.

He brought up the needler, and again felt them react,
build a resistance. But suddenly, something reached out
and squeezed at the Shield he had long since raised, the
mental Shield that was supposed to protect his mind and
body from Skill manipulation . . .

"Asher Tye," Ceal Carnak said then, and her voice
sounded as if it was amplified in a cathedral of bells. It was
lower than a woman's voice, and it echoed in his head like
a steel wrecking ball, banging from side to side. "You are

Asher Tye," the voice hammered. "We enter you; we read you; we peel away your mind."

"No!" Asher screamed, and tried to strengthen the Shield. He dropped the blaster and called into himself, and the Green Flame would not come. He reached frantically for other Skills, but they were being squeezed, too. It was as if the Network was catching his fist just as he was about to punch, catching it before he could put any strength into it.

The Word . . . Asher reached for it deep inside himself, the hypnotic Word implanted in every Apprentice as a hedge against rebellion—the Word whose utterance would turn an October student into a frozen statue unable to move or speak . . .

He quailed. His mind! He was being buffeted back and forth. They had gleaned his name already, but he had never known any of them when he was in training on the October World. He called up the Word.

But he could not say it. And now he sensed . . . amusement?

"You are greater than any of us," the voice said. "But against us combined . . ."

He had not expected this! He had known that his own Skill was beyond that of any single Apprentice. But was it only fractionally so, born of his mental and physical discipline, with nothing added that made him really, truly unique?

He brought the point of a fiery mental sword, like a giant icepick, crashing onto the ruby barrier.

It slid off as if it had encountered a greased glass ball.

He put a physical Shield around their bodies, and squeezed. They felt it and reacted instantly, turning their purely mental Shield briefly into a physical one. Instantly he fired the needler, and simultaneously delivered the mental icepick again.

The needler beam disappeared into a nothingness; the icepick again bounced off. They seemed infinitely reactive when focused on him, secure in their Network, able to change from physical to mental Shield forms in an intuitive instant, as if they could read his plan of attack a moment before he executed any part of it.

Ceal's voice came in that eerie, monstrous hollowness: "We will now determine where you were trained, and who else may have been trained with you."

Asher couldn't believe it. In their gap-ridden Apprentice Skills they apparently lacked the collective ability to hold a duplex Shield—one that would protect against mental and physical attack all at once—but they did seem to be able to anticipate whatever he thought and react against it. He knew the source of their strength over him, and he feared it, for their combined Power enabled them to enter his mind like a flood of water that covered him and, as if he were a thousand feet down, force its way in through combined pressure, each leak a pencil stream of mental force boring in and around . . .

Asher shrieked and fell to his knees. They concentrated on him, moved in on him.

"Feeble Shields he has taught others," fat Larla observed. "They can be of no concern," Sanda said with disdain.

"Yet there is one named Clemmy . . ." Ceal began.

Asher screamed again, and beat his fists against his head, but consciousness would not fade, would not be shaken, would not go away . . .

"The Guild of Personal Protectors," Score's thought came. "He is, in fact, the only one with true Skill among them."

"Other than this Clemmy," Larla thought.

"Whose Skill is so weak that any of us could take her," said Sanda, again contemptuously. "Yet," Ceal Carnak thought, "we must kill her, too . . ."

Asher was bent over now, tears streaming down his cheeks.

"Do you sense the training?" Larla thought. "Do you see the Power in him? Might he not be one of us, if only we could bring him in?"

"Nay," Ceal thought sadly. "Look at the impossible ethics . . ."

"Let's kill him now," Score's thought came, hissing like a tidal wave.

Ceal's mental sigh came. "I suppose we must . . ."

The ruby wall suddenly brightened. The enlightened

eye of Asher's mind quailed before it, even as his physical eyes saw its intensity and knew what it meant. The feeling of drowning suddenly grew sharper, more urgent, more suffocating. He brought one hand to his throat, gagging even though there was plenty of air around him. And they kept pressing in, pressing, pressing. He felt them fingering around the autonomic portion of his brain, the part that controlled his heart and lungs, and he knew that he was moments from death.

Always he had expected that in this moment, this particular moment between life and death, he would be able to accept what was about to happen, to resign himself to the inevitable destiny of every living thing, and pass with cordial grace into whatever awaited him on the other side.

But no, not this time, at least. This time he was raging inside, calling upon all his training, both Skill and warrior, looking for a weapon, any weapon, conjuring up technique after technique, battering against destiny like a rooster in a cage . . .

"Keep hold of the Com thread," Ceal Carnak thought to the others. "Don't let it go even for an instant. Now, a little more focus, please. Exclude all else around you but the Com and this. Now, join with me on this . . ."

Here it comes, thought Asher, and still he fought. Above his head there raged a brilliant aura of mental fire . . .

FZZZHHTTT! Something burned the air to Asher's left. He hadn't expected to hear the killing blow.

And then, with incredulous, gasping relief, he felt the Network explode into chaos.

Ceal Carnak felt it go and couldn't grasp the reason, for the first, briefest moment. But suddenly she was feeling heat, and her eyes were seeing Larla's massive midsection dissolve into a red and black swirl, and then she felt the woman's life disappear like a balloon popping in the night. And she felt the Com thread disappear with a mental sound like breaking bones.

Each of them hit the cushions with a thump. The tight mental ring that they had ruled only moments ago was gone as if it had never been.

FZZZHHTTT! Another blast, then another. Asher felt

his ears pop suddenly and saw Score and Dal Gaskin lifted into the air as if by puppet strings in an entangled, sickening, bloody mass, hurled back against the far wall. Then there was a whistling sound, and Asher saw black marks on the relux glass. There screamed inside him an instinctive space-age reflex thought: what idiot was firing a blaster near the outer wall of a ship? If not for that, of course, he would now be dead. But the air of the room was whistling out through scatterholes in the bubble, and out in the corridor an alarm was sounding shrilly. The edges of the door Asher had blasted into atoms tried to shut, to throw a bulkhead between the compromised bubble and the outer corridor, and failed.

Asher shot his attention to the remaining Apprentices; he was barely in time. The hammer blow that Ceal Carnak delivered was vicious, and it might have killed him had he been unprepared. He saw it coming at the last possible instant and blocked it with a Shield, and felt himself catching only a part of it, because it was not . . .

Asher realized that the blow had not been directed at him at all, but at the unseen person in the doorway, the one who had fired the blaster three times, destroying the Network, killing three wizards, holing the bubble.

He turned and saw her then—a red-haired head, a pair of shoulders and two arms—as the woman, on hands and knees, tried to shake off the numbness that had hit her brain. Asher's block had partly protected her. Yet even now, with her hands on the floor, hit by something she could not have understood, she still had the will to keep hold of the blaster clutched in one hand.

Asher took a long step toward her. He was no longer worried about the October agents; there was no chance that the remaining two could Network effectively against him. But who was this woman? An agent of Cleos?

She sensed him coming. Asher had seen warriors with slower reflexes. She rolled onto her side, the blaster in her hand, and Asher had only the briefest moment to react.

The awful fire ripped into nothingness; somehow, as he had done in the skirmish with the Downermaster, Asher brought up a hole into which the blaster fire poured and

disappeared. It was a technique that he had not learned on
the October World, but must have picked up during that
long ago, hypnotic time when he and the October One's
Teacher had shared a starship.

Warrior trained . . . he reacted. But his hammer blow
was gentler than Ceal Carnak's, and not calculated to kill.
She of red hair fell in a loose sprawl, face down, on the
floor of the bubble.

He stood over the fallen woman and kicked the blaster
away. A Downer, by the look of her. And it made sudden
sense for someone who had spent a life in the bowels of
Dade Station to make unthinking use of a blaster here, on
the filmy edge of space. But what was a Downer doing
in the upabove? Hadn't the Network indicated that the
attack was over?

He remembered his dazzled eyes when the corridor
lights had gone on, and the Cleos attack that had followed.
Had it been she that he had dimly sensed behind him
when he had wanted to scan his backtrail?

He felt another hammer blow. It cascaded off Asher's
Shield like water off a duck. He turned and looked at
Sanda and Ceal Carnak.

Sanda had one fist to her mouth, and seemed to be
chewing. Ceal was on her feet.

"Careful, woman," Asher said, "that those holes don't
suck you out."

Ceal glanced at the blackened rings in the relux bubble,
through which air was still whistling.

"Yes," Asher said, knowing her thoughts. "It would take
more than air to blow that wall apart. Still . . ."

The alarm in the corridor was bothering him; he reached
out with his mind and disconnected it.

"Many people are coming," Asher said then, and sighed.
"I have had no peace on Dade Station. Now, I suppose, I
have to take you both in Shadow to some out-of-the-way
place where I can work out who you are and how many
more of you are out there."

"We will never tell!" Sanda shrilled.

"Shut up," Asher said wearily. He ran his mind over the
two women, and paused at Ceal Carnak's pocket. Some

kind of a grenade? No, more to it than that. He would disable it . . .

At his feet, the woman groaned. Asher glanced down.

Ceal Carnak knew that she was beaten, and that she had only one more weapon to bear. She also knew that Asher was aware of it and was about to reach into it. So she shot a hand into her tunic and switched on the Skill jammer . . .

Asher's hands leaped to his head, and Sanda screamed. To Asher, it was as if a trapdoor had been opened and all his Skill had fallen into it. His Shield went down. He reached for the Power to bring it up again, and failed. He could not reach it. It was there, but he could not reach it.

This was not some living use of Skill, he realized; this was something mechanical. He had thought it impossible, but someone had taken machine intelligence and scrambled it and amplified it . . .

Again his brain was in chaos; again he felt the bizarre, almost-forgotten sensation of being helpless, his most important weapons stripped away.

Who could have done it? Who could have built a machine like this? Only the October-trained, Asher knew. Only they would be able to tell if such a thing worked in the first place. Under the One, such a thing had never been considered, for it might have been used against the One herself. But under this cabal of Apprentices . . .

Asher reached down with his hand and picked the blaster from under the red-haired woman's hand.

"Stand back," he said, pointing it at Ceal and Sanda.

"Come now," Ceal Carnak said. She seemed composed again, in charge of the situation, despite the buffeting that was going on in her head. "We have been inside your mind."

Asher flushed. What they were saying was that they knew he could not shoot someone down in cold blood.

"All right," he shouted. "And I'm proud of it! But turn off that damned bomb in your pocket before it blows us all to Caldott."

Ceal Carnak tensed. "Bomb?" she said, her voice suddenly hoarse.

"Haven't you ever probed it?" Asher yelled at her. "I felt its insides." He bent and seized the red-haired woman's tunic collar. He began to pull her into the doorway.

"Probing machines is not among my Skills," Ceal said with a rasp. Sanda was staring at her, her whole body trembling. Ceal drew the mechanism out of her pocket.

She looked toward Asher. Her composure was gone and her mind was racing, and there was pain in her eyes. This wizard, this near-Adept—was he fooling her in some weird way? Was he simply trying a trick born of a quick mind and the knowledge that he couldn't defeat the machine?

But there was a logic in his words that was not his at all, but the Seventeen's—they who had sent the four of them on this errand, Ceal thought. Why would they send a bomb with us, too?

To kill us, she thought. Because we know too much, she thought. Because if we were forced to the point of turning this machine on, it would mean that we were close to the unknown Adept, in a situation our Network could not control. Killing the four of us was not the important thing; it was a side effect to killing the Adept.

And all we wanted were the Ressies, she thought. She glanced at Sanda.

Then she spun around and hurled the machine at the relux, at the black-edged holes through which air was still shrieking. And then she turned toward Asher and began to run, Sanda, whimpering, close behind.

The pint-sized juggling club hit one of the larger holes, and was sucked against it like a plug, the narrower end sticking out into space.

Ceal had known what she was doing. The impact against the glass could not set such a device off; only its timer could. But if it exploded in a place of suction, its force would be partially directed away from them; and if she could reach the corridor, there would be a chance.

There was no chance. The explosion was loud, but not as loud as it could have been, for its first effect was to blow away a quarter of the weakened and holed relux dome, and sound cannot travel in a vacuum.

Asher was blown by the first blast of the explosion into

the corridor, hand still clutching the woman's tunic and dragging her with him. Then, as if it were the same motion, he was hurtling backwards through the doorway in a howling current of air.

He saw Sanda's body erupting through the gaping bubble opening into space, and then Ceal Carnak's.

Air exploded through the doorway, a living current that hurled him and the woman backward and into the hole. Outside the stars awaited, and a vacuum that was almost perfect; and Asher and the red-haired woman, like leaves, were blown outside.

Chapter 19

I ought to be dead, thought Asher Tye. I ought to be a burst-open chunk of frozen meat headed away from Dade Station into another orbit around the planet.

What orbit would I have finally settled into? I cannot guess, but one thing I do know is that Dade Station's feeble gravity wouldn't have had anything to do with it, for I came out of that hole at escape velocity, at least.

I should be dead. But instead, I live, and I can't complain, though I'll be dead in a few minutes more if I can't reach and open an airlock in time.

Instinct. Asher knew that it had been instinct that had done it: trained instinct, fostered instinct, instinct honed by hours and days and months of practice. Action and reaction, attack and repulse, routine and surprise, until he had finally reached the point in his training toward which all warriors strive—the point at which mind dies and no-mind rules. No-mind, in which the body reacts alone, unfettered by the contradictory static of the neurotic, dualistic body/mind personality. The no-mind of aikido, karate, kendo, and dozens of lesser disciplines, in most of which there was not even a label for it. It was a state without a name, though every top athlete knew exactly what it was.

The Shield, Asher thought. In this case the response had been the raising of a Shield the instant the mind machine had exploded into fragments and broken mental contact. And the raising of the Shield had been of such unconscious immediacy that Asher knew that he had not "decided" to raise it, that his totality had instantly grasped the need and just as instantly met it, without the dubious assistance of his battered and shell-shocked mind.

And now . . .

Now he "flew" in a bubble of air, held in by the Shield his mind had raised while still within the Station's atmosphere. In one hand he still grasped the collar of the woman with the red hair, the woman who had saved his life, and then had tried to kill him.

It was a sensation of falling. First his dazed brain was telling him that he was inside a pea in a giant pea shooter. But then his sense of up and down failed, and he seemed for a moment to be shooting upward toward the tangle of transtubes, and for another moment to be falling like a stone toward them. The tubes shone like elongated soap bubbles before him, iridescent shades of purple and orange and green. And as he looked back at the Station, he saw white and dark faces, open-mouthed, staring and pointing at him from inside their bubble hotel rooms. The women's mouths all seemed to be wide open in gigantic, unheard screams, though now that he thought about it, the men's mouths were open, too.

Suddenly he and the woman were among the tubes. He could see empty guide rails inside them, and at one point the receding end of a transbus heading toward the Station. They passed one tube, two, and then he and the woman slammed against the side of a tube and ricocheted at an oblique angle as the tube's curvature directed them.

It was quite beautiful, Asher thought. The pimply face of Dade below (or above) him, the lucid green of the planet glimpsed from moment to moment through interstices of the tubes, the tubes themselves in their color and splendor. And, of course, the scintillating stars in their own peculiar hard, bright colors, hung against a background of the deepest black, a black that might be the annulment of substance itself.

Brightness, from the planet and from the hard edge of the bloated systemic sun, which was invisible somewhere behind a tangle of tubes. But its presence was all-pervading in the red edge of light it forced through the tangles, defining a blinding puckered line of demarcation on the Station itself. In the bright half, the bubbles seemed black as they polarized out the dangerous brightness and selected spectral lines of the light; and in the darker areas, which were somewhat lit by the sunlight's reflections off the sunlit side to the tubes and back again, the bubbles shone their own light, colors of all kinds, depending on what the occupants were doing in each particular room.

Alarms, Asher thought, must be clamoring all over Dade. Its surface is holed, its Com is compromised, its major sectors are at war with one another. He also knew that they would eventually come out after him and the woman, and that all they would expect to find would be bloated corpses, perhaps bouncing among the tubes like pinballs in a computer game.

Won't they be surprised, thought Asher. But of course, I can't wait for them.

He reached out with his mind. It was a question of one of the simplest of all Skills, a mere application of telekinetics—moving matter with the mind. Nothing to it. Gamblers do it all the time.

He reached out and pushed; their long bounce toward another tube slowed. He pushed here and pulled there, and then he cast his eyes and mind around for any hint of an airlock.

He had two people breathing air in a constricted shield perhaps twenty feet in diameter, and it would not take long for the air to become so foul from their own exhalations that Asher would lose consciousness, and the woman too if she had revived by then. And if Asher lost consciousness, then they would lose something else a moment later, together:

Their lives.

Or . . . he could always jettison the woman through the bubble. She would die, but he would have twice as much air then . . .

He pulled his hand, drew the woman up effortlessly in the near-null gravity until her face was a foot from his. Were this woman ugly, Asher thought resolutely (she was not; he noted the way her cheekbones highlighted the shape of her closed eyes); were she the deadliest enemy in the galaxy (maybe she was, for all he knew, but she couldn't hurt him now); were she one of the Networkers themselves (by comparison, they had been a scurvy-looking bunch, though Ceal Carnak's soul had had something . . .); were she all those things and more, he could not have pushed her into space any more than he could have pushed himself.

At least, he hoped so.

He found himself staring hungrily at the half-open lips, the sheer feminine shape of her . . . I must be losing consciousness already, he thought. Had he been away from Clemmy for so long? Romance among the stars, he thought. Except that the woman is unconscious and we are being watched by a busload of gesticulating tourists right over there, who seem amazed at the sight of two people maneuvering among the tubes without any sign of a space-suit, or even a mask.

Asher sighed, lowering the woman. There were, he noted, airlock strips all over the place. The tubes had been constructed in sections, and the builders had installed many protection rings throughout, for if a micrometeorite holed a tube, as one inevitably would several times a year, the rings would close suddenly and isolate the damaged section, preserving the air in the remainder of the tube. And there were maintenance airlock strips at every one of those rings.

The woman is passive enough, Asher thought. Were she fighting or excited she would be using air at a fearful rate, as would I; but we are both rather calm, for different reasons. Hers is obvious; mine, that the Network is gone, and I now know exactly what is bedevilling the Bodyguard Guild.

The transbus had ground to a stop to let the passengers enjoy the unusual sight. Asher looked at the woman and thought: is this what it means to be twenty-two? That every third thought is sex, and there's almost no rest from it? Is that what it means? No wonder the ancients had covered themselves like tents, and put their women's faces behind veils. All they had wanted had been a little peace of mind.

Shaking his head again, wearily, Asher moved them toward the nearest airlock strip. He would tuck himself and the woman inside that distendable plastic, run his fingers along the sealant edge, and then open the inside seal.

"Survival more important than sex, Asher Tye?" a thought came to him. He paused. Nothing further came.

"Ceal Carnak?" He said it aloud, but the thought went out, too.

"Not for long, I'm afraid," the thought came again. He noticed then the weakness in it.

"Hang on," Asher beamed. It was easy to work out the direction. He pushed on a couple of nearby tubes with his mind and he and the red-haired woman shot away from the airlock strip. Later he would wonder why he hadn't pushed the red-haired woman through the lockstrip into the air beyond. He had had hold of her for so long that it had never occurred to him. The watching people stared from their stalled bus as Asher and the woman receded purposefully into the labyrinth.

"Forget it, Asher Tye," came the thought. Asher was maneuvering them around one of the tubes nearest the Station. The tube snaked almost horizontally above the surface of Dade, headed toward the central reception area where most of the tubes ended like a gigantic, multi-stranded umbilical cord.

"Forget it," the weak thought came again. "Nothing you can do can put me together again; and, in any event, I cannot go back to Surcease now. The mission is a botch and my partners are dead."

Asher saw her then. She was on the next tube over, a gap of a thousand yards separating her from the two of them. She seemed spread-eagled against the tube, facing Dade like a fly on the ceiling.

"Just break away," Asher thought, for some reason trying to reassure her as he launched into the gap, the red-haired woman firmly in his grasp. "My Guild would be happy to have you. You led your three Apprentices very well."

"And Your Guild would like my mind," Ceal thought. "After all, there's only one of you among them. With me they'd have it twice as good."

Asher winced. That was a piece of intelligence that the Network had revealed, and would no doubt have been of great importance to whoever on Surcease had sent the Network after him.

"Is it the October One?" Asher thought. He was beginning to make out more details as he came closer to her. There was red among the clothes she wore, and one of her legs seemed oddly askew.

He sensed now that she, too, was in a Shield bubble; of course she must be, or she would be dead.

"Dead," her thought came, echoing his. "Dead like Larla and Score and Sanda. Did you know that I saw Sanda die, Asher Tye? She was never any good at Shields. If I could turn my head, I might see her off to the side, the far tube over there. I saw her hit, Asher Tye—saw her hit the tube—and by that time it was all over for her. Her body was an erupted bloody thing that hit the tube and stuck there like a swatted fly, and her congealing blood had enough stickiness to hold her there until it froze a moment later. There she is, stuck against a tube like me, with her ridiculous bald head shining in the starlight, and her eyes popping out, and all the bloody rest of it . . ."

Asher realized that Ceal was in shock, babbling like a waterfall. And she was weak, heaving for oxygen. She had been closer to the explosion, had entered vacuum sooner. There probably hadn't been enough time for her Shield to trap much air.

"I will be like Sanda in a moment," she went on. "I can feel my mind going, Asher Tye. I don't want you to see it; I don't want anyone to see it. If I had the strength, I'd throw myself into space, at that planet down there. Somehow it seems an attractive thing, to fall endlessly into greenness, around and around the planet in a spiral orbit, closer and closer, until after a thousand years the greenness reaches up and I burn as a falling star. And no one will see me—no one—and that's what I want . . ."

He was drawing near now, and he could see that her

neck too was at a peculiar cant to her body. The explosion had riddled her with chunks of relux, which had broken some of her bones and ruptured her inside. Her anorexic body looked as if it were made of pipe cleaners.

"But I want to hurt THEM, Asher Tye. Ask me anything. Ask me anything you need to know. They didn't need to blow us up. They could have done it some other way."

She was gasping, her thoughts coming in disjointed jerks. Her mind was slipping. Little puffs of air were escaping her Shield at each slippage, and the Shield was drawing inward, barely covering her body now.

Like a robin settling on a branch, Asher landed next to her and let his Shield cover and envelop hers. And then, with infinite tenderness, he reached into her mind and turned off her Shield.

She gave an explosive gasp, and drew a lungful of Asher's air into her. Increasingly foul, it still felt like a bucket of cold water to her, as if she had been thirsting for days.

Asher's eye was attracted by a tiny puff of something, far off against the skin of Dade. Air. An airlock had been opened on Dade proper. Someone on their way to pick up corpses?

Thoughtfully, he threw the three of them into Shadow.

He let his Shield lift Ceal Carnak off of the tube and, thrusting away, he brought the three of them out into the gap between the tubes and that faraway airlock.

"If I bring you into the tube, we'd have to wait; we can't risk being run over by a transbus." Asher heard his own voice; it was soothing, as if he were talking to a sick child. "But if I can get you to Dade proper myself, I'll have a medico unit around you in five minutes."

"Don't tell me there's hope, Asher Tye," her ironic thought came, remarkably clear. Nevertheless, he did feel a tiny surge of hope. Her injuries were profound, but they were hurtling across the space as fast as he could push, and it hadn't taken long to pass the other way when they had exploded outward. "Don't tell me there's hope," she repeated. "Because I am going to die this day. I can feel it. I know it. I want it."

"You don't want it!" Asher hissed. He was using part of his mind to probe her deeper wounds, closing off arteries and veins when he could, compressing the flesh to abate the internal bleeding. But he was not well trained in this sort of thing.

He looked at her face. She was looking straight at him, and in the thinness of her face, the pinching of the nose and directness of the gaze, he suddenly saw Clemmy, and he found himself choking. "Don't say that," he said. "Please don't say it; you are going to live." He said it savagely, as if his will could make it so.

Her lips twisted in a pained, mocking smile. "Nay, Asher Tye," she said hoarsely, and then abandoned her lips for her mind alone. "Nay," she thought. "I feel death's shadow on me, and I welcome it. You are trained for this, too. You too will feel your own death when it is close, and you will not want to escape it."

He shook his head, but she continued: "But now, Asher Tye, ask me. Ask me. I will tell you all I can."

Her thought had trailed off, and he had felt a wave of pain engulf her. He moved to isolate her brain from it with a few delicate probings, but the input came from almost everywhere in her body. Still, he did what he could.

She gasped, and this time there was a bubbling in the gasp. "Thank you, Asher Tye," she said. "I had been doing some of that, but I was slipping. Now, ask!" She thought it almost fiercely.

Asher kept trying to keep life in her body as his mind took hold of the train of thought she was forcing on him.

"Er . . ." he said. "How many Apprentices are there on Surcease?"

"Around three thousand," she thought instantly. "But most of them are at Com Central by now. All have different stages of training. Have not advanced since October save for Networking. Another few hundred scattered around the human part of the galaxy doing Surcesean work."

"What do they know about me and the Bodyguards?" Asher asked, distracted by the bleeding of her right kidney and what it was doing to nearby organs.

"They guess that the Bodyguards have one or several Adepts," Ceal thought. "They don't know that you're just an Apprentice like us." Absently, Asher flushed. "You could stand up to any one of them. You've had further training somewhere. But if they Network against you . . ."

She didn't have to elaborate. Asher popped in a key question, almost as an afterthought, his mind concentrating on tiny, probing fingers.

"How many at the Concourse jimmying the Encyclopedia?"

"Four shifts of five hundred twelve each," she said.

"What? Is that all?"

"Is that all to distort the information flow of the galaxy?" she mocked him. "You saw what five second-rate Apprentices could do with a Network. And all the four of us wanted . . . I thought Score was a snivelling baby, and Sanda too, and I thought if I never heard that screeching voice again, it would be too soon, but you know what, Asher Tye? I loved them. I really did. You can't Network with someone and not see into them and see what pushes them to be what they are. And I loved Larla too, the fat genius. She was the best of us, I think."

Babbling. Not enough oxygen was reaching her brain. Asher was trying to keep the blood from filling up her lungs, but there were so many alveoli involved, so many seepage points. He was sweating in clammy profusion now.

"Why? Was there so much profit in Candy?"

And she laughed. She laughed with her lips. Her diaphragm heaved, and half a dozen seepages in her chest became spurting rivers before Asher could again bring them under control.

"Candy?" her mind said. "Did you think all this time that it was Candy?" Her mental laugh was derisive, but it was also weak.

"What else then?" He was intent on the questions now, but still frantically working on her body with his mind. He saw, absently, that a vehicle had moved out of the onrushing airlock and was headed toward them, but on a course that would pass them by. They would reach the airlock long before the vehicle could stop, open up, take them in (and it didn't seem large enough, anyway), and return to the Station. Thank heaven that in Shadow, he didn't have to worry about them trying. Ceal was best left for the moment as little disturbed as possible.

She was babbling again. "All Sanda wanted was her Ressie," she said. "All I wanted was my Ressie, too. That's all we wanted. Was that too much? That's all any of us want. Everybody should have a Ressie. Then you wouldn't think it was so weird, Asher Tye." Asher started; had she sneaked around in his mind when he wasn't paying attention? Or was this just a remnant of what the Network had found in its relentless probe. "Don't blame your Clemmy, Asher Tye. She knows what she is doing."

"I can understand Skilled people trying to dominate a part of the human galaxy," Asher said, trying to draw her out further, "even by distorting the Encyclopedia. But you could have done it a lot better; that's what I don't understand."

"All we wanted were our Ressies," Ceal thought dreamily. Images came into her mind, and Asher realized that she was reliving a session with the aliens. Blast it, he thought. I've got to get her on track or . . .

A blood vessel occluded suddenly near her heart, and Ceal Carnak stiffened.

No. No! Asher thought, reaching it with his mind and trying to force it open. Blood moved sluggishly through then.

"We just wanted to be left alone," Ceal thought, her mind splintering into fragments. "And the only way we could do it was to make everyone see . . ."

No! No! No! Asher thought frantically, probing around for the immediate cause, trying to find the one thing out of the hundreds of damaged parts that would restart the flow again, prop up the cards that were already tumbling down.

In the end, he stood on the surface plates near the airlock, the unconscious red-haired woman still with him, the air around them foul, and pushed Ceal Carnak's body outward with his mind, through the interstices in the tubes, far, far out, with as much force as he could as he weak-

ened in the carbon dioxide-contaminated air. He thrust
her broken body, already freezing, against the orbit of
Dade.

Fall, Ceal Carnak, he thought. Fall into greenness, as
you wished, for a thousand years.

Then he took the red-haired woman and cycled up the
airlock.

Chapter 20

They entered in Shadow, but no one was watching the apparently self-cycling airlock from inside. Asher became conscious that they were in a private bay for someone's personal shuttle, a kind of short-range space car, doubtless the one that had passed them outside. There was no sign of the medico emergency units he had expected.

The hangar was richly appointed. Asher took a step into it, and nearly wrenched his arm off. He looked down, and saw that he still had hold of the red-haired woman's collar. But now they were in full gravity, and she was sagging like a sack of bowling balls, her face turning a mottled blue. As if he had touched a hot skillet, he released her collar and she collapsed onto the deck, and began to breathe again.

Alarms. He could hear them from somewhere behind the smaller safety lock that led into the Station itself, not too far from where he stood. Why they weren't sounding off in here, Asher did not know. He wondered now where that shuttle had been going. Not to pick them up, for sure. No, probably to get away from Dade Station for some reason.

He activated his wrist computer. Immediately a quiet voice spoke inside the receiver imbedded behind his ear.

"Please remain in the cabin in which you are now located," the voice said; it was the impersonal voice of Station Com. "Interference with normal Station operations has brought about the need for self-repair. Certain areas of the Station will be unsafe while self-correcting mechanisms operate. Please remain in your cabin until the problem is resolved."

"And how long might that be?" Asher demanded belligerently, as any guest would.

"Sir, the inconvenience will be short," the Com said. "Dade Station's tradition is one of service. Please make yourself comfortable. Automatic cuisine delivery is unaffected by the problem, and during the interim all services will be provided without charge."

Without charge? Asher thought incredulously. Wasn't that something of an overreaction to the holing of a single cabin?

"What is the nature of the problem?" Asher demanded. "Give me a holo image; I want to see what's going on." And, as an afterthought: "I want to be entertained."

All over the Station, guests would be engaged in similar dialogs with Com, Asher thought.

"Station security and channel overload do not permit the fulfillment of your request," the Com said. "Please remain in your cabin."

No doubt, Asher thought, the Com was continuously scanning for newly activated wrist computers and delivering the same message to owners as they climbed out of baths or awoke from foggy, drug-ridden sleep to the klaxon sounds from the corridors.

Asher picked the woman up more gently now, cradling her in his arms, and moved toward the inner doorway. The hangar smelled faintly of ozone and grease. The doorway sensed their coming, checked for hangar atmosphere, found it, and opened smoothly before them.

The room beyond had been a luxury apartment. Even through the debris, Asher could see the opulence—knotty pine panelling, a real nylon carpet, and small sculptures that living hands had wrought out of actual organic soap. But now objects were strewn in broken disarray—a couch overturned, a hypnotic holo image dancing unattended in the corner, a smoking pile of plastic circuitry huddled dysfunctionally in the center of the plush, grass-imitating carpet. The smell of smashed perfumed soap hung like sweet sewer gas in the air.

What in the world had gone on here? Asher thought.

Yet even in the mess, there was a certain harmony, and Asher then realized that it was in the colors themselves, the shades of pigment and shadow with which everything had been put together. Nothing clashed; everything blended subtly and relaxedly, and the torn-apart room exuded an aura of satiated peace.

He turned the couch upright, and stretched the woman out on it. Once again he admired the turn of her cheek, but only briefly. He looked into her sleeping mind, again only briefly, and saw that she was nearing wakefulness. The colors distracted him, and he had seen something in the farther corner of the room that interested him more than the woman at that moment, if such can be believed.

"A private tachyonic holo booth," Asher muttered. "Who-ever lived here liked first class."

Asher moved over to it, then paused. "Com," he said out loud, "are tachmitters operational?"

"Yes, indeed," the Com said, as if relieved to be able to bring good news. "Full and free traffic with the galaxy has been restored."

Full and free, Asher thought. Odd that it would stress that.

Far away, the Concourse techie said: "Dade is online again, sir."

"Good, good," the depollinated alien said woozily. "I told you the humans could handle it."

"Not exactly, sir," the techie said uncomfortably.

"Why not?" his boss said languidly.

"Sir, Dade reports October manipulation of its Com," the techie said.

"What!" The satiated lassitude was suddenly gone.

"And the Encyclopedia is disagreeing."

It was coming apart. Cleos could sense it, feel it, as the Com moved to realign the power structure of Dade Station, back to the ways the Seventy had dictated so long ago.

The Servicemaster had been the first to break allegiance. Then the Foodmaster, then the Drugmaster, then a dozen others. The Colormaster had taken off in a private shuttle with a hundred million credits encoded somehow. Eight others had disappeared too, probably to convenient ships in nearby space, placed there thoughtfully for just this sort of emergency. For Com had given them all the ultimate threat: they would be cut off from their Station tasks if they persisted in alliance with Cleos. The rats among them were jumping ship; the mice were capitulating.

The Station Police had begun to move for the first time since Cleos had forced it into subservience.

The Downermaster was gloating openly. Her domain was the least affected by the change, for she had been holding her area against Cleos ever since he had begun using the Surceasean agents against the Com. She would gain no power from the realignment, but was having the great satisfaction of saying "I told you so" to everyone she could reach by shouted voice over every circuit she could find.

To Cleos himself, the agony was that the Com was taking over his fiber optic network of personnel. The great electromagnetic mind was stirring throughout the very molecules of the Station, retaking control of the vast, intertwining molecular memory of the Station, retaking control of everything electromagnetic.

"The medico units will remove the optical threads from each Cleos agent," the Com informed Cleos. "You too will be deactivated. You will return to your former position of Greetermaster to incoming guests."

Cleos, attended in his cabin only by the tall, austere lieutenant, groaned, weaving from side to side. A sudden transmission broke in:

"Cleos, baby!" the rasped voice shrieked, like an iron bar across a chainsaw. "You're through! I won, you many off-color remarks. I won I won I won!"

It was beyond tolerance. Greetermaster! And now the likes of the Downermaster taunting in his ear.

"Shut up!" he screamed at her image, holoed in the air

before him like a short, grey-haired buxom demon. Behind her he saw the image of Ponger the Great, tending to her.

"Remember," Cleos screamed at the Downermaster's gloating face. "All my agents are wired; all wired are my agents!"

She turned a puzzled face toward Ponger, her blasted eyes bright.

"What does he mean by that?" she demanded.

"Beats me," he said.

Above: it was all lost, Cleos thought. He would hesitate no more. Revenge on the Downermaster would be sweet if he could see it, but he would not. Let it all end. Now.

He thought a certain thought, doubled it, redoubled it. A suggestion that a Surceasean had planted in his brain at his own request focused the neural energy of his mind on a certain bit pattern, and transmitted it simultaneously through the great fiber optic network of his collapsing universe even as, at the same moment, it triggered his own destruction.

The message reached only a third of his dwindling forces, blocked from further reach by the Com. In the other two-thirds, the tiny bits of superplastique at the end of certain of the brain-imbedded optical fibers were eventually taken out unnoticed with the fibers themselves by the medico units as, in succeeding weeks, the Com erased all traces of the Cleos empire. But now, in the one-third Cleos still controlled . . .

Cleos died fractionally first, his head erupting like an overripe melon. He fell, darkened fibers flying in red and grey confusion in all directions, splattering the walls, his body hitting the floor at the same moment as that of his gaunt-faced lieutenant.

The Downermaster was still looking at Ponger when the brown man blew up, too. She kept looking, staring, not understanding at first what had happened, not believing what she had seen. His head bulged suddenly, a crack splitting redly along one side of his forehead, blood spurting from the nose, and body falling like a sack of wet cement in a sodden thump on the Downermaster's floor.

She kept looking. Ponger . . . a spy? Ponger, whom she had loved after her fashion, who had been so useful to her in so many tactical and physical ways, who had served her long and well . . . Ponger the Great, one of Cleos' eyes? Cleos had had her all along, then?

She kept looking. In succeeding days, weeks, months, her mind played it over and over, an unreal image of vivid death, the suddenly distorted face of her lover, the suddenly ruined face of her universe and the place she had thought she had belonged.

She kept looking, long after her eyes had left Ponger's body and turned inward upon the image that floated there like the flickering, repetitious reality of a broken holo, showing the same scene over and over.

Eventually, it drove her insane. Cleos had his revenge. But it didn't do him, or anybody else, any good.

The *Bonnie's Best*, Asher found out, was in interspace somewhere between Dade and Surcease, if such spatial relativity as "between" could have any logic before the illogic of interspace. Asher was tired beyond exhaustion, but he wanted before anything else to pass on the knowledge he had gained, so that whatever might happen, the Bodyguards would at least know what they were facing in the Surceasean Sector.

Clemmy first, Asher decided. There was a real-space stop on the interspatial road to Surcease, and she would pick up the message there. If only he could see her, talk with her, see her standing before him in the vivid, intangible reality of two-way holo transmission. But a ship in interspace was cut off as completely as if it had entered another universe, which in fact it had.

He entered the necessary codes, specifying image storage at *Bonnie Best*'s next stopover, and began.

"Clemmy . . ." He faced the imager, and thoughts fled from him. There was vast emotion in him, and its unaccustomed power interfered with the gathering of his thoughts. All the dying had shaken him. He felt as if he were with Clemmy already, and yet felt the aching loneliness of a man without a home.

"Clemmy," he said again. He tried to put a brave face on it, tried out a smile or two, then settled on one that he hoped was confident, loving, reassuring. "Clemmy, I've had some trouble here . . ." He paused. "Trouble" seemed feeble, but he didn't want to scare her by saying that he had been near death at least four times in twenty-four hours.

He dredged up the smile and said: "Clemmy, darling, lover, mine . . ." Again he paused. Endearments did not come easily for him, and they sounded hollow. "Clem, Clem . . ." No, that didn't sound right either. "It's like I'm being watched by a billion people," he muttered, and then started and looked at the imager. He laughed, and it began naturally, but he cut it off. "I'm stage-struck, I guess," he said, and felt a sudden fierce anger at his own inadequacy.

He tried again. "Listen, Clemmy, please. Don't go on to Surcease; you cannot win there." It was coming more fluidly now, thank heaven. "The planet is overrun by October Apprentices." Maybe "overrun" was an exaggeration when referring to three thousand out of five billion people, and most of them off-planet, but he wanted her to see the seriousness of it. "I've trained you in some Skill, and you could fight most of those Apprentices one-on-one and win each time, but Clemmy, they have a Skill that I never knew about, something they figured out after the October One was taken away. What I'm about to describe to you is called a 'Network' . . ."

Behind him, the red-haired woman stirred on the couch. As he launched into detail on the power of a Network and how five second-rate Apprentices had almost taken him, the woman stretched unconsciously, languidly, the movement of her hard body stirring the last traces of sleep away.

Consciousness. She opened her eyes, making no sudden move, body immobile at the apex of the stretch. She turned green eyes toward Asher Tye.

"Clemmy, they will eat you alive," Asher was saying earnestly. "You cannot depend on Nisha and Spimmon's

Shield; I just don't know what a Network of seventeen, or a hundred, could do to it. I can't break through, and it becomes a question of raw force."

The woman moved in a single fluid motion, carefully controlled to bring her body upright with the absolute minimum stirring of couch fabric or air. Asher kept talking as she reached her feet, and when she saw that he was not reacting, she smiled ferociously and reached into her bodice for one of the fingerneedlers hidden there.

"I'm not telling you, Clemmy, I'm ordering you," Asher was saying. "As Squad Leader, I'm ordering all of you . . . oh!"

For his constant background hypermind scan had perceived the newly awakened mental energy nearby. He half-turned: "You're awake," he said, looking at her.

"Yess," she said, voice throaty from disuse. Asher saw her smiling face, and thought: Clemmy is watching this. "And I want you," the woman said. And as fast as thought itself, she drew the needler out and fired.

Perhaps if she hadn't been mentally hammered and then dragged by the neck inside and outside of Dade, her first shot would have holed Asher's body. But her aim was a hair out of true, just enough to miss him by the slightest hissing margin, and even as her hand moved to slice the beam across Asher's body, to cut him in half like an orange, he shot out his mind and seized the weapon and crunched it into slag.

She looked in amazement at the thing in her hand that had twisted itself into wreakage, and then back at Asher. "No," he said. She had moved as if to spring at him, her green eyes pools of verdant fire, but he reached in and paralyzed her.

"Stand there," he said. "I'll be right with you."

He turned to wrap up his transmission to Clemmy, and stopped short.

The activator light that usually shone red beneath the imager during a transmission was gone. In its place was a four-inch smoking line.

"End of transmission," Asher muttered, feeling a trace

of irritation. He turned back to the woman. He could feel her straining inside, and could feel an icy certainty that she would someway, somehow, see this October Adept dead.

"October Adept?" Asher inquired mildly, stepping toward her. "No, I am sorry to say that I am no Adept, and not sorry that I am not October either."

Then he heard her voice again. Perhaps the constant assaults of danger during the past few days had desensitized his reactions, for he found himself neither angry with this woman for wanting to kill him, nor frightened that somehow, in her determination, she had nearly succeeded, weakened as he was by the spacewalk in the putrefying bubble of air.

"You *be* Adept," she said. "You *be* October; you *be* Cleos. Cleos has killed my Glaxzy, and *you* have killed my Glaxzy, and you I will kill now, later, zoon."

He saw it, then. The scene leaped out of her head, an image of startling clarity, and for a moment he was with her, high in a grav shaft in which full planetary gravity had just been switched on. He felt her straining, felt her strength, as she hung on while others fell, as she hung on and felt a surge of sheer joy as she saw her Glaxzy hanging on too, dangling above her. And now one of her needlers was out and she was climbing. And then there was a horrible moment as she shot at Cleos thugs across the shaft, seeing one of them holed, then seeing a needler beam slice across the forearms of Glaxzy and feeling his body fall past her, without even a glimpse of his face for the last time. And then . . .

Asher gasped. "You fell in full gravity, and controlled it solely by grabbing at handholds on the way down?" He saw it in her mind as it left the scene, for the part important to her had been replayed already, and he said: "Why, that's incredible; most Bodyguards would have lost it and fallen. What kind of training did you have, woman?" But now he could see flickering images of her and the man named Glaxzy as her mind flicked past tender times, loving times, times in which her love for the dashing Downer lieutenant had been so great that she had wanted to laugh and cry, scream and weep, all at the same time.

He just stood there and looked at her. In a day of emotional chaos, he was now shaken again. The force of her love shook him, and so did the force of her grief. And so did the force of her hate. For she and Glaxzy and the others had been sent against wizards, and they had died, and now she was facing a wizard.

"I . . ." he said then, "I'm sorry . . ." Her blazing eyes seemed to erupt, and the raw hatred that poured from her sent him back a step.

"Zorry!" she spat. "I killed zree of you, and if it was a zouzand of you it would not make up what you did to me." Asher opened his mouth to say that he had done nothing to her, and then closed it. The waves of hatred were still coming, and he felt sick and hopeless in their surflike pounding.

"Actually, you killed all five of them," he said, and immediately regretted it. For there was a surge of feral joy, with the hatred piercing through like a spear of blinding light.

"Did I?" she hissed.

"But I was not one of them," Asher said desperately. He was fascinated by her eyes; he had never seen anything so intensely green. For a moment, he could not place the association that they stirred in him, and then he had it. They reminded him in their blazing clarity of the green, green planet below them, the planet into which Ceal Carnak would fall someday a millennium from now. "In fact," Asher said, "by killing them you saved my life. And then I saved yours."

She was still straining against her mental bonds, and Asher feared that she might hate so much that she would center, and then she might be able to break his hold on her, and he would have to employ some other Skill that might hurt her. He found, to his amazement, that he felt guilt toward this woman, and that his guilt was mixed up with desire, of all things.

She was a thoroughly handsome woman, and she hated him and would kill him at the first opportunity.

I could, he thought, overcome her and treat her any way I wish. And the thought itself soils me.

"You zaved my life," she mocked. "Pray tell how. Amuze me wiss your lies, zen give me five zeconds free from your wizard's grazp."

He thought of telling her about the explosion, the space-walk, Ceal Carnak's death, the Com revolution going on all over the Station, but he sensed it wouldn't do any good. Only time could do what his self-justifying explanations would never be able to. There are few things more frustrating than being unable to show someone the truth, and Asher felt the futility of it, and the pain.

So, finally: "Woman, what is your name?" Asher said.

The name leaped into her mind. She would not give him satisfaction of any kind, even an answer, but he read it easily despite her searing decision that he not.

"Lillian," he said. Her eyes blazed brighter with even greater hate. "Lillian, if you ever want to get off Dade, dial up the code I'm planting in your mind."

The blaze flared suddenly as she felt the mental touch.

"It will give you enough money to reach the Bodyguard Planet. With a little more training, you could be as good as the Nin herself."

She had never heard of the Nin, and the last thing she wanted was the dirty touch of his thoughts in her mind.

"Get out!" she screamed. "I will kill you! I . . ."

"As you wish," he said, as tired as he had ever been. He withdrew from her mind and passed into Shadow.

She felt the release and shot her hand into her bodice again, looking wildly around. The corridor door opened. She pointed her second spare fingerneedler and blasted at the opening; and like the touch of a kitten, she felt her hand pushed gently aside.

Good-bye, she thought, and then realized that it had not been her own thought, but had come into her head from outside.

"You head-freaked baztard!" she screamed.

Asher sought out another holo booth and tried to reach the Nin.

"We are sorry," the Com told him, and Asher wondered who "we" was. "There is unprecedented disruption of tachyonic transmissions in certain galactic regions. No one has been able to reach the Bodyguard System in over forty standard hours."

They're meddling with Concourse, Asher thought.

"The only thing I can guess," Asher said aloud, "is that something is interfering with the galactic Com." Then he realized that he was entering into deliberate dialogue with the Station Com.

It waited a long moment before replying. "That is an explanation," it said at last. "There have been certain irregularities in the Encyclopedia . . . Wait. Wait. Something is coming from the Concourse . . ."

Asher waited, and the answer came in only a moment.

"Dade is being interdicted," the Com said emotionlessly. "Our transmissions are being eliminated from priority scan."

"What!" Asher exclaimed. "That means that from this moment no one will find out about the Apprentice attack on Dade Station Com, on *you*."

"A Galactic Police squadron is being separated from the Bodyguard Planet and ordered to secure Dade," the Com said.

" 'Separated from the Bodyguard Planet?' " Asher quoted, horrified. "How many other squadrons are at that planet?"

"Classified," the Com said.

"What!" Asher said again. "There's no such thing as 'classified' when it comes to tach."

And then, in sudden inspiration, he asked for any stored messages and saw the appalling transmission from the Nin.

He knew what was happening between the Police and Dade. It was a replay on a galactic scale of what had happened on Dade Station, what had been thought by 400,000 races to be impossible: interference with a Com. Only now, the goal seemed to be to extinguish the knowledge that such a thing could, in fact, happen. And at the same time, the Bodyguard Guild was being set up for destruction.

"I want to buy a ship with full robotic repair facilities," Asher said. He gave the account number and slapped down his palm. "Provision it for a run to the Concourse; route me to it as quick as you can."

And it was done; the Station Com saw no reason not to. After all, his name was Warren, and he was a paying customer.

Part III:

RECKONING

Chapter 21

What happened next made first-priority galactic news in tach transmissions and stayed there for weeks, a greater shock after the big shock of the probable genocide of twenty-five races. Most of the 430,000 Concourse races took notice, studied the event, worked out the implications, murmured at a danger that they had not known to exist, and murmured too at its apparent elimination. Many analyzed the machine involved and built one for themselves. Insurance, they proclaimed. They, at least, would be safe from wizardry. That's why most planetary systems today are routinely equipped with mind-numbing satellites. Nothing like October can ever threaten the galaxy again.

The run from Dade to Central had been a straight one, with no intermediate spatial exits. With apparent shipboard time of eighteen days, Asher had had plenty of time to retrieve from latent memory the glimpse of the Skill jammer as he had perceived it lying in Ceal Carnak's pocket. He had analyzed it, described its apparent workings to the engineering robots on his newly acquired ship, and supervised the duplication of a vastly larger version—without the explosive add-on that had blown through the bubble wall of Dade Station. To make certain the machine worked he used a test subject: himself. With his Power-aware mind, he would know whether the thing worked or not.

But it did. With the blankness of interspace all around his ship, Asher had dampened output and turned on the machine—and it had nearly destroyed him. He had in-

structed a two-minute test, and the timed cut-off had
saved his life. He woke up thirteen hours later with the
sense of recovering from a ten-day drinking jag, head
pounding like an ocean ship in a hurricane.

Grimly he had contemplated what it would do to him
when he entered Concourse Central space and brought it
to full power. And so he prepared . . .

The five hundred twelve Surceaseans, alerted as they
had been by the events on Dade, nevertheless had had no
real warning. All they knew was that the Dade Network
had failed. Who or what had caused the failure had not
been learned. The Surceaseans stationed at the Galactic
Concourse pursued their tasks of rearranging information
flow, reprioritizing news channels, redefining certain areas
of the Encyclopedia.

And then an incoming ship broke interspace, and their
minds erupted into mental cacophony. The Network collapsed. Central, freed at last, reacted with the blinding
speed of machine thought. The source of the Com disruption was located and identified. Galactic Police poured out
of their barracks and converged upon the human-inhabited
islet.

The Surceaseans had time to arm themselves, and they
fought viciously, but the ship, with its din of mental noise,
kept coming closer, closer, and every instinctive reach for
the Skill was met with mind-numbing confusion, a confusion that carried over into the physical actions the Surceaseans were trying to perform.

Central Com was quite logical, as were all computers
everywhere, no matter what race had constructed the
particular unit. It did not yet know exactly why its bond-
age to the Surceaseans had been broken, and it could not
chance a recurrence.

The protective dome over the human enclave was shattered. Atmosphere laced with hydrogen cyanide rushed
into the breach, and aliens stormed in to mop up any
survivors. All humans were suspect, hence all were killed.
Several hundred innocent humans died along with the
Surceaseans, along with a score of Trarrian ventropods and

a few other aliens. An interspecies diplomatic crisis began that took years to resolve.

It took a little less than four hours to erase everything the Surceaseans had created. The logical patterns of Central realigned themselves. Distorted facts in the Encyclopedia were repaired, filled in, rebuilt. News priorities became objective again.

The interdiction of Dade Station was lifted.

The interdiction of the Bodyguard Planet was erased.

A collective shudder passed through 430,000 races as illogical gaps in the Encyclopedia disappeared and facts emerged to astound and frighten the previously complacent and secure.

For despite their minimalist care, the Surceasean interference in Com Central had had effects far beyond the particular facts that had been suppressed or changed for the convenience of Surcease. One of the sharpest jolts to collective awareness had been the exoneration of the Bodyguard Guild from the crime of planetary destruction, and the identification of the race which had in fact brought about the genocide of five other races and the first dip ever known in the Galactic Index. The Index now rose by one. The race in question:

Ekans.

Asher lay in the Death Trance for a dozen hours. He had timed his revival nearly to the minute that the mind machine turned itself off, his ship in near orbit around Central. In his cabin, Asher's body began a series of autonomic twitchings that would bring his mind back from the Trance. For the first time in twelve hours, heartbeat resumed, blood flowed, breathing came online.

He came awake tensed, half expecting an attack from Surceasean agents if, by some chance, his machine had failed. But as he scanned the Power background of Central space, he felt only the aftertastes of the Surceaseans, nothing more. They were no longer there, but the taste of their dying was, to leave bitter gall in Asher's mind.

His ship was one of thousands that had broken out of interspace about the time that the Network had failed.

Central had had no way of knowing what had brought about that failure. It had not, until now, even suspected the presence of Skill. It knew that it had been released, and now it was vastly busy in reestablishing its integrity and trying to come to grips with the interference that had distorted the information background of the galaxy.

Because the Death Trance involved the shutting down of Asher's body, he had believed that the mind machine, whatever its proximity, could not reach him. He had been wrong. Had he been awake, he knew, his hypermind would have been shattered by the force of the mental jamming the large machine had produced, but even in the Trance he had felt it, and he remembered it as a series of violent nightmares that haunted him for years afterwards. Now, however, the machine was off, and he was the only October-trained mind in Central space.

There were perhaps nine hundred thousand ships in the Central solar system, from half as many races, and they were in chaos. All felt the effects of Central's realignment to greater or lesser extent. Some were rushing to reach their home worlds; others were pushing in to occupy nearer orbits, and still others were emerging from interspace at every moment to confront the confusing scene. Asher ordered his robo-servants to eject the mind machine into space and to turn their attention to a second one which, half-built, awaited their impeccable attention. The solar cells would reactivate the original machine once Asher was safely out of Central space, a precaution against the arrival of any incoming Surceasean Apprentices on a routine shift-change perhaps, or a Surceasean task force on its way in reaction to the events on Dade. And the machine would also alert Central as to its presence, its function, and the need for it to be physically protected.

As Asher sent his ship outbound he called up Surcease in the Encyclopedia, and Candy. Clemmy . . .

The Surcesean Com, and that of most of its Sector's planets, was either compromised or off line. Central Com detected illogic now where it was occurring, and the Surceasean stars were riddled with it. Coherent information from that particular human Sector was fragmented and suspect; it would take days to put the pieces together, and a tool of which Central was not yet aware, but soon would be.

Candy was still listed as a minor problem whose flow had long since been effectively restricted.

Asher should have looked up "Ressies," but he did not. Instead he spent futile time scanning for a message from Clemmy, but there was none. She must have received his own transmission from Dade space by now. Why, then, had she not replied?

Dov, he thought. Jealousy twisted him, and he scanned for a message from any of the other squad members.

There was one. From Dov.

His face, insolent, appeared in holo image before Asher; just the face, disembodied.

"Clemmy didn't tell me to pass this on, old boy," Dov said; he appeared pale, but intensely satisfied. "But I'm going to anyway: Have fun with your red-haired harlot. Know what I mean?"

The message ended. Asher sat back, stunned.

In the meantime, the Encyclopedia collated long-suppressed information on the Ressies. Asher should have called it up, but didn't. Clemmy . . .

The galaxy is not a simple, self-contained spiral of stars. There are remnants above and below it, like cobwebs hanging over the curdled milk of the central disk. Old and tired stars lie in a shroud above and below the plane of the Milky Way like puffs of still sparks around an ancient fire. Were the shroud stars as dense as the spiral arms, the galaxy would look like a football, an SO-class oblong of gleaming brightness among many others in the galactic landscape.

But the shroud was neither dense nor bright. Whiteness attracted the eye here and there, for the dimness was punctuated by globular clusters, each a million or more equally ancient stars in a crowded sphere. But these were mere aggregate sparks in the shroud itself, scattered sterile starfields lacking the nebular gases which were still forming new stars in the main galaxy. The stars of the shroud had sucked in the surrounding gases long ago. Now they were dying, with only an occasional nova to vary the long, slow dissipation into darkness.

Perhaps the civilizations that had risen in the early days of the shroud were now among those teeming quadrillions of the Galactic Concourse, having long abandoned their iced-over ancestral worlds for the vigor of the main galaxy. No matter. Here and there in the shroud were living worlds still, worlds that had been moved by mighty technologies from their original orbits into closer proximity to the dimming suns. And in other places, where novae had flared, ruined worlds had been left behind, and many others consumed in the exploding starry violence.

As, with a slowness measured in millions of years, the shroud stars faded into redness and toward the black, some close-in hell planets cooled. Some of them then spawned life, for whenever the environment permitted life sprang up, a fundamental rule of the natural universe. On one such world the Ressies had come to be, and evolved rapidly as their planet spun around a star that was gasping out its last.

The planet cooled and the rains came, rains that lasted thousands of years. The chemical soup stirred, and things moved and grew. The first Ressie was a parasite on the back of a small sea creature, both leech and host boasting the intelligence of an earthly slug. But the primordial Ressie had, even then, exhibited its species' fatal flaw, for it had consumed and eaten and moved on, until there were no longer enough of its special host to sustain the Ressie numbers. So with desperation prodding it toward thought, the Ressie moved on to another species, and another, and another.

When the first amphibian crawled out of the drying muck during one of the sun's cyclical flare-ups, a Ressie rode with it.

Once man had colonized all available stars in its sector of the outer spiral, there were only two directions to go. With the teeming hordes of the Concourse all around it, mankind had headed outward. Above and below the disk of the galaxy the restless ventured, finding slim pickings in the worlds of the shroud, but once in a while finding a planet worth having.

Far "above" the Castor/Pollux Sector, the Ressie world was encountered. Its star was so weak that the chance of a livable world had been rated low, and hundreds of stars around it had been checked and some colonized before the Ressie world was visited.

By that time the Ressies had stirred toward primitive intelligence, pushed by recurrent disasters of their own making. By now each full-grown Ressie was as large as a softball, and for life each needed a large animal. Unfortunately, there was only one on its own planet that was large enough—a ruminant descended from cow-like sea creatures that no longer roamed the cooling oceans of the Ressie world, for they had been wiped out by the ravenous early Ressies. The seven-legged ruminants had evolved into an amazing fecundity, luckily for them, for it was the only way to stay ahead of the Ressies. As long as there were more ruminants than Ressies, both species could survive and prosper.

But such growth could not continue forever. The environment of a planet is finite, and eventually the ruminant population came to occupy every field and valley and eat up every green thing within reach of its prehensile seventh limb. Then the Ressie population began to catch up.

The Ressies ate; they couldn't help it. No Ressie could avoid eating for something so abstract as the long-term benefit of the race; the thought did not occur. When every ruminant had a Ressie, sometimes more than one, the ruminant population plunged, and the Ressies turned on each other in ruthless cannibalism. Finally, after crashing to near extinction, the remnants of the two species began the cycle again, populations growing as the planet recovered its vegetative health, waiting for the next gorging and the next collapse.

Dozens of such cycles were what finally awakened the strange, gap-ridden intelligence of the Ressies. They began to communicate with one another through feeler-touch; they began to analyze the problem and look for solutions. But ages-bred inclinations flared up again and again, and for all the pleasure the Ressies gave their hosts, eventually the Ressies would gorge themselves, and no host could withstand the feeding frenzy of a Ressie. And then each individual Ressie would split into fragments by mitosis, and each new little Ressie would roll the planet, searching for a host.

The first starship shuttle to visit the Ressie world brought a dozen Ressies to the main ship. It took only a few Ressie sessions to convince the humans aboard that they had encountered something of great economic potential. For what the Ressies gave, humans would be willing to pay.

And the Ressies . . . star travel had never before occurred to them. They had no technology, and had never even thought of it. The idea that there were other worlds in the cosmos was a revelation, if such a term can be used for such a self-centered, dim, and alien race. Now, for the first time, the Ressies saw a way out of their trap. In a galaxy crawling with life, it would be a long, long time before the limits of the new environment were reached . . .

Chapter 22

"Now remember," Clemmy said to her four partners. "The hardest thing will be to avoid raising Shields. Asher said that that's the one thing that would give us away to sensitives on Surcease, to raise Shields and cause a rippling in the Power."

"Or to do anything else, Skill-wise," Dov put in. Clemmy glared at him.

"Yes," she said, "or do anything else, if you know how to do anything else."

No one said anything. Nisha Scalli was, as usual, exuding contempt for everything around him. But this time there was a sort of sweaty exhaustion to it as he swished his tail from side to side and fidgeted uncontrollably. His Ressie, Clemmy noted, seemed larger than hers or Dov's. Did that mean that he was using it more often—feeding it more frequently, as it were?

Spimmon was sitting on the table like a little stick man. Adio-Gabutti was just planted there on the floor, as immobile as a granite boulder. Clemmy sighed. If only she could read their faces, though only Nisha and Dov had any. Or if she could read their minds—but that would stir up the Power. She wondered what it was like to feel a stirring of the Power. It would have to be in volcanic eruption before she'd feel it, she thought.

"Don't worry," Clemmy said. "I won't use the Green Flame on you, Dov, unless I have to."

Dov didn't say anything. He seemed rather drawn, eighteen days into their journey from Dade to Surcease. They

231

had been in interspace for a straight dozen days now, the last layover having been at a planet which most spacers called "The Planet of the Gnats" after an indigenous, very common native species. None of them had felt like shuttling down. In orbit there, Clemmy had finally received Asher's transmission from Dade Station.

The bar around them was in its usual uproar, but everyone was keeping a wide berth from their table in deference to Nisha Scalli.

"We'll be in contact by wrist computer if any of us finds anything," Clemmy said. They had decided early on to separate by ability, with Dov and Clemmy acting as rich and dissolute sightseers. They would be able to penetrate human places where the aliens might not be welcome. Nisha and Spimmon would mask themselves as a trade delegation, an arrangement of convenience to keep their joint Shield-raising abilities together. And the Therd would simply hole up in the spaceport hotel, keeping his knack for mental invisibility in reserve.

"If I understand correctly, Squad Leader Ms. Clemmy," Spimmon piped, "Nisha Scalli and I will refuse to talk with anyone except the top leadership of Surcease."

"Absolutely," said Clemmy. "That will guarantee that you'll talk to almost no one for a long time. The lower echelons will want to know why, and what you're selling, and you won't tell them. They'll badger you if they can, and cut you off otherwise. No bureaucrat likes to hear that you want to see his boss."

"But what are we selling?" Spimmon said plaintively.

"Shields," Nisha hissed.

"None of that!" Clemmy said sharply. Nisha didn't even glance at her; his eyes seemed to be following an invisible fly around the room. "Use your Shield only if you must," Clemmy said authoritatively. "It will protect you against anything they can throw at you, Asher says. But then you have only about twenty-four hours to reach interspace, before you get so tired that they'll break through. So don't even play with it, unless you have to. Keep your minds on the mission, all of you: who killed Randolph Tarney? And why?"

Dov seemed feverish. "Man," he said, "from what it sounds like, we're jumping into a nest of October wizards. This is one time I'd sure like to have Asher and his hypermind around."

"Indeed," Clemmy said tonelessly.

"You all stay close enough to cover us with that Shield of yours," Dov said to Nisha and Spimmon.

"We will be in contact via wrist computer," Spimmon intoned. "We are able to Shield you from several thousand meters away, as well as ourselves."

"Look, let's hope we don't need it," Clemmy said. "Now, I want to see each of you in my cabin, one at a time, in the time we have left before planetfall . . ."

There was a jolt through the ship, and they all felt as if they had been turned inside out and then put right again.

"There," Clemmy said. "We're out of interspace. I think I'll see Adio-Gabutti first . . ."

In her cabin, waiting for the Therd, Clemmy gripped her courage and called up the ship's Com. Her Ressie sat contentedly on her left calf, and for a moment she was tempted to give herself over to it, as she guessed both Dov and Nisha Scalli were doing with theirs at that very moment in their separate cabins. No, it would interfere with her planning, with her efforts to get her first command in readiness for the task ahead. Still, she almost didn't care.

She ran a hand through her black hair and wondered if she looked as ragged as Dov. She hoped not. He had stopped bothering her, and she was content with that. But she worried about him, too. She had to; he was under her command.

"Messages for me?" she said shortly to the Com. Now that they had left interspace, the local planetary Com might be holding something for them.

There was an unusual pause. "None detected," the ship's Com said in its professional voice.

"None *detected*?" Clemmy said impatiently. "Why don't you say 'no' straight out?"

"There is disruption in the Com traffic flow of a sort

that is unfamiliar to me," said the Com after a moment.
"The flow is at odds with Com Central in some way. It is
most difficult to sort through the confusion."

Whew, Clemmy thought. If a machine with a giga-
terabyte memory can't sort through whatever it is, then it
must be a mess indeed.

"Well, keep watch," she said grumpily. "I am expecting
something."

And it had better not be like the last one, she thought
bitterly. She had been tempted, oh so tempted, to call
Dov to her bed because of that last transmission of Asher's.
She felt her belly tighten at the memory of it, the shame
of it, and at the fact that she had, in her ignorance,
allowed Dov to watch it with her, thinking that maybe
Asher had some tactical advice to add to what he had told
them as they had departed Dade.

She remembered it as if she had played it twenty times
a day since the Planet of the Gnats. In a way, she had, in
that playback device that was her memory. There Asher
stood, in some kind of a luxury suite on Dade, stammering
nervously about trouble, but looking just fine, thank you.
"Clemmy, darling, lover, mine," he had said. And then
the feeble joke about being watched by a billion people.
Because she was focusing on the scene behind Asher, the
scene that the holo unit was picking up. There had evidently been a wild time in that apartment, and there, on a
couch along the far wall, was a woman lying as sleek and
languid as a kitten.

"A sex kitten," Clemmy had hissed in a sudden rage.
Dov had turned his green eyes on her, and for once he
had wisely held his tongue.

She had almost ignored Asher's exposition on the Network thing, her mind and gaze fixed upon the unknown
woman. Perhaps it was her own guilt, she thought, for
having toyed, even momentarily, with the idea of taking
Dov. Or maybe it was a deeper guilt over what the Ressie
was doing with her nightly. Whatever. The ferocity of her
jealousy came from somewhere, and every time she tried
to examine it, it overwhelmed her with feral, raw emotion.
"It's an animal, dammit," she whispered fiercely to her-

self, and then blanched. "No," she whispered, even more fiercely, "it's more like a blanket—an electric blanket. Oh, I don't know!"

Then the woman had moved, had stretched, and had risen to her feet, every motion marked by a fluid grace. Clemmy could see that she was wonderfully formed, beautifully proportioned, and her own skinniness seemed shabby to her then. The woman was smiling, stepping toward Asher.

The transmission had not shown the needler; Asher's body had blocked a view of it.

Asher had turned with the inane observation: "You're awake." And the siren had said: "Yess. And I want you." And then the transmission had gone blank.

I just bet it did, Clemmy thought. I would have turned it off myself if I had been in Asher's shoes. Dade Station!

Even now, when she had lived with it for a dozen days, she was still raging inside, she realized, as if she were just seeing it for the first time. The Ressie beckoned to her; she almost took it up on the offer.

Most of all, she thought in sudden despair, I am so tired.

The door buzzed then, and she led Adio-Gabutti in.

"Sit down . . . er . . ." she began automatically. She had to get control. If the Therd actually put his weight on any of the furniture in the room, the piece would splinter into fragments as if made of dry spaghetti.

The session was unproductive. The Therd seemed quite content about everything, with no worries about the upcoming probe into Surcease. "I have lived a fruitful life," the alien said solemnly, "and I would like to live it longer. But if I can do some good for the citizens of the galaxy, my end would be a worthy trade."

And he lives his entire life on such bromides! I'm not so phlegmatic, Clemmy thought as she sent the Therd away. I used to admire thinking like that; now I'm not sure of anything.

Nisha Scalli was next. Clemmy felt as if she had let an acrobatic monkey into her cabin. He didn't bounce off the walls exactly, but he was so hyperkinetic that she ordered him to sit on one of the open-backed chairs, and repeated the order until he finally acceded to it. This behavior in an Ekans signaled exhaustion rather than invigoration, she guessed.

"Is the Ressie doing that to you?" Clemmy inquired curiously. The Ekans half rose, and for a moment, Clemmy braced herself to ward off a physical attack.

"You speak of things private to me," the alien hissed.

"It's my business too if it jeopardizes the mission," Clemmy rasped.

"That it will not do. My mission is clear to me," he said enigmatically. She probed him further, but he was not willing to discuss tactics other than to repeat her instructions back to her verbatim. Finally, she had to let him go.

Moments later, Spimmon was in her cabin. He said: "Yes, I do worry about my partner Nisha Scalli, Squad Leader Ms. Clemmy."

"In what way?" she asked him, trying to look professional and competent, and suspecting that the pose was entirely wasted on the Ghiuliduc.

"He does not talk about the mission," Spimmon said. "Instead he talks only about returning to his home world, and taking me there with him."

"Taking you with him?" Clemmy repeated.

"Taking me with him," Spimmon fluted. "That is the strange thing; it be all he talks about, taking me with him. He tries to persuade me in a hundred ways. It does no good for me to say that I be indentured to the Guild for fifteen more years, and then must return to Ghiuliduc to take my place in the pantheon."

"The pantheon," Clemmy muttered. She had no idea what that was. She had been lax; she would have to look up Ghiuliduc's social patterns in the Encyclopedia.

"He wants me to summon other Ghiuliducs, too," Spimmon said. "It be to teach the impenetrable Shield, he says. He believes it to be a very valuable thing for his people."

"What—is he afraid that the Surceasean October wizards are going to attack the Ekans planet?" Clemmy asked. "But there are three alien Sectors in between!"

"No, Lady. I think that he feared Asher Tye in the

beginning, only Asher Tye. Now . . . Lady," Spimmon said, picking his words carefully if she were understanding his mood correctly. "He be, if you forgive a comment about a fellow trainee, of a paranoid race. That be why he is so aggressive; his people must be that way, too."

"Not necessarily," Clemmy said.

"I think so," Spimmon said. "But now, I do not believe that he fears Asher Tye anymore, because he believes that he and I can Shield against him. Other things occupy him now, and the most important one is his Ressie. Beings of violence are often sensuous, and I think that he highly values his Ressie. If Surcease is the place to get Ressies for his people, then he will have to find a way to protect his people from the Skill abilities of the Surceaseans, even as they open trade for Ressies. I think he sees each Ekans trader accompanied by a Ghiuliduc, with constant Shielding whenever a Surcease be near."

"Do you want a Ressie, too?" Clemmy inquired curiously.

"Alas," Spimmon said, spreading apart two of his various limbs, a human gesture he had picked up somewhere. "I am afraid that a Ressie would absorb me in one session, and that would be the end of me."

"You're probably right," Clemmy murmured. But her thoughts were whirling in a dozen different directions. She found the analysis of the Ekans mildly interesting, but not a threat to the mission insofar as she could see.

"Well," she said, "all this bears thinking about. Thank you, Spimmon." And she ushered the Ghiuliduc out.

It bears thinking about, she thought. She pressed the heels of her hands against her temples. What a mess! All she wanted to think about was Asher Tye, her husband, her lover, and how he had betrayed her, and was probably betraying her even now. And he had ordered her to abort the mission. Hah!

No, no, no, she thought. This is wrong; I should not feel this way. I haven't even asked him about that woman. What if there is some explanation? But I saw it with my own eyes!

Is this what being married is all about? Clemmy pounded

her fists against the wall. Or is it just me, paranoid as hell, afraid I'll botch the mission, strung out by the Ressie . . .

The door buzzed and Dov strode in.

"What do you want?" Clemmy shouted at him. He stopped abruptly.

"It's my turn," he said. His voice was as meek as a child's with one hand in the cookie jar.

Hysterical images flashed into Clemmy's mind.

"Your *turn*? You . . . you . . ." She swung a warrior-trained palm at his face. He took a warrior-trained step back and let it fan the empty air.

"My turn," he repeated helplessly. "First Adio-Gabutti, then Nisha, then Spimmon, and now me."

Clemmy paused, her hand poised for the backhand.

"Your turn," she repeated. She let the hand fall. "Your turn. Of course. Sorry." Then she yelled at him. "Now go away!"

Baffled, he scurried out of the door, which opened smoothly before him and closed smoothly behind him.

Clemmy fought back tears, and a wild impulse to call up the Ressie. They were nearing planetfall.

Chapter 23

Surcease had no moon, not even a space station worthy of the name. The dingy stations that it did provide had all the elan of inner-city bus terminals. Luxury vessels like *Bonnie's Best* preferred direct shuttling to the surface.

This annoyed Nisha Scalli a great deal, but the others accepted the situation and soon found themselves spiralling down to the planet on which Randolph Tarney had died. It seemed to Clemmy, as she gazed out of the shuttle window at the clouds and colors of the planet, that she had set out years before, for so much had happened on the way. But they had left the Bodyguard Planet hardly more than a month ago.

They had no way of knowing the chaos going on below. On-planet, the Surceaseans were trying valiantly to keep up appearances, while at the same time cope with the twin disasters on Dade and Central. Com Central was broadcasting to the galaxy that wizards from Surcease had been controlling the galactic Com, and it, now freed, was advising planetary authorities how to build large-scale versions of the Skill jammer the Surceaseans themselves had invented.

The end of wizardry in the galaxy could be clearly foreseen, for it would only be a matter of time before the Galactic Police brought to bear one of the jammers against Surcease herself. That would be the end of the predominance of the wizards. It would be only a matter of time before every canny planet had a machine of its own, with the Police moving portables among the lazier or stupider which didn't. There soon would not be a place in the galaxy in which a wizard could maintain Skill control.

Oddly enough, most of the 158 remaining Surceasean wizards (excluding the Seventeen), failed October Apprentices that they were, were not unduly exercised at the prospect of losing the effective use of Skill. They hadn't been among those sent to Central because their use of Skill was primitive in the best of circumstances—there were solid reasons for why most of them had failed the Tests—and Skill was more a nuisance than a blessing. Perhaps alone on a populated planet, each could have used Skill to reach real power, but in the company of three thousand failed students, few of them had felt unique or invaluable. And then the Ressies had brought them solace and commerce. They were no longer interested in power. They went about their tasks by rote, doing routine jobs they had done many times before. One group of them still rotated into a desultory Network for contolling the Surceasean planetary Com. Others watched the spaceport, kept the traders in line, and controlled the actions of various politicians. Those off-planet were resigning themselves to the coming of the jammer to their areas of space. They sought solace in their Ressies.

The Council of Seventeen, the Network of the most powerful and capable of the failed Octobers, was still a formidable instrument of control on Surcease—or would be until the Police brought in a machine. Fat and naked, the Seventeen sat in their circle and considered, their Ressie band humming around their ankles.

"We have to face it," Ash Medai said, sweating uncontrollably in the sweltering atmosphere of the inner room. "If we stay on Surcease, we will be absorbed. We will not have a Network, nor will we be able to employ Skill for anything. Ordinary humans will compete with us for control."

"Yea," the young fat man across the table on his left wheezed. "But if we leave, what about the one hundred fifty-eight?"

"We can't take them with us," the big man said, gravel in his voice. "It's all over for them. Our only hope, the only hope of saving our own hides and retaining Skill, is to subserve once again."

" 'Subserve?' " quoted one of the women, whose hair looked as if it had been groomed with a rake dipped in axle grease.

"Yes," said Ash Medai. "Have you been following the Com data scan? There is a rumor afloat in the galaxy, and I fervently hope that it is true. The rumor is that the tachyonic interruption from the Sculptor is a sign of the October One's return."

The room fell dead silent. Conflicting thoughts flowed. Whatever came now, October One or Police, their independence was at an end. But with the October One, there was still a chance for power.

"Subserve," repeated the man. "We have no choice, unless it be to wander off into space looking for some planet no one has discovered yet, and I don't have to tell you that there aren't many of them left in the main galaxy. A blind search of the shroud . . . No, if we are to function in this galaxy, in this galactic civilization, we have to defeat those infernal machines that we, to our eternal sorrow, designed to protect ourselves from each other. We haven't the Skill, haven't access to sufficient Power, even Networked, to beat the machines—unless the rumor is true and the source of all our Skill has come again. You all know that She had access to Power beyond our wildest imaginings. If somehow the Teacher has freed her, or she has broken away and come back, we can be the nucleus of her renewed power in the human end of the galaxy, at least. We can be her new Adepts. And She can deal with the machines."

"The October World?" another woman inquired.

"Yes," the big man said. "We will lose our autonomy, but our Skill will grow. She will teach us, and October will be great again."

"But the one hundred fifty-eight!" the fat man moaned.

"They are Ressie bound, of no use to us—not even the local Com controllers." The big man put all the contempt of the congenitally strong over everyone else into his voice. "They let the Ressies feed on them like cattle

grazing on mud. They hardly eat or drink. They are no
different from the rest of the population of this insipid
world, which has let the Ressie become like whisky to the
alcoholic—something thought about every minute, experi-
enced every chance. Only we Seventeen among the entire
three thousand have control of our Ressies. Look at us!"

The sixteen others regarded each member of the circle
with a combination of disgust and awe. "Look at us," the
big man said. "The Ressies don't use us; we use them. We
don't grow thin; we grow fat, giving them more surface on
which to graze, and more skin for us to feel within. We
control them and heighten them. They are ours; we are
not theirs."

He stopped. They all had known it for a long time, but
they now could look at their own superiority and be pleased
with it.

"We must leave forthwith," the big man said. "To the
October World . . ."

Disaster struck Clemmy's party almost at once.

Dov and Clemmy had disappeared in an aircar, headed
for town. They had hired a space car, too, as any rich kids
would, in order (Dov told the autoagent) to explore the
system's spectacular asteroid ring a few A.U.'s out; the car
was waiting for them just outside one of the embarkation
terminals. It had been Spimmon's and Nisha Scalli's intention to follow them in another rented car. As for Adio-
Gabutti, the Therd had wandered off just after landing.
He had had the appearance of a being with all the time in
the world.

"Wait," Nisha said. Spimmon, riding on his shoulder,
asked: "Why?"

"This is why," Nisha said, and struck Spimmon a sharp,
sudden blow with his tail. He had finally figured out which
way the Ghiuliduc's vision was pointed at any given time,
and he struck from the blind side. Spimmon was hurled off
Nisha into a broken heap on the floor.

They were in the nearly empty spaceport concourse,
and no one had been looking toward them. Nisha gathered
up Spimmon and raced for the nearest autoteller.

"I need passage for the Linder Sector immediately," he hissed rapidly. "And my friend has been hurt; I need an emergency medbed right now."

The automatic teller summoned the medbed while it almost simultaneously issued tickets.

As the medico wheeled up, Nisha sprang over and opened its lid. He thrust Spimmon inside.

But the spaceport was still being watched. One of the watcher rotations was still on duty—four Apprentices of varying Skill.

One of the watchers was now wondering why these two aliens had stepped off one shuttle only to ticket themselves onto another, outbound. He keyed the spaceport Com and it identified the two as a "trade delegation." The watcher frowned.

Nisha was wheeling the medbed into the long embarkation corridor. He was in an agony of guilt, but overriding it was exultation. His mission had succeeded beyond his wildest expectations. He now had in his hands the means by which Ekans could Shield themselves from both the single Bodyguard and the Surceasean wizards—he had no knowledge, of course, of the Skill jammer. He had probed the Bodyguards and they had not suspected him. He had studied their training and knew that any Ekans would normally defeat any Bodyguard. And, of course, he now had a Ressie, and knew that he could parlay that into a multi-million-credit operation, serving his fellow Ekans.

"I am sorry, little friend," he hissed at the med unit as he pushed it forward. And he really was sorry. He had respected Spimmon, and the bond of their shared Shield-making had grown on him. He would have taken this step long since, with or without the Ghiuliduc. But at Dade, Asher had been close to him during the critical time after he had bought his Ressie and emerged from its first embrace, until the *Best* had peeled out of its position near Dade. At the Planet of the Gnats he had fully intended to jump ship, only to find that the single route to his Sector went through Surcease anyway. And then the *Best* had failed to stop at one of the shabby orbiting stations, and he had had no choice, and had to shuttle down. Now . . .

The medbed was telling him that Spimmon had been critically injured; it would freeze him cryogenically pending treatment by a unit that specialized in Ghiuliducs. That was exactly what Nisha had hoped it would do— freeze the little stick man. He was relieved, he realized with surprise, that the Ghiuliduc was not dead.

The watcher reached out with his mind and entered that of Nisha Scalli. What type of trade caused the behavior that he had just witnessed? He had not seen the blow to Spimmon, but no trader he had ever seen turned outbound the moment of planetfall.

Nisha felt the mental touch and, with the instinctive no-mind of the warrior, threw up his Shield. It was exactly the wrong thing to do, and Nisha knew it instantly. Without Spimmon the Shield was faint, wobbly, weak. And he had given himself away.

A Shield? the watcher thought. And what I saw in that mind before it closed was no trader, but a Bodyguard . . .

WAUMMMM! Nisha felt it like a concrete sack hitting him from fifty stories up. WAUMMMM! He fell to his knees on the moving walkway, hissing, tail whipping, trying to bring the Shield back up again. WAUMMMM! WAUMMMM!

At the far end of the walkway, another watcher was waiting. He gathered up the fallen Ekans and carried him through a hidden door into the sunlight. There were no life signs. The watcher's attack had been swift and merciless, and Nisha's brain was as dead as the plasteel walls of the spaceport terminal. The watcher had squeezed the life out of the Ekans like a fist squeezing a grape.

The second watcher unceremoniously hoisted Nisha's body into the open mouth of a trash disintegrator, its safety grating removed. With Ran, the Surceasean wizards had learned not to ship bodies back to their home planets.

The disintegrator whirred, and of Nisha Scalli there was finally nothing left but atomized dust.

The second watcher went back inside to fetch the medbed unit in which the second alien was encased. There was no question of the alien's mind, but it could be assumed that it was another Bodyguard. That body, too, would go into the trash.

But the medbed was gone. The watcher gaped, and ran back and forth. There was no trace of the use of Power, no evidence of another nearby mind. But the medbed was gone!

Adio-Gabutti was already gone in the private space car, having slipped by the watcher as the latter reentered the building. It was handy, the Therd reflected, to have a mind so invisible, even if he had to move his heavy body as if it were made of feathers. He looked into the transparent bubble that covered the medbed unit, clutched to his own lumpy body, and felt, in his alien way, sorrow.

Chapter 24

Dov and Clemmy wandered through the streets of the capital city of Surcease, feeling as though they were alone on a deserted planet.

There were people around. They heard them moving behind crumbling apartment walls, inside shabby houses, and here and there, they encountered one or two of them. They had never seen anything like what they were seeing now.

The people, all of them, were as gaunt as concentration camp inmates, and every single one had a Ressie attached to his or her leg.

Children? They were around, looking wild and unattended, but they didn't have Ressies. A gang of them followed the two Bodyguards for a while, hurling clods of refuse and screaming at them. There seemed to be no children at all less than four years old. "When the Ressies came," Clemmy muttered.

Still they felt alone, different from these people. "Why?" Clemmy asked. "We're just like them; we have Ressies, too."

"No, we're better by far," Dov insisted. "They're weaklings; we are trained not to be."

They still could not make sense of the planetary Com as it carried on its futile war of information with Central. It didn't matter.

"It should have been obvious from Dade," Clemmy said hoarsely. "There is no Candy problem and never was. It's just that the symptoms are much the same: no motivation, no ambition, no desire other than to huddle every available moment with a Ressie and forget the world."

She shuddered. Dov looked at her out of haunted eyes. "And I suppose you are ready to tear off your own Ressie?"

"No, no," she said, echoing his assurance of a moment ago. "These people are the walking dead; they have no strength inside. We are Bodyguards. If anyone can control their Ressies, we can." But it sounded fatuous to her even as she said it.

Dov said nothing. His cheeks were hollowing; his mind was avoiding logic.

"Ran died because he saw through the Candy thing," she said, "and the Surceaseans wanted nothing to interfere with their efforts to spread Ressies around the human galaxy. Or maybe it was simply that Ran found out that there were October leftovers here, and they did not care to have that known."

Dov grunted. They were deep in the lower levels now, the setting sun casting weird shadows from the cavernous streets all around them. Nets of skylip roadways snaked far above them like spider webs made of tinsel.

The city smelled. Here on the lowest level, puddles of rancid water and machine oil huddled each other off, while detritus of every description stirred and swirled in the stale air. In the residential sections, rodents screamed at them from piles of refuse that had apparently been simply tossed down from above.

Once they came upon a skeleton lying pressed against the base of a building. "I wonder where its Ressie went," Clemmy said. She looked around, and shuddered again. This was the type of area that in most cities would be full of muggers and derelicts. But there was nothing human to fear here; the humans were all holed up inside the buildings, cuddling with Ressies.

"Let's get out of here," Clemmy said. She tried her wrist computer again, but there was no response from the other three. "I hope that Nisha and Spimmon are nearby somewhere; I have a bad feeling."

A rising walkway, still functional—they had seen many others motionless—carried them upward at a long slant.

"It's so sad," Clemmy said. "The children running wild,

the parents so bound up in their Ressie pleasure that they don't care."

"It's been the way of history," Dov said then, "Ressies or not."

She glanced at him, surprised that he had offered any comment at all. But his gaze was inward, and it wasn't liking what it saw.

"We should kill our Ressies," Dov whispered. She didn't think she had heard him right. "But I . . . I . . ."

Every night, she thought. Every night for eighteen days, the Ressie had carried her to heights of sensation she had never dreamed of, never imagined: taste, color, odor, sound, touch, everything. Each night had been better than the last, each day more exhausted. But even now, her palms sweated and her pulse quickened as she thought about it.

She filled in his words: "But I don't think I can."

She waved at the dying planet around her. "I will not end up like them!" she exclaimed suddenly. Dov merely shrugged.

After another moment: "This mission is fulfilled," Clemmy heard herself proclaim, as much to herself as to Dov. "We know why Ran died. It doesn't matter which of these millions did it; they're all dying anyway. We know the wizards are here, and we know how to neutralize them. I'll report to the Nin: we'll need teams of Ekans and Ghiuliducs to Shield the Police.

"And then . . ." she said. "And then we'll find a way to stop the Ressie advance—just close it down like drug traffic. Let those who already have Ressies keep them, but keep them away from everyone else. Take the children out of here, too. The human worlds will have to work together on this for a change."

Dov flashed a crooked smile at her. "I like the part," he said hoarsely, "about letting those who have them already, keep them."

"Is this all you could get?" the fat man complained, looking at the twelve-seater in front of them. All seventeen were there.

"It will be cramped," Ash Medai conceded, "but it's the

fastest rig I could get on short notice. We've had five temporary seats welded in."

The ship was the perfect cone demanded by one type of interspatial technology, with a tiny, perfectly smooth bore down its central axis. That was the gripper, the thing that somehow took hold of the interspatial strings that allowed shortcuts between the folds of real space, enabling the speed of light relativistic limitation to be bypassed.

"We're losing control of the planet already," one of the woman murmured. All of them were reasonably, if poorly, clothed. "Not long ago we could have commandeered the fanciest liner in the skies, and no one would have been able to stop us."

"Most of the Surceasean liners are grounded for repairs," the big leader said, "or off in interspace."

"Grounded . . ." the woman said. "Because people could not break away from Ressie action to fix them."

"You want to give up your Ressie?" the man said. But she did not answer.

"Com Central says a Task Force is on its way here with an October jammer," Ash Medai said. "There's no point in waiting for it; let Surcease go to hell. We're for October and a new dominion."

They climbed aboard the small ship.

Clemmy finally reached Adio-Gabutti from her hotel room. Dov was with her, and they were drinking electrolytes as fast as the machine could pour.

Clemmy sat down heavily on the bed.

"Dead?" she cried. Dov looked sharply over at her. "Dead? Oh, no. Please, no."

The tiny voice seemed to thunder in her ears, carried by the audio implants in her mastoids.

"Dov, switch over," she motioned to him. He did so, and at the other end, Adio-Gabutti repeated the story of Spimmon and Nisha Scalli.

"That snaky bastard," Dov growled. But Clemmy cut him off:

"He was my responsibility!"

There was no longer any thought of a relaxing evening

in their respective suites. They headed out to the spaceport. They had to get a message to the Nin, but the local
Com was still dysfunctional. They had to go off-planet.

"Have you heard? The Seventeen are going off-planet.
They are fleeing from the Police." The whisper began at
the spaceport, spread like wildfire through the city. Some
of the wizards left behind cursed and waved their fists, as
if they could scare their rulers back to the ground. But
most of them turned back to their Ressies within a few
hours; nothing else seemed really important.

The spaceport watchers left their posts and headed back
to their homes in the city. There didn't seem any point in
watching anymore.

Passing them on one of the skylips came Clemmy and
Dov, hurrying in a rented groundcar. They reached the
spaceport, and soon found Adio-Gabutti and the private
space car they had rented on arrival. Clemmy looked at the
frozen, broken figure of Spimmon inside the medico's transparent bubble and cried for him, and for Nisha Scalli too.

They lifted off. If necessary, they would pop into interspace and out again—anything to get enough distance
between themselves and the Surceasean Com for a clear
communication with the Nin. Or even, Clemmy conceded,
with Asher Tye.

Just then, on the fringe of the solar system, Asher and
his repair ship flared out of interspace, Asher lying coma-
tose in a Death Trance he had raised moments before.
And the new Skill jammer aboard his ship switched on.

"Ahhhh!" There came a collective scream from the Seventeen. Their cone ship had been thrusting away from the
planet, headed out to jump point. The partially trained
October minds reacted to the jammer with violence.

"Network. Network!" the big man screamed as, inside
the small cabin of the twelve-seater, the Seventeen tried
to raise Shields against the jammer, tried to fight it any
way they could. They tried to form a Network, their
Ressies quivering on their ankles, but the mental chaos
was too great.

The big man thundered: "The Trance. Go into the Trance!"

"For how long?" the mohawk-haired woman wailed.

"Just do it!"

One by one, the Seventeen fell into a slumber filled with nightmares and terror.

On the planet behind them, the desultory Network controlling the planetary Com simply ceased to function and, like a swimmer finally grasping at the sand after a shipwreck, the Com seemed to gasp and then gave itself over to its own logical circuitry. Machine thought moved in incredible speed, and logic reasserted itself over the dissipating remnants of Skill control.

On Surcease, the few remaining wizards clutched at their heads and screamed. The jammer was not mind-destroying. As they lived longer and longer under its field, they would grow to tolerate it, and then ignore it, for their Skill would close itself off inside and eventually become unreachable as their minds protected themselves. But they didn't know this yet, and for the moment the mental scrambling was like a horrible, drug-induced hallucination.

"Hey," Clemmy exclaimed, as the shuttle left Surcease's atmosphere. She had some Skill, and she could feel the jammer as an annoying noise in the back of her mind. But she was functional, and her mind was still working. "The Com has cleared up!" she said. She placed a call to the Nin.

The Nin's holo image formed before them. Was it a computer amalgam, or the real thing? It didn't much matter. At last, Clemmy was able to report what they had found.

"But what of the Seventeen?" the image of the magnificent woman asked them. She looked haggard but triumphant; why, Clemmy did not know.

"The Seventeen?" Dov asked. Clemmy was frowning; a headache was forming in her that seemed to want to split her skull.

The Nin told them what she had heard from Asher, who had in turn learned it from Ceal Carnak. "The core of

Surceasean power is a Network of Seventeen. Where are they? Neutralize them, and this battle is won."

"We never even heard of them," Dov exclaimed indignantly.

"Is Clemmy in pain?" the Nin asked. Dov and the Therd glanced at her. She was hunched over with both hands on her forehead.

"I guess so," Dov said. Then, lower: "She's been depressed over Asher Tye."

The Nin seemed to be thinking. "What led you to get through to me?" she asked finally. "Was your local Com out of service up until now, by any chance?"

They allowed that it had been, and the Nin said: "Now I understand—Asher Tye is somewhere in your space."

Clemmy jerked her head up; the effort made it feel like the clapper in a bell.

"The Police Task Force isn't due in Surceasean space for at least a day," the Nin pursued. "Believe me, I know about Police Task Forces. They would have a Skill jammer with them, but so does Asher Tye. He hasn't reported in, and your Com is suddenly free . . . it has to be him. Scan for this ship . . ." She gave them the registry of Asher's repair ship. "Find him, Clemmy, and if he doesn't know it already, tell him the worst is happening. The October One is said to be returning to her world. We have to brace ourselves for all-out warfare with her."

The words were ominous, but the idea that Asher was nearby . . . a sudden throb brought her head back down again.

"Dov, Adio," she croaked. "Find him . . ."

Chapter 25

The machine turned itself off. Asher had set it for a two-hour assault on Surcease; now he would awaken from the Trance, examine the situation, and proceed on the basis of what he found. Mostly, he wanted to communicate with Clemmy.

He opened his eyes and found himself looking into hers.

Dreaming? No, his mind was working, his Skill intact. Her eyes were like pools of obsidian, deep and dark, glazed over. The expression on her face was unreadable. He sought for thoughts, and found almost nothing, just fleeting traces, confused in their complexity.

He sat up, and she stepped back from him. She was very thin, he saw.

And then he saw Dov, lounging in the captain's chair, studying him; and Adio-Gabutti, planted like a rock in one corner.

Wonder swirled through Asher like syrup in ice cream.

"How," he managed to say at last, "did *you* get *here*?"

Then Clemmy's eyes rolled upward and her legs gave way. Dov leaped forward and caught her as she sagged toward the deck.

The sight of Dov's hands on his wife brought Asher's awakening mind to full alert. He climbed off the couch on which he had slept, took Clemmy roughly from Dov and carried her back to it, stretching her out gently. With disquiet he noted the Ressie affixed to her left leg.

"What's wrong with her?" Asher croaked.

"You are," Dov said. Asher turned on him and Dov stepped hastily away.

"Keep your hands off of her," Asher shouted.

"Calm down, old boy," Dov said. "This is about the only time I ever had my hands on her. She took a good dose of that mind jammer of yours, is all. It about tore her apart the closer to your ship we got. You should go in more for automatic defenses, Asher, old pal. We just cruised right up, docked and walked in, and your ship's Com didn't do a thing but say 'Hi'."

"I haven't had a lot of time to work on anything except the jammer," Asher muttered.

"Listen, Your Squad Leadership," Dov continued relentlessly. "What if we were Surceaseans, hm? Suppose we were employees, as it were, of those Adepts down there? We could have cut your throat and taken the machine apart."

"Yeah, well," Asher said. He was looking down at Clemmy, a riot of emotions in his mind. "I told you," he said softly, and Dov realized that he was speaking to the unconscious woman, "not to come to Surcease. Why?"

Dov moved up to Asher's shoulder and looked down at Clemmy. "Because," he said, more gently now, "she got her directions from the Nin herself. You, my friend, haven't the authority to contradict them, husband or no."

Asher said nothing. Looking down at her, he felt, instead of love, a great sadness. None of this should have happened, he thought. We should never have been separated. The Nin might be a tactical master, but she should have kept us together.

He called up a deck chair and sat down heavily next to Clemmy. "Fill me in," he said, not looking at Dov, not taking his eyes away from his wife.

And so, for the first time, Asher heard Clemmy's conclusions about the death of Ran; heard about the death of Nisha Scalli; heard about the freeing of the planetary Com and their conversation with the Nin.

"Nin Tova said something about the return of the October One," Dov concluded. "That seemed to worry her a lot. I think she thinks that the top Surceasean honchos are going to team up with the One somehow, and it will be war between them and the Bodyguard Guild."

Asher looked sharply at him. "She's convinced that the One is returning?"

Dov nodded. He had no idea what the news would mean to Asher Tye, who had been a part of the October trainees so long ago. He was rather afraid of the reaction.

"The One has such access to Power that she could defeat the Skill jamming machines, am I right?" Dov ventured hesitantly.

"Maybe she could, I don't know," Asher said shortly. He said more loudly: "ShipCom." The ship's Com answered in its business-like voice. "Take us out."

" 'Out'?" Dov repeated.

"Out," Asher said. "To the October World, my friend. It is time for us to confront the last of the Power."

"To the *October World!*" Dov gasped. "You're kidding me."

"I wish I were," Asher said. "The Police will be here in a day with another machine. We know what we need to about Surcease now, and it is no threat anymore."

Asher moved over to Adio-Gabutti. "It goes well with you?" he asked the alien.

There was no response. Asher looked more closely at him.

"I think he's asleep," Dov ventured. Asher grunted softly.

Near the edge of the galaxy, the October World spun. A dry planet, it had some vegetation supported by underground aquifers, but no open bodies of water. Its oxygen was supplied by several species of dry algae imbedded by the trillions throughout the sands of the planet. Ever since the defeat of the October One the world had fallen into insignificance, an out-of-the-way place with a small population of human tradesmen and miners, visited seldom by starliners, desired by no one. The megalithic castle-like fortress that the October One had caused to be built was now partly occupied by the planetary administration, but vast halls and chambers stood empty, gathering dust.

The administration on the planet was in a panic over the rumor of the One's return; there were tiny warships in space, waiting. The rare ship was challenged and searched, though the administration had the despairing knowledge that if in fact the One did return, their weapons would be for nothing.

If she did come, it would be from the Sculptor, whither she had gone with the Teacher these years past, to retrain and review and eliminate, one would hope, the lust for domination from her and her sisters' hearts.

Was she coming? No one really knew. The Sculptor subgalaxy itself was still showing an anomalous tachyonic silence radiating from its amorphous shape, a silence covering the entirety of its million stars. But there was no other sign of anything unusual in it, or in any of the other subgalaxies of the Milky Way.

The ship of the Seventeen reached October space first, of course. The seventeen Apprentices had awakened in interspace, groggily, from their Trance, a Skill they had rarely used and in whose technique they were rusty in the extreme. They ate, they enjoyed their Ressies, and ate again; then they Networked, and awaited the exit from interspace.

When it came, even as the incandescent flaring still glowed behind their ship, they probed October space with all the power of their Network, trying to locate the October One.

The big man, feeling the Power flow like water through his mind, gloated and glowed, and his ecstasy carried along the others. They were Strength such as the galaxy had not seen since the fall of October. Underlying it all was the unuttered sense that perhaps, maybe, they themselves in consort would be the equal of the One herself; and that, all together, they could resist any Skill machine. For they themselves had designed it, and they knew its inner workings.

"I don't feel Her presence," one of the fat women breathed to the group circled around. And indeed, strain as they would, they could feel no rippling of the Power— certainly not the massive stirring that the presence of the One would entail.

One of the small, watching warships hailed the newcomer. The Network turned its brief attention to it, and the ship suddenly lost control, its Com in disarray, its crew stunned or dead.

The October World lost four other ships that way, until, finally unopposed, the twelve-seater settled into the atmosphere and dropped toward the landing site the One herself once had used, inside a flattened portion of the mile-high castle walls.

And at that moment, Asher Tye's ship burst out of interspace.

"There," he said, watching as a robotech made a last adjustment on the Skill jammer. He was in the hold of the ship with Adio-Gabutti, examining the machine. "Now the thing is as powerful as I can make with the tools at hand. When the Surceaseans come through, as I think they must, chasing for the October One, we'll be able to cope with them whether or not I'm conscious . . . or alive." He looked up as if his eyes could pierce the bulkhead of the hold in which he was working, to look in on Clemmy, still in a deep sleep on the bridge. "The machine will turn on at five-minute intervals unless I give the verbal signal not to. And our ship's automatics are set to seek the Surceaseans out, to bring itself close in. The closer it gets, the worse it is for a sensitive, believe me . . ." Suddenly he stopped. His mind had sensed a stirring of Power in this local space.

The Network felt him as well, and with instant precision found his ship. They felt as if they could move the October planet itself merely by an effort of mind.

"Focus!" the big man ordered. "Stun whoever's on that ship; I want them alive. I want to take them apart into little pieces, one by one. Now . . ."

Asher, Dov, and Adio-Gabutti fell like stones. Asher had had a Shield up, but the power of the Network sliced through it like a knife through a soap bubble, and he didn't even have time to feel surprise.

The new ship came steadily inward, and the Network probed it for life.

"We did it," a fat woman breathed. They all could sense Clemmy's and Asher's and Dov's stunned minds, and even a trace of Spimmon's frozen one. Of Adio-Gabutti they felt nothing, but he lay as inert as the rest, for when he was caught in a wide attack he went out like anyone else.

"Let the ship reach orbit, and we'll send someone up to get it," said the big man. "And when the October One comes, we'll hand their heads and their machine over to her . . ."

At that moment the Skill jammer, having heard nothing from Asher Tye, switched on. The impact on the Seventeen was like a freight train hitting a barn.

"Oh, no; not again," groaned the fat man.

"But we are in Network," Ash Medai thought desperately at them. "Quickly—a death blast at the machine—kill everyone around it. Tear the machine itself to pieces."

The Seventeen gathered Power, felt the ecstatic surge of mental energy, turned it on the incoming ship . . .

But it just would not come. They could not focus properly. The blinding racket of the jammer jangled in their minds like ball bearings in a can. They couldn't think.

They strained, their sweating bodies tensing, rippling, to the delight of the Ressies below. They fought and heaved. The Network wavered and finally, in a long despairing wail, collapsed into seventeen individual minds, fleeing the noise of the gigantic version of the machine they had once designed. For Asher had built well. In his own sleep, the nightmares chased him again, like phantoms on a death ship.

"Damn!" the big man screamed. They went into Trance, even as their ship touched ground.

The planet's administration was cowering in hiding, its warships scared off by the first strange ship. But the planetary Com was functional, and it quizzed the repair ship's Com as the ship reached close orbit around the October World.

"No, we are not armed," the Com flashed. "You may read my memory . . ."

The repair ship spiralled down and set itself gently next to the twelve-seater.

Asher was the first to awaken, for his Shield and experience had given him some protection. But his mind immediately felt the jammer, and forced itself into the Death Trance.

Dov awakened on the deck of the bridge. Woozily he looked around, and it took much consulting with the ship's Com before he realized that they had in fact landed, and that their enemy lay within feet of them. That brought him fully conscious, and he demanded readouts and details.

He ran down to the hold and found Asher Tye deep in the grip of the Trance. He knew it was the Trance from the lack of apparent breathing. And he saw that the jammer was full on.

"That means," he said out loud, "that the Seventeen are immobilized as well, right outside our ship. But I need Asher . . ."

Adio-Gabutti suddenly said: "We will go in and take them."

Dov spun around. He hadn't even noticed the Therd.

"You're awake," he said foolishly.

"Evidently," the alien said. He suddenly headed toward the bridge on his three stumpy legs. "We will go in and take them," he said again.

"We can't," Dov said. "Their Com won't let us in; I already checked. It has no current orders, but will obey no one but those inside."

"Then we will do the opposite," the alien said. "We will weld them in."

Weld them in? Why not? Dov wondered. This, after all, is a repair ship; there are plenty of tools at hand.

"Why are you so ruthless all of a sudden?" Dov asked.

"I, too, knew Randolph Tarney," the alien said.

And so Adio-Gabutti and Dov stepped outside with robotechs and welded the airlock of the twelve-seater shut. They chopped pieces out of its antigrav scoops, then welded plasteel plates over its observation relux bubble, its waste disposal units, its cargo loaders, and finally, the central grabber hole. They made sure that the ship would not fly by any method. They left a few air ventlocks still able to open.

"Now?" Adio-Gabutti asked.

"Now we turn off that damned machine and hope to hell we can wake up Asher before those bozos wake up in there," Dov said. The castle walls loomed around them, and he felt as if he were in a gothic romance.

Asher did wake up before the Surceaseans; his experience with the Trance and the jammer was much more extensive than theirs, and his mind more readily sensed the turning off of the machine. The device lay silent now, with Adio-Gabutti standing by it, ready to turn it on at the slightest sign of trouble.

"I can't go through this up-down cycle much longer," Asher groaned as he came erect. Then his mind told him what must have happened, and Dov told him the rest.

"Very, very good," Asher commented, and Dov flushed. He rarely heard any praise from anyone. "Yeah, well, what do we do now?" he asked truculently.

"I've got to immobilize their Skill without destroying mine," Asher muttered. "I thought about this on the trip out from Central, but . . . Adio-Gabutti."

The two of them, alien and human, turned to the machine. "What are you going to do?" Dov asked.

"Rewire this thing," Asher said, looking somberly at the Skill jammer, "so that it turns on instantly whenever it feels a mental touch."

"What good would that do?" Dov demanded. "All they'd have to do is aim a killing blow at us and it would be all over."

Asher turned his cold brown eyes on Dov. "Except for one thing. Our minds are much cruder and slower than a machine's." He turned back again and set to work, calling up a robotech, which came stalking like a rooster out of a side compartment.

"But—" Dov said. Then: "Wait. I get it. Our brains won't react to a killing blow before the thing turns on. Are you sure that will work, Asher? I mean, just because we don't know we're dead, doesn't mean we aren't."

"Yes, yes, I've thought a lot about that," Asher said, bending to his work. "But my theory is that it takes at least a fraction of a millisecond for the full effect of a mental blow to hit, and in that instant, the jammer will intervene and prevent most of the blow."

"Your *theory*?" Dov said. "Listen, Asher, let's just inject some cyanide into their air system and forget the whole thing, all right?"

Again, the cold eyes. "Not all right," Asher said. "Enough have died . . ." It seemed to strangle in his throat; he turned back to his work. "Call up the Nin if you like and get me overruled, Dov. Right now I've got to get this done as fast as I can, because if they do wake up in the next hour and strike at us, then we will be dead."

Dov called up the Nin and laid it all out before her.

"The Police want them," the Nin said shortly. "Do it Asher's way."

Dov decided, after bitter reflection, to seek out one of the crew berths. If he was going to die in the next few minutes, he wanted a last chance at the Ressie.

Minutes later, Asher felt the waves of pleasure in the mental background, and moved his mind outward until he found the source. Disgusted, he wrenched his mind away and concentrated on the task at hand. Sure, it was enjoyable, he thought. But don't they see what it does to them?

Chapter 26

Clemmy finally came awake. Her sleep hadn't been a Death Trance, but had begun in exhaustion and lapsed into normal REM sleep, only slightly disturbed by the recent blastings of the Skill jammer. The jammer was on again, and it was that which had brought her out of sleep.

But Asher was unconscious this time, and so was everybody else. The Seventeen had emerged from their drug-induced sleep and attacked. Clemmy's sleeping brain hadn't been much affected. Dov and Asher and Adio-Gabutti had been felled like oxen.

"Blast it," Clemmy said, her head pounding now from the jammer. "I've been parsecs away from him for eighteen days, and the minute I get close to him I discover that we're on alternate sleep cycles!"

She knew it wasn't exactly that, of course. She thought about turning the machine off, but reconsidered. She did not yet know what the tactical situation was, where the enemies were and in what condition.

Luckily, the jamming wasn't as painful as it had been in Surceasean space. Maybe she was getting used to it.

She stumbled over to Asher, who lay in a heap in the hold, and examined him. No visible injury; just that blasted Trance again. She hoisted him by the armpits and dragged him up into the repair ship's tiny bridge. With some effort, she lifted him up and maneuvered his body onto the same fold-in couch where she had found him upon boarding his ship from the shuttle in Surceasean space, and on which she had found herself a moment ago. She tried to enter his mind and call him back from the Trance despite the jammer. She felt something give, like a lever

262

pushed back, but Asher didn't move and she had no idea if she had done any good.

Dov was lolling in the pilot's chair, and Adio-Gabutti was at his side, as immobile as a granite slab.

Clemmy surveyed the situation. ShipCom told her that they were on the October World, side by side with a shipful of mortal enemies, the October One likely to arrive at any moment. She frowned at that one. Central didn't seem to be particularly excited, and by probing further, she found out why. The whole thing was still an unsubstantiated rumor, a piece of gossip plucked out of the morass of galactic information that Central spewed forth every day. In all the time the rumor had persisted, there had been nothing to corroborate it. Still, a Task Force was being readied for a cautionary trip to the October World.

Won't do us any good, Clemmy thought; it will take over a week to get here.

Where in the devil is the planetary government? Clemmy badgered the planetary Com, but it wouldn't say because it didn't know. The whole population seemed to be in hiding; even a hint that the One might return had sent it into a hysterical panic.

She grew thoughtful. The jammer was jangling at her, interfering with her concentration, but she knew that above all else she wanted a conscious, alert Asher Tye. And she could think of only one way to get it.

She lifted the ship and headed for interspace.

By the time Dov and Adio-Gabutti came out of it, the repair ship had left the atmosphere and was already nearing the interspatial jump point. With weightlessness available to them now, they maneuvered the jammer into the airlock and ejected it, still full on. Then they brought their ship into interspace, into a static universal bubble, going nowhere. When they reentered real space, they would still be in the vicinity of the October World.

And then they waited. It seemed a long time to Clemmy before Asher groaned and sat up. He looked wildly around. His eyes saw Clemmy, but the warrior in him was uppermost, the preservation of life transcendent over love.

"Report!" he barked. "The jammer . . . the Network . . ."

She met his stance and, in a few clipped sentences, told him what she had done. His mind, even as it saw the sense in it, began suddenly to veer. No crisis was imminent. Now . . .

He took a deep, shuddering breath. Clemmy had no idea what he was going to do next; but she knew what she was going to do.

"Clemmy," he said, gyrating mind coming to rest. Then: "Clemmy!" He leaped off the medbed and his legs gave way; he landed on his knees. Grinning foolishly, he pushed himself erect and swayed, wondering where his balance was, but overwhelmed with the sight of Clemmy alive, Clemmy with him.

He did love her, he realized. More than that—he *liked* her.

"Hug me, Clemmy," he said. "I don't think I can reach you."

But she didn't move, regarding him with a peculiar mixture of doubt and confused contempt. Then he saw the Ressie affixed to her leg, and his own mood altered.

"Take it off," he said. She looked down at the Ressie.

"Is that an order, sir?" she inquired sweetly.

"Yes, dammit," he said. Dov and Adio looked at one another. They decided in silent harmony that they had urgent business down in the hold. They turned and melted silently away.

"I think," Clemmy said, ignoring the order, "that you can never give me orders again, Asher Tye, and I think further that it is over between us, don't you?" Her voice rose through the words until she caught herself, and then dabbed at something liquid in her eye. I'm really angry, she thought.

"What are you talking about?" Asher demanded.

"You have your red-haired poppsie," Clemmy said, still in that controlled, saccharine voice. "And I have my Ressie. Kind of makes us even, doesn't it?"

"My . . . What in the world *are* you talking about?"

She showed him the holo clip. His eyes grew larger and larger as he saw the double meaning in everything the clip showed. She regarded him with a sardonic smile, waiting

for his breakdown, waiting for him to beg her for forgive-
ness. Which she would withhold.

"She blew the guts right out of that holo booth," Asher
exclaimed. "Isn't there anywhere that we see the needler?" But there wasn't.

" 'I want you,' " Clemmy said dryly.

"I want you *dead*, is what she meant," Asher said desperately. "Look, Clemmy, we made a bargain when we
married that we would never go inside one another's mind
without express permission. Well, I am giving that permission right now. Look inside, Clemmy; I'm going to
open everything to you."

She tried to find some demur, but in the end, looked.
And saw what the red-haired woman meant to Asher.

"You admired her," Clemmy said accusingly. "You
thought she was beautiful. You even thought about . . .
about . . ."

"Yes, Clemmy, yes. But I didn't do it, and I could have. I
could have forced her; at that point I could have been the
supreme power on Dade if I had chosen to be. She was resourceful and quick and she had saved my life. Yes, she attracted me, but good heavens, woman, I'll fight it if you will."

"What do you mean?" she asked suspiciously. She was
unwilling to give up the scene that had led her thoughts in
such grim directions for half a month, for it had become a
habit, but reality was forcing her to.

"I mean, what have you been doing while I've been
resisting temptation on Dade? Can I look into your mind
as you did mine?"

For a moment, she felt ashamed. She had no reason to
feel that way, she thought; anyone seeing that holo would
have drawn the conclusions she had. But she was ashamed
anyway, and not entirely about her unfounded suspicions.

"All right," she said meekly. She opened her mind to
him and, in doing so, became aware that she was afraid
what he saw would cause her to lose him.

He studied her. For a long time he studied her, gently
lifting memory to the surface—desire, need, emotion—
loving her, yet seeing the morass she had been drawn
into. He could see why she and Dov and Nisha Scalli had

been so immersed in it, oh yes, he could see. In their place, maybe he too . . .

Finally he drew back, sweating. "You must," he whispered hoarsely to her, "you have to get rid of it."

She turned and looked out of the observation bubble. "I don't know if I can," she said. "It's my body and my decision."

Time passed. They had to return to the October World; they all knew it. Asher struggled inside himself, cast about for other solutions, but at last he had to face it: as long as the jammer was their only effective weapon, he himself was out of the action.

"All we can do is go back in and turn the jammer off," he said at last. "And see what happens. Try to talk; make them give up. *Don't kill them.* Clemmy, you are in charge." He struggled with his mouth for an instant, then said: "I know you'll do a good job." Lame, lame, lame, he thought. Then, with a tired sigh, he settled himself down on the couch and reached for the Trance.

He didn't see the aurora of pleasure creep up Clemmy's neck and onto her face. Smartly, she brought the ship back into real space. They picked up the jammer and turned it off. Then they headed for the October World.

Asher roused himself. Inside the other ship, the Seventeen were able to bring themselves alive more quickly than before; one among them was mastering recovery from the Trance, and the rest were learning from it. They began gathering themselves together, waking up the deepest sleepers, preparing . . .

And even as the repair ship landed next to the twelve-seater, even as Asher felt himself finally come fully awake, they struck again with a violent crashing mental blow. All four on the repair ship fell like stockings full of sand. The Skill jammer screamed.

Four days passed—the October World's cycle was 26 hours 40 minutes—and whenever the jammer was off, the Surceaseans tried everything they had. They tried to burn through the welded door of their airlock with a Networked

Green Flame; the jammer turned on. They tried to levitate the ship; the jammer turned on. They tried to throw up a Networked Shield; at the touch of their minds, the jammer turned on.

In between bouts, they sweltered in the close confines of their cramped ship. The Ressies loved it at first; the free sweating was exactly what they tried to stimulate at every opportunity. But soon the water tanks were dry, and all the food they had had for rations was gone. The Seventeen began to starve.

It was hard on the occupants of Asher's ship too, but at least they were well supplied. The off-and-on jammer disoriented Clemmy, with Asher retreating into Trance on a near-permanent basis. Only Dov and Adio-Gabutti withstood the jammer without effect. When, however, the attack was another mental blow, then they too felt it enough to lose consciousness, while the jammer intervened and saved them from mutual, simultaneous death.

Clemmy tried to reason with them via holography, but they would have none of it. The One will soon be here, they insisted. And even if she never arrived, they would not become slaves to the loss of their Skill through that infernal machine.

And in the daytime, the sun of the October World, in its cloudless sky, beat down upon their ship, and inside the heat was suffocating.

It was in midwatch on that fourth day, the sun high overhead, that it happened. The atmosphere in the Surceasean ship was as thick as butter. The welded plates outside had inhibited proper air filtration, and the air was foul with the reek of Seventeen overweight, closed-in bodies.

The big man was giving them one of his endless pep talks.

"She will be here, I know it," he was saying, his tongue thick, the words barely coming. Some of them had been working on cutting through a rear plate to the outside. They could only operate the cutter for a few minutes at a time; the fumes became so bad that they had to wait for the partially blocked air flow to do its job.

"Another six hours, and we'll be out," the big man

croaked. "Let them try then to use the jammer to track us down; we'll be free at least."

Hunger and thirst were interfering with the clarity of his thoughts, as well as the others'. During the last Network, he had felt their wavering weakness, and knew that they could not even raise a Network for much longer. And every time they tried it, it set off that damned machine.

The quality of their sweating had changed as it had faded with the lack of water. They were not particularly aware of it, but the Ressies were. After millennia of absorbing bodily secretions, they knew the chemical signs of dehydration and starvation. Fat though the people were, their bodies were crying out for food and water. The Ressies had heard that cry many times during their endless cycle of growth and starvation.

It was time, one of them decided, and all of the Ressies seemed to decide so at the same time. It was time to reach for the rest of the fluids in those diminishing bodies.

"No," one of the women said distinctly.

Ash Medai jerked his head up, having not realized that he had been nodding off. "What is it?" he asked, hearing something more than annoyance in her voice.

"My Ressie seems to want a session," she said, and giggled nervously. The Ressie was expanding upward from her leg, just as if . . .

"Well, let it," one of the others said. "You need a little relaxation, sweetie."

It spread upward, reaching her neck with unusual speed, without that slow, gradual massaging for which Ressies were so famous. It reached her mouth and nostrils, and without preliminaries forced its way in. The woman began to gag.

"Hey!" the big man said. He leaped over and tried to grab hold of the Ressie, tried to insinuate his fingers under its pulsing ochre body, spread like paint over the woman's torso; but the cilia dug in, and his fingers could not get a grip.

The woman was thrashing now, her eyes bulging. Ash Medai became aware of cries of horror, and looked to see all of the others trying to fight off their own Ressies.

Something filled his own mouth, forced its way down his throat, blocked his nose.

Then someone reached for the Skill, and tried to use it to pry the Ressie away . . .

And the Skill jammer turned on.

Asher came out of the Trance to find Dov watching him sardonically, and Clemmy shaking her head from side to side as she sat in the copilot's chair. "I think Adio-Gabutti's asleep again," Dov observed. Indeed, the alien did not seem conscious, though it was hard to tell.

"How long was I out this time?" Asher asked wearily.

"Only about two hours," Dov said. "You're waking up quicker and quicker, old boy."

Asher looked out the observation bubble to the other ship. "I just wish they'd give up and get it over with before the Police get here," he said. "I don't want to have to answer a lot of fool questions . . ." He paused. Something was wrong. It took him a moment to figure out what it was.

His mind was no longer feeling mental activity in the other ship, not even the slow rhythm of sleeping minds.

"What's wrong?" Dov demanded, seeing his expression.

Asher bolted for the airlock, the two humans following him. Both Clemmy and Dov grabbed their weapon belts as they ran, but Asher carried no weapon other than his mind.

Outside, the sun glinted blindingly off the cone-shaped ship, its lux-metal body polished brightly by the recent descent through the atmosphere, and the air was hot and calm. They circled the Surceasean ship warily, but there was no sign of any opening.

"They're still in there," Dov said, trying to reassure Asher. But it only seemed to make him more frantic.

"Come on!" he yelled. "We have to cut those plates loose and get that airlock open." But, sick in his heart, Asher knew that what he would find would not be life.

They got the big plate off the airlock, and this time when the ship's Com refused them entry, Asher sent Dov back to the repair ship. "I want you to keep the jammer turned off; you'll find a power lever on the lower right side of the machine."

"But—" Dov protested.

"Do it!" Asher said.

When his wrist computer told him that Dov was in place, Asher closed his eyes and said: "Now, ShipCom, old fellow, I am going to change your orders . . ." He reached out with his mind.

The airlock clicked and cycled open.

Clemmy and Asher climbed inside. Clemmy wrinkled her nose: "Sure is ripe in here," she said. She had her weapon out, and Asher saw that it was a blaster.

"You won't need that," he said sharply as the inner door began to cycle open.

"I feel better with it, Asher," Clemmy said quietly. Then the door opened full. She looked inside and screamed.

Asher leaped through the doorway, mentally ready for anything, and then quailed back before the scene that met his eyes. Scattered around the cramped cabin of the twelve-seater were seventeen bodies, but the faces were invisible. Each one looked like a painted, ochre dummy, without distinct features, eyes and nostrils and mouth merely outlined by the layer over them, bodies bloated by the Ressie-enhanced heat. And the layers pulsated, throbbed, heaved, and fed.

Clemmy staggered outside. She looked at the blaster in her hand, and then at the Ressie on her leg.

From inside Asher heard the blast of the weapon; Clemmy screamed.

He rushed out and found her sitting on the rock-slabbed ground.

"I did it, Asher," she sobbed, looking at him. "I did it, but I'm a lousy aim."

Asher looked, and saw that her foot was attached to her leg by nothing more than a strip of scorched skin. There were pieces of her calf, and of her Ressie, smoldering around the tiny crater the blast had created.

Chapter 27

"It's ended, Nin," Asher said. He was standing before the pilot's seat, staring at the woman who stood as if real before him. Behind her image, Clemmy slept in an emergency medbed, her leg encased in a bulbous regeneration pouch, which would do until they reached the Bodyguard Planet again.

"It's not ended until the October One is dealt with," the Nin said quietly. Her peculiar brown and blonde hair was dishevelled today, and it was that and that alone which suggested to Asher that this was the real woman he was talking with, holoed across the parsecs, and not her well-programmed computer amalgam.

Dov, in front of the bridge readouts, glanced out the observation bubble of the ship as if the October One were sailing over the near horizon at that very moment.

But he saw instead a smoking pit in the ground where they had dumped the Ressie-covered bodies and, unceremoniously, turned their blasters on them.

"That's seventeen Ressies who will never again kill a human being," Asher had said. Dov had said nothing.

"Why should she be dealt with?" Asher said flatly. "She isn't here."

"The rumors . . ." the Nin began.

"Were planted by me," Asher interrupted, "to lure the Seventeen away from Surcease and a potential Network of one hundred seventy-five—all the remaining Apprentices, on and off-planet, plus the Seventeen."

The Nin regarded him in amazement, and then began to

271

laugh. "And that's why her return is not big news throughout the galaxy—why it's still labelled unsubstantiated and unreliable? Even the thought of it is sending thousands of worlds into panic." She laughed again, and Asher was abruptly conscious of her as a woman. Wearily, he put the thought out of his mind. Would the images never stop?

Adio-Gabutti, standing nearby, said in his solemn voice: "Pardon my intrusion, Nin Tova, but having seen its effect on my own colleagues, I must tell you that the Ressies are as big a threat as the October One herself would be. For they strip away all drive from a human, make him lazy, make him refuse to work. He wallows in a sea of pleasure, and he accomplishes nothing."

"Oh, the Police are going to interdict Surcease and its dependencies at the request of the human governments," the Nin said dismissively.

"And the Ressies will spread underground, like any drug," Asher said harshly.

"No, I don't think so. I have a refugee emperor on my side, among a few kings, dukes, regents, and presidents," the Nin said. "I'm talking with four of them at this very moment." By computer amalgam, Asher thought. "We'll give the people of Surcease the chance to throw off their Ressies, and we'll care for the children of the ones who don't. You have to realize, Asher, that their whole system's information input was distorted for several years by the Apprentices. The people of Surcease never realized that their own blasted lives were mirrored planetwide. The Apprentices themselves never admitted it. All they really wanted was the riches that Ressie trade would bring, and after that to be left alone to wallow in their own private Ressies.

"In the meantime, Asher, I want you home."

Asher broke in sharply. "Nin, I'm getting tired of saving the galaxy. I'm tired of killing; I'm tired of death. In any event, I won't be able to function in this galaxy soon now, as the Skill jammers spread from planet to planet."

"We won't elect one on the Bodyguard Planet," the Nin said soothingly.

"Oh, fine," Asher said, "and I'll spend my days teaching rebellious students how to survive in street fights."

"As I was saying, Asher," the Nin said stiffly, "and I say this to each of you: you have performed a tremendous service for the Guild of Personal Protectors and for the Concourse of Races as a whole, and on behalf of the Guild, I thank you now, and you can expect suitable rewards upon your return."

"Nin," Dov broke in. "I have a request." He looked sheepish and defiant at the same time.

"Go on," the Nin said.

"Make me Bodyguard rep on Surcease. There hasn't been a Bodyguard there since the Apprentices took over."

Asher eyed Dov narrowly. Why this? And then he understood. It put off for Dov the day when he would have to face what the Ressie was doing to him. He hadn't had a marriage to fall back on, as Clemmy had had.

"You made a mistake, Nin," Asher said quietly, "of not marrying Dov off before this mission."

Dov looked outraged, but the Nin seemed to be considering what Asher had said. "I suppose so," she sighed at last. "I have only the barest understanding of men, even though I've associated with hundreds of them over the years."

Asher and Dov looked at each other.

The Nin sighed. "I'm going to sign off now. The Ekans crisis is occupying the Guild right now, and the Police have asked for our help, which we're bound to give, though how to deal with such an aggressive race in a way that won't incite them further frankly escapes me. What I don't understand is how they arranged for the Surceaseans to hide the genocides behind the Guild. Insofar as I can determine, Nisha Scalli was the first Ekans ever to visit Surceasean space, and no Surceasean has ever come near Ekans."

Asher said: "I've thought about that, and I think you'll find that there was in fact no contact. The Surceaseans merely used the worst event of the time as a mechanism for attacking the Bodyguard Guild; the Ekans were just lucky. They probably couldn't understand how they were getting away with it. It probably made them harbor even greater contempt for the Concourse than they already had.

"But as for dealing with the Ekans," Asher said, "a suggestion, if you will."

"Please," Nin Tova said.

"This sounds crazy, but why not solve two problems at once?" Asher said. "Gather up all the Ressies you can find on Surcease and anywhere else, and ship them all to Ekans. Poor Nisha Scalli seemed to like his. Maybe it will enervate them all, in the end, as much as it did him, and the Surceaseans as well. The Ekans have no real aptitude for Skill, despite the strangeness with the Ghiuliducs, and anyway, the jammers will be in place. There is no chance we'd end up facing an Ekans/Ressie Network."

The Nin considered, smiled, smiled again, and looked up at Asher with a twinkle in her eye. "Asher Tye. Not bad at all. Let me think about it. They might consider it an act of war if we tried it; I would, if I were them. But maybe they'll go for it once they've tried a few Ressies."

There was a pause. The Nin watched Asher, and waited for the words she was sure would come. Finally she said: "And you, Asher Tye?"

Like water through a floodgate, the words poured out of him: "I'm going to take my wife, and take one of your ships, Nin, and find out what the silence in the Sculptor is all about." Asher forced himself to pause. He found he was breathing hard. It wasn't just departing from the Guild; it was the idea itself. For a starman used to the incredible scale of interstellar distance, the idea of the vastly greater intergalactic emptiness was appalling. In a way, it was agoraphobia, the fear of open space, Asher thought, of emptiness beyond imagining. It meant ghastly isolation for years, perhaps, as they tried the long, long jump between galaxy and sub-galaxy. And he didn't even know if Clemmy would agree to go.

"I do not think technology permits such a thing," the Nin said soberly. "The sub-galaxies are too far away, and the few who have tried it have never come back."

"Nin, I can no longer function in this galaxy; my Skill makes me anathema, and I cannot live with a jammer clanging overhead on every planet I visit. Someone will make it out to the sub-galaxies some day; it might as well be me."

"We'll talk about this when you return," the Nin said. "And now, I must go, Asher Tye."

She regarded them all, and they all could see why Guild members on four hundred thousand planets obeyed her.

"You've done well, all of you. Tell Clemmy I said that," she said. And then her image flickered and was gone.

The Galactic Index was 434,703, and going up. And then the ship rose into the atmosphere of the October World and headed for the stars, Asher Tye stepped over and looked down into the face of his sleeping wife.

Here is an excerpt from the new novel by Timothy Zahn, coming from Baen Books in August 1987:

TIMOTHY ZAHN

TRIPLET

The way house had been quiet for over an hour by the time Karyx's moon rose that night, its fingernail-clipping crescent adding only token assistance to the dim starlight already illuminating the grounds. Sitting on the mansion's garret-floor widow's walk, his back against the door, Ravagin watched the moon drift above the trees to the east and listened to the silence of the night. And tried to decide what in blazes he was going to do.

There actually *were* precedents for this kind of situation: loose precedents, to be sure, and hushed up like crazy by the people upstairs in the Crosspoint Building, but precedents nonetheless. Every so often a Courier and his group would have such a mutual falling out that continuing on together was out of the question . . . and when that happened the Courier would often simply give notice and quit, leaving the responsibility for getting the party back to Threshold in the hands of the nearest way house staff. Triplet management ground their collective teeth when it happened, but they'd long ago come to the reluctant conclusion that clients were better off alone than with a Courier who no longer gave a damn about their safety.

And Ravagin wouldn't even have to endure the

usual froth-mouthed lecture that would be waiting when he got back. He was finished with the Corps, and those who'd bent his fingers into taking this trip had only themselves to blame for the results. He could leave a note with Melentha, grab a horse, and be at the Cairn Mounds well before daylight. By the time Danae had finished sputtering, he'd have alerted the way house master in Feymar Protectorate on Shamsheer and be on a sky-plane over the Ordarl Mountains . . . and by the time she made it back through to Threshold and screamed for vengeance, he'd have picked up his last paychit, said bye-and-luck to Corah, and boarded a starship for points unknown. Ravagin, the great veteran Courier, actually deserting a client. Genuinely one for the record books.

Yes. He would do it. He would. Right now. He'd get up, go downstairs, and get the hell out of here.

Standing up, he gazed out at the moon . . . and slammed his fist in impotent fury on the low railing in front of him.

He couldn't do it.

"Damn," he muttered under his breath, clenching his jaw hard enough to hurt. "Damn, damn, *damn*."

He hit the railing again and inhaled deeply, exhaling in a hissing sigh of anger and resignation. He couldn't do it. No matter what the justification—no matter that the punishment would be light or nonexistent—no matter even that others had done it without lasting stigma. He was a *professional*, damn it, and it was his job to stay with his clients no matter what happened.

Danae had wounded his pride. Deserting her, unfortunately, would hurt it far more deeply then she ever could.

In other words, a classic no-win situation. With him on the short end.

And it left him just two alternatives: continue his silent treatment toward Danae for the rest of the trip, or work through his anger enough to at least get back on civil terms with her. At the moment, neither choice was especially attractive.

Out in the grounds, a flicker of green caught his eye. He looked down, frowning, trying to locate the source. Nothing was moving; nothing seemed out of place. Could there be something skulking in the clumps of trees, or perhaps even the shadows thrown by the bushes?

Or could something have tried to break through the post line?

Nothing was visible near the section of post line he could see. Cautiously, he began easing his way around the widow's walk, muttering a spirit-protection spell just to be on the safe side.

Still nothing. He'd reached the front of the house and was starting to continue past when a movement through the gap in the tree hedge across the grounds to the south caught his attention. He peered toward it . . . and a few seconds later it was repeated further east.

A horseman on the road toward Besak, most likely . . . except that Besak had long since been sealed up for the night by the village lar. And Karyx was not a place to casually indulge in nighttime travel. Whoever it was, he was either on an errand of dire emergency or else—

Or else hurrying away from an aborted attempt to break in?

Ravagin pursed his lips. "*Haklarast*," he said. It was at least worth checking out.

The glow-fire of the sprite appeared before him. "I am here, as you summoned," it squeaked.

"There's a horse and human traveling on the road toward Besak just south of here," he told it. "Go to the human and ask why he rides so late. Return to me with his answer."

The sprite flared and was gone. Ravagin watched it dart off across the darkened landscape and then, for lack of anything better to do while he waited, continued his long-range inspection of the post line. Again he found nothing; and he was coming around to the front of the house again when the sprite returned. "What answer?" he asked it.

"None. The human is not awake."

"Are you sure?" Ravagin asked, frowning. He'd once learned the hard way about the hazards of sleeping on horseback—most Karyx natives weren't stupid enough to try it. "Really asleep, not injured?"

"I do not know."

Of course it wouldn't—spirits didn't see the world the way humans did. "Well . . . is he riding alone, or is there a spirit with him protecting him from falls?"

"There is a djinn present, though it is not keeping the human from falling. There is no danger of that."

And with a djinn along to— "What do you mean? Why isn't he going to fall?"

"The human is upright, in full control of the animal—"

"Wait a second," Ravagin cut it off. "You just told me he was asleep. How can he be controlling the horse?"

"The human is asleep," the sprite repeated, and Ravagin thought he could detect a touch of vexation in the squeaky voice. "It is in control of its animal."

"That's impossible," Ravagin growled. "He'd have to be—"

Sleepwalking.

"*Damn!*" he snarled, eyes darting toward the place where the rider had vanished, thoughts skidding with shock, chagrin, and a full-bellied rush of fear. *Danae*—

His mental wheels caught. "Follow the rider," he ordered the sprite. "Stay back where you won't be spotted by any other humans, but don't let her out of your sight. First give me your name, so I can locate you later. Come on, give—I haven't got time for games."

"I am Psskapsst," the sprite said reluctantly.

"Psskapsst, right. Now get after it—and *don't* communicate with that djinn."

The glow-fire flared and skittered off. Racing along the widow's walk, Ravagin reached the door and hurried inside. Danae's room was two flights down, on the second floor; on a hunch, he stopped first on the third floor and let himself into Melentha's sanctum.

The place had made Ravagin's skin crawl even with good lighting, and the dark shadows stretching around the room now didn't improve it a bit. Shivering reflexively, he stepped carefully around the central pentagram and over to the table where Melentha had put the bow and Coven robe when she'd finished her spirit search.

The robe was gone.

Swearing under his breath, he turned and hurried back to the door—and nearly ran into Melentha as she suddenly appeared outside in the hallway. "What are you doing in there?" she demanded, holding her robe closed with one hand and clutching a glowing dagger in the other.

"The Coven robe's gone," he told her, "and I think Danae's gone with it."

"What?" She backed up hastily to let him pass, then hurried to catch up with him. "When?"

"Just a little while ago—I think I saw her leaving on horseback from the roof. I just want to make sure—"

They reached Danae's room and Ravagin pushed open the door . . . and she was indeed gone.

August 1987 • 384 pp. • 65341-5 • $3.50

Here is an excerpt from PYRAMIDS, Fred Saberhagen's newest novel, coming from Baen Books in January 1987

YOU ARE HERE TO ROB THE PYRAMIDS? COME THEN: THE MONSTROUS GODS OF ANCIENT EGYPT AWAIT YOU . . .

Whether or not that monstrous, incredible mass of stone up on the hill was the original Great Pyramid of Giza, it was still there when Scheffler went back again to take a look at it through heat and sunlight. Still there, in the broad daylight of what was either mid-morning or mid-afternoon, though it had been dusk in Illinois when he pulled the tapestry-curtain back into place and closed himself into the elevator once more.

Standing in the savage sun-glare on the lip of the rocky fissure, he pulled the cheap mass compass out of his shirt pocket and established to his own satisfaction that here it was mid-afternoon and not mid-morning. For this purpose he was going to be daring and assume that, whatever else might happen to the world, the sun still came up in the east.

So the river was east of him, and the pyramid about the same distance to his west and a little south. Last night Scheffler had done a little reading on the geography of Giza, the district of the Pyramids just east of modern Giza, and he had to admit that the situation he was looking at here seemed to correspond exactly. Everything he could see indicated to him that he was standing on the west bank of the Nile.

The hardest part of that to deal with was that if Khufu, or Cheops as the Greeks came to call him, was still building his great tomb, the year ought to be somewhere near three thousand B.C.

Whatever, and wherever, *here* was.

A Fascinating New Twist on the Time-Travel Novel, by the Author of The Book of Swords, Berserker, *and* The Frankenstein Papers.

JANUARY 1987 • 65609-0 • 320 pp. • $3.50